"Rod Duncan's *The Bullet Catcher's Daughter* is a magic box pulsating with energy. Compulsive reading from the get-go, the blend of steampunk alternate history wrapped in the enigma of a chase makes for first-rate entertainment in this finely crafted novel."

Graham Joyce, author of Year of the Ladybird

"The winner of the 2018 Leicester Book Prize was Rod Duncan, for his novel *The Queen of All Crows*. This was a hugely imaginative, compelling and ambitious work of speculative fiction, which frankly I loved, start to finish. I've never read anything quite like it."

Jonathan Taylor, author of Entertaining Strangers

"Steeped in illusion and grounded in an alternative history of the Luddite Rebellion, Duncan's strong supernatural mystery serves ably as both a standalone adventure and the start to a series. Strategically placed steampunk tropes inform but do not overwhelm Elizabeth's headlong quest to find a missing aristocrat sought by the Patent Office, which is fixated on both achieving perfection and eliminating 'unseemly science.' A hazardous border crossing into the permissively corrupt Kingdom of England and Southern Wales provides ample excitement, and a glossary at the novel's conclusion hints enticingly at a much more involved story to come."

Publishers Weekly

"Rod Duncan's writing is a joy because his pseudo late-Victorian narrative runs along the smooth rails of a framework powered by an invisible, but well-oiled word engine that hums away in the background making sure the reader gets all the thrills and spills while retaining a good sense of the story as it relentlessly barrels along."

Strange Alliances

"It's all steampunk and circus wonder as we follow the adventures of Elizabeth Barnabas. The double crosses along the way keep the plot tight and fun, and the conclusion sets us up nicely for book two."
The Washington Post

"A tumultuous and utterly wonderful series."
Smorgasbord Fantasia

"I'm one of those people who only grudgingly give a book five stars. But when I was finished with this book, I knew there was simply no other rating for it. *The Custodian of Marvels* was simply the perfect book for me. Whereas I had anticipated an exceptional book, I instead was gifted a rather extraordinary one, filled with action, suspense, and returning characters that left me cheering. I sincerely endorse the Fall of the Gas-Lit Empire series for your next reads!"
Victorian Soul Critiques

"Any writer who can, without infodumping, bring me directly into a fantastical and outrageously unlikely alternate steampunk world earned their scarce book-buying dollars. He gave such reality to the conundrum of how to simply exist as a woman in the world he's made that I was wincing, squirming, and blushing for the privilege that being male has always brought. Please believe me, this is powerful storytelling talent working so smoothly you can't feel the strain."
Expendable Mudge Muses Aloud

"Elizabeth Barnabus might just be one of my favourite female characters of all time. *The Bullet Catcher's Daughter* is an exciting, intriguing novel, full of theatrical wonders and sci-fi spectacle."
Why Words Work

BY THE SAME AUTHOR

ROD DUNCAN

The Outlaw and the Upstart King

BEING VOLUME TWO *of*
The MAP *of* UNKNOWN THINGS

WITHDRAWN

ANGRY
ROBOT

ANGRY ROBOT
An imprint of Watkins Media Ltd

20 Fletcher Gate,
Nottingham,
NG1 2FZ • UK

angryrobotbooks.com
twitter.com/angryrobotbooks
The cunning needle

An Angry Robot paperback original 2019

Cover by Amazing15
Map by Argh! Nottingham
Set in Meridien by Argh! Nottingham

Distributed in the United States by Penguin Random House, Inc., New York.

ISBN 978 0 85766 703 8
Ebook ISBN 978 0 85766 704 5

Printed in the United States of America

9 8 7 6 5 4 3 2 1

THE OUTLAW &
THE UPSTART KING

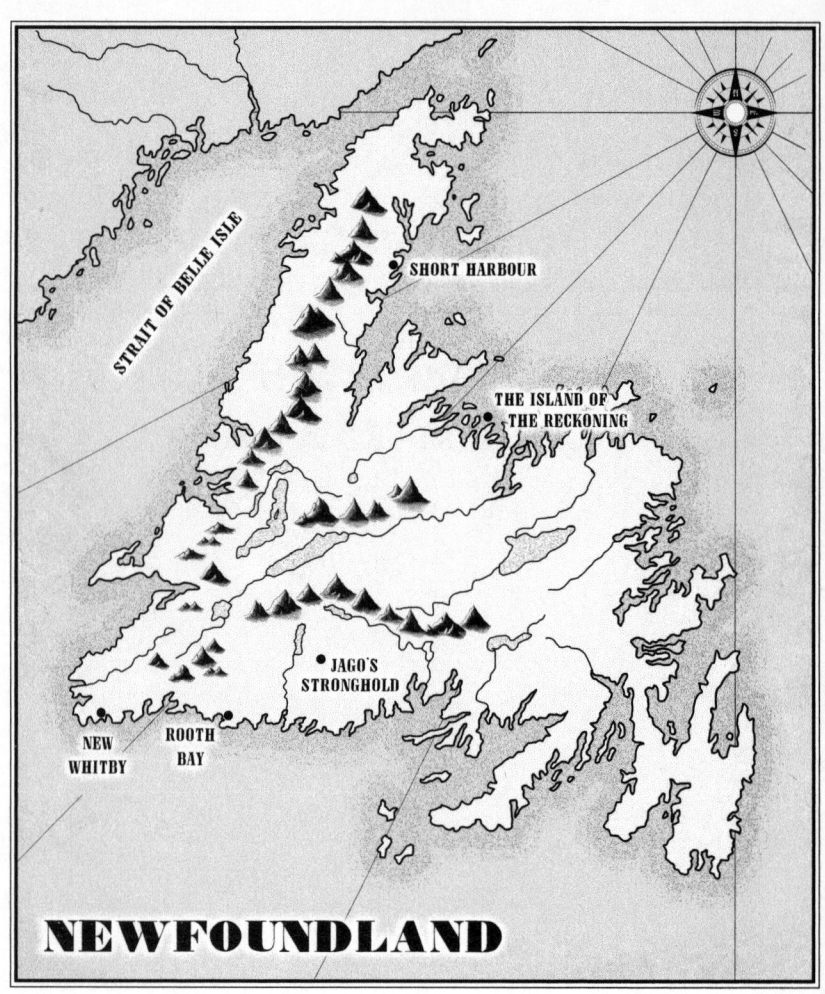

STRAIT OF BELLE ISLE

SHORT HARBOUR

THE ISLAND OF
THE RECKONING

JAGO'S
STRONGHOLD

NEW
WHITBY

ROOTH
BAY

NEWFOUNDLAND

PART ONE

The bookmaker and the gun smuggler: brothers in a way, rivals without a doubt. Each knows enough to recognize himself in the other. They would be the humble servant, always, of gambler and warrior. Loss is the subject of both trades. But not their own. Their payment is a peppercorn. Who would be without such servants?

CHAPTER 1

Elias chose a booth at the back of the Salt Ray Inn. Furthest from the lamps. Hiding against the risk that one of the other drinkers might have known him from his life before. His eyes were the giveaway. Their upward tilt came from his grandfather, the gemstone blue from his mother.

Setting down his tankard, he hid his hands under the table and set to watching the room. A young trader here, a fishwife there. Most would be carrying knives. But no big weapons. Modest folk of modest means. No men of the Blood. Hushed talk made a gentle hubbub. He would be safe enough.

Even with those distinctive eyes, Elias would have been hard to recognise. His face had weathered in his time away. His rich clothes too, thinning and fading. The cloak had been a fine thing once. Now there might be only a year left in it. But tomorrow he'd buy himself a new one. It would be hemmed with silver thread. There'd be garnets big as blackberries in the clasp. Tomorrow he'd have the money. Tomorrow he'd get even.

Always tomorrow.

With enough time, he might have earned such silver and gold by regular means. He could have set up a place of his own. A fixed address with house rules and a roof that didn't leak. He could have sold liquor and hash instead of paying to sit far from someone else's fire, next to a wooden pail already half-full from dripping rainwater.

He sipped the bitter ale, just to wet his mouth.

On seeing a man carrying three flagons from the tap, he beckoned. The man faltered, as if the "come hither" might have been meant for someone else.

So Elias asked him, "Have you seen this one?"

The man glanced to the booth where his friends were waiting for beer. Elias lifted a Lucifer from the uneven table, gripping it between two fingers. The man approached. Elias took a second match with his other hand, the same awkward finger-grip. He turned them until they were end on end in a vertical line, then let go the top one, as if attempting a balance. It fell. No surprise there.

"What?" the man asked.

"I bet I can make one stand on top of the other." This spoken in a whisper, so the man had to come closer to hear.

"How much?"

Sliding a clipping from a silver coin over the table, Elias took a deep breath and held out the matches again. The man set down his flagons. He sat, leaning closer for a clearer view in the low light. Some people want their money taking.

"Ready?"

The man nodded.

Elias struck one match on the rough wall and held the flaring head against the other, lighting that also. He blew out the flame. The phosphorus of the two match heads had fused forming a single lump of ash, fixing them together.

"You cheated!" the man said. "They're not balanced!"

"I never said they'd balance. I said they'd stand. And they do. Look."

The man balled his fists. "I did not agree to the bet!"

Elias leaned back and waved in dismissal. "No matter," he said. "I don't want your silver."

"You don't?"

"No," he said. It must never be him against them. "But I'll teach you how to play the same trick. Then you can bring your friends over. If it works, you can give me a tip. What do you say?"

So it began. The playful bet of matches first. Then cards. He did the setting out of them, so the men could be sure there would be no double dealing. For an hour he had them. Until their tempers frayed. With each other. All he'd done was take the dealer's cut, once in a while, when the hands scored like for like.

After they left, stomping out into the squally night, Elias began drinking the rest of the half pint in his pint flagon. He'd planned to make it last, then head out to the back and sneak past the stable boy so he could bury himself in straw. Shallow enough to not be smothered. Deep enough not to freeze. Newfoundland could be cold in any season.

But the three gamblers had proved richer than their clothes and drunker than the hour. They'd carried real American coins. He'd made enough to take a room for the night if he wished. Even a bath.

He was thinking on the sweetness of life when a squat man stepped into the Salt Ray Inn, leaving the door swinging, as only one could do who'd forgotten what it felt like to need to be polite. His hair was long on one side. But as the wind pulled it back, Elias saw the scarring and the missing ear. On the other side, the man's head had been shaved to stubble.

The rain outside had turned to snow. A flurry swirled in. Drinkers near the door hunkered down into cloaks and coats. They wouldn't complain. The town was unaligned, meaning a fighter of any oath could show his face.

He took a couple of paces, peered into shadows here and there, as if checking for threats, then beckoned towards the open door. In marched half a dozen men with swords or pistols at their belts. The last of them had to stoop to pass under the lintel. His left coat sleeve had been knotted below the elbow. A missing forearm. Most had lost something: a finger, a hand. Hazards of the oath-bound life. But not the man they guarded. That was Jago: unmistakably barrel-chested. No other Patron would have dared to travel with so small a band.

Elias had already scooped the hacksilver and foreign coins from the table. He hoped the shadow had covered his move. The drinkers in the best seats had been evicted. They stood, bowed and gestured for the warriors to take their places, as if making the offer by choice.

Patron Jago sat, propping his feet on a stool near the fire. His muddy boots steamed. The men sat with him, but for the knot-sleeved giant who remained on guard in the draft near the door. Elias watched it all over the rim of his empty tankard, trying to seem more casual than he felt. The owner of the Salt Ray was hurrying across, arms laden with bottles. Imported wine, most likely. She wouldn't risk offering them the ale they brewed at the inn. A dark-haired barmaid followed with glasses and a tray of something. It made for a fair distraction. The girl bent to serve food. The man at the door leered at her arse.

Elias picked up his hat and slid out from behind the table. A narrow passage led towards the rear yard. It was the first thing he had checked on arriving. Patron Jago was a man he'd need to speak to. But not here. Not yet. Elias would need to choose his own place and time.

Lifting the latch, he slipped out into the night. A storm lantern squeaked as it swung on its bracket, lighting a halo of drifting snowflakes. Slipping the winnings and cards into the pocket at his belt, he drew the old cloak tight around him. One more night in a hayloft wasn't going to hurt. He started across the yard towards the stables.

But a figure loomed from the shadow to block his way. A gatherer. One of Jago's men. Damn, but of course he'd left a guard at the back.

"Where are you going?"

"Going for a pish," said Elias, adding the slur to seem more helpless.

"Then you're going wrong," said the man, pointing towards the latrine with a long knife. "The pisser's over there." He must have done something to displease his Patron or he wouldn't have been given that dismal watch.

"Drunk too mush," said Elias.

"Show me your face," said the man.

Elias removed his hat and scrunched his eyes in a squint that he hoped would seem drunken.

"Have I seen you before?" asked the man.

"Dunno."

"Got any money?"

Without waiting for an answer, he patted down Elias's side with his free hand, finding the pocket inside the cloak. Metal chinked.

"There's a fine for being drunk," said the man.

"Never heard of it," said Elias.

"Yeah. It's new."

"How mush?"

"Show me what you've got."

There was nothing to do but obey. Elias opened his cloak and poured the silver from the pocket. A couple of ounces all told. He held it out on his upturned palm: four fingers delicate and long and the stump that had been the base of his thumb. If only he'd had time to pull on his gloves.

"Show me your other hand," said the gatherer.

Elias did.

The man licked his lips and grinned in the manner of one who's just found a way back into the warmth. "I know who you are," he said. "You're Elias No-Thumbs. Jago's been wanting to speak to you."

Being spoken to by a Patron Protector didn't mean a conversation. Not for someone like Elias. It meant lying in the mud while three or four gatherers took turns to kick him in the guts. A reminder of his place in the world. In case he needed it.

Oath-bound to no man, Patron Protectors were the un-ruled, doing as they wished, upholding their rights through war. There was honour in that. But there was still a seemly way to go about things: a custom and practice for which Jago showed little respect. The others wouldn't have killed him there on the unaligned land of New Whitby. But with Jago it was hard to know.

Steered by pricks from the gatherer's long knife, he stumbled back down the passage into the saloon, his hands raised. The other drinkers couldn't look away quickly enough. At least he got to be next to the fire, though kneeling on the flagstones with a blade touching his shoulder.

Jago smiled that fickle smile of his. "Well met, Elias," he said. "It's been a long time. Eighteen months pass so swift. Though not for you, eh? But here you are, back in the motherland." The underside of his boots were caked in horse shit.

Elias bowed.

"How's business?" the Patron asked.

The gatherer held out Elias's winnings, or some of them. "Found this in his pocket."

"A wealthy man!" said Jago.

The others laughed.

"Who did you rob?"

"No one."

The gatherer with the knife handed over Elias's playing cards. "He had these."

Jago flicked through them. "Do you deal with your teeth?"

"They're a keepsake," Elias said.

"A reminder of the old days, eh?"

Elias nodded. His cloak was steaming. His back and shoulder were getting too much of the fire. Jago shifted his feet and some of the drying horse shit dropped to the floor.

"When did you get back to the Mother Land?"

"Two weeks ago."

"You should have come to see me. Enjoy your travels?"

"No, Patron."

"Where did you go?"

"West. The Hudson Bay. Churchill."

"And what did you see there?"

"Bears and drunk trappers."

Jago laughed. Elias wasn't sure if this was a good sign. He tried to lean away from the fire but the gatherer behind him jiggled the knife at his neck so he had to kneel straight again.

"You didn't go any further west then?" Jago asked.

"No."

"Why not? Churchill's a shit-hole."

"No guide would take me," Elias said.

"That would be the stink of you!"

The gatherers laughed again.

Elias could smell burning cloth. He lowered his head, as if to abase himself, but in truth to allow a glance to where the trailing edge of his cloak lay in the hearth. An ember had landed on it and a thread of smoke was rising. He bowed lower still, placing his forehead on the cobbles next to the drying filth. In the same movement, he pulled his cloak clear of the fire.

"Have mercy," he said.

"Why? What have you done?"

"I don't know. But if I've displeased you…"

"You have me wrong, No-Thumbs. You weren't man

enough to die back then. Now I've the pleasure of seeing you reduced."

The blade lifted under his chin, forcing him back to a kneeling position.

"Eighteen months are up. The outlawing over. And back you crawl to New Whitby. Back to your old ways. But not up to your old tricks, eh? Can't play your old tricks without thumbs."

Jago's feet clomped down onto the flagstones and the great man stood. He turned and Elias risked a glance around the room. All the other drinkers were looking down into their flagons and beakers.

"See this man," Jago said, his voice loud. "You're not to show him your money, unless you want to be losing it. He's a liar and a cheat." He flourished the worn pack of playing cards by way of proof. Not that anyone dared to look. "And don't you go pitying him. He was born with a silver spoon up his arse. The famous Elias No-Thumbs."

So saying Jago tossed the playing cards towards the fire. Elias watched them catch. He'd rather have taken a beating.

"Now clear out, all of you. Blame No-Thumbs if you like."

His cloak was no longer steaming. All the moisture had gone from it. He was so hot it felt as if his flesh might be next to smoulder. The giant one-armed gatherer held open the door and all the drinkers trooped out into the snow. All the witnesses.

Jago kicked it closed after them, then strode back to the fire. "What else have you got to give me?" he asked.

"I've nothing."

Jago took the knife from his gatherer and ran the tip around Elias's ear. "Some other amusement? Will you bark like a dog?"

Elias might have done it: yapped and rolled in the dirt for them. Anything so they'd leave him alone. But he'd seen enough of the courts of the Patrons to know better than that. Bark and he'd be given a worse test. Something more humiliating, more dangerous, searching for his limits. It would end badly.

"Well? Will you not bark?"

"No."

Jago would kick him, for sure. He braced for the impact, tensing his stomach muscles. But the blow came to his head and from behind. Lights burst in the air.

He became aware of the uneven meeting of two damp flagstones under his cheek. Saliva must have run from his slack mouth. He hoped it was saliva. He'd forgotten about the gatherer standing behind him, the one who'd caught him trying to leave. Jago's voice drifted somewhere above. The Patron Protector was addressing his men. The words seemed far away but they were sharp and angry.

Elias blinked, clearing his vision. The flagstones were the floor of the Salt Ray Inn. Only a few seconds could have passed. That surprised him. It felt like longer.

Someone grabbed his collar and hauled him upright. The room heaved. So did his guts, but he didn't throw up. One of the gatherers chucked a cup of wine into his face. Somewhere in his mind, he marvelled at how good it tasted. It paid to be oath-bound to a wealthy man. He closed his mouth.

Jago's face loomed. The Patron must be bending down.

"See what happens when you don't do what you're told?"

"Shorry," Elias managed, the slur real this time.

"You should know. You, of all people."

"I'm a shlow learner."

Jago frowned, as if his kindness was being mocked. Elias braced for another blow, but it didn't come.

"How did you get away when you were outlawed?" This the Patron asked in a whisper, as if not wanting his men to hear. It was the real question, the reason for the talking to. How does any outlawed man get across the straights to Labrador?

"I stole a boat."

"And no one saw you?"

"It was a very small boat."

"Jokes get men killed."

Jago was very close now, his voice little more than a breath. He smelled of something sweet. "A boatman helped you to get away. I want to meet him, Elias, whoever he is. Bring him to me and you'll have a reward. You need to know who your friends are. I'll give you one week."

CHAPTER 2

In Labrador they joked that more Newfoundlanders had been killed in arguments over fish than had ever been killed over women. But what did they know? Feudal Newfoundland was a place apart, even in the wilds. The thing they fought for, died for, was to hold a stretch of coast. Fish, seals and seaweed would be part of it. Whales, too, if the gods were kind. But the meat of it was this: someone might try to smuggle weapons across. Without a harbour at his command, a Patron could do nothing to stop such a crime. Nor could he try to do it himself.

They were dangerous waters.

The coastline of Newfoundland that no Patron could hold was Cape Ray and the bays and inlets around New Whitby. Whichever of them had tried to thrust his will on it in the past had been laid low by the swords of the others. It wasn't a law exactly. That would have been impossible. It was merely custom and practice: an understanding born of history.

This tract spanned twelve miles and two furlongs east to west as the raven flew, marked with cairns at either end, with a hinterland of seven miles and five furlongs northwards from the coast. A boat docking there could be inspected by any free man. If the cargo wasn't contraband, the owners would be left to go about their business. A graveyard of smuggling ships lay out in the bay, rotting timbers showing at low tide like the ribcages of drowned men. Such was the price of freedom.

Contraband was chiefly weaponry and powder. But also women or men bearing oath-marks. And the outlawed.

That was the problem with being outlawed. You couldn't stay, because you'd be found and killed for sure. You couldn't sail, because no captain would risk his life for such a cargo. Many were the outlaws who, against all reason, made their way to the coast where the straits were narrowest, and there gave up. They would be found sitting on the rocks, watching chunks of ice flowing past and on the other side, unreachable, the land of safety.

But not Elias. When his time came, he'd found the means of it.

He woke to an eerie silence and the memory of being dumped in the mud outside the inn. At first he thought it must still be night, but he could make out the silhouette of his hand when he held it in front of his face. Pushing the layers of straw aside, he clambered out from the muggy warmth of his sleeping place. The smell and cold of fog hit him. One of the horses snorted as he climbed down the ladder from the hayloft. There was no one below to give trouble, though scores could have been standing a few paces out and he wouldn't have been able to see them. Stepping into flat greyness, he trailed his hand on a damp wall and began to skirt the yard. The back door of the Salt Ray Inn was locked,

as was the front.

He rapped his knuckle against it, then waited, picking straw from his hair and brushing it from the shoulders of his cloak. The spyhole cover pulled back. The owner's brown eyes stared out.

"What?"

"I was here last night."

"I saw it," she said.

"Can I come in?"

"Why?"

"I left something." When she didn't answer, he added, "I'll do any work you want to give me. A trade."

All he needed was for her to open the door. A promise meant nothing.

"What work can a man do who's no thumbs?" she said.

He could have made a joke of it or crafted a wise answer to shoot back. But she was right. The spyhole cover thudded closed. Then he heard the bolts slide within.

"I thank you," he said, when the door was open.

She shook her head. "Don't."

The fire was out, the ashes cold. A dozen or so of his playing cards lay scattered around the hearth. Those that had fallen closer to the fire were singed at the edges. Three had burned half away. Sifting the ash, he found more. Some had blackened but seemed whole until he picked them up, whereupon they crumbled to dust. All told, he gathered twelve full cards, three that were half or less and six odd corners. He'd hoped for more. Laying them on the flagstones, he found more clubs than anything. He might have been able to draft the missing ones, copying from what was left. He'd had a way with a likeness once.

"Here," said the owner, holding out a hearth brush. "There's a shovel and bucket in the scullery."

He took it, holding the handle in that clumsy grip between fingers and palm.

"I lost half a night's trade thanks to you," she said. "I want you gone in an hour."

He'd been planning to walk away there and then with what was left of his pack. But few enough inns were safe for him. Making an enemy of the mistress of the Salt Ray wasn't something he could afford. And her case was fair. So he set to work, shovelling out the ash pan. He found the pit at the back of the stable block and then returned to wipe down the flagstones where he'd been made to kneel the night before, and the glazed wall tiles of the edging.

By the time the mistress came back, he'd got the place looking good, to his own eye at least. She gave his work a token glance then marched away. Some reward, he thought. His knees were black. But as he scrubbed his hands in the scullery, the dark-haired barmaid came to him with a wooden bowl of barley soup. "From the mistress," she said.

"Thank you."

He lifted it two-handed, feeling the heat in his fingers and mouth. And then in his belly. A man can bed himself so deep in hunger that he no longer knows the feeling for what it is. But as Elias drank, he did know. He'd been stocky when he fled from Newfoundland. His broad shoulders still made him seem that way. But opening his cloak revealed the truth. The weight had fallen from him.

The barmaid cocked her head, watching as he drank. "What will you do?" she asked, pointing to the pile of singed playing cards on the floor.

"Buy a new pack," he said. And then, more gravely, "Has the mistress a flat file I could use? A saw maybe?"

The barmaid didn't know. She refilled the bowl before going to ask.

Newfoundland was a great place to buy a longbow, a blunderbuss, a mace or all manner of edged and spiked weapons. If one had money – which one day he would. But not a silk shirt or a book, not glassware nor the kind of finery they made over the border in the Gas-Lit Empire. And truly not a pack of playing cards.

Her question had been a good one. What was he going to do? His eighteen months were up. He'd returned from his outlawing with a task and limited time to do it. For two weeks he'd been hanging around in unaligned bars, treading water so to speak, gathering news. He needed to know the gossip of the clans: who was up, who was down, what battles had been fought. He needed to map the births, alliances and deaths that were the warp and weft of Newfoundland's ever-shifting power games.

The irony was that before his exile, the knowing of all this had been in his hands. But he'd had no interest in it. He'd lived the life of wealth. When his Patron said fight, he'd fought. Other than that, he'd been happy to drink and play. But with the task before him, life rested on the knowing of things.

The barmaid came back, lugging a heavy toolbox. "The mistress says you can use it. So long as I'm here to watch."

Ash wasn't the only thing Elias had seen at the back of the stable block. On this second visit, he knelt and put his hands in among the filth. First he pulled out a piece of yellowed bone that squirmed with maggots, the jaw of a hog, he thought. There was no part of it thick enough in any case. He threw it aside and sifted the dregs of the pit until he found the leg bone of an ox. It had been smashed open to get at the fatty marrow. But the joint was whole. In size it was like Elias's clenched fist. And it was old enough that all flesh had rotted away.

The maid told him to scrub it in the yard, and his hands too. When at last she would let him back inside, he knelt gripping a saw between his knees, sliding the bone up and down along the toothed edge. When the cut was through, he turned the bone and began again. White dust gathered in cracks between the flagstones.

The maid talked to him as he worked. For the most part he let her words flow. After a time, the mistress of the Salt Ray stepped into the saloon to watch.

"We open at dusk," she said.

"I'll be done in time."

"But not in an hour?"

"I'll pay you back," he said. "When things go better, I'll find a way."

She said, "What innkeeper hasn't heard such promises a thousand times? You'll need to clean the hearth again."

"I'll get Tinker to do it," the barmaid said.

A look passed between the two women, which Elias couldn't read. The mistress walked away.

While he worked, the barmaid set kindling and small sticks in the fireplace, then lit them with a taper. He was happy to have the warmth. The flames had grown to a fine blaze by the time he'd carved three small cubes from the bone, and filed the surfaces smooth.

The last part was the hardest. He took a long iron spike from the toolbox and rested the tip in the bed of embers. Sitting on a low stool, he pulled off one of his boots, and then the sock. The sharp point of the iron spike had begun to glow in the fire. Gripping one of the bone cubes between his toes, he pressed the red hot point down into the very centre of its upturned face. He could feel the heat on his exposed skin. One slip and he'd brand himself. A thread of acrid smoke twisted in the air as the iron burned a small black circle in the bone. When the spot was wide and deep enough, he turned a new face up and burned three dots in a slanted line. Four marks done. Fifty-nine to go.

"Why do you gamble?" asked the barmaid.

"I don't," he said.

"You had cards. Now you're making dice."

"Others will use them. Not me."

"You're a bookmaker, then?"

The iron had gone black. Elias returned it to the heart of the fire and looked at her straight on for the first time. She and her mistress had been kind. In fairness he should give back the same. But he'd left his conscience three thousand bloody miles to the west, frozen in the permafrost of the Yukon alongside the long dead bodies of mammoths and musk ox.

"Why do you want to know?" he asked.

"I'm curious."

There was something about her that bothered him: her voice or her questions, he couldn't pin it down.

"Why is it you're making three dice?" she asked. "Most men gamble with two."

"Look," he said. "Thanks for your help. But I'll make these marks and then I'll be gone."

He turned the cube again and began burning more holes. Six dots this time: two lines of three. This face was made from the dense bone at the surface of the joint. A feeling troubled him, that the barmaid might have seen through the trick.

"How did you get away?" she asked. "When they outlawed you, I mean."

And there was the question again, the one thing everyone wanted to know, from Patron to peasant. But the answer was a coin he could spend only once.

Smoke spiralled from the bone dice as the hot metal faded. "Do you admire my work?" he asked.

CHAPTER 3

The odds were one in six that two throws would add up to seven. If the dice were true. But there was no way to judge the odds of a smuggling run between Newfoundland and the coast of Labrador.

A faster boat would cut the danger, or a quieter one. The captain could set out after dark on a moonless night, steer by the compass. The lanterns that guided him in could be hooded, casting only narrow slits of light.

It would work, most likely. Nine times out of ten. But on every run, the captain would be thinking about that one other time, which would surely come. A cannon might pick him off, if he was lucky. It would take only a minute to die in the freezing waters of the Strait of Belle Isle. His body would go into shock. He wouldn't even know it when he breathed water into his lungs.

But if a Patron Protector's ship caught him, or caught the land crew trying to guide him in, then his family and theirs would die. Only when he'd witnessed his life's loves passing through every horror would he be allowed to follow them into the fire. Nine cargoes safely delivered could never pay for that.

An oath-bound man could be ordered to do it. But even oaths had limits. Ask a boat captain to take the trip again and he might choose to sever his bonds instead, whatever the cost.

The question that had lurked under the surface of Newfoundland politics for two centuries was this: what if someone found a way to change the odds completely? Would death once in a hundred times be worth the risk? It took a gambler to reckon it. But what if the risk could be so blunted that any cargo might be carried with easy mind? That was the nightmare of every Patron Protector. Unless he could find such a path for himself, in which case it was his fondest dream.

The others would set upon him if they knew, banding together to bring him low. It was easier to defend than to attack in the bare hills. But numbers would tell in the end. They'd surely break him.

The trick would be to keep the secret close. If he could smuggle in a great treasury of powder and weapons before being found, he'd be able to wage war on all of them. He'd be able to win. A crown was the thought that none of the Patrons could abide, though most might dream of wearing it.

Smuggled weapons did turn up from time to time. The year before his outlawing, Elias had found an off-island sword, pulled it from the cold grip of a corpse on the battlefield. The edge cut wonderfully keen. Elias had had no thought for the politics of smuggled weapons. He just wanted to keep it for himself. But his uncle insisted they yield it to Patron Calvary. That had been little more than three years ago. It felt like a different lifetime.

Before the outlawing, his duties had been to obey Patron Calvary, his great uncle, to fight with the clan when ordered, to practise with sword and pistol, to hone his powers of battle. Beyond that, his needs had been simple. In the way of men who are given most things they want, he desired only to win at everything.

The odds of two thrown dice adding to twelve was one in thirty-six. If they'd been cut true. But the chance of all four kings turning up in a poker hand were smaller than Elias could figure. He should have known better.

Arriving at the Reckoning two years before, still a man of the Blood, whole in body and with blatant wealth, Elias yielded his weapons to the oath-wrights for safekeeping. That was the way of things, custom and practice, which enforced each year a short-lived break from war. He couldn't have guessed how closely his pistol would be inspected once he was gone. It was a fine thing. He'd been given it freely by Fitz, a childhood friend. There was no cause to think it might be the death of him.

His mind was elsewhere. The Reckoning was a time when he could meet with men from other clans without it being in battle. And girls too, women of the Blood who weren't his cousins. They strolled in fine clothes, swaying rumps or breasts or whatever else their gifts. It would be a feast for his eyes. And his hands, if he could only find the means to woo them.

They made camp on a promontory projecting from Newfoundland's northern coast. It had been the site of the Reckoning back to the time of his great, great grandfather. The Island, they called it, though it wasn't quite. Each of the twenty-three clans took up its old place, forming a kind of map, as if the Island were the wide span of Newfoundland itself. The Calvary tents were pitched at the northwest tip. The Locke clan pitched immediately to the south of them.

As the days of the Reckoning passed, Elias did his best to be seen and heard. He wrestled and drank and showed off and flirted. And he gambled on cards: a skill with which the gods had marked him.

For once, no man of the Blood was playing. That gave him

the pride of dealing and the top seat. He thought nothing of it.

He'd always had a feeling for the odds, Elias, and he liked what lay before him. The other players seemed awkward at the game. But they'd no shortage of gold. That should have been a warning. They were only the sons of councillors.

They flashed their money and slapped it down on the oak board. He spread the cards for everyone to see and then flipped them over. The pack whispered to his shuffle. They played and they drank, or pretended to. He won three hands then lost the four that followed, but was still up on the night because he knew when to fold. The others hadn't the same wit. With his next strong hand, he pushed up the stakes and won more than he'd lost on the previous four.

Some men want their money taking.

A crowd gathered. There's no sport like watching another man lose. The higher the stakes the better. Among them were two women of the Blood, but rosy-skinned and with arses that drew his eye. Their clans were distant enough that he'd not spoken to them before. Yet not so distant that an alliance would be impossible. Patron Calvary might let him have one of them. As the heap of his winnings grew, they favoured him with their eyes and the angle of their bodies.

He flashed the pack, spreading it one-handed between fingers and thumb, showing off his skill, then made another perfect dovetail shuffle.

When a break was called, Elias made a show of going off to the cliff edge for a piss, staggering as if half-drunk. On the way back he blundered into one of the others, making it seem a mistake. But in the clumsy righting of himself, he'd felt the man's purse and guessed its weight.

It was going to be a good night.

Then came a hand of three kings. He swapped out the other two cards, hoping they would think it a long-shot at a flush or a straight. In return he drew a five and the final king. A wiser man might not have trusted such a run. But luck can seem the way of things when it's been a friend for so long. There was gold to be won. There were men to be beaten. And there were pretty girls watching.

Four kings wouldn't make for a big win. Unless others round the table thought their hands better. He tossed down an American silver dollar, a cagey raising of the stakes. One by one they followed, but with gold. He frowned, as if thinking to give up, hiding the stir of excitement building in his chest.

The pile of gold and silver grew. So did the crowd. There was so much treasure on the board that the heap of it was taller than the drinking beakers. Such a prize might change even the life of a man of the Blood. The women moistened their lips and flashed their eyes.

When there was no more gold to put down, he laid out his cards; four kings and a five. The crowd clapped, but not wildly. No one likes to see the highborn win. A few cheers had come from men of his own clan.

He looked up, expecting defeat in the other players' eyes. But one of them was snarling with anger. Down came his cards. A flush of spades; the two, the seven, the eight, the ten and last the king. Five kings lay on the oak board, and he, Elias, had been the one to deal them.

The crowd rushed him, turning the table spilling the treasure on the turf. They had his arms pinned. A fist went into his gut. Another caught him on the side of the head. Then he was on the ground and kicks were coming in from all sides.

There were no guns or knives on the Island. But the boots were hitting hard enough to do the job. He might have died, but a group of Patrons happened to be strolling close by. One of them shouted and the beating stopped.

That night, Patron Calvary came to the place they'd chained him. "What have you done, boy?" he asked.

"Nothing."

"You cheated."

"I did not!"

"There's eight men standing witness against you."

"I left the table. Just for a minute. One of them must have changed the pack. It was all set up."

But the more Elias begged, the darker the Patron's gaze. "You're either a cheat or you've been played for a fool. Which is worse?"

In the morning they took him to where the Patrons had gathered and pushed him to his knees. Men came then, to tell what they'd seen. Each swore Elias had been crooked in his dealing of the cards. After the fifth had spoken, Patron Locke called it to an end.

"Who will witness for this man?"

No one came. Not even his own kin.

"Patron Protector Calvary, one of your blood has shamed the Reckoning. You must pay the price of it."

But his great uncle stood and shook his head. "He's no more of my blood. He's no more under my protection. Last night I cast him out. I have men to swear it."

Patron Locke failed to cover his disappointment.

"Then this Elias is of no affinity. He is severed. Let it so be marked. And let him be put beyond the law."

"Aye," said each of the other Patrons in turn.

It was a grim mark, the tattoo they gave him: the likeness of a rope wrapping his arm high above the elbow. But there was no one to speak for him. No one to argue his case that it be inked on some less needed limb. The oath-wright worked with jabs of the needle. It took all the day to finish.

Through the hurt of it, Elias was planning the way of his

escape. Outlawed, he'd be given a warrant of eighteen hours to put miles between himself and the many who'd want the sport and pride of slaying Patron Calvary's great nephew. None could shelter him without suffering the same forfeit. Nor could any give him aid.

Most would reckon he'd flee down the road to New Whitby, where a boat might be stolen. A few, knowing the way his mind worked, might think he'd turn south to the end of the track and hope to be more swift than them over the rough land beyond.

But whichever way he turned, they'd snare him soon enough. They would have horses and dogs, weapons and food. He'd have only his wits, his feet, his hands and such clothes as he was wearing.

A narrow spur of rock connected the Island to the cliffs of the mainland. If he followed that, the hunting dogs would pick up the smell of him. But he knew another way across: down a scree to a little cove then around the base of the cliffs, wading to the mainland when the sea was low, climbing the cliffs on the other side. He'd done it as a child, hunting for seagull eggs.

If he did it unseen, the dogs wouldn't know where to pick up his scent. He could make a wide circle and then cut north with scant chance of being followed.

Then to leave Newfoundland. There was the rub. But Fitz knew a way. Fitz could get things brought in from Labrador and Nova Scotia. Things no one else could get. The pistol had been one of them, a beautiful weapon with a snakeskin pattern acid-etched into the barrel and the same design picked up by a dark wood inlay in the walnut stock. It was too lovely to have seen but not held.

"You must never tell where it came from," Fitz had said.

"I wouldn't!"

"I smuggled it. You know the trouble we'd be in."

"How did you smuggle it?"

"I'll show you one day. I promise. But swear now never to tell. On your life."

So the oath was sworn. On the honour of the Calvary name.

Now was the time for Fitz to show him the secret of how the gun was smuggled, which might also be a means for him to leave Newfoundland. Fitz would help. They'd been like brothers. Even when wealth and standing had taken them apart, they still found ways to see each other from time to time. Fitz would save him. He always did.

All at the Reckoning came out from their tents for the sport of seeing him brought low. They lined the sides of the track and jeered as he was dragged through. None had the right to do him harm until the eighteen hours were spent. But they could pelt him with rotting food. They cheered when a boy ran from the crowd and reached up to rub filth in his face.

The women whose eyes the night before had offered pleasure, now whistled and spat. The truth, laid plain by the morning light, was that they too had been plotting his downfall. And every other player around the table. The Patrons hadn't just happened to be passing when the fifth king was upturned. He'd been the only one who hadn't known the play in which he acted. Yet he'd spoken his lines to the letter.

He clamped his jaw tight, cursing his own dull wits, inwardly vowing to never trust long odds again. He would get away. Somehow. He'd see his enemies weeping. After eighteen months of exile in Labrador, he'd come back stronger. They would fear him in the end.

"Wait!"

Everyone turned. A man was marching down the track: Aaron Weaverbright, eldest son of Patron Weaverbright.

"I've a complaint against Elias! I demand he pay me back for what he's taken by trickery."

It was the claim of a simpleton. Elias might have laughed.

"He was found out," said Patron Locke. "He's being punished."

"He's being punished for last night. But last year he won gold from me. And the year before. Now we know him as a cheat. Let him pay me back for those times."

Patron Locke turned to Elias. "Will you pay him what you owe?"

To be outlawed was to be cast loose with nothing. The Patron would know he couldn't pay. Everyone would know.

"I note your silence," Locke said. "Therefore the plaintiff must take settlement in flesh."

Elias fought like a wild thing, though there was no chance of escape. In the end, they lifted and carried him to the fire. His great uncle among them.

"Stay still or you'll lose your whole hand." He spat the words.

Elias never saw the man who did it. Dread had overwhelmed his reason. There was a blur of angry faces and the pincers, crystal clear, pulled red hot from the fire. He closed his eyes after that.

Shards of the ordeal would afterwards flash in his mind unbidden: the blades clamping over the base of his left thumb, not knowing if it was hot or freezing cold, the stink of burning flesh, the hiss of boiling fat. He'd no wits left when they pulled his other hand across and strapped it down. It seemed they'd got it wrong because he sensed both thumbs, as if they were numb but still attached. He couldn't scream. There was no breath left in his lungs.

As the crowd cheered for a second time, the truth hit him that this too had been part of the play. The pincers had been ready for him, waiting in the fire.

CHAPTER 4

With bone dice cut and marked and stowed in the pocket at his belt, Elias No-Thumbs, returned outlaw, stepped from the Salt Ray Inn. Three door-bolts scraped shut behind him. The morning fog had melted away, leaving a blue sky bright enough to hurt the eyes. Newfoundland could span four seasons in one morning.

Squinting against the light, he scanned the houses that made up New Whitby: weather-sanded timbers and fading paint, stilts holding shacks flat over rocky ground, here and there a square of glass catching the sun. It wasn't much of a place compared to the towns of Québec and Labrador. It sprawled round the bay and over the low hills, with no clear end or beginning, its angles wayward.

But under the sun, with low billows rolling into the bay, the place kindled something in his heart. The scent of childhood perhaps. The sting of home that only a wanderer can know. However bad the way of things, however low he'd sunk, his feet were standing on Newfoundland soil. If he had to die, and he owned that all men did, then it was here his bones would bleach. One way or another.

But not yet.

A scattering of men and women were out working the shoreline, gathering the gifts of the last high tide. Seaweed and small pieces of driftwood for the most part. But on the other side of the bay a horse had been roped to lug something large from the beach. It seemed to be a tamarack, complete with roots and branches. Who knew how such a tree could have come to land in the bay and where it might once have grown.

The ocean was a mystery, both curse and blessing. It gifted the food that for the most part kept the peasants alive. It made the rock of Newfoundland into a fortress that no attack could breach. But it also stopped the Patrons from getting the things their hearts were set on.

Scanning the eastern sweep of the bay, Elias at last found what he was looking for. Not trouble, exactly, but a hint that it would come. A boat had tied to a jetty two furlongs distant. The crew were unloading casks.

Elias had stayed hidden since coming back, biding time, gathering news. His face and frame, now lean, had been their own disguise. But Jago had found him out. And Jago had given him a week. That had shrunk to six days and a few hours. He'd no choice but to act.

Setting off on the path at the top of the shoreline, his long legs carried him towards the jetty. Eyes were always watching in New Whitby. But it still surprised him how quickly a crew could arrive to rummage through the boat and its cargo. Cantering hooves clattered the stones behind. He stepped off the track but didn't turn to face them. Three riders passed, and then a small pack of powder dogs. He held his breath, but they gave him neither look nor sniff. The horses bore the brand of the Locke clan. Elias shuddered. He'd caught a glimpse of the same mark inked across the cheekbone and ear of the rearmost rider.

He was too far away to hear the challenge when they arrived at the jetty. But he saw the captain bowing. The powder dogs sniffed around for a moment then leapt into the boat. Two riders had jumped down and were knocking on the barrels, testing them by sound. The third rider, Elias knew: Nathaniel Grimundson, who was married to Patron Locke's great niece. He wasn't of the Blood himself, or he wouldn't have been doing such menial work.

Closer now, Elias could hear the voices.

"I don't care. Open the barrel or I stave it in. Not that one. This one! This one, idiot!"

The boat captain said something to his mate and tools were brought. He'd begun to drill a hole in the top of the cask by the time Elias drew level. The dogs, having done their work, leapt back to the jetty, tails wagging. One of them, some kind of lurcher, bounded towards him. It nosed around the hem of his cloak then jumped up to smell the tote slung from his shoulder.

"You," said Nathaniel, from the saddle of his horse. "What do you carry?"

There was no recognition in the man's eyes. But then, Elias was a ghost of the warrior he'd once been.

"Clothes," he said. "And food and soap."

The dog was still sniffing. It hadn't sat, which would have been the sign of contraband. But it was there, moving around him, bothered by some smell.

Nathaniel swung himself down, landing double booted in the shingle. As he stomped closer, Elias raised his hands, gloved for disguise, to show he held no weapon. Nathaniel circled him, head cocked, eyes narrowed.

"Empty the bag."

So Elias did, spilling his things onto the path. There was little enough: a few rags to wrap himself in should the weather turn colder, strips of dried meat, a scratched pewter bowl, a tin with his last few rubbings of tobacco. Nathaniel used a boot to spread the scanty treasures.

"What's your clan?" he asked.

"I'm unaligned."

Nathaniel's lip curled in a sneer.

The dog was getting close to the strips of dried meat. Elias stooped to grab them; it was a good enough excuse to break the man's gaze.

"What's that?" Nathaniel asked.

"Mipku," Elias said, holding the meat above the dog's reach.

"Speak English, damn your eyes!"

"I don't know another name. It's dried caribou."

There'd once been great herds on Newfoundland. But they'd been hunted out a generation before.

"Where did you get it?"

"On the mainland."

The dog had found a small jar, which had rolled free from the rest of Elias's things. It shifted its body first to the left then the right, but always with the button of its nose pressed against the wide cork, sniffing. Nathaniel picked it up and peered through its dull green glass. A bean of something rolled within. It could have been a roughly formed ball of clay. Elias tensed as Nathaniel shook the jar next to his ear, then pulled out the stopper. It came away with a quiet pop.

"It's medicine," Elias said, too quickly.

Nathaniel sniffed, recoiling with an expression of disgust. "What manner of medicine?"

"They call it glycer-fortis."

"Well, the dog doesn't like it. I want to see you use it. Show me."

Elias drew the long pin from his cloak and with great care dipped it into the jar, which Nathaniel was still holding. A greasy crumb of the contents came out, stuck to the pin's tip. Elias wiped it off on the underside of his tongue. A familiar chemical buzz and heat filled his mouth, flowing down to his chest. For a moment he felt light headed.

"What's it for?"

"My heart."

"It makes you strong?"

"Yes," said Elias.

"Then I should take some for myself." The man seemed set to dip his little finger into the jar.

"No!" Elias blurted the word.

"No?" There was an edge in Nathaniel's voice.

"It might kill you," Elias said. "Even a touch of it on the skin would make you sick."

"You saying you're stronger than me?"

"No. It's the way of this medicine to make a strong man weak, but to keep a weak man alive."

For a moment Nathaniel Grimundson seemed interested. Then a call came from the jetty. The hole had been drilled in the cask, as ordered. Inside was merely salt. The dogs jumped and yowled, sensing it was time to run once more. He took a last look into the green glass jar, then replaced the stopper and seemed about to thump it down. Elias clenched his teeth. But instead, Nathaniel tossed it in the air. Elias grabbed at it like a drowning man snatching for a rope. It jumped from his grip and looked set to fall, but he grabbed again, and this time pulled it to his chest.

Nathaniel mounted his horse. "Glycer-fortis," he said with a sneer. He pointed down to Elias, as if his fingers were a gun. Then he kicked in his heels and was thundering away, followed by his men and the dogs, back along the coast path the way they'd come.

The boat captain began to spike the hole he'd been forced to drill. His mallet made a dull drum of the cask. The sound echoed from a low rise of rocks to the east, while waves scoured the shingle below the jetty.

CHAPTER 5

Glycer-fortis. Elias had first tasted it in the time of his outlawing. There'd been ten of them working in the factory, servants of the chemist's glassware. Three stirred the oily liquid in the flasks. Three added fuming aqua-fortis, a few drops at a time. Three brought snow and ice to pack around the cooling tubes. And one kept watch on the thermometers. That job went with rank, they said. Not to the oldest, but to whoever had been longest in the job: months perhaps, but seldom years.

They walked a knife edge. Too cold and nothing happened. But the reaction made heat. The hotter the flasks, the quicker the chemicals did their magic, making more heat yet. Too hot and it ran away with itself, they said. Though no one who had seen it happen had lived to tell.

Given a knock, or a spark, glycer-fortis would blow like gunpowder. But more than gunpowder. A thimbleful could take the door off a safe. A cup would turn a house to splinters. That's why they made it. Not to treat a sickness of the heart, but to detonate, to shatter, to destroy.

Standing in front of the overseer's hut for the first time, Elias had turned a full circle, taking in the vast white valley. Everything seemed outsized. The mountains, the trees, the Yukon River itself, icebound below. Escape in winter would be impossible. But paths might come clear when the snow was gone. The camp and the factory had been built on a terrace some sixty feet above the river, safe from spring floods. South looked to be the best way out. Forest cloaked the lower slopes. There would be places to hide.

The overseer told him about punishment, seeming bored with the words he was speaking. When the lecture was done, he walked Elias to a low heap of rocks and earth, his mood darkening as they climbed to the top. It was the rim of a crater, Elias saw, perhaps twenty paces across. Snow had drifted in the hollow, but only on one side, so he could see the true depth.

"Think about it," the overseer said. "This was the last glycer-fortis factory. We couldn't find anything of them that worked it. There was nothing to bury. So you listen to the thermometer man. He says stop, you stop. He says stir, you stir. He says pack ice faster, then that's what you do. Understand?"

"Yes sir."

Elias had already learned to say sir or feel the overseer's baton.

"You want to live?"

"Yes sir."

"Then stay wakeful, you hear? And watch the others. One of them closes his eyes, you shout. And if you start to thinking one of them's tired of life, you let me know. Got that, boy?"

"Yes sir."

The new factory was a wooden shack with earth heaped round, so that from the outside all Elias could see was its sloping roof. If they made a mistake, the explosion would be directed upwards, not out at the surrounding huts. *When* it blew. That was the one sure thing. It would happen. The only goal worth holding was being alive at the end of a shift. One day at a time.

The others, three men and six women, were thin and dressed in rags. A sickly yellow light came from storm lanterns on the walls. At first, Elias didn't see that the other workers were themselves coloured yellow, each to a different shade. For some the yellowness was in their fingers only. But the thermometer man had it in his lank grey hair as well and it tinged the whites of his eyes.

On stepping out into the daylight after that first shift, Elias saw it properly. He must have made some sound of dismay because the old man laughed.

"You should be so lucky," he said.

"Lucky?"

The man touched a hand to his hair. "This takes time."

Packing the ice was gruelling work. It froze the hands until the fingers were numb. Within an hour Elias's back was aching. But when he slowed or knelt on the earth floor to catch some rest, the others shouted at him. At least he got to leave the hut, to fetch more ice. There he could breathe deep and try to get rid of the acid fumes from the bottom of his lungs.

The headaches started halfway through the first day. They weren't like anything he'd felt before. When he stood up from packing ice around the pipes, the world started closing to black, as if there wasn't enough blood flowing to his brain. So he knelt again and put his head down on the dirt, until they shouted at him to get on with it.

"That's why we don't have you stirring," said the thermometer man. "Don't want you toppling in!"

There was a laugh from the others at that.

"I'm sick," Elias said.

"We've all been there, son. It'll pass."

The old man was right. After the third week, Elias was strong enough to try out the work of stirring. This he did with a small paddle, wooden so there'd be no chance of it making a spark. That was another way the glycer-fortis factory might blow.

One morning Elias woke to find the camp quiet. Others in the bunkhouse were sleeping, though it was well after dawn. He stepped outside. There was no one around, so he sat in a splash of sunshine and let its warmth seep into his bones. Lost to thought, he didn't notice the thermometer man step out to join him.

"You're turning yellow," said the man, lowering himself next to Elias.

It was true. The colour had started in the beds of his nails and spread out over his skin.

"How long before I get to be like you?"

"You'll never catch up."

"Why aren't we at work?" Elias asked.

"It's the commander's birthday. Everyone rests. But for the house servants. They cook the feast. We might even get a taste of the leftovers, if his dogs aren't too hungry."

After a time, Elias said, "How do I get out of here?"

"Try walking."

"I'm not joking. Haven't you thought of it?"

"And I'm not joking neither. Guards might have the day off too. But it's dangerous out there. If the wolves don't get you, the wild men will."

"Where would you go?" Elias asked.

"I can't," said the thermometer man. "Here…" He dug in his pocket and pulled out a small jar of green glass.

Elias took it. A lump of something rolled within. He was about to shake it, but the man put his hand on Elias's arm.

"Gently," he said. "Gently."

So Elias pulled out the wide stopper. Putting it to his nose, he breathed in a familiar smell. "Glycer-fortis?"

The man dipped the tip of his little finger into the jar,

touching the lump, then put the same finger to the underside of his tongue. "They soak the glycer-fortis into a kind of dirt. Makes it safer. But not safe. You don't get the headaches no more?"

"No," said Elias.

"Your body's gotten used to it. But tomorrow, when we're back to work, you'll get the headaches all over again. Just from one day off."

Elias dipped his finger into the jar and then wiped it on the underside of his tongue as he'd been shown. His mouth and throat buzzed from the chemical taste. He felt his heart put in an extra beat.

"That's the way," said the man.

"Where would you go?" Elias asked, again. "Where's home to you?"

"Oregon. That's where I grew up. Ah, you should see it. I still do, up here." He tapped the side of his head. "And I can hear the woodpeckers drumming in the forests. It's a sound like nothing else. I'd love to hear it one more time. Before I'm gone."

"So come with me. The two of us together. Spring's near. It's warmer every day. Right now we could walk over the Yukon. They say it's going to break any time. If we got it right, we'd be on the other side and the ice would be cracking. They'd not risk following us. If we walked out in the night, we'd be ten miles gone before they knew it. You understand the country. The two of us together – we'd have a chance."

While Elias had been whispering this, the thermometer man gazed off into the distance, as if picturing it. His face wore a sad smile.

"I would like it," he said. "Very much. And I would do it. But…" He shook his head. "We'd neither of us live."

"You can't be sure!"

"Oh, I can."

He held up the glass pot so the sunlight came through it, tourmaline green. The glycer-fortis was a pea-sized lump within. "This would last us a few weeks. Then it'd be gone. For all the danger of this stuff, our bodies come to need it. You could live for a few days, maybe. But I've been here longer. Without it my heart would stop. They don't need guards to keep me."

By the time Elias had been working in the factory for eight months, the yellow tint had crept into his own hair. One day he saw the thermometer man staring into the oily liquid in the reaction flask with a kind of longing. Then he seemed to notice Elias watching. He looked around, almost guiltily, smiling a smile that was false.

It had lasted only a second, but that night Elias couldn't sleep. He kept circling the memory, trying to find a way to explain it other than the one that had hit him at the time.

"Are you feeling well?" he asked the next morning in the canteen hut, as they shovelled oatmeal porridge into their mouths.

"I'm good," the man said. "Always good."

"You're sure of that?"

"I said so, didn't I!"

"It's just... yesterday, I thought, perhaps..."

"You know nothing!" the man shouted. It was almost a confession. Neither of them spoke again.

The next day a gangly boy arrived to learn the backbreaking job of packing ice. No one said anything. But they all looked at Elias, who'd been promoted to watching the thermometers ahead of his time. He didn't know if they were accusing him or if they'd just wanted the job themselves. The mercury inched upwards towards the red line, then crept back down.

No one could have known that he'd done it. Not for sure.

He'd told them he was fetching more wood for the stove. From the woodpile, he'd circled the camp, keeping out of the lamplight.

"What do you want, boy?" the overseer had asked.

"You said I should tell if one of them was tired of life."

When Elias's first shift watching thermometers was done, he hurried ahead to the bunkhouse before the others. The thermometer man's blankets had been stripped and folded. The crate at the foot of the bed was empty. As an afterthought, he felt under the thin mattress. His fingers closed on something small and smooth. He knew what it was even before pulling it from its hiding place. The green glass jar with its stopper, holding a small lump of glycer-fortis. The thing the old man couldn't live without.

The others trooped in and dropped themselves to their beds. The gangly boy was in tears. There were scowls from the old hands. *I saved you*, Elias wanted to say. *You don't know it, but I saved you all.*

CHAPTER 6

Sitting on the beach at New Whitby, Elias watched the sun setting over the western headland. He'd been remembering his time in the Yukon: the ordeals that had formed this new version of the man he'd once been. When the months of his outlawing had been almost complete, they let him go. He was free, they said, laughing. And from the generosity of their hearts, they gave him a lump of glycer-fortis to keep him alive. For a little while. There would be more to follow, they said, if he went back to Newfoundland and did their bidding. Two small tasks would be the price of the drug.

Turning his hand, he inspected the skin. The yellow had faded, though a tint still remained in the beds of his nails. Nothing that would be noticed. He picked up a pebble and cast it towards the water. It landed short, skittering across the rocks. So he tried another and this time got it to splash into an incoming wave.

He'd enough of the drug to last a month. Slender time, which he'd planned to use to the full. Then Jago had turned up and demanded to meet the smugglers who'd taken him off Newfoundland. Elias had no choice but to obey, much as he hated the thought of it. One month had shrunk to seven days.

At least Elias had completed one of his tasks. And without

pain. The dogs might be able to sniff out gunpowder, even a few grains. But they didn't know the scent of glycer-fortis. The stuff could be smuggled without fear. That was news he could trade with.

He held the glass jar up to the pale western sky, tilting it so the small lump rolled within. He'd been rationing himself. But too long between doses and his heart picked up that irregular beat, leaving him short of breath.

The stopper came away with a muted pop. He loved the sound and the smell of it. And he hated them. Dipping his cloak pin, he wiped it on the underside of his tongue then lay back on the shingle, feeling the chemical warmth seep through his relaxing chest.

With his head on the ground, the wash and draw of the waves sounded different. Three gulls flew overhead. One held something in its beak. The others swooped on it, trying to snatch the morsel away.

Elias's time had been stolen. But there'd been fortune also. Jago was unusual among the Patron Protectors. An upstart, the others called him, a man careless of custom and practice. It was always going to be Jago to provide for Elias's second task. Only an upstart could wish for the world to be turned on its head. And that is what they were going to do.

He waited until full dark before returning to the Salt Ray Inn. There were fewer drinkers than the night before. News of Jago's interest in the place must have spread. That would be a black mark by Elias's name, though it hadn't been his fault. He stepped to the tap, where the dark-haired barmaid eyed him with suspicion.

"A pint," he said, sliding his last half coin over the smooth wood. "Please."

She pulled the pump. Beer frothed in the tankard. He tried a smile but it felt false and her expression stayed icy. He was about to ask if the mistress could spare him a minute, but the barmaid cut him off, saying, "I've been told not to talk to you."

Before he could get a word in, she'd grabbed a cloth and ducked down to the floor. Elias had to lean over the bar to see her. She was wiping the flagstones under the tap, giving them more sweat and muscle than ever they deserved.

"Excuse me?" he said, but got no answer.

Money might have seemed the least of his worries. But he still needed some if he wasn't to starve. If the mistress of the Salt Ray wasn't going to speak with him, he'd be needing it all the more.

He stayed clear of the table he'd used the night before. Only fools believe lightning doesn't strike twice. People were watching him as he took a table in the lamplight. How long, he wondered, before news spread beyond New Whitby that Elias No-Thumbs had returned. Jago wouldn't be the only one wanting a piece of him.

The dice were too white. Too conspicuously new. If he'd had some fine oil, he could have worked it into the surface and started building up a patina. Bone becomes more like ivory with age and handling. The rough edges of the cubes annoyed him too. It would take time for them to wear pebble smooth. But for all that, his new dice did sing a beautiful tune. He cast them onto the table. Oh, the soft clatter of them. Heads turned. The sound would be a lover's whisper to any gambling man.

He cast them again and again, counting the throws and the number of sixes. He pretended to not see the glances of nearby drinkers. They'd be wanting to know how a man could play dice against himself. Someone would pluck up the courage and ask. By then they'd be ready. A man needs beer in his belly before he'll slap silver on the table.

He cast the dice, read the spots, added the numbers. If they were true, they'd turn up sixes one-sixth of the time. The more throws he took, the closer the numbers came to being right. Not bad work for a man with no thumbs.

It was a woman with a lopsided nose who took his bait. She made it seem as if it was just a trip to the bar. But Elias had caught her watching. On the way back to her table, she skewed off course for a closer look at him.

He held out the dice to her, palm upwards. She acted surprised.

"Do I know you?" she asked.

"I don't know. Do you?"

And then: "Why do you play dice on your own?"

"I'd play solitaire, but my cards were burned."

"I…" She glanced around before continuing in a whisper, "I heard about that."

She might be a fisherwoman, Elias thought, to judge by her clothes. Or a small-time trader. Not a peasant, yet not exactly comfortable. There was a curl of Irish in her accent, a hint that she might be knit from the early settlers. She was older than him by a few years. He cast the dice again. They tumbled to a stop near where she stood, showing a six and a three. She licked her lips and then slid onto the bench opposite him. They were full lips.

"Do you play?" he asked.

"I… That is… I haven't. But…"

"Would you like to?"

"How do I do it?"

This was a surprise. A gambler should know such things, even if dice wasn't her regular game. She might be play-acting. But if so, she'd made a good pretence.

He scooped the dice from the table's edge and held them out to her again. "Try it. Just let them roll."

She nodded. As she took them, her eyes lingered on his for a fraction too long.

"They're lovely," she said. "Did you... Did you make them?"

"Yes."

"How... I mean... with your hands like that?" And then, when he didn't answer: "I've heard stories about you. They say you've come back to take revenge."

"Who says?"

"I don't know. Someone. My brother heard it. We don't believe it. Unless you say it's true. Then we'd believe it, of course. But I'm not asking."

"I've come home. That's all."

"That's good then," she said, though seeming disappointed. "Where do you sleep? I mean, do you have a house or something?"

Elias was sure now. If the light had been stronger, he'd have been able to see her cheeks glowing. It wasn't the song of the dice that had called to her. It was him. Or the things people had said about him.

"I don't have a place," he said

"I do," said she, too quickly.

The topmost laces of her bodice were loose. He hadn't noticed that before. She leaned forwards and let the dice roll from her hand. A two and another six. Damn, but he'd lost count. He found himself gazing at her breasts.

"You live with your brother?" he asked.

"Yes."

Elias had opened his mouth to say something, he wasn't sure what, when a shadow fell over the table. The woman with the crooked nose sat back suddenly and grabbed her tankard. Elias looked up to see the mistress of the Salt Ray Inn.

"Well met," the mistress said.

"You too," said the woman with the crooked nose.

"How's the beer?"

"Fine. Good. Thank you," she said.

"No. Thank *you* for your custom."

The woman with the crooked nose clearly wanted to go, but the mistress of the Salt Ray Inn was standing with folded arms, solidly blocking her escape.

"How's trade?" the mistress asked.

"Good."

So, not a fisherwoman after all.

"And how's your husband?"

Elias could see the blush in the woman's face this time, even in the lamplight.

"He's good. Thank you."

"I hear business keeps him in Labrador?"

The woman lifted her tankard and pushed her way out, hurrying to get back to her table at the other side of the saloon. Elias watched her go.

"I'm told you wanted to speak to me," the mistress said. "I hope I didn't interrupt anything important."

A doorway behind the bar let them into an earth-floored room of shelves and barrels. A lantern, flour sacks and cured meats hung from hooks in the central beam. The barmaid stopped carving strips from a ham and stared at him. He expected the mistress to send her away, but the two women stood shoulder to shoulder facing him, arms folded.

"Thank you for seeing me," he said.

No response.

"I'm grateful for this morning. I'm in your debt already. But there's something more I need. It'll be your boon if I get it. I didn't want to see Jago last night. But he came to your bar and you saw what happened."

"You're blaming me?" The mistress's tone was sharp.

"No. No. But I'm saying it wasn't my fault either. It just happened. And now he's wanting something. If I don't give it, he'll be back in six days."

A glance passed between the two women. No more than a flick of the eyes, but Elias had seen it. The thought of having Jago at the Inn had panicked them.

"I need to get a message to Short Harbour," he said.

"Then you'd better start walking."

"I need to get an answer back before the six days are up."

"Try walking faster."

"Jago took my winnings, or I could pay."

"But you still have silver for beer." This from the barmaid.

"That was my last scrap," he said, directing his answer to the mistress. "It's what it took to get me here, face to face with you."

The two women turned to each other: a consultation of small expressions and nods, which he couldn't read.

"I could send a message," the mistress said, at last. "Carrier pigeon to Stephenville. From there, another to Woodstock. Then a rider to Short Harbour. Two days, if you're lucky with the weather. Two days back. Twenty American dollars would see it done. It'd only happen on my good name. Folk know I pay my debts. What would I get in return?"

"Jago's going to give me a reward."

"You think so?"

"Maybe. But if I can't do what he asks, I'll have no choice but hide. He'll come looking. He'll come here."

"You ask much," the mistress said. "But all you offer are hopes and threats."

"I have nothing else."

"That's not true," said the maid.

The mistress nodded. "You're Elias Calvary?"

"I'm Elias. But not Calvary anymore." He didn't like the way the conversation was going.

"They say you were outlawed."

"My time's spent."

"But you *did* escape. You got away from Newfoundland."

"Yes."

"I'll have your message taken to Short Harbour. But in exchange, I want to know how you got away."

First Jago, then the maid, now the mistress. Everyone wanted the same thing. It was a coin he could spend only once.

"If I give that, I'll have nothing left," he said.

"That," she said, "is our price."

CHAPTER 7

Elias woke with a start to the unaccustomed feeling of linen beneath him, a down-filled cover above, and his left side warmer than his right. Inching out a hand, he met the naked skin of a woman's hip. She sighed and rolled towards him, bringing those full lips and that crooked nose close to his face. Her kiss began as something lazy but became more urgent. Her mouth smelled of sleep. His must too. She pushed him onto his back, her weight squeezing the breath from him.

When they got back to her house the night before, she'd wanted stories of his time as an outlaw. The more he spoke of reckless deeds and hardship, the hungrier her eyes had become. He'd no wish to re-live the shame, but stories were the price of a bed. So he told her of a day on the journey back towards Newfoundland when he'd held a piece of wood to the neck of a trapper, told him it was a knife and robbed him of a plate of beans and bacon. It had been a bad time. But hearing it, she launched herself at him. They started against the kitchen wall. Then she took his hand and led him up to the sleeping loft.

He'd guessed the truth already, but found proof of it in the way she took him. It wasn't Elias she wanted, but the desperate outlaw she imagined him to be. Straddling his hips, she'd closed her eyes, as if for a better view.

Perhaps she'd been dreaming of outlaws because, with the morning light streaming in through the gable window, she needed no more stories. This time her eyes were open and, in the end, his were closed.

There were eggs for breakfast – he ate three – and toasted bread and butter and blueberry jam and coffee. Her name was Charity, she said, as she slid another slice onto his plate. He chuckled at that, taking it as a joke, but stopped when he saw her frown. So Charity it was. Finding her smile again she kissed him on the forehead and returned to the stove.

Afterwards, leaning back from the table with the odd feeling of a full belly, he watched her washing the breakfast things in the sink. She wasn't fat, few on Newfoundland were. Strongly built might be a better way to put it. Her arse swung from side to side as she dried the plates and shifted them to the rack. Before his outlawing, he'd had the pick of the serving girls. They'd been happy enough to take a tumble with a young man of the Blood. Sometimes he gave them trinkets: a ring or a necklace, red glass cut to look like rubies. Back then, he wouldn't have given Charity a second glance. Now here he was, trading his body for a bed and a plate of food. At least the serving girls had gone away with something that lasted.

The mistress of the Salt Ray Inn had asked after Charity's husband. Elias had seen a pair of man's boots just inside the back door. There'd been mention of a brother as well. The boots could belong to him. It would have been good to know if there was a chance of another night in Charity's house. But it seemed the wrong time to ask.

"What do you know about the Salt Ray?" he said.

"They're pricy," she said. "But the beer's not watered. The mistress don't hold with fighting. I guess folk go there if they want a quiet time."

"Where's she from?"

There was a lull in Charity's washing of the cutlery. "She's from up north, they say. Moved to New Whitby ten years back. Bought the Salt Ray – it wasn't called that then. Twelve years, maybe. Why do you want to know?"

"I'm curious. What about that barmaid?"

"The pretty one?"

He caught the warning note in her voice.

"I hadn't noticed," he said.

That seemed to be the right answer. She carried on brighter. "She's new. Turned up a few months back."

"From where?"

"Does it matter?"

"I saw the mistress look to her. It felt wrong. Like their places were the other way about. Like the maid was the mistress. Could she be family, do you think?"

Charity turned to face him, wiping her hands on her apron.

"You're sure you didn't see how pretty she is?"

"I need something from them," Elias said. "That's all." And then, knowing he could press her no more, he changed the subject. "Do you have children?"

"I was never so blessed," she said.

"And your brother?"

"The line ends with us."

"I meant to ask where he is. You said he lived with you?"

"Oh. Yes. But he's away." She looked to the floor, blushing. "Was it him you wanted to know about, or my husband?"

Elias blushed too, and felt foolish for it. "Both," he said.

She met his gaze. "They're away together. On business. Couldn't be back until tomorrow. That at the soonest. So I'll be on my own tonight. Unless you're wanting to stay?"

The great wonder of Charity's house was a copper tub. More than large enough for Elias to sit in, and deep enough to soak to the bottom of his chest, it had been made with a high sloping back, so the bather could rest in comfort.

At the woodpile, he found the axe handle too fat for his grip. The saw was more to his liking. As he worked, he wondered about the other men she must have bedded. If the husband and brother were traders, they might be away for much of the time.

When enough logs had been cut to heat the water, he split them with a hammer and spike. Then, feeling guilty for his thoughts, he cut two loads more.

Stripping off in the kitchen he was aware of her eyes on him, reading the words of the law tattooed across his chest. Only a man born of the Blood had such marks. He turned away before pulling down his long johns and casting them to the floor with the other clothes.

"You weren't so shy last night," she said.

He lowered himself into the water. "Why are you staring?"

"Sorry. It's just, I'd never thought to see a highborn man stripped naked."

"I'm not of the Blood. You've seen the severed rope on my arm. They cut me off."

"Do you think it makes a difference?" she asked.

It was a stupid question. "Yes, it makes a difference!"

"But not to who you are."

"Ink is everything," he said.

"Ink is ink," she replied, almost fiercely. Then she tipped a stream of water over him. The shock of the heat made him gasp.

When the bucket was empty, she was smiling again. She threw him the soap, giggling when it slipped out of his hands and splashed into the tub.

"I'll wash these for you," she said, gathering his clothes.

Alone in the kitchen, Elias stared at the limewashed wall, seeing but not seeing. Charity was unaligned. She lived in the unaligned land. She would never go to the Reckoning or understand the meaning of oaths and honour. He was merely a story to her.

He slid lower, allowing his face to dip beneath the hot water. His heart slowed as he let breath escape through his nose. When he sat up again, his thoughts had cleared. It was the barmaid he needed to think about, not Charity. The barmaid held the key.

Her voice had been bothering him from the start. The Newfoundland mix was almost right. He might not have caught the foreignness. But her vowels slipped on some words. A different accent hid underneath. It had been prickling at the back of his mind. But only with his body relaxing into the steaming water did a memory come to his aid. He'd heard a similar accent once before, in the Yukon when he was an outlaw. A European man had travelled through, stopping at the glycer-fortis factory. Elias never learned how that man had ended up in Alaska. Now he wished he'd asked.

In Europe, all matters of life were controlled, they said. Anything you did might risk gaol or the gallows. Lawmen stood on every corner. And spies. Easy to understand a man or woman in that place wanting to escape to the free wilds beyond the Gas-Lit Empire. But not to Newfoundland. Newfoundland was a place apart. Hard to get to. Harder to leave.

He guessed the barmaid was in her early twenties. If she *was* an off-lander, the only way for her to be living in New Whitby was as a slave. Yet he'd seen no slave marks on her skin.

They could be lovers, he thought, the two women. The mistress might have met her in Labrador or Quebec, away from Newfoundland but not yet in the Gas-Lit Empire. She could have found a way to smuggle her lover back. That would explain the closeness, the way the mistress had yielded to the maid. But more than that, it would answer the riddle of the look the women had shared when he told them Jago might return. They'd been afraid. Pity the barmaid if Jago found out she was an off-lander but not yet owned. He'd have his oath-wright marking her skin before anyone else could put in a claim.

Elias lifted his leg over the side of the copper bath and let it dangle, dripping water onto the tiles. He might go back to the barmaid, he thought. But if he demanded to see her oath-marks and found them in order, he'd have burned what slim welcome remained for him at the Salt Ray. If, on the other hand, the mark was missing...

With a crash, the kitchen door slammed open behind him. He lunged his hand out of the tub. But his knife had been taken with his clothes. He was set to leap out and grab the skillet as a weapon, but Charity's giggle made him stop.

"Did you think it was the husband?" she asked, wickedly.

He turned and saw that she was alone. "I thought just that!"

He lowered himself back into the water, trying to calm the uneven beat of his heart. If the glycer-fortis had been in reach, he'd have given himself another dose. She stepped around the tub and looked down at him.

"Your things are drying in front of the fire," she said. And then, holding his gaze, she began to undress. Her chemise was the last to fall. She stepped into the tub and crouched, scooping up water onto her breasts. For the first time he thought about her unmarked skin.

Salmon-pink veins ran through the rocks behind the Salt Ray Inn. He sat above the place where the outcrop plunged into the shingle of the beach. A small fleet of fishing boats were out in the loop beyond the shelter of the bay. The furthest headland shone dizzyingly clear in the distance. The beauty of it was almost too much to hold. It felt like a knife cutting into his flesh.

If Charity weren't married, he might move in with her. He let himself imagine the ease of sleeping in the same bed from day to day, knowing there'd be hot food. Not that she'd want him like that. He might dream of a simple life, but she'd bedded him for a taste of the opposite. She was being unfaithful with him. But she could just as easily be unfaithful to him. It was a fool's dream. Even if she could change, he could not.

It was mid-afternoon, judging by the sun. They'd be scrubbing down the saloon in the Salt Ray, getting ready for the night. All the windows had been thrown wide, making the most of the good weather. He could hear tables and chairs being dragged around within. Then a shovel began to scrape over flagstones. Someone was mucking out the stables. He didn't turn to look. Not even when the back door of the inn opened and a bucket clanged near the ash pit.

Eyes would be fixed on him though, and not just from the inn. The windows of New Whitby might be small, but someone was always watching. Jago's wrath would be white hot at the end of the week if he didn't get what he wanted. It wouldn't take him long to find out that Elias No-Thumbs had spent his days loitering around the Salt Ray. He'd force his way in, say he was searching for smuggled weapons. If the mistress had nothing to hide, she'd have nothing to fear.

Elias rummaged for his smoking things. The tobacco was from Georgia, or so said the man who'd traded it. He prised open the tin and breathed in the sweet scent. He'd been holding off, but there might not be a better time, so he tipped the last rubbings onto a paper and began the rolling.

The good thing about having no thumbs was the way people thought he could do so little. He'd come to relish the chances that gave him. Life's little pleasures. He had workarounds for most every task. Like rolling the twist, which he did on the palm of one hand with the fingers of the other. The result was misshapen. But it would taste every bit as good.

A launch steamed into view around the headland, the smoke from its funnel smudging the horizon. An inspection crew would ride out to it as soon as it made fast at one of the jetties. Elias wondered what kind of craft Charity's husband and brother used for their trading. Nothing so brash as the steam launch, he thought. It would be modest but solid and reliable.

A scuffing of shoes made him turn. A skinny boy had scrambled up onto the rocks and was staring at him.

"Show us your hands," said the boy.

Damn, but everyone in the whole dump of a town must be talking about him. He held them out anyway.

"It *is* you," said the boy, sounding impressed "Mistress says you're to go to the stable."

Feeling a stir in his heart, Elias put the unlit twist in the tin and snapped closed the lid. The boy jumped back down from the rocks and beckoned.

Elias would have waited there all day if needed, and the next. With Charity's husband back he'd have been looking for a new place to sleep. And scrounging for food. There was a crock of coins in Charity's kitchen, hidden behind the flour and the oats. He'd have felt bad dipping into it. But none of that mattered now. The mistress had panicked. She'd shown the weakness of her hand. She'd never have made a gambler.

They reached the yard. The boy pointed to the stable doors then scampered away. Elias considered the dark opening before stepping inside. He couldn't see much after the bright sunshine. He could smell the horses though. One of them stamped and snorted as he stepped further in.

Then something clicked against the flagstones behind him. He started to turn but a sack rammed down over his head.

He tensed, about to swing his elbow back into whoever it was, but a sharp point jabbed against his right kidney. A hand pushed on his shoulder. Obediently he knelt.

CHAPTER 8

It was one of Jago's men. The thought flashed into Elias's panicked mind. Or another Patron. They'd all be after the same thing, to know how he'd smuggled himself over the water.

The grip on his shoulder hardened, fingertips digging into muscle, the jab of pain deadening his arm.

He could only see a shadow through the hessian of the sack. It was a man, though. And he'd caught the sound of iron hobnails striking the cobbles. A working man, then. Perhaps not one of Jago's after all.

"I came to see the mistress," he said, trying not to cough. The sack was thick with barley dust.

A whack on the side of the head left his ear ringing. But the man wasn't a gatherer. Elias was sure of that now. If it had been a gatherer, the blow would have left him sprawled on the stones, lights popping behind his eyes.

"I came to see the mistress," he said again, his voice stronger this time.

The sack ripped away. He tried to blink the dust from his eyes. An old man stood in front of him, bald and wiry. The sharp point had been the spike at the head of a bill hook. It was sweeping the air in front of his face.

"You're to get gone!" said the man.

"But I was told to come here."

"Gone! Out of New Whitby."

"Who says?"

"I do."

"What if I don't go?"

"I'll cut y' fingers off and stuff 'em down y' gullet."

"Is that what the mistress told you to say?"

"You'll leave her out of it!"

The man swung his free hand. But without the sack over his eyes, Elias saw it coming clear enough and shifted to the side so the blow landed soft. The bill hook jabbed air, as if to threaten worse.

"Do you want me to go now?" Elias asked.

"Yes!"

He raised his hands and stood, taking each move slow. His first panic had been replaced by fear. But now that, too, was leaving him. He was taller than the old man. And broader in the shoulder.

"Do you work for the mistress, then?" he asked. "What are you – servant or slave?"

"Shut y' mouth!"

"I just want to know," Elias said. "I shouldn't like to do damage if you belong to her."

The bill hook pricked him in the belly. There'd be a drop of blood on his clean washed clothes. But the man had put no force behind it. Elias had been taught how to use a knife in battle: picturing the hand going right through the body and coming out the other side. The old man wasn't a killer. But he was armed and that had to change.

"What else does the mistress make you do?" Elias asked in a mocking tone. "Does she make you clean the floor of the pisser with your tongue?"

It was enough. Hatred flared in the man's eyes. He lunged properly this time, taking himself off balance. Elias sidestepped, smashed down on the wrist. The bill hook clattered to the stones. The old man was bending to grab it, but Elias trapped his arm and twisted it back.

"I don't think so," he said, kicking the blade away into the straw.

The man whipped his head round and spat but Elias easily kept behind him, out of harm's way.

"Should we call the mistress, do you think?" he said, then twisted the man's wrist an inch or two higher, making him yelp.

A shadow moved into the sunlight by the doors and the mistress of the Salt Ray stepped inside. "Enough!" she said.

"He tried to stab me."

"It was a warning."

"On your orders? He's put a hole through my clothes."

"Let him go. Please."

This time Elias did. The old man staggered away, rubbing his shoulder. It might be sore for a day or two, but the real damage was to his pride. He seemed about to take up the bill hook, but the mistress shook her head. He stared hatefully at Elias as he backed into the stable-yard.

They were alone.

"I want you gone," she said.

"I was happy where I was."

"Those rocks, everything from here to the shore, it all belongs to me. You can't sit there."

"We're neither of us aligned," he said. "I can sit where I like, unless you want to make a challenge of combat."

"He was only supposed to warn you. I can have someone mend the cloak, if you like."

It was an offering of help. Little enough, to be sure. But it showed her weakness again.

"What about my shirt?" he asked.

"I'm sorry. They'll mend that too."

"And my skin?"

"Look – I'll make it right. You wanted money. I can give you money. Compensation. For the misunderstanding."

His nerves steadied. His heart beat strong and even. He wondered how much silver he could take her for, if he pressed his case. But it wasn't her silver he needed. It was her credit.

"Send the message for me," he said. "Then we'll call it even. You'll be shot of me. I won't come back."

She straightened to her full height. He hadn't noticed a stoop before, but she'd added a couple of inches.

"Well?" he asked.

Another shadow blinked out the light in the doorway and the dark-haired barmaid stepped in from the courtyard.

"Is everything good, mistress?" she asked.

There it was again: the look passing between the two women.

"I can't give you my credit," said the mistress.

"Why not?"

"You're snared with Jago. I don't know how. But if I let you have my name for credit, I'll be putting the Salt Ray in the same trap. Folk drink here because it's safe. I can't do it."

"Then we have a problem," Elias said. "Your credit's the one thing I need."

"I have friends," she said. "If I put out the word, they'd come to drive you away. They won't be gentle."

If it had been the truth, she'd have done it already. The maid was an off-lander, and not yet owned. He felt sure of it now. The two women were staring at him. A horse stamped again in one of the stalls.

"Show me her oath-marks," he said, pointing to the maid's neck. "Do that and I'll be gone."

The mistress stiffened, but the maid began to unwind her neck cloth. After three turns it hung loose in her hand. Then she undid the top buttons of her bodice and spread the collar.

Her pale skin seemed milky in the half-light of the stable. And there they were: blue-black letters where her neck met the shoulders. His heart threw in an extra beat. She had to be an off-lander. She turned. The letters ran all the way around, a necklace of writing.

"Are we done?" the mistress asked. There was a catch in her voice.

Thoughts swarmed in Elias's mind. It couldn't be! He'd gambled everything that the maid was unclaimed. *I am bound to Maria Rosa.* The line of writing ended with the design of two fish made to look like a circle.

"Maria Rosa." He spoke the name aloud.

The mistress nodded. "That is me. Now go. Go to your fate, whatever it is. From this day, you'll never be welcome here."

Elias beat a palm against his forehead, as if a jolt to the brain might reveal a better truth. The mistress, Maria Rosa, strode out into the yard. The maid started to button up her bodice. But it wasn't right. It couldn't be right.

"Stop!" he said.

He caught the flicker of fear in her face.

"Turn!"

She didn't move, so he stepped around her. "Who was the oath-wright? Whose mark is the two fish?"

He gripped her shoulder to keep her still then spat on the pad of his finger and rubbed at the back of her neck. The skin stretched and the mark stretched also. It didn't fade. He dragged her towards the splash of daylight by the door. She tried to pull away. Desperate. He looped his arm around her. It couldn't be right.

In the courtyard, the mistress was shouting for help. Servants came running from the inn. Catching the flash of steel blades, he turned the maid towards them, making a shield of her.

The old man held a crossbow.

Everything was going to hell. Elias brought his head behind the maid's. It was then, with his eye close to her neck and the daylight on her, that he saw it. There was a sheen on her skin over the lettering. The blue-black pigment lay on the surface, not underneath it. It wasn't a tattoo.

He let go of her and raised his hands. He stepped into the courtyard. The old man aimed the crossbow.

"You want I kill him?"

It was an empty threat. Elias had put himself in the open. The many eyes of New Whitby were surely watching. He'd be safe enough, so long as his hands were up.

"Away!" The mistress spat the word at him. But she was shaking and her face had drained of colour. Perhaps she'd seen the calm in his eyes.

"I don't think you want me to go," he said. "And I don't think you want me to say why. Not out loud."

They were standing in the storeroom behind the bar, the mistress, the maid and Elias. The door had been pulled closed, but thumbs or no thumbs, he would be more than a match for them if it came to a fight.

"Her oath-marks are false," he said.

The mistress was crumpling. The maid gripped her hand, as if to give support. Strangely, the young woman had stood taller as her truth was brought to light. Her level gaze unnerved him.

Elias said, "I can tell Jago what I've found. Or you can lend me your credit so I can get my message to Short Harbour. There's still time, if we do it now."

All this he said to Maria Rosa, who nodded in response, her eyes on the earth floor, defeated.

But the maid folded her arms. "No," she said.

"Do you understand what Jago would do if he found out you're an off-lander?"

"I do."

"I'm giving you a way out," he said. "You can't turn it down."

"I don't believe you'll give up my secret," said the maid.

"Why in hell's name not?"

"Because if Jago put his mark on me, I'd have to tell him what I know about you. You've been cheating at cards. I watched you that night in the saloon. Before he marched in."

"Those men played each with the other," Elias said and tried to laugh. The sound stuck in his throat. His heart had caught that irregular beat. The glycer-fortis was in the pocket at his belt. He could feel it against his leg. He wanted to reach for it.

"You dealt the cards," she said.

"I wasn't gambling. They were."

"You still dealt. What would happen if Jago found out that Elias No-Thumbs had been back to his old tricks? What do you get for cheating a second time?"

"No one would believe you!"

"You'd be outlawed again," she said.

"It'd be your word against mine. And here are my witnesses." He held up his mutilated hands. "No one would believe I could cheat."

"What about this witness?" she said, reaching two fingers under her cuff and extracting a playing card from the sleeve. It was one of his. He snatched it away and was about to tear it to pieces.

"I have more," she said. "Safely locked away. Trick cards, shaved narrow at one end. That's why you came back. A few burned cards would be no use. But you had to get them. They prove you were cheating."

The maid was right. But it was impossible that she could have seen it.

"Who are you?" he asked.

"My name is Elizabeth," she said. "Elizabeth Barnabus. And I think we can help each other."

PART TWO

CHAPTER 9

The longer Elizabeth Barnabus spent on Newfoundland, the less she seemed to understand it. It was the most brutal place she could imagine. And yet she'd witnessed kindness and generosity on a heroic scale. Many said they were proud to have so few laws, to be free. Yet she saw their fear at the casual violence of the lawless land.

It was the opposite of her home in England. Back across the waters, in what she'd thought of as the civilised world, the nations had long ago been bound together by a treaty of mutual security. It wasn't an empire, because no single government ruled over it. Yet so tightly were they bound that it was described just so: the Gas-Lit Empire.

The waging of war had been banned, as well as technologies that might be detrimental to the wellbeing of the common man, which meant all new developments that might lead to weaponry. There'd been great advances in the science of medicine. Barriers to trade and travel had been dismantled. Goods and people could move without let or hindrance from Samarkand to Carlisle, from New York to Timbuktu.

The price of such freedoms had been the overbearing authority of a new legal system, with the International Patent Office at its centre, like a spider in the middle of a web. Patent Office judges decided which technologies were unseemly and should be blotted out. No one knew the number of its prison camps. Its agents were everywhere, gathering information about every aspect of life. The innocent had nothing to fear, they said.

Some fled in the early days: those with means, those who couldn't abide the new laws. The 1830s saw a trickle of British, French and Americans arriving in Newfoundland. Their numbers swelled as the controls of the International Patent Office spread from nation to nation. No one had invited them. But hospitality was the way of things in old Newfoundland. Homesteads opened their doors as the boats arrived.

The Gas-Lit Empire reached out after them. The people of Newfoundland gathered to decide whether they, too, should join this new alliance and submit to its laws. The vote could have gone either way. The promised benefits were great. But it was the votes of the new arrivals that carried the day. They outnumbered the earlier settlers. And they would never submit to the things they'd so recently fled.

Amputation was the most visible evidence of the Newfoundland way. The peasants were less afflicted by it. But in the middle ranks it seemed almost universal.

"You mustn't stare," Maria Rosa had whispered, after Elizabeth had first ventured into the saloon of the Salt Ray Inn, carrying a tray of cold meats to men seated near the fire.

"Why didn't you warn me?"

"Of what?"

"They... They're all... That man – half his face is gone. And the others... Were they in a battle?"

The confusion on Maria Rosa's face was replaced by understanding. She brushed a stray lock of hair from Elizabeth's brow. "This is Newfoundland," she said. "When an oath is made, it is marked onto some part of the body. For the oath to be broken, that part must be removed."

• • •

After three months serving and hiding at the Salt Ray Inn, Elizabeth had become accustomed to the mutilations. They still appalled her, but her initial revulsion had been replaced by curiosity. A story lay behind each cut, if one had the knowledge to read it. Maria Rosa said she should put such things out of her mind. But that had never been Elizabeth's way.

Elias had interested her from the moment he walked into the saloon, though not for his missing thumbs, which had been hidden at the time. It was his actions that marked him out. There were warmer seats he could have chosen. And brighter. Instead he placed himself in the settle next to the drip from the roof, which was also the least well lit. He paid for half a pint of bitter ale but asked her to pour it into a pint tankard – the sign of a sober man giving the appearance that he was drinking.

He'd been wearing gloves when he approached the tap. The thumbs must have been stuffed with something rigid. Picking up his drink, the grip had seemed almost natural. It takes one trickster to recognise another.

Not that he'd noticed her. She made a point of passing close to his booth on her way to pick up the empties and when carrying out plates of food. She was behind him when he brought out the matchbox and slipped off his gloves. He must have thought himself unseen.

Missing digits were common enough. But she'd never before seen a man who'd lost both his thumbs. Unusual though that was, it was his hiding of them that intrigued her.

He tipped out the matches onto the table and selected two from the heap, holding them between his first and second fingers. A clumsy grip. Deliberately clumsy, she thought. The deformity that he'd hidden before was now becoming the centre of his trick. But only for a select audience.

There'd been moments of terror during her time as a barmaid. The risk of discovery and its consequences could never be forgotten. But for the most part it had been a time of excruciating boredom. Watching the man with no thumbs and trying to guess his secrets presented her with a stimulating distraction.

It was a private show, for no one else in the bar would have the knowledge to decode his actions. As a connoisseur of misdirection, Elizabeth found particular satisfaction in seeing something new. She watched him as he watched the room, searching for a suitable mark, some gullible drinker with silver in their pocket. The missing thumbs put a novel twist on his work.

First, he performed a proposition bet: the placing of matches on top of each other. She'd seen it before, though by tricksters with fully functioning hands. She imagined that a demand for money might come next. But instead, he used the trick as bait, drawing in the mark's friends from another table.

Elizabeth's admiration grew. And her enjoyment.

With the three of them assembled, he brought out a pack of playing cards and dealt five to each man. Seeing it, she had to suppress the urge to laugh out loud, such was the elegance of his work. The trick was precisely that there could be no trick. He had no thumbs. The players knew that sleight of hand would be impossible. The dealing was clumsy but they trusted him. They gambled against each other. Only when their cards were balanced did he take the money on the table. They might have been irritated when it happened, but his money never stayed in view so they never had the sense of how much he was accumulating. Their eyes were on each other.

He wasn't earning a fortune. But the risk was never his. She couldn't keep count precisely, but he was earning a fair night's pay. For a man with no thumbs. And the players saved their anger for each other.

"Be careful," said Maria Rosa, when they passed each other in the storeroom. "Patron Jago's ridden into town. The boy saw his men over at the High Rat. With luck he won't come near us."

Elizabeth had heard the story of Jago and his upstart family. His grandfather had been a fisherman, they said. And then a mercenary. But he'd bought a tract of seven hundred acres with a sliver of coast and a mountain in the middle. Then he'd got himself an oath-wright and set the family up as a clan. The old clans didn't accept it, of course. Money wasn't the same as Blood. They launched a few attacks, but the mountain was easy to defend. The others gave up trying to dislodge him. Two generations later, the feud still rumbled on. Everyone knew Jago was a Patron Protector, though the other clans hadn't given him full rights at the Reckoning. He was "new power" to them. They still called him a little shit, but no longer to his face. None of them would have dared to ride into New Whitby without a small army to stand guard. In doing it himself, Jago mocked them.

"Be careful," the mistress said again, as if a second warning were needed.

As she turned to leave, Elizabeth caught her arm. "There's a man running a card game out there. Do you want me to stop him?"

"How do you read them?" Maria Rosa asked. "Are they fighting types?"

Elizabeth thought for a moment before answering. "I don't see it that way."

"Then let them play. So long as they're buying drinks. But keep your eyes open. Tell me if anything changes."

When Elizabeth stepped across to clear the empties from the table, she asked if they wanted food brought. But the players were intent on the cards and waved her away without looking up. The dealer looked, though. He'd shifted his hands from the table as she approached.

After that she was careful to be more discreet, clearing the tables behind him, watching over the top of the settle, from which angle he couldn't see her.

Tempers had started to wear thin. One of the players was winning more than the others. They were staring each other down when the dealer made his move. It might have seemed impossible for him to cheat. He still had the stub of a thumb on his left hand. But it was less than half an inch of the lower joint.

With his deformity, he was obliged to scoop the cards to the edge of the table to pick them up. The action seemed natural enough. But as he did it, Elizabeth caught him brushing the stub of his thumb along the side of the pack, stripping out a few cards from the middle and setting them on the top. It was done in a heartbeat. If she'd blinked she would have missed it.

Then he began to deal with that laborious two-fingered grip, placing in front of the men the very cards he'd just stripped. At first she was certain of what she'd seen. But when the cards were turned up at the end of the round, there was nothing special among them. King-high facing a pair of twos. A pair of sevens won the few coins on the table.

It was little enough. But all the small losses added up and one of the men had raised his voice. He thumped down a fist. Elizabeth glanced back to the storeroom. She knew she should be telling Maria Rosa. The men should be thrown out before it turned into a fight. But she didn't move.

The thumbless man had started off as a bookmaker. But now he seemed to be pulling a confidence trick. Either way, he'd surely be trying to match risk with reward. He'd only choose to act if the laws of probability were in his favour. If the card players had seen his sleight of hand, all their anger and fight would have come his way. He'd be lucky to escape with his life. That was the risk. But there seemed to be no reward. No card sharp should act in such a way.

She'd just convinced herself that she must have imagined the move, when he stripped the pack again. This time two players folded and she never got to see the cards. But there could be no more doubt. It was a tapered deck, shaved to make one end narrower by a hair's breadth. Simply turning one card around enabled the holder to strip it out with a stroke of the finger. Or, in this case, the stub of a thumb.

One of the men stood and drew back a fist. She'd left it too late. The men were shouting at each other. Everyone in the saloon was watching. She had to act, but surprise and indecision had paralysed her. Then Maria Rosa swept past. There was a heavy iron wrench in the mistress's hand, held close to her skirts so the men wouldn't see it coming. But the man who'd raised his fist now dropped it to his side. The fight was gone from him. The other two were still casting each other dark looks, but seemed more sullen than angry. One of them was swearing as they tramped out into the squally night.

"Gods protect us!" Maria Rosa hissed. "Why didn't you call me?"

Elizabeth took her hand and led her back into the storeroom. "I saw something," she said. "I've got to tell you."

As it happened, there was no time to explain the details or why it was significant. For in marched Jago, as they'd feared. Elizabeth re-tied the cloth to cover the marks around her neck, as any real slave would do, though hers were merely painted on.

The two hours that followed were the most frightening she'd experienced on Newfoundland. The Patron's men were following his lead, showing off in front of each other. At first she managed to position herself to avoid their hands. Then the one-armed giant by the door grabbed at her. She could have had the point of a knife pricking his groin before he knew what was happening. But a slave doesn't do such things. So she stepped behind him, breaking his grip on her apron.

Jago threw his privileges around as if he'd been descended from the founding fathers. Perhaps, Elizabeth thought, he was loud precisely because of his family's humble origins. As if brashness might one day yield respect. For his children, perhaps. Or for theirs. And who was going to stop him?

The one-armed gatherer had been left standing in the draft by the door. No food or drink were ordered for him, so she easily stayed clear. Until he came looking for her. From the bar, she ducked into the storeroom, her heart beating fast and strong. She could have called out for help, but that would have made trouble for Maria Rosa. Instead she wrenched the meat carving knife from the ceiling beam. He had to stoop to pass under the doorway lintel.

If she stabbed him, it would make more trouble still. But she wouldn't need to. She backed away, ducking behind a sack of flour and a leg of ham. He pushed them aside as he advanced, leaving them swinging. She sidestepped right. He mirrored her move, as if they were dancing. But as he dipped his head to pass under the central beam, she jinked the other way, under the stump of his missing arm. His head hit the beam with a dull thud. She could have been away. She should have. But fear had made her angry. She wheeled, bringing the tip of the knife to his back, stopping him mid-turn, pressing hard enough for him to feel the prick of it.

"Want to lose a kidney as well as an arm?" she hissed.

As she stepped away, she knew it had been a mistake. He emerged from the storeroom, eyes fired with hatred. She rounded the bar, certain he was about to charge at her.

And then it happened: the rear door slammed open, bringing a waft of freezing air. And the thumbless man, hands raised above his head. Behind him followed a gatherer with a long knife.

The giant took one more furious look at her, then skulked back to his place by the door, playing the part of the dutiful gatherer.

The prisoner was made to kneel in the hearth. She watched his humiliation unfolding, relieved that they'd found a different victim to focus on, and guilty also for having thought such a thing. His name was Elias, Jago said. A man not to be trusted. That part was true enough, she thought.

When the doors of the Salt Ray Inn were finally bolted, Maria Rosa hugged her close. "What happened in the storeroom?" she asked. "The way he looked at you after! What did you do to him?"

Elizabeth broke free from the embrace and rushed to the hearth. The Patron had thrown Elias's playing cards towards the fire, but they had scattered as they flew, many landing short. She gathered up the ones that hadn't burned, then slid her fingers along the side, stripping out a few, which she then turned and put back so that all the shaved edges were in alignment.

"What is it?" Maria Rosa asked.

"That man was cheating," Elizabeth said.

"That's how he lost his thumbs in the first place," said Maria Rosa.

"You know him, then?"

"I know of him. He was outlawed."

"But he managed to get away?"

"I shouldn't have let him drink here. It was a mistake."

"If he got away, I need to speak with him."

"It's a bad idea."

"He's the first person I've met on Newfoundland who might be able to tell me how to escape!"

"He's trouble. You don't want to be seen with him. Big trouble. There's no surer way to have a Patron notice you!"

"I need to talk with him!"

"And I forbid it! You'll bring ruin to us both."

Maria Rosa's voice had grown shrill. Elizabeth could push no further.

"I know you want to protect me. But there's no safety unless I can get away. And no escape without danger. I'll be found one day, if I stay. So will my friends. The clock's ticking."

"There'll be another path," Maria Rosa said.

Elizabeth rubbed the backs of the cards. They might have had a wax coating once, but it had worn away, leaving the surface rough to the touch. "What if he were to come back?"

"He won't."

"But if he did… Would you give me permission to talk to him then?"

There was a hesitation. Then the mistress nodded.

Elizabeth knelt and began to position the playing cards around the hearth at odd angles, as if they'd fallen at random. "He'll come tomorrow," she said.

CHAPTER 10

If the wind hadn't been north-easterly, Elizabeth might have made landfall in Nova Scotia, within the borders of the Gas-Lit Empire. Then she and her friends would have been safe. If fog hadn't been surrounding the boat, they might have had a sense that they'd steamed a hundred miles too far north. Not that they could have done anything about it. They were down to the last few pints of oil by the time the keel scraped the Newfoundland shingle. There wasn't enough left in the tank to take them across the straits.

But by another measure, they'd been lucky. The fog had also hidden them from view. It had muffled the sound of the engine. Otherwise they'd have been found and enslaved like so many shipwrecked sailors had been before them. The oath-wrights would have marked words around their necks, binding them to one Patron Protector or another.

Luck, then, had saved them. And yet luck had marooned them also. For, without the oath-marks of a Newfoundlander, no one would give them passage across the straits. But with those marks, they'd not be allowed to cross the border into the Free States of America.

There were three of them in the boat: Elizabeth, Julia and Tinker. Also the corpse of a fourth, a victim of their journey. They'd buried the body in a marsh just behind the beach. It was the only place with ground soft and deep enough. They'd said some words and cried, partly from sorrow. But also from relief, for they still believed they'd reached the safety of the American Free States.

A track ran parallel to the coast, following the top of the cliff. That took them southwest, which seemed the right direction. After an hour of walking they came upon a peasant man baling seaweed on the beach.

"How far to Nantucket?" Elizabeth asked.

"You'll be slaves before tomorrow," he said, then laughed, showing the stumps of yellowed teeth.

That's when they understood their mistake.

He put two fingers in his mouth and blew a piercing whistle. There was no one else in view, but Elizabeth and her friends turned and ran. On the path they'd been exposed, so they cut inland, climbing a hillside tangled with wind-twisted spruce. Once they thought they heard the voices of men in pursuit, far behind them and below. The land levelled off and they began to descend. The sounds of the sea faded, leaving only the hiss of the wind among the rocks and branches. At the bottom of a valley, they changed course again, following a stream, trying to lose their pursuers. But in the process they were steadily losing themselves.

By the dawn of the next day, they were cold and exhausted. They might have starved, Elizabeth, Julia and Tinker, but for another chance event. Staggering through that wilderness of bogs and woodlands, they heard a cry of distress, which seemed to be a child's, but which proved to be an old woman, lying on the ground. She'd been collecting crowberry leaves when she'd caught her foot and fallen. Her ankle was swollen so badly that she couldn't even crawl.

Some say that the wild lands are devoid of virtue. The truth is the opposite. Kindness and loyalty are empty words on a day of safety and comfort.

Elizabeth built a fire to warm the old woman, who was near to death. Through one night and one day they kept it burning, using the driest wood they could find, so as to make little smoke. When the woman had at last come back to full consciousness, she told them of a shepherd's hut which they were able to help her to. From there, after two more days, she was able to send word via a peasant shepherd to her daughter in New Whitby, who was Maria Rosa, the mistress of the Salt Ray Inn.

On the morning after the incident with Jago and Elias in the saloon, Elizabeth was busy plaiting dough on a tray. She had three loaves already in the oven and three more on the rise. Fog had rolled in during the night, so the windows had to stay closed. Her eyes stung with the bitter fumes of baking yeast.

Elias No-Thumbs, the man who'd successfully escaped from Newfoundland, had not returned to the inn. Elizabeth had been certain he would. She'd put off cleaning the hearth in the saloon. But it would need to be done in the next hour if the place was to be made ready. It took time for a fire to warm the room through.

Thinking she'd heard a noise in the courtyard, she paused in her work. Then the handle of the rear door rattled. A shadow moved in the white outside the window. She rushed the last three turns of the plait, making a bad job of it, then hurried from the kitchen, wiping her hands on her apron as she went.

Maria Rosa was seated in the counting room, the ledger open on the table in front of her and the bag of coins and hack silver, which were last night's takings.

"He's here," Elizabeth said.

"Where?"

"Outside."

"You saw him?"

A knock came from the front door. Maria Rosa tilted her head, questioning.

"It is him," Elizabeth said. "Trust me."

She stood to the side, out of view, as the mistress pulled back the spyhole cover.

"What?"

"I was here last night," Elias said, his voice muffled by the door.

"I saw it," Maria Rosa said.

"Can I come in?"

The mistress hesitated. Elizabeth willed her to pull back the bolts.

Instead she said, "Why?"

"I left something." The mistress hesitated again. "I'll do any work you want to give me. A trade."

"What work can a man do who's no thumbs?"

Maria Rosa slid the spyhole cover closed.

"Let him in," Elizabeth hissed.

"It'll bring down a sword on both our necks!"

"Just open the door."

"How did you know he'd come?"

"You promised!"

Maria Rosa turned her face away for a moment, then her hand went to the topmost bolt. Elizabeth ran to the storeroom, from where she could listen but not be seen.

"I thank you," Elias said, when the door was open.

"Don't," the mistress said.

There were two safes in the counting room. One stood in the corner. It had two keyholes, a lever handle and an intricate pattern etched on the door. In short it was a conspicuous and expensive import. Elizabeth entered to find Maria Rosa kneeling before it, placing the coin bag on one of its shelves.

"Close the door," the mistress said, getting to her feet.

Elizabeth did. "I told you he'd come."

"And now what? He's not going to tell you how he got away."

"We can talk to him. I might discover something. What he's doing for Jago, maybe."

"We?"

"I."

"It's bad business. All the Patrons are dangerous. But Jago's worse. You can't know what a man like that will do next. How can I protect you, Elizabeth, if you won't listen to me? You don't understand this place."

"How is he different?"

"He's got no respect for practice and custom."

"It's not your job to protect me."

"My debt won't be paid till you're safe across the water."

Elizabeth extracted five playing cards from the sleeve of her blouse. She fanned them, one-handed, as if performing a trick. "We can use these. They prove he's been cheating. We threaten to expose him. He can have the cards back if he tells us how he escaped."

The mistress held out her hand. "Give."

Elizabeth pulled back the cards. "Why?"

"Give them here now!"

"I don't understand."

"You try to blackmail him, and he'll make it his life's work to destroy you. And me. And your friends. And everyone who works here, if he can. He's of the Blood. You never do that to a man of the Blood."

"You told me they threw him out."

"It's their nature. They're born to it. A mark on the skin can't undo a lifetime of training. And he'll have been schooled in fighting. Now give them to me!"

Elizabeth snapped the cards closed, passed them from one hand to the other, then held them out. She wasn't practiced. A card sharp would have spotted the sleight of hand, or counted the number of cards to check. But not Maria Rosa, who accepted them with no comment.

She was bending, as if to place them in the corner safe but then seemed to change her mind. Instead, she stepped to the counting room's cold hearth and knelt. Eight blackened bricks came away from the rear wall of the fireplace. She reached in with a key. A crude metal door swung out, revealing a void beyond. Two shelves stacked with the bags and documents that were Maria Rosa's real wealth. In went the playing cards.

Elizabeth had keys for the corner safe. But not for this hidden one. While the mistress was replacing the bricks, she slipped back into her sleeve the single card that she'd palmed.

Cold meats were for the inn's paying guests. Servants ate simple fare, as did the mistress. Barley soup, with carrots, turnips and onions, fortified with pork fat. Elizabeth ladled some into a bowl and tore a hunk from her new baked bread.

She found Elias in the scullery, washing his hands. He drank the soup straight from the bowl, slowly at first, as if he wasn't hungry. He was tall for a poor man, though he'd been wealthy once. He had broad shoulders but his shirt hung loose. Hollowed cheeks made him seem aloof, yet they were not unattractive. He wasn't the kind of man to be free with words, she thought. But she had to get him talking somehow.

He'd left the remains of the playing cards on the floor next to the basin.

"What will you do?" she asked, pointing to them.

"Buy a new pack," he said, handing her the empty bowl. And then, "Has the mistress a flat file? A saw, maybe?"

• • •

Elizabeth stood in the rear doorway, hands on hips, barring the way. She'd watched him grubbing in the ash pit. Now he wanted to bring the end of a long bone into the saloon. His hands were covered in filth.

"What?" he said.

"You're never coming in like that!"

She fired the words at him, deliberately sharp. A man of the Blood should have resented the tone. But there was no spark of reaction in his eyes. He seemed to expect a barmaid to look down on him. His shoulders dropped a fraction.

"What should I do?" he asked.

"Wait."

She added an inch from the kettle to a bucket of cold water then carried it out into the yard. Not wanting to touch his hands, she placed the bar of soap on the cobbles. Obediently, he knelt to wash.

It was hard to imagine him as one of the haughty men who strutted along the tracks of New Whitby, vaunting the power of their Blood over peasants and traders. Perhaps his time of wandering had taught him humility. Maria Rosa might change her mind if she saw him like this. Or maybe the mistress was right and being an outlaw had just taught him to hide his true feelings.

When he was done, he stood, soap in hand.

"Empty the water into the drain," she said.

Meekly he obeyed.

She sat on one of the chairs near the saloon fireplace and watched him work, running the bone along the blade of the saw. He'd reached the third cut before she understood what he was making.

"Did Jago take all your silver?" she asked, trying to start a conversation.

He didn't answer.

"I'm sorry for you," she said. And then, "Where did you sleep? I mean, since you've no money."

His eyes were dazzlingly blue against that weather-beaten skin. "Are you offering?"

Feeling a blush starting to rise, she looked away. The sound of sawing resumed.

Perhaps the mistress had been right after all. His pride was still there, lurking under the surface. He was more dangerous for having learned to hide it.

He'd finished two of the cubes and was working on the third when Maria Rosa came to inspect. He expressed his indebtedness again, but the mistress brushed his words away. Elizabeth knew her well enough to understand what she was doing. Any ties that Elias No-Thumbs implied between them would be dismissed, coolly but not impolite.

Elizabeth built a fire while he worked. When the wind was wrong, it brought smoke back down the chimney. But today it was drawing well and the flames grew quickly. When a bed of glowing embers had formed, he put a soldering spike into the heart of it and began burning dots into the faces of the bone dice. The smoke smelled bitter, like burning hair.

Soon his work would be finished and he'd walk from the inn. She might never see him again. She had tried being superior, searching for his arrogance. This time she decided to turn it around and present herself as ignorant.

"Why do you gamble?" she asked.

"I don't."

"You had cards. Now you're making dice."

"Others will use them. Not me."

"Are you a bookmaker, then?"

"Why do you want to know?"

"I'm curious."

Those clear blue eyes turned back to his work. He began burning a line of holes in the bone.

"Why is it you're making three dice?" she asked. "Most men gamble with two."

"Look," he said. "Thanks for your help. But I'll make these marks and then I'll be gone."

The chance was slipping away from her. It might never come again. Smoke spiralled from the bone gripped between his toes.

"How did you get away?" she asked. "When they outlawed you, I mean."

He fixed her with those pale eyes. "Do you admire my work?"

After Elias had gone, Elizabeth felt a hollowness in the pit of her stomach. In all the time of her hiding, his story had offered the first possibility of escape. He wouldn't return, she thought. Even if he did, Maria Rosa had forbidden her to speak with him. The mistress of the Salt Ray Inn was indebted to her. And yet, there were limits to how far Elizabeth could push. In risking herself, she would also be risking the people around her.

When he did return that night, and began to play his tricks with the dice, all she could do was watch. It was the mistress who confronted him, calling him to the storeroom behind the bar. It was there that he made his impossible request, to borrow the mistress's credit and thereby get his message to Short Harbour.

Knowing it would be the last chance, she pressed her case, which again came to nothing. Except that Maria Rosa berated her afterwards for foolishness and disobedience.

"I told you not to speak with him!"

"I did no harm. And it was you who brought him to me."

"That was for fairness' sake," the mistress said. "But now he knows of your interest."

"Yet he still doesn't know why."

• • •

On the third day, the boy, Tinker, came running, clattering
into a chair as he skidded to a stop in the cold saloon.

"It's him!"

"Who?"

"Him with the hands!"

Maria Rosa swore when she saw him through the window,
sitting on the rocks behind the stable block. "See what you've
done!" she cried.

"This isn't my doing. It's your credit he wants. He's using
your fear as a lever."

"How can I make him go away?"

Elizabeth hesitated before answering. She didn't want him
to leave. But nor could she lie to the woman who'd risked
so much to help her. "Ignore him," she said. "Wait for long
enough and he'll have to go."

But as the morning wore on the mistress became
increasingly agitated, returning to the window twenty
minutes later and then again a quarter of an hour after that.
Eventually all she could do was stand watching, though there
was nothing to see.

"Put him out of your mind," Elizabeth said.

But at last the man with no thumbs defeated the mistress
of the Salt Ray Inn, through his patience and through her
lack of it.

"You're making a mistake," Elizabeth told her.

She might have been able to argue it, to explain the ways
of gambling and the importance of the bluff. But there came
a point where Elizabeth knew she was arguing against the
outcome that she wanted for herself. At last she gave in and
the mistress devised her disastrous plan, setting one of the
servants, who was entirely devoted, to threaten him with a
bill hook.

But Elizabeth had watched Elias as he worked in the
saloon. Even with no thumbs, there had been a kind of grace

to his movements. Not a dancer. Not on Newfoundland. A trained fighter. Even with mutilated hands, he would never be beaten by a working man.

And so it proved.

It seemed they'd been moving towards this moment from the first time he stepped into the Salt Ray Inn: a confrontation of vulnerabilities.

"Her oath-marks are fake," he said.

And she responded: "You've been cheating at cards."

They could have walked away from each other. It was the perfect stalemate. They could have gone to opposite coasts and vowed to never see each other again. For each of them held knowledge that would have destroyed the other. But fate can make allies of the strangest kinds.

"I think we can help each other," she said.

CHAPTER 11

On the day of Elias's dozen, his twelfth birthday, they took him to the oath-wright to have the words of the law tattooed across his chest. He turned his face away while they were doing it, so his father wouldn't see the tears. It wasn't so much the pain that made him cry, but the fear of it, and of crossing the threshold into manhood.

Afterwards his head swam. His father gave him a horn of whisky. He still remembered the catch of it in his throat, the heat as it seared down into his belly. Then his older brothers and his best friend, Fitz, had taken him off to do what young men do.

By the time he was twenty, his shoulders had grown broad. His chest widened, stretching the letters on his skin. But they'd been written large, to be clear throughout all his life, however long or short that might be.

As it is inked, so shall your oaths and bindings be.
This is the fullness of the law. Death to those who seek another.

Those twenty-four words had been Newfoundland's cry of freedom. They were its constitution and all of its legal code. The idea was simple. And beautiful. If an oath was sworn, it would also be inked. Staying true to it was the highest duty of the oath-bound. To read a man's skin was to know who owned his promise. No lawyer was needed and no contract.

Elias woke with daylight glowing red through his eyelids and a hand stroking his chest. They had stacked the kitchen stove with peat the night before and closed it down for a long, slow burn. The heat of it drifted up to the loft. They'd lain together naked, without even a cover.

He blinked to clear the blurriness of sleep. Charity was looking at him, her head propped on one hand. Dawn's light softened her. She stroked his chest again. As she moved, her nipple brushed against his ribs. But it wasn't sexual. Not this time. She seemed lost in thought.

"You should write a book," she said.

"About what?"

"Everything. You've been places. Seen things."

"What would it be called?"

She didn't answer, but started writing on his skin with the tip of her finger, following the words of the law. Her touch tickled like the legs of an insect. He wanted to push her away. But it seemed as if that might reveal something he didn't want to share. The closeness hadn't troubled him before. Not even when she was riding him.

"When will your husband get here?" he asked.

She rolled away to lie on her back.

"You're safe till midday. Can't say beyond that."

"He won't guess?"

"I could wash the sheets," she said. "And change the straw. Where will you go?" There was a slight catch in her voice.

"I'll find a place. At the inn, maybe."

"The Salt Ray?"

"A couple of days. Then I'll be gone."

"And the pretty barmaid?"

"I'll be sleeping in the stables."

"Call it *Confessions of a Bad Man*," she said.

It took him a moment to figure out that she was talking about the book again. "They taught me to read," he said. "But there were people who did the writing. I never learned it for myself. And now…"

He held up his hands and turned them in the grey light for her to see. They seemed like hands made from clay, the thumbs pinched off while it was soft. That would have been a gentle change, he thought.

She took one in hers, brought it to her lips, put a kiss on each finger, soft as breath. Then she guided it across her body, having him touch her there and there and there, and then making him roll towards her.

"It's not me you want," he said.

"And how do you figure that?"

"A woman like you…" He wanted to say that she was wholesome, but that sounded like another way of saying plain. Ink is ink, she'd said. It was the truth of a good person. "You deserve better. Better than me."

She was slow this time. A different kind of hunger. And when he opened his eyes to see if she was almost done, he caught the brittle pain in hers.

After he was dressed and washed, he put a finger to his neck to feel the beats of his pulse. For once they came strong and even. He unstoppered the green glass pot and put it to his nose, filling himself with the smell of it. Once that smell had made him feel sick. Now he felt sick without it. But today, perhaps he could miss the morning dose. He could always take some later if things went badly.

"What was that?" Charity asked, as he slipped it back into the pocket at his belt.

He hadn't heard her climbing to the loft.

"Nothing," he said. And then, "It's medicine."

"You're sick?"

"It doesn't matter."

"I brought you this." She held out a package of brown paper tied in twine. "It's dried cod. And there's some bread. It'll last you a day or two."

He took it. Smelled it. "Thank you."

"You've no fat on you, Elias. How can you live if you've no fat?"

He climbed down the ladder ahead of her. When they were both in the kitchen, he nodded towards the back door. "I'll keep low along the wall. When I get to the track there might be no one looking."

"Thanks," she said. "But this is New Whitby. Someone always sees."

"Will you be in trouble?"

The words hit her strangely, he thought. Then she seemed to get the sense of them and shook her head. "You'd better be along."

A boat sailed into the bay. Or it could have been called a ship. Afterwards, people argued about that. It had one mast and one triangular sail of brown canvas. But it was bigger than what you'd call a boat. On another day, it might have taken a crew of five. But only two men got off when it tied up at the eastern jetty: a captain and an old man with milky eyes.

The powder dogs jumped aboard and went sniffing round the cargo: wheat flour from Ontario, sacks of apples, four barrels of tar, lengths of good timber, a load of coffee, bales of hash and tobacco. Nothing to worry anyone.

The dogs jumped out, work done. But the chief inspector still wasn't happy. There was wealth in the cargo. The goods were to go to several different clans. Why, he wanted to know, hadn't such a cargo been put in the care of a full crew?

He sent the powder dogs back to try again. They found

nothing. He had the sacks and bales laid out on the jetty. Then came the timber and the barrels. It was the barrels that worried him most. He had them opened. The tar was solid. He demanded a fire be built so it could be melted.

"You can inspect my cargo," the captain said. "But you can't destroy it."

He was a free man. Unaligned. So there were limits to what the inspector could do. A rider was dispatched, who brought back a young man of the Blood from the Wattlington clan.

The captain had no choice but to back down. The tar was melted. But it was merely tar. The chief probed the barrel with a wooden stave but found none of the guns he'd thought might be there. The captain demanded payment for the damage. The young man of the Blood began to panic, offered money. The boat captain agreed. But he hadn't haggled.

The inspection team left and onlookers drifted away. That would have been an end to it. No one would afterwards have bothered to argue whether it had been a boat or a ship. But the inspector still felt the wrongness. Boat or ship, the captain should have haggled.

The moon set three hours before dawn. That was another cause for suspicion: the timing of it. There were stars, but only in the gaps between the clouds. They gave so little light that the chief inspector couldn't have walked to the jetty. But from his hiding place, he saw shapes moving and heard a tapping noise approach. The old man with the milky eyes led the way. The tapping was his stick on the ground. The captain followed behind, one hand on the old man's shoulder.

Out along the jetty they walked. The secret cargo was not in the boat. It was outside, secured along the keel. The captain stripped off, lowered himself into the icy water, came back a few seconds later with the first bundle. After each dive he had to climb to the deck and warm himself. It took an hour and a half to finish the job.

The blindness of the old man would have been another clue, had anyone picked up on it. Night or day made no difference to him. It was he who went off to fetch a packhorse. When it was led back and the bundles had been loaded, the two men began their journey away from the jetty. They ran, when they heard the inspector shout, abandoning the horse. When dawn came, riders galloped off to track the smugglers down.

The bundles were guns, wrapped in tarred canvas: ten precision rifles mounted with optical sights, weapons of assassination. The blacksmith saw to them, in front of witnesses, hammering each to uselessness.

They found the old man with the milky eyes hiding in a ditch on the edge of town. The dark had made him powerful. But once the sun was up he was just a blind old man. The dogs scented him out and he was hauled away, whimpering. The captain had got further. They caught him a day later, trying to escape along the north road.

Neither man had family. That's why they'd risked it, people said. There were only the two of them to be killed. But the Patrons would make it last.

Alone in the kitchen of the Salt Ray Inn, Elizabeth stared through the window glass which ran with condensation. Earlier she'd gone to stand and watch as the smugglers were laid out on the beach, tied to stakes so the waves would first reach their heads. It would be another five hours before the high tide drowned them. And that, slowly. To have not gone would have marked her out as strange, something she couldn't afford.

She wept for them. And she wept for her friends, Julia and Tinker, trapped on Newfoundland. Or perhaps it was for herself.

Tinker had managed to blend in with perfect ease. He

was a quiet boy by nature, speaking little, and most of that in grunts. No one could have caught the temperate hills of England in his voice. He also seemed younger than his age, small from years of malnutrition. As such, the lack of oath-marks were easy to explain. Not that anyone asked. He was just the lad who groomed the horses at the inn. That made him almost invisible. But most of all, he seemed to fit because he carried no cares, having complete faith that she, Elizabeth, would work things out.

Julia had been the other member of their party, beached unwontedly. She was the opposite of Tinker. Her accent could not be hidden and her fair hair drew men's eyes. She couldn't have lived at the inn. Yet Elizabeth wished for those comforts above all things: her dearest friend to confide in, someone to test her thoughts and plans, someone to hold.

In the time of their separation, all that she'd seen of Julia had been letters. And those could not contain anything of substance, since they were passed through the hands of many messengers.

Julia was well, though. At least Elizabeth knew that. She was living with Maria Rosa's mother, in a remote cottage. When travellers passed, Julia hid indoors. This happened seldom. But on washing days her clothes had to be hung inside to dry, just in case. Her letters described the wildflowers that grew in the hills. She drew them. And the moths, which she'd learned to trap at night with a lamp and a sheet. So did Julia bide her time.

It was to Elizabeth that the task had fallen, to find the means of their escape. If she did not manage it, then no one could. And thus she wept.

CHAPTER 12

The reply from Short Harbour came on Friday, one day earlier than predicted. The mistress handed the paper to Elias, who broke the wax and read. Elizabeth watched, waiting for the verdict. At last he nodded.

"He'll do it," he said. "There are conditions. But he'll do it."

Elias had fascinated Elizabeth from the first time she saw him in the saloon. He was a gambler and a trickster. Every conversation with him had been a game of hidden motives. Hers and his. She seldom knew whether the feelings he displayed were real or part of the game. But this time she felt certain that his relief was true. Elias really had doubted that the message sender would agree.

"Now you'll be wanting to send a message to Jago," the mistress said.

But Elias wouldn't have it. "I'll see him face to face. He's not going to like the conditions. If I put them on paper, he'll come to find me anyway. But if I speak it to him direct, it might go better for me. For us."

"Well, he can't come here!" the mistress snapped. "He did enough damage the first time. And I'll not risk Elizabeth."

"You want me to go to his court, then?" Elias asked.

"Meet him where you like. But I want you gone."

Through this exchange, Elizabeth had kept quiet. Over

the previous days, with the messenger dispatched to Short Harbour, waiting for a reply, she'd been thinking through the twists of the argument. Since beaching on Newfoundland she'd been trapped at the inn, held there by the relative safety that Maria Rosa could provide. Every time she wanted to venture out or ask someone a question about boats and cargo and travelling to Labrador, the mistress would warn her of danger.

"You'll make them suspicious," she'd say. Or, "I can't protect you out there."

And it was true. But without taking those small risks, she'd never find a way for her and her friends to escape. Her safety at the inn wasn't complete. They would find her one day, if she did nothing.

Elias refolded the paper and slipped it into his tote. "I'd better be going, then," he said. "It's a long walk to Jago's fortress. I'll say goodbye."

"No," said Elizabeth.

They both turned.

"If you're going, I must go with you."

Maria Rosa favoured Elizabeth with a patient smile, as if she was a child who'd not understood the conversation of the adults. "You can't. Not to Jago's land."

"I must."

"You've seen the Patron. And his men. Remember that giant gatherer? No. I won't hear of it."

"Once Elias has gone, he won't come back. He won't keep to his deal."

Elias frowned, as if offended, but made no complaint. There was nothing he could have said. They each knew secrets that could ruin the other. But to use them would bring down destruction on both. The promises they'd made to each other were tenuous enough. Add distance to the mix and they would be useless. Each might bring the other to ruin. But only if they were ready to embrace it for themselves.

The gentle smile on Maria Rosa's face had been replaced by anxiety. Now she seemed terrified. "You can't go!"

"I have no choice. Unless you let the meeting happen here."

"There is a third way," Elias said. "If you'll permit it. Send a cart along the East Road, as if you're trading goods. And a small party to go with it. It won't seem strange that Elizabeth's there, as a serving girl. If we time it right, we can meet Jago at one of the hamlets on the way. There'll be enough witnesses to make it safe. Or safer. We'll be on Williams Clan land. An attack on Elizabeth would insult their Patron Protector. I don't think even Jago would do that. It'd be better than meeting him here, unaligned. Far better than going to Jago's fortress."

"And better for you?" Maria Rosa said.

He acknowledged the truth of it with a half-smile, which made Elizabeth think he'd been angling for it all along.

The East Road earned its name only in that it was more east than any other bearing. The meanders of bay and headland always came back to the travellers facing the rising sun. But to call it a road was to overdress the truth. Grass grew thick along the middle ridge while the ruts on either side were deep enough to ground the axles of the cart. Again and again, they had to work it free, men pushing behind, beasts straining at the front.

There were five of them in the main party: a carter, who looked like the oxen he cared for; Tinker the stable boy; the old man who'd pricked Elias with the bill hook; Elizabeth the barmaid; and Elias himself. They'd loaded the cart with barrels of ale brewed at the Salt Ray and wedged them in with straw.

A young man had been sent to ride on ahead, scouting the land. From looks and mood, Elias figured him to be of the same family as the old man. A grandson, perhaps. Both of them scowled whenever they looked in his direction. Elias made sure not to let his own feelings show. But he kept his knife in easy reach. You can break a man's arm and he'll forgive you. But wounded pride will always fester.

The East Road was an ordeal by headlands. Each one meant another climb. When the axles stuck on the way up, he and the old man had to go behind and lift while the oxen did the pulling. Once, when there seemed no chance of it being shifted, the old man took out the side planks and used them as levers. That lifted the cart another couple of inches and it lurched forwards again.

At the top of each ridge they'd catch their first view of the next stretch of coast, a bay and a headland, the measure of the journey's next ordeal. Tinker, whose eyes were the sharpest, had been given a small brass telescope. At each summit, he climbed onto the cart and spied the land ahead for dangers.

It was a day of clear air and fast-moving cloud. Elias had been keeping watch on a storm over the sea. Once, he'd looked back and seen a double rainbow blazed on the slate grey sky. There'd been only a few drops of rain through the morning, but it could spill out at any minute. If they couldn't reach the shelter of a hamlet, they'd be forced to make camp. Rain would slow Jago as well. Parts of the East Road would turn to rivers and foul the Patron's mood. There were risks, whichever way he counted it.

They were climbing again. His heartbeat came irregular, so he stopped to breathe and look back. No rainbow this time, but a glimpse of New Whitby far off around the curve of the coast, lit by a beam of sunlight. He felt in the belt pocket for his glass pot. Taking the pin from his cloak, he dipped it and wiped a smear of glycer-fortis on the underside of his tongue. His mouth filled with that chemical buzz. Relief flowed down through his neck to his chest.

"What's that?" Elizabeth asked.

Damn, but the woman could be quiet. He put on a careless half-smile and turned to face her.

"Medicine," he said

"For what?"

"It's a tonic. That's all."

"May I see?"

"No." He stoppered the pot and slipped it away. "Where did you learn about cards?"

She folded her arms, a sign that the question had unsettled her. "My father taught me."

"He was a gambler?"

"No."

"A bookmaker?"

"An entertainer," she said. "Where did you learn to fight?"

He found himself folding his own arms now, mirroring her defence. "My father taught me," he said.

"He was a fighter?"

"This is Newfoundland. We're all fighters."

"He taught you to fight without thumbs? Or did you lose them *after* you learned?"

"It makes less difference than you'd think," he said. And then, "How did you come to wash up here?"

"An accident."

"You were sailing somewhere?"

"Steaming."

She began to walk, setting off towards the cart which had pulled ahead.

He followed. "Where were you steaming to?"

"From," she said. "There was a battle. Out there somewhere." She pointed to the horizon. "Men were dying. And women."

"You deserted?"

"It wasn't my battle."

"That's what all deserters say."

"And every tyrant disagrees." She flashed him a wounded glance. That jab had got under her guard.

They walked on, but slowly, as if by some agreement, not closing the distance to the ox cart, keeping beyond the earshot of the others. The air between them felt heavy.

"I'll offer you a trade," he said. "A truth for a truth."

"You'll tell me how to escape from Newfoundland?"

"Not that. Not till the end of this. But anything else. I tell you whatever you want to know. In return, you tell me what I ask. Do you want to know how I lost my thumbs? Most folk do. I don't tell them."

"No," she said. "But I want to know what you're planning to do to the people who cut them from you."

The cart had reached the brow of the headland. A patch of sunlight swept over the sea towards them. Then they were all bathed in yellow light, and the puddles in the wheel ruts turned golden. At the top of the rise, the boy's telescope caught the sun. Then he turned towards them and was waving with both arms.

Elizabeth set off up the hill, running faster than Elias's heart would let him follow. They'd danced around each other's questions. But he'd got something out of it: the glint of a brilliant mind. One word out of place and she might be made a slave. And she didn't look the type to use a sword in battle. Yet she was dangerous. He felt it in his gut.

He took his time climbing to the crest of the hill. It was too soon for Jago and his men to have reached them. Ahead lay another desolate beach. But there was no driftwood on it and no seaweed lines, which meant that it was being worked. Smoke smudged the sky beyond the next headland.

He followed behind as the others rushed on towards their hoped-for rest. Elizabeth led the way, putting more distance between herself and him. And she would do nothing by chance.

The rain hit them as they were climbing the final rise. Sudden and hard, it swept in from the sea, driven by a gusting wind. Elias felt the sting of it on one side of his face. Head down, leaning into the blow to stop himself being thrown, he pushed on. The wheel ruts turned to rivers. Gritty water sluiced over the top of his boots.

Elizabeth had already thumped on the door of the first hovel by the time he caught up. A woman carrying a baby on her hip pointed them inland along a track, which led at last to a stable with a stone wall at the front and a turf roof that leaked.

From cloak through to underwear, Elias could not have been more soaked. The others seemed little better. The carter found empty stalls for the beasts and while he was giving them food, the owner of the stable ran in from the rain to greet them. There was no inn nor any house big enough for them all. The old man and his grandson were sent to a nearby shack.

"I'll bunk with the boy," said Elizabeth.

"Right you are," said the stable owner. He pointed to a hovel closer to the sea. "They'll take you in. And you two…" He nodded to Elias and the carter. "You can go to the shack at the end of the row."

The boy ran off ahead. Elizabeth looked set to follow, but Elias grabbed her wrist. "I think not," he said. "I'll be going with you."

Her eyes were on him. It seemed she might try to pull free. But then she nodded. "Very well."

The sun would still be up. Somewhere. But a sky full of storm had turned the afternoon to twilight. The owners of the hovel must have been warned of their coming. A lantern swung from a nail in the wall, turning the rain to dull yellow streaks. Elias led the way across the deepening puddles of the yard.

The door opened as they came close. A woman with grey strands in her hair beckoned them in. Elias had to stoop to get inside, where his clothes dripped onto a floor of irregular and ill-fitting flagstones. The woman bowed low, as people once did on meeting him.

"Most welcome. Most welcome," she said. She seemed perhaps thirty, but weatherworn to look older. "You'd take soup?"

"Thank you," said Elias.

"And the lady wife?"

"She's not…" he began.

"I'm not," said Elizabeth.

"Oh," said the woman, flustered.

The shack's one room served as both kitchen and work space. A great mass of fishing net covered the table and the floor around it. Mending needles rested on top, hooked into a roll of twine.

A sluggish fire burned in the hearth. Some of the smoke went up the chimney, the rest drifted under the beams of the roof, where dried fish hung from racks, together with sacks and rope and gardening tools. One end of the loft space had been sectioned off with boards to make a sleeping platform.

"The rats don't much go there," the woman said, as if to coax them up.

Elias was first to climb the ladder. He found a box bed half-full of straw and a roof so low that it was easier to crawl on hands and knees than go about stooped. A small pile of blankets lay folded on the floorboards next to the bed, which would just be wide enough for two. Elizabeth clambered up after him.

"I didn't know," he whispered, feeling suddenly shamed.

"No?" There was a barb in her tone. "You thought there'd be two spare rooms in every shack?"

"I didn't think."

"Turn!" she ordered. "And if you even think of looking, I'll bury my dagger in your eye."

Facing the wall, he listened to the slap of her sodden clothes dropping. Her shadow moved. Charity would never believe it had happened by mistake: him and the naked barmaid next to the bed they were about to share. Plain-faced Charity with her crooked nose.

Elizabeth was a different kind of woman. Young but with depth in her eyes. She had a mind that might cut glass. He couldn't help imagining her body, just behind him. She might not have the speed of hand to stab him, or the killer's heart. But he still resisted the urge to steal a look.

The floorboard creaked.

"I'm done," she said.

She had wrapped a blanket around herself, over one arm and under the other, gathering it around at the waist with her neck scarf. If the woman below saw the ring of false oath-marks, she'd think Elizabeth a slave. His perhaps.

"Don't go down," he said. "I'll… you know."

He gathered up her clothes and dropped them over the edge, then clambered back down the ladder.

The woman had already tied a line in front of the fire. She took the wet things and draped them. Finding himself staring at Elizabeth's underwear, he looked away.

"And yours?" asked the woman.

He was about to fetch a blanket and wrap himself as Elizabeth had done. But to hell with it all. He had no need. The woman turned her back to him as he stripped. He caught her sneaky glance at his cock as he handed her the clothes. Then her eyes shifted to his chest and arm. She'd never have seen those oath-marks. Not together. He left her gawping and climbed back to the loft.

Elizabeth was lying in the bed, eyes closed, facing the edge of the box, the blanket tightly round her. He wrapped himself as she had done then lay down with his back to hers, pulling the other blankets over the both of them, trying to keep their body warmth within the bed frame. It would be a cold night. He wriggled deeper into the straw, getting comfortable. His feet were sore from thin soles and a rough road. Tiredness washed over him and he closed his eyes.

"What happens in the end?" Elizabeth asked.

"I thought you were asleep."

"You promised to tell me a secret."

He felt too aware of her nakedness under the blanket. He was too tired to think straight anyway. A bad time to cross swords with Elizabeth. "Tomorrow," he said. "We can talk tomorrow."

"What happens in the end?" she asked, her tone a challenge.

"The end?"

"The mistress is helping to get you sorted with Jago. The deal is, you'll introduce me to the smugglers who helped you get away to Labrador. But what happens after that? For you, I mean?"

He turned onto his back. "Why do you want to know?" It was a mistake. He should be the one to choose the time of this conversation.

"They say you came back to take revenge. Is that true?"

"That's the secret you want from me?"

"Yes."

"In exchange, I can have any secret from you?"

Instead of answering, she turned over, bringing her face uncomfortably close.

"I think you're going to gamble with them," she said.

"Who?"

"The people who cut off your thumbs."

"How do you figure that?"

"When I saw you stripping cards from the deck, I couldn't work out why you were doing it. There was no gain for you. But then I thought, what if you're practising? That made sense. But you had to be practising for something."

"To get better," he said.

"To win," she countered. "And why does a man want to win at cards?"

"For money?"

"If you wanted money, you'd make something to sell. Or you'd do some service and get paid. With that kind of trade everyone ends up with the thing they wanted. But gambling's different. It's the only trade where one person ends up poorer. Gamblers don't do it for the money. Not really. Not even to win. You do it so someone else loses."

He didn't know how she'd built so much truth on so little ground. No one else had managed. Every answer he made was giving her more. He had the feeling that even should he lie, she'd gain from it.

"What if I can't make something?" he asked, holding his free hand for her to see. "What if gambling is all I'm good for?"

Her eyes mocked him.

"It won't do," she said.

He really had to stop talking or he'd let slip something that mattered. He'd think sharper in the morning. But those keen eyes were fixed on him.

"What won't do?" he asked, knowing he'd bitten on a baited hook. Hating his own lack of will.

"You're not so good at cards," she said. "Not so good as you think."

"They didn't see!"

"They were half-drunk! But I saw. And I wasn't even in the game. Real gamblers would be looking for it."

If he'd known for sure that she was wrong, the sting

wouldn't have been so sharp. He stared at the roof beams, trying to ignore that oh-too-beautiful face. "I'm good enough."

"You're fooling yourself," she said. "A man never looks so keenly at the deal as when he's got money on the table."

"I want to go to sleep now."

"Liar."

He rolled to face her, his anger beating his wits; they were inches apart. "You dare to say that?"

"I dare because it's true. I dare because if you're driving yourself to ruin, I need to know. I need to get out of the way."

"I'm good with the cards!"

"You are," she said. "You're outstanding. For a man with no thumbs."

He took a breath. His fists were bunched under the blankets. Her gaze held his. His knife was on the floor, just outside the box bed.

Afterwards he'd try to tell himself that she was at fault. He was teaching her a lesson. But at the time, there'd been no such thought in his head. The whim came to him and he acted. Dipping his head close, he placed a kiss plumb on her mouth. To stop her goading.

Her eyes went wide. For a second neither of them moved. Then she twisted away, breaking the warm contact of her lips and he was left cursing himself for a fool.

CHAPTER 13

Elizabeth's first view of Rooth Bay was from the crown of yet another headland. The village comprised a bunching of mean-looking shacks and stables, a quayside and slipway and, incongruously, a corrugated iron church, complete with corrugated iron bell tower surmounted by a rusting cross.

Rooth Bay would have been just another desolate inlet on Newfoundland's southern coast, but the homestead fortress of Patron Protector Williams lay five miles inland. That made the bay a natural anchorage for his small fleet of warships. Where there are boats, there will be trade. And where there is trade, there will be crumbs from which the impoverished will try to eke out a living.

Smoke rose from stovepipes on the shacks along the quayside. Some of them might be in the business of selling food, she thought. The track had been even harder going after the rainstorm of the day before. Her feet ached. And she hadn't slept.

She started to lead the way down the hill. But Elias called out, "Wait!"

It was the first word he'd said to her all morning. She stopped but didn't turn.

"We should arrive at the same time as Jago," he said.

"Why?" asked the old man.

"So it looks like an accident."

"For what?"

"So it doesn't seem we're meeting him on Williams land on purpose. He'd take that as an insult. We'll pull back behind the ridge. When he comes into view, we can move."

"Might be hours," said the old man.

"Might be days," said Elizabeth, under her breath, then set off down the hill.

"Wait!" Elias shouted again.

She pretended to not hear. But the others didn't follow.

Sparring with him hadn't bothered her. She didn't mind that he was hiding his own agenda and looking after his own needs. She didn't mind that he saw her as an adversary. When he mistakenly arranged for them to share a bed, it had played more into her hands than his. He'd been unsettled. Feeling empowered by his discomfort, she'd pressed her advantage, trying to get some truth from him.

And then the kiss. She didn't know why it had made her so angry. She'd had her knife hidden in the straw. She'd wanted to hurt him. But only afterwards. At that moment, when his lips pressed against hers, the shock had taken all strength from her hand.

She lay awake afterwards, facing the edge of the box bed, thoughts churning. She knew he'd done it to throw her off balance. But a thought kept intruding. Perhaps he'd done it because he admired her in that particular way, as a man will admire a woman.

It wasn't fair. Maria Rosa had said he was a rogue with a woman in every town. Elizabeth had only ever been with one man. And that man was an ocean away. She tried to picture his face. John Farthing was his name. An honourable man. A man of passion who desired her for what she was in spite of all the forces of the world that had tried to pull them apart. But John Farthing's face was hard to picture now. And in the end, the forces of the world won. She might never escape from Newfoundland. She might never see him again.

Round the thoughts tumbled: the kiss, his eyes, the unfairness, John Farthing, lost pleasure. It was ridiculous. All of it. She would escape. They'd be reunited. Somehow. And this Elias No-Thumbs would help her to do it. Her anger would be a whetstone. With it she would sharpen the blade of her resolve.

She'd reached the first shacks of Rooth Bay. Three children ran into the trackway, skidding to a stop when they saw her. They were girls, she thought, though it was hard to tell. The whites of their wide eyes were the only clean thing about them. For a heartbeat they stood gawping. Then they spun on their heels and scampered back the way they'd come, shouting as they went. It was a wonder that children so thin had so much running in them.

The quayside was deserted. Unlike everything else in the place, it had been built to last. Great stones made up a wall facing the water. Iron dock cleats had been built into the quay every ten yards or so. No ships were tied up, but a burnish on the metal suggested the cleats were well used.

Lobster pots had been stacked against the walls of the harbour-facing shacks. She could smell salt and fish and rotting seaweed, but roasting meat as well.

"Can I help you, miss?" asked a man standing in a doorway. He was almost as ragged as the children.

"Do you have food to sell?"

"There's bread and fat," he said, then cast his eye on her boots. "But there's mutton, if you've got the silver."

Her stomach gurgled. "I have."

He nodded towards the lobster pots. "Sit yourself down."

She was about to step towards them but stopped. "There is something else," she said. "I'll have a bucket of hot water, if you please."

• • •

The meat had been cooked long and slow, waiting for customers perhaps. A more delicious feast might not have been found in the restaurants of London or New York. She used her own knife to cut slices from the loaf and fashioned a rough kind of sandwich. It was too thick to eat with good manners. The children came out from their hiding places to watch her get smears of mutton fat around her mouth and chin.

She didn't mind. Her feet were soaking in steaming water. It had been almost too hot at first. But as she ate, it cooled. Putting the empty platter aside, she leaned back against the wall of the shack and wriggled her toes in pleasure. Just then the sun came out. She hoped Elias would arrive, tired and hungry, to see her sitting there. With that in mind, she lay her left arm over the top of the lobster pot by her shoulder and upturned her right hand, resting on a low pot on the other side. She'd once seen a painting of a French peasant sitting in front of a cottage, just so. He'd seemed contented. That's what she wanted to be: a picture of careless ease against weatherworn planks and the flaking blue paint of the door.

Gulls sat in a line along the edge of the quay wall. They cried their mournful song. The sun went behind another cloud. A gust of wind shifted Elizabeth's skirts. If Elias didn't give up his vigil soon, she'd have to move and it would spoil the whole thing. The water in the bucket was growing cool. She turned her head and looked along the line of quayside shacks.

A man was standing there: a giant of a man, his left coat sleeve knotted at the elbow. Panic hit her like a blow to the stomach. He was the same man who had cornered her in the storeroom. She wanted to fill her lungs but couldn't. She wanted to grab her boots and run. His gaze seemed to have taken her in, but he was still turning. He stepped to the edge and looked down, as if checking for small boats in the water below.

The pile of lobster pots must have partly hidden her. Or her stillness. He might not have seen her at all. The slab of his back was towards her. Standing, she lifted one foot from the water and placed it on the stones.

Then a gust of wind blew, bringing a scent of salt from the wave tops. All the seagulls took off, crying. The gatherer turned to look. She panicked, jerking her other foot from the water and catching her toe on the rim of the bucket. It toppled. Water sluiced over the ground where her boots lay. He stared directly at her, his expression blank for a moment. She saw the recognition breaking in the bitter twist of his face. Then he looked down at her bare feet and his teeth showed in a kind of grin.

She ran, knowing the stones would tear her feet but not feeling the pain, diving between the shacks, a narrow space that might put him off. Then she was out at the back. A chicken run lay to the left, cordoned with a fence of sticks. She vaulted it, sending the birds into panic. Scrambling over the fence on the other side, she heard the splintering wood as he smashed through in pursuit. If she could find a path of thick mud, it might slow him down and let her run full tilt. But it was all stones around the yard so she ducked under a line of washing and swung herself through a doorway into the nearest shack. In the dark she heard a child crying. Then she was out on the quayside again.

She'd been able to beat him before because of the low roof. Small spaces and tight turns were her only chance. She'd never outpace him in a straight race. In five steps she was back at the lobster pots where she'd been sitting. Grabbing her boots, she ducked inside the building. Any commotion would tell the giant where she'd gone.

The man who'd served the mutton was staring at her.

Crouching, she brushed the soles of her feet. They felt sticky. Manure, not blood, she hoped. Breathing deeply, she tried to slow the racing beat of her heart. But her hands still shook as she tied the laces.

One of her feet was throbbing. Bruised at least. But with the boots on, she felt less vulnerable.

Elias hadn't come down the hill. He might not have seen the giant gatherer. He'd certainly know him if he did, even at a distance. Perhaps the gatherer had been in the village all along. If she could get to the track leading to the headland, she could wave her arms in signal. One of her friends would see.

Unsheathing her knife, she stepped to the side of the rear door, keeping out of the light. The hens had quietened down. She stepped into the sunshine. Ten swift paces took her to the wall of the privy. She edged around it. The village seemed deserted.

Her hand ached from gripping the hilt too hard. Breathing deeply, she started out towards the main track, forcing herself to walk not run, placing her feet carefully to make less sound. Gulls swirled overhead, riding the wind.

She must soon be in Elias's view. If he was looking. She couldn't make out the ox cart. But they'd have rolled that back behind the ridge.

Somewhere behind her, small stones scattered. She bolted. He was after her, accelerating. She sprinted to the track but could hear him gaining. Elias must surely see her now. He must come. But there was no time to hail him. No time to wave.

She'd been heading for the track but now veered off towards the rusty iron church. She'd get there before the gatherer. But not by much. She slammed into the double doors and grabbed the handles. They wouldn't budge so she launched herself towards the corner of the building, grabbing a downpipe to slingshot herself around. A smaller door lay to the side. This one opened. As she barged into the church, the giant was racing towards her. She slammed it shut and got the top bolt in place before the shudder of his impact. A crack of light opened at the bottom as the frame flexed. When it sprung back closed, she slid the lower bolts.

Backing away, she waited for the next impact. A man that size could turn the door to splinters. And the walls were nothing but a skin of corrugated iron over a wooden frame. He might break through anywhere. Unless the fact that it was a church was stopping him. There couldn't be a law of sanctuary. But it might be a taboo. A place of worship, not war. There was so much she didn't know about Newfoundland.

She turned to survey the space behind her. Light from high windows fell on four rows of pews. The altar lay at the front, complete with altar cloth. On top of it lay a man, head propped on one arm, a leg of chicken in his other hand. He smiled as he chewed. A dangerous smile. It was Jago, the upstart Patron.

CHAPTER 14

Damn the woman. Elias watched as Elizabeth strolled down the track into Rooth Bay, careless as if there'd been no plan and no Patron. Damn her eyes. She hadn't spoken to him since that kiss. Hadn't given him a chance to say he was sorry. She'd spoken to everyone else though, touching the old man on the arm as she whispered something, giving the boy Tinker a share of her food, shining her smile on the carter. They all smiled back, not seeing the way she played them. Elizabeth, the darling of their hearts. Elias No-Thumbs, the enemy of a helpless woman.

"We'd best follow," said the carter.

The old man picked up his pack, readying himself for the last stretch.

"We wait," Elias said. "It's your mistress made the plan. Not Elizabeth Barnabus. We're to wait here until we get sight of Jago's men approaching from the other side."

"But…"

"But nothing. We wait!"

They didn't like it. But however much they wanted to go with Elizabeth, Maria Rosa's name had the power to hold them. Elizabeth may have dreamed up the plan, but it was the mistress who had the knowledge to understand how it could be made to work. Rooth Bay wasn't Jago's land, so the

Patron would need to watch himself. To kill there would be a slight on the Williams clan. Elias's safety would come from the villagers, who could stand witness. And yet it had to seem as if the place of the meeting had come to be through chance. Otherwise it would be an insult to Jago, who'd need to lash out to save face.

Elizabeth was a foreigner. She didn't understand the politics. Not that she'd have listened to Elias anyway.

"Give me that," he said, taking the telescope from Tinker. Twisting the eyepiece, he brought the woman into focus. She'd reached the bottom of the hill. The carefree spring had gone from her step. She'd walked like that just to irritate him, he thought. But alone in a strange village, she'd grown less sure of herself. Good. He hoped she was miserable.

He turned the focus ring a fraction. The high collar of her coat would hide the neck cloth from the villagers. Else they'd see it and think her a slave. She'd get different treatment, then. Any of them might order her to show the marks around her neck. The forgery was good, but not good enough to bet her life on.

Damn the woman. And damn his own conscience.

There was a tug at his sleeve and he lost sight of her for a moment.

"My turn," said the boy.

It was warm enough in the sunshine. He'd worked up a sweat heaving the cart over the ruts of the last climb. But sweat cools quickly on a hilltop, doing nothing but watch and worry.

Tinker found a rocky hollow off to the left side of the track, dry enough to lie in. The fringe of fireweed around the edge bent over and danced as the wind gusted around the headland. The carter lay at the edge with the glass aimed down into the village. Hot food would have been good, but they couldn't risk the smoke. The others lay close to each other for warmth, but didn't ask Elias to join them. After a time, the boy took the watch.

"Should've followed her," said the carter, when he was settled with the others.

"We can't," said Elias.

"The beasts need shelter. They'll freeze up here."

"We're staying!"

The wind hissed in the grasses. It seemed no one else would challenge him.

Then Tinker called out, "She's there!"

Elias scrambled up to the rim to look. The others followed.

"Keep your heads down!"

There was movement between the shacks, but he couldn't make it out. He tried to grab the telescope. The boy yanked it back.

"She's running. And there's a man!"

Tinker leapt, as if to set off down the track, but Elias grabbed his ankle and felled him. With the glass to his eye, he could see the deserted village, but with the boy's struggles he couldn't keep the picture still.

"Someone hold him down!"

The carter did.

"Where did you see her?"

"There's a man! With no arm! Jago's man!"

Just as Tinker said it, Elias found her in the circle of his view. She was walking from one of the shacks towards the privy, not running. He let out a steadying breath. How did Elizabeth tangle things to such a knot? He lowered the glass.

"Where did you see the man?"

The boy pointed. "There!"

A bulky figure was charging after Elizabeth. She ran towards the church. Tinker scrambled free and sprinted. The carter was after him, following down the hill. Then the old man. Elias put the glass to his eye once more. This time he saw the gatherer clear: the tied coat sleeve, the giant frame.

Swearing under his breath, he scrambled after the others, angry with Elizabeth. Angry with himself. He'd been stupid. He hadn't thought that Jago might leave a man in Rooth Bay to watch the road.

"Wait!" He had to stop the others charging into trouble.

"Wait, damn you!"

The carter looked back, stopped.

"We walk in!" Elias growled.

"But Elizabeth…"

"Go fetch the cart."

The old man had stopped as well. And his son. But Tinker was running, out of earshot, flailing his arms as he tore away down the hill.

"What about Elizabeth?"

He wanted to say, to hell with her. She'd brought it on herself. But he'd been part of it, at least. He should never have done what he'd done.

"If we go running in, it'll make more trouble than good. If Jago sees we care for her… If he sees I care for her…"

"Do you?" said the carter.

Elias didn't answer.

"We'll work it your way, then. But if she comes to harm…" His eyes narrowed to slits.

It took five minutes to harness the beasts and fetch them over the brow of the hill, five minutes that felt like an hour. At last they were lumbering down the rutted track towards the village. He caught no sight or sign of her, nor Tinker, nor the giant gatherer. The spaces between the buildings were empty.

Jago: the thought hit him as they were approaching the first shack. What if the Patron hadn't just left a man to keep watch? If he were there himself, it would give meaning to the eerie quiet: the people too scared to be seen out.

His heart started missing beats. The air seemed too thin. The glass pot felt smooth and welcoming in his pocket. But he'd already taken the morning dose. He couldn't keep using it so fast.

"Move," the carter said, close behind.

Elias hadn't been aware that he'd stopped. He stepped forward again, light-headed, trying to slow his breathing.

There was no building grand enough for a Patron. Except the church. It would be just like Jago to make camp in a church.

He could check the stables. Jago's stallion would be easy to spot. Then he'd know for sure. But that would take minutes. He hated himself for thinking it, but delay could be the difference between slavery and freedom for Elizabeth.

"Go to the stables," he said. "All of you."

Before they could ask why, he turned on his heel and set off towards the corrugated iron door.

A missionary had visited the Williams clan in the last years of the nineteenth century, having the good luck to arrive as the Patron lay dying. The old man converted. Some would later say his new faith had been false, that his order to build the church was a joke to gall his son and heir. Either way, the building had seen little use. Peasants might like the idea of a Lord above but Patrons did not. Each winter for a hundred years they'd begged the storms to break it down. Yet there it stood.

With his ear pressed to the side door, Elias heard voices.

He needed witnesses from the village, men and women who bore oath-marks of the Williams clan. But inside the church he'd be hidden. All that planning and care to confront Jago in the safest place would come to nothing. Unless he waited for the others to come from the stables. They could make a loud argument together. If Jago heard, he would step out. Barging inside was too great a risk. Elizabeth would have to eat the meal she'd made.

Then, cutting through the murmur of male voices within the church, he heard a woman's cry of alarm. His hand shot to the door handle.

He was inside in one step, trying to take in the strange scene. Jago paced along the front of the pews. Two gatherers were holding Tinker over the altar. His shirt had been pulled up over his head. His skinny back squirmed like an animal. The giant gatherer was standing off to the side.

The wind took the door, slamming it against the frame. Everyone turned.

He saw Elizabeth then. The giant had his one good arm tight under her neck, pinning her fast against his chest.

Other gatherers who'd been lounging on the pews now stood.

"Mr No-Thumbs!" Jago called, flourishing his arm as if to bow, but doing no more than nodding his head. "We're honoured by your presence."

Elias did bow. Deep. "Patron Protector."

"Are you here to join our entertainment?"

"My week's almost up. I was coming to see you. To spare you the trouble of the road."

"Oh so generous. But I say again – are you here to share the entertainment?" Jago nodded to one of the men at the altar, who raised a stick and brought it down with a fierce snap. The boy writhed under the blow but it was Elizabeth who gasped, as if her own skin had been cut. Three red weals lined the boy's back.

Elias's eyes darted around the gloomy church. He counted six gatherers and Jago. Sticks had been piled on the flagstones between the pews, as if ready for a bonfire.

"Lost your voice?" Jago asked.

"No. I'm sorry, Patron. I… I just don't understand."

"And why would you? You didn't see these two sneaking in to steal from us. We'll get a confession from the boy. Or from the girl if he holds his tongue. Hard to forget a body like hers. Was she not with you at the Inn?"

The stick came down again. A mewling sound escaped from Elizabeth's throat.

"I can explain," Elias said, trying to make his words sound casual.

"You can?"

"They're with me. That is… I'm with them. And others. We sent these two ahead to look for a place to rest. I said they should try the old church. It was my fault if they bothered you."

Jago gestured to the man with the stick. Down it snapped on the boy's back. This time Elizabeth remained still. One of her hands was pressed unnaturally against her hip, as if something were held there, hidden by the folds of her skirt. He turned his head away so Jago wouldn't follow his gaze. It would surely be a knife. Things would go hellish bad, hellish quick if she tried to use it.

He spread his arms wide and stepped towards the Patron. He could feel the gatherers tensing. One sprung up from the front pew. Hands went to weapons.

"I bring news," Elias said. "I have the information you asked for. All can be arranged as you wished."

Jago cocked his head. "All?"

"Yes, Patron."

"You were rushing to my homestead to share the good news?"

"Yes, Patron."

Jago moved towards him, but seemed to change his mind and stepped to Elizabeth instead. Elias saw her draw breath, as if readying for a strike.

"What's your name, girl?" Jago asked.

"Elizabeth," she said, her eyes downcast.

"You served us in the Salt Ray." He took a lock of her dark hair and felt it between finger and thumb, as if testing the quality of a garment. He stroked her cheek with the back of his fingers then dropped his hand to her neck, spreading the coat collar

"Who owns you?"

Jago had only to slip a finger into the cloth and pull it away for all to be lost. That close, he'd know the untruth of her marks. And all she had to do was jerk her knife up under his ribs. Anger for the boy would give strength to her arm. In her mind, she'd see her blade burst out through his spine. Her hand would follow to make it happen.

"I belong to the mistress of the Salt Ray Inn, sir."

"And what's Mr No-Thumbs to you?"

Elias tensed. His heartbeat swapped from fast to slow and back. He felt that constriction in his neck. Damn, but he needed another dose to get through this.

"He's a customer, sir."

"He says he sent you ahead."

"We're trading beer from the inn, sir. He said he'd protect us on the road."

Jago leaned towards her. His finger had been toying with her neck cloth. Now he brought it under her chin, tilting back her head. The Patron was so close to her that Elias could no longer see her knife hand.

"He offered to protect you?"

"Yes, sir."

Jago opened his mouth, as if to ask another question, then closed it again. His chest shuddered. Elias's own heart seemed set to explode. But then the Patron stepped back and Elias saw a grin on his face. The shudder had been the beginning of laughter.

"No-Thumbs the protector!" Jago spluttered. "No-Thumbs

the guardian of sour beer!"

The gatherers were throwing themselves into the mirth, doubling over, wiping tears from the corners of their eyes.

"Is this true?"

Elias bowed. "Yes, Patron."

"How much do they pay you?"

"Board and food. A ride on the wagon."

"How will you perform your mighty deeds? If a bear charges the beer barrels will you slap it with the flat of your hand? The mistress should come to me if she needs protection. My word will see her safe. She'd easily afford my payment."

His eye roamed over Elizabeth. Then he nodded and the giant let her go. The gatherers who had been holding the boy let go also and he ran to her. She gathered him in, cradling his head rather than his back.

"Tell me your news, No-Thumbs," Jago said.

"You wish me to speak it in front of them?" Elias nodded towards Elizabeth and the boy.

"No," Jago said. "No. We'll speak alone. But… She's pretty, don't you think? The boy's not your bastard, is he?"

"No, Patron."

"No, Patron?" Jago seemed to taste the words as he repeated them. "But I fancy she means something to you." He pointed to the gatherer with the stick. "Go fetch medicine for the boy's back. Mr No-Thumbs has a liking for him. And the wench. We must treat them with particular care."

CHAPTER 15

The church had seemed to be a single hall. The east window let in light from twenty feet above the altar. Smaller windows lined the side walls at the same height. The wind had been strengthening. Now it rattled the glass and flexed the corrugated iron sheets, making them groan against the wooden frame. If Elias hadn't known how long the place had stood, he might have thought it about to split down the middle.

Jago led him to the side of the altar and pulled back a threadbare wall hanging, leading him through into a small sacristy. The low roof sloped away from the main body of the church. The room had been furnished with a table and wash basin, a pot-bellied stove, a row of coat pegs on the wall and a travelling chest, which lay open. Splintered wood marked the place where its lock should have been. Jago folded down the lid and sat.

Elias had been practising his speech all the way along the road from New Whitby. But now he came to it, the words didn't seem so wise. One thing, though, had fallen to his gain. None of Jago's men could hear what he was about to say. Even if the Patron didn't like it, he wasn't going to lose face.

"Tell me your secrets," Jago said.

"You told me I'd get a reward."

"Afterwards."

"You didn't say what I'd be given."

"You don't trust me?"

Jago leaned back against the wall. His mouth had curled downwards. Elias waited. At last the Patron said, "This is a dangerous game, Elias."

"But I have something to offer. Everyone wants the secret of how I got to Labrador. I told you I'd stolen a boat."

Jago grunted. "A small one, you said. You're nothing but a scabrous dog. It vexes me that you don't seem to know it."

Elias bowed, as if he'd just been praised. "The tide could have carried me across," he said. "By good fortune. Patrol ships might have missed me. A one-in-a-thousand chance. But I'd nothing to lose. It might have been true.

"What you hope is that I found a more certain way. Other people are thinking it too. You're not the only one to ask me. I've left them to guess. But now I'm going to tell you the truth. There *is* a way to cross. It got an outlaw from Newfoundland to Labrador. But it could just as well bring a cargo of weapons the other way. All in sure safety. Twenty cargos. One hundred."

"How?"

"Through a person I know."

"I'm not a patient man, Elias. Be careful."

"If I told you everything here and now, it'd still do you no good. But..." Elias had reached the heart of it. The words he planned to say were turning his mouth dry and tight. They would be treason against the very words tattooed across his chest, and Jago's. He dropped his voice to a whisper. "But... if this man... the one I know... if he decides to help... no one will be able to stop you. You could have it all. You could be the first king of Newfoundland."

Jago drew his head back. He blinked three times as if clearing his eyes from sleep. "I should cut out your tongue!"

But his pupils had dilated with lust. "I should have you torn apart by horses." He was whispering too. "If I let it be known…"

"Then should I say no more?"

"You play a dangerous game!"

When he'd said those words before, they'd been a threat from one man to another. Now they spoke of others not in the room: tens of thousands of warriors, all the layers of feudal Newfoundland from Patron to slave. It had been the subject of their dealings from the start. But in giving voice to the idea, Elias had broken a taboo.

Jago got to his feet. He paced to the other end of the small room and stood facing the rusting corrugated iron. Elias waited, keeping his own mouth clamped tight.

"Who sent you to say this?"

"You did, Patron."

Jago wheeled to face him. "The old clans hate me. They'd love nothing better than to see me thrown down. Your words reek of their plotting. Is this a trap? I've got your woman and your boy."

"They're not mine."

"Others want this knowledge, you say?"

"Yes, Patron."

"Who?"

"Everyone who knows enough to have guessed part of the story."

"You refused them?"

"Yes."

"Then why offer it to me?"

Jago was right to fear the snare of his enemies. If Elias's story wasn't convincing, his end might come in that small room.

"I'm talking to you because of the reward," he said.

"The old clans are richer."

"But they wouldn't give me what I want."

"Which is?"

"A new cloak," Elias said. "With garnets big as blackberries sewn into the clasp. And hemmed with silver thread."

Jago's expression darkened.

"I could sit with Patrons wearing a cloak like that. I could sit with their sons and their ministers."

"That's all you want?"

Elias shook his head. "No. That's why I'm not talking to them. They have money. They have fine clothes. But none would give me what I really need. I'll help to make you king of Newfoundland. And in return, all I want is for you to dress me in finery and set me up in a game of cards."

"With who?"

Elias held out his hands, palms upwards, fingers and what remained of his mutilated thumbs spread. "With the men who did this." He could have asked for anything else and Jago might not have believed him. But the man had a taste for revenge in the same way others have a taste for wine.

Elias's heart thrummed, painful in his chest. He needed to smear glycer-fortis under his tongue. He needed to get out of the sacristy, out of the church, to feel the fresh wind on his face. But there was no way back from what he'd just said.

"My contact agreed to meet you," he said. "If you want this, we'll take the north road. But... you can't bring more than two gatherers. That's what he said. If we go to him – you and two gatherers and me – he said he'd give you what you want."

A smile grew on the Patron's face, starting on one side and spreading until his teeth showed sharp between his lips.

"I agree," he said.

A shudder rose from Elias's belly. He couldn't tell if it came from loathing or relief.

CHAPTER 16

After his outlawing, after his thumbs had been cut, Elias had set out to escape. He knew a way down from the Island of the Reckoning to a shingle beach. He scrambled it in the dark, wading around headlands, the water close to freezing.

The hardest part was the climb back up. He tore strips from the lining of his cloak and wrapped them around his wounded hands. He made hooks of his fingertips and lodged them in crevasses in the sea cliff. When he scrambled over the top, he found himself hidden between tangles of tuckamore. He must have passed out, then. But when he woke it was still dark. His jaw rubbed against the dirt as he spoke.

"Sit up," he said.

It was an order, so he did.

He stood, fell, stood again, swaying. He shifted one foot in front of the other, moving away from the cliff. When he didn't stumble, he took another step. Then another. Movement seemed to help. His mind began to clear. The sensation of walking pulled him away from the numbness in his hands. When at last he looked back, he saw that the campfires on the Island of the Reckoning had grown distant.

To follow the track would mean a swift death, once the eighteen hours of grace were up and hunting parties set out in pursuit. He knew the dangers of crossing rough ground in the dark: bogs and hollows. But they were the odds he'd been given.

When the sky started to brew sunrise, he crossed a stream and headed up the valley side, finding a rocky gully to shelter in. And just in time, because a party of horsemen and dogs raced along the road below, the way he might have walked.

Lying at the lip of the gulley, hidden by long grasses and low brush, he watched. If the dogs ran past the place where he'd crossed the track in the night, he would be safe for a few hours more.

A bilberry hung near his face. He plucked it with his teeth. The sharp juice puckered his mouth. There were riper ones nearby. Far below, the dogs were running ahead. If they hesitated with the finding of his scent, the riders would see.

He unwrapped the binding from around his right hand. His guts churned at the sight of it, but he didn't throw up. He could feel the thumb even though it wasn't there. Reaching out, he took one of the riper bilberries between his first and second finger. But in pulling it from the bush, it burst. He'd squeezed too hard.

Below him the dogs had reached his crossing point. Two of them ran on but one stopped to sniff the ground, running in a circle. The riders had reached it.

Elias took another of the berries between his fingers. This time it came away clean.

Only one of the riders reined in his horse. Ahead, the other dogs were picking up speed. They began to bark. The last rider gave up. He dug in his heels and galloped away, catching up with the rest of the party. The last dog followed.

Elias looked at the berry held between his fingers. He put it to his mouth and bit. The juice ran sweet.

Once over the ridge, there was no more chance of being seen from the road. Berries and stream water kept him alive, and the heat of walking. After a time – it might have been the third day, he'd lost count by then – he came again to the coast and a cluster of shacks. The peasants who lived there would pay their rent in food. Such families could never catch or grow enough to work themselves out of hunger. Yet it was their sweat that stacked the tables of Patron and gatherer. Elias had known all this before. But it had never hit him so hard.

He waited until the men had set out in their fishing boats before creeping towards the drying racks. There were chickens around him and an old dog with grey hairs at the muzzle, whose growl was only a token. It was the geese that gave him away: a flock of them in a pen between the shacks. They set up a great noise, which drew out the women and children.

Elias grabbed three salmon from the nearest rack, gripping two between fingers and palms, the third he held in his mouth, as might an animal. He backed away. None of them followed. There was no fight in them. Hunger and pain left little room for pity. But Elias felt it still.

Afterwards he'd think that he could have asked for help. They might have given it freely. They knew what it meant to suffer.

He ate the salmon raw, tearing the flesh, grinding the bones with his teeth, eating every part. But only a little each day. It was enough to keep him alive until he could stumble along the road into Short Harbour.

Under moonlight and from deep memory, he walked the rocks next to the bay, finding Fitz's house, and the boatshed that belonged to it. The land door was locked, so he clambered round onto the wooden slipway, crusted with barnacles at the edge. The sea door swung open to his touch, the creak of it quieter than the waves scouring the cobbles behind him. It was too dark to see but he felt the curving side of a skiff and followed it until he found the ladder to the loft, just where it had always been. With the trapdoor laid back down, he stretched out on the floorboards. It had been their hideaway as children. It brought a kind of peace.

He woke to cracks of sunlight between the shingles above, and drifting dust motes lit yellow.

"Why didn't you use the bed?" asked a familiar voice.

"Fitz?"

"I made one for you. Just in case."

Elias sat. His old friend rested cross-legged, back against the end wall. He saw now that straw had been laid out for sleeping, and blankets. A jug and horn beaker lay next to it and a plate of dried fish. Elias grabbed it and began stuffing his mouth.

"Gods, but look at you!" Fitz said. "Your hands are the best kind of mess! Didn't you think what might happen when you cheated? But you were lucky. They'd have done worse if it were me. And they'd do it now, if they knew I was helping."

He filled the beaker from the jug and passed it across.

"I didn't cheat," Elias said. Then he drank. He'd expected water. It was wine. Still cold from the night.

"We had riders come through two days back," said Fitz. "They flashed gold for any news of you. I figured you might follow. You must have pissed someone off proper."

Elias shook his head. He'd been circling the question through his long walk but had found no answer. He'd fought battles for his Patron. They all had. He'd wounded men, but not killed them outright on the field. There should be no grudge against him. He went to the Reckoning most years and played rough like all the young men. But few would have known him away from that place.

In truth, he'd never spared a thought for his great uncle's politics, beyond the fighting of battles. Against which clans they fought was never his worry. And if he'd used his position to tumble a girl or two, what man would have done different?

"Who'd have thought you'd end up poorer than me?" his friend said.

"Can you help?" Elias asked.

"Perhaps. But you'll need to keep a secret."

Having filled his belly on that first morning, he'd slept for thirteen hours straight. And then, waking only to relieve himself and eat again before sleeping for another ten. After three days in the loft, he could stand without trembling. The blisters on his feet were hardening into calluses and the sores around his mouth had begun to heal. Most remarkable though were his hands. Skin was returning over the wounds, growing in from the sides. He could already make a fist without sending jolts of pain up his arm, and had started to learn to use his fingers on smaller things: picking up morsels, fastening the buttons on the new shirt and hose that Fitz had brought him. Simple tasks had become puzzles, even aiming his piss into the chamber pot.

When Fitz climbed into the loft on the fourth night, it was not with food and drink, but a tote bag stuffed with provisions. "This is the day," he said.

"I'm not ready."

"It'll be a month before the next chance."

Together they pushed the skiff down the slipway. Fitz took the oars, dipping them without a splash, rowing out through the calm of the bay to the chop of open waters where he turned to skirt the coast.

"How do you find your way?" Elias asked.

Fitz gave no answer, but every few strokes he turned his head as if to sight between landmarks.

"Thank you," Elias said. "I don't deserve this." Lying in the boathouse attic, he'd had time to think about their shared childhood. It hadn't seemed that way at the time, but privilege of birth had tinted all their games. They might not have seen it, but they'd been an uneven match. "I'll pay you back some day."

"I know you will," said Fitz.

He didn't see the other boat until they were almost alongside. It seemed little more than a raft at first; a flat oval, dipping down into the water at the edges. In the middle sat a protrusion like a barrel. Strangely, the swell washed over the flat part of it, as if it were not floating, but had somehow been fixed to the bottom of the sea.

Fitz gave the oars one last heave, driving them up onto the strange craft, as if grounding on a sand bar. The keel grated against it, whereupon a man stood up in the middle of the barrel, as if he'd been crouched there waiting to surprise them.

"You're late," said the man. "I was about to go." Then he looked down into the barrel and called out. "Bring up the cargo."

Only then did Elias understand. They had not beached on a raft, but on the back of some much larger vessel, which lay mostly beneath the waves, like the body of a whale.

Two other men climbed up from below, with safety lines attached. Out they came, onto the flat back of the craft, forming a line so that when a package was passed up they could hand it one to the other and then to Fitz, who stowed it in the skiff. Elias couldn't see the nature of the cargo. But smuggled across from the mainland, it would be contraband for sure.

When there was little room left in the bottom of the skiff, a purse was passed to Fitz, who counted the coins and nodded. Then Elias was being helped along the back of the craft.

Fitz pushed off with one of the oars, timing the move so the swell would carry him clear.

"Come," said one of the men.

A ladder down from the barrel took him into a dark space

below. It smelled of body odour. The last man in sealed a hatch. Then a match flared and caught the wick of a lamp. As the flame grew, he started to make out the details of a small chamber.

His mind was buzzing with questions. How often did they make these smuggling runs? Which Patron did they serve? It was clear that Fitz had been involved with them for some time. But even with a boat so low in the water, they might one day be seen.

A hum like the sound of a wasp vibrated through the floor and walls. He heard the bubbling of air and water in pipes. The craft began to move. Not forwards or backwards, but down.

"Underwater? It travels underwater?" The idea of a submarine boat was so simple and beautiful that he laughed. It was a smuggling boat that would never be found.

"Through there," said one of the men, shoving him towards a door.

Elias rounded on him, annoyed. But the man was holding a knife, pointing the tip towards his chest. "Through there," he said again.

They chained him between barrels and wooden crates in what must have been the hold of the submarine boat. The manacle chains were short, allowing him so little movement that there was no way to raise his arms or lift himself from the outward sloping wall of the hull.

At first he'd shouted, calling Fitz's name, as if the words might somehow reach his friend. But after a minute, the truth came to him. Fitz had known what would happen. He'd known it all along.

Through all that followed, Elias had tried to find a person to blame. Without Fitz, he would have been killed. But from the action of his childhood friend, such suffering had followed: the long march to the Yukon, slave work in the factory, the journey back across the frozen lands of Canada, through Churchill and Labrador. Then across the waters to Newfoundland. But not as the same man who had set out.

PART THREE

CHAPTER 17

Every story has its price, depending on meaning and rarity. News of Elias's return to Newfoundland might have been worth a handful of hack silver when he arrived. But after he'd been exposed by Jago, it wouldn't have been worth an old ship's nail.

The punishment he took in the saloon was no news at all. Dust is beaten from a carpet, they say, and secrets from a man. What Patron wouldn't have taken the same chance? Not that Elias would have talked.

But if he was then glimpsed walking unharmed next to Jago, a spy could name his own price. Such news would be proof of an alliance between the outlaw and the upstart Patron.

"Hold him," Jago had said.

The giant gatherer did just that, his one arm trapping Elias's neck, in the same way he'd held Elizabeth before. The two gatherers who'd beaten the boy took turns to throw fists. Three went to his stomach. Then they started on his face. He lost count after that. They hauled him out through the side door of the church then swung him by a leg and an arm. For a moment he felt weightless. Oh, the bliss of it. Then the dirt slammed him on the side of the head. They were laughing as they closed the church door.

It was a slow and lonely walk back to New Whitby. He'd had no sight of a mirror. But peasants on the track winced when they saw him and turned away. He felt his nose: tender but not broken, he thought. He'd lost a tooth. The gap in his mouth felt huge. One of the others was loose. But that would heal. Swelling had closed his right eye.

He might have thought that Jago had decided his story was a trap after all. But as he'd lain in the mud, the Patron bent down to whisper in his ear. "You can thank me later. I'm saving your life. I'll see you at the North Road turning in four days."

Somewhere in the beating, Elias's knee must have taken a knock. Stepping up the hill out of Rooth Bay, it hadn't been too bad. But coming down the other side, each step gave him a jab of pain. He couldn't remember being kicked on the ground. But it felt like that kind of damage. There were other bits he couldn't remember, so he figured he must have blacked out.

Somewhere on the climb towards the second headland, his thoughts cleared enough to send a wave of panic through him. He fumbled in the pocket at his belt. It wasn't there. At first he couldn't find it in his tote. Then his fingers closed around the smooth glass pot. Trembling, he pulled out the stopper. His hands refused to obey him so he gave up trying to unclip his cloak pin. Instead, he dipped the tip of his little finger. The chemical buzz filled his senses. He felt his heart slowing.

Elizabeth. They still held Elizabeth and the boy, hostages against the chance that he might change his mind. There'd been no way for him to talk with her. No sooner had he been out of the sacristy than Jago had ordered the beating. She must think their plan had gone to ruin. That had been the point of it. Everyone would think he'd insulted the Patron in some way. Even Jago's own men.

When dusk began to gather, Elias left the path and searched out a stand of birch saplings. Bending them over, he wove a makeshift frame of living stems, like an overturned basket. Between the withies, he stuffed armfuls of dead bracken until the space below was dark and still. Then he crawled in, pulling more bracken behind him to stopper the doorway. It was cold. Yet not so cold as it might have been.

The problem came in the morning when he tried to straighten. His muscles had tightened from the beating and the rough sleep. At least his hands were steady. He took another dose of glycer-fortis. How small the remaining lump had shrunk. On the way back to the path, he cut some willow branches. The bark tasted bitter as he chewed on the undamaged side of his mouth. It didn't seem to take the pain away, but after a mile or so he found himself walking faster and more evenly.

With the final headland climbed, he started down towards New Whitby. On seeing him, a fisherwoman turned on her heel and sprinted back to town, trying to be first with the news, he thought. Running would do her little good. He walked directly along the main cut, aware that faces watched him from windows on all sides. Let everyone see that Elias No-Thumbs had come back, beaten.

Turning left, he headed for the Salt Ray. The inn was the last building on the track. He knocked on the door, knowing the danger he brought. But the mistress had to be told. Trying to sneak in would only make things worse.

The spyhole cover slid back. He heard the gasp from within. Then the door was unbolted and Maria Rosa pulled him inside. She demanded to know what he'd done with Elizabeth. Instead of answering he asked for soap and a basin of hot water, for food and drink. She waved a hand and the kitchen girl rushed off to bring them.

There was only one cut that he could find: that on his

scalp. A small wound but a lot of blood. As he dipped his head in the basin, his stiff hair began to soften. When at last he could run his fingers through it, he looked down and saw the redness of the water. He didn't take the hand glass they offered. Nor the bread. It would be a few days before his teeth were up to such a crust. But the soup was delicious and he felt the energy flowing back into his body. He sat in the best seat of the empty saloon and let the warmth of the fire seep into his bones.

Maria Rosa had hovered close to him all the while, her face washed of colour. "Don't make me wait longer!" she said, when his soup bowl was still half-full.

His eyes flicked to the servants. Taking his meaning, she snapped her fingers and pointed to the door. They filed out.

"She's safe," he said, though he didn't feel it.

"Where?"

"With Jago."

Maria Rosa's hand darted to her open mouth.

"He's keeping her as a hostage against my actions. If he killed her, she'd be no use."

"There are things he can do that aren't killing! Men! You have no thought but for your own selves!"

"He won't hurt her. He has too much on the table."

Maria Rosa stood, as if to walk away, but sat down again immediately. "Where is the boy?"

"He's with Elizabeth."

"My gods. How can you make so light of this disaster?"

"They're safe," Elias said, not letting his own fear show, banishing the picture of the boy's injured back. He leaned closer to her and whispered, "I'm meeting Jago on the North Road. He'll have your barmaid and the boy with him. We'll go to meet my contact. That's what Elizabeth wants to do as well. It's her chance to get off Newfoundland. She'll want to be there. And this way she gets taken by a Patron Protector."

"That man is the worst of them," Maria Rosa said. "The worst of all of them. Look what he did to you!"

She picked up the hand glass and angled it so that this time he couldn't help seeing. A distorted face looked back from the mirror, more blue than skin tone, a swollen mouth and brow. Only on the right hand side could he see his own self. How hidden he had become.

"Now tell me Elizabeth is safe!" Maria Rosa was crying.

He wanted to ask why she cared so deeply. But then, Elizabeth was a strange creature. She moved people in one way or another. He still didn't know why he'd kissed her that night. It hadn't been from arousal or lust. He'd been annoyed. But deeper than that, and harder to admit, he'd been fascinated.

"Elizabeth is safe," he said yet again, not liking how deeply he wished it was true.

The mistress wouldn't give him a bed for the night. But as she pushed him from the door, she whispered that the stable master was still away. Within the hour, all in the town would know that he'd been thrown out.

When it was dark enough, he followed the beach around and came to the stables from the rear. His knee was feeling better already. There was hardly a twinge as he climbed the ladder to the hayloft.

He made himself comfortable, his tote a lumpy pillow under his head. As an afterthought, he set his knife in the hay next to him, in easy reach, another comfort. It wasn't that he'd an enemy in mind. Jago had been right about that. The beating had saved his life. If he'd walked out of the church unharmed, every other Patron would know an agreement had been struck. They'd all be after him.

He woke in blackness to the creaking of the ladder and then a vibration as someone climbed onto the loft boards. His hand searched, but the knife must have sunk deeper in the hay as he turned in his sleep. His every move sounded loud in the dead quiet. He couldn't see the figure, but whoever it was had stopped moving.

Then a voice whispered, "Elias?"

"Charity?"

He felt rather than saw the hay shifting as she pulled away the layers and widened the sleeping hollow. Then she was next to him, her breath smelling of alcohol. Her kiss landed on his cheek. It didn't hurt too badly.

"Your husband…" he began.

She placed a finger over his lips and pressed it down. That did hurt.

"Sleep," she said. "It'll be alright."

He woke to find her pulling on the clothes she had sloughed off in the night. When she saw that he was watching she smiled.

"I have to go. Before the town wakes."

"There's always someone watching," he said. "Will you get in trouble?"

"Not so much."

"Is… that is…"

"Yes," she said. "My husband's home."

She tilted her head, as if to see him from a better angle, searching his face until he had to look away. She ran a finger along the length of her own crooked nose, then clambered out of the hollow they'd been sleeping in. The ladder creaked. And then she was gone. She hadn't asked for sex.

CHAPTER 18

It might have looked like a dining table: a cloth to cover it, six chairs around and plates of meat and fish steaming in the chill air. But there was no space for knees underneath the church altar. That meant sitting back. Elizabeth found herself in a constant battle to stop meat juices dripping onto her skirts. Jago, sitting next to her, had simply tucked the edge of the altar cloth into his shirt. Gold embroidery caught the candlelight.

Elizabeth had been baptised in a country church in Devon when she was three years old. She wasn't sure if it was a real memory or if she'd built it from things her father had told her. Either way, it had become part of her.

She watched as Jago tossed a bone over his shoulder and reached for another rib of pork. The setting seemed to be sharpening his enjoyment of the food. It had quite taken hers away. Three gatherers shared the feast. Plenty of wine was being drunk by all. She watched and kept count. The more they drank, the better her chance of escape. But also the more unpredictable they would become. When one laid a hand on her shoulder before the meal, Jago had ordered him away. The giant gatherer, who held a grudge against her, had been left on guard duty outside. He'd have his wits about him still.

Jago proffered a morsel of food towards her. "Eat," he said.

She reached for it but he shook his head and moved it closer to her mouth.

"Eat!"

Her instinct was to spit on his hand. But it's a fool who lets her enemy choose her battles. And she'd seen what he'd done to Elias. So she shifted her head forward and took the food between her teeth, trying not to let her skin brush against his.

"Good girl," he said. "Got to keep your strength up."

The others laughed. Jago wiped his thumb across her lower lip, as if to clean it. The touch left a smear of grease.

"Tasty, yes?"

She nodded. He ripped another piece of meat from one of the joints and seemed about to hand feed her again.

She swallowed quickly. "When can I go?"

An expression of disappointment creased the skin between his eyebrows. His hand hovered over the serving plate. "You don't like the food?"

"It's not that."

"You don't like the company?"

The gatherers had stopped eating, their eyes fixed on the Patron.

"I have work to do for my mistress."

He shook a drop of juice from the food in his hand and held it near her mouth once more. "Don't worry. I'll pay her well enough. She's got other maids."

She took the food but when he turned away she spat it out again, covering the move with a cough, dropping it under the chair. They hadn't searched her. Not yet. They hadn't found the knife she kept in her boot. She'd heard it said that a man can't cry out if his throat is opened in a single, deep cut. It wasn't in her nature to hurt or kill. But she'd do it for sure if this Patron tried to take her to his bed.

Tinker had been set to work bringing plates of food and clearing away the empties. She knew him well enough to be sure that not all the food the villages provided was reaching the altar. He'd find a way to eat his fill. The problem would be getting him out of the church once she'd done whatever she was forced to do.

"To bed!" Jago announced.

His gatherers applauded him as he stood. She couldn't tell if it was for the feast he'd given them, or for the way he grabbed her wrist and led her towards the sacristy.

It could be both. They were drunk enough to cheer at anything. Jago pushed her through. She could feel the edge of the knife handle against her calf muscle. She turned to see him letting the cloth fall back into place, covering the entrance. Furs had been laid out on the floor, making the form of a bed. A candle burned next to the wash basin. The stove made the small room oppressively hot.

He sat himself on the wooden chest. She felt his eyes examining her. He wasn't as drunk as his men, though he'd been acting it. She'd kept count. He'd had two beakers of wine, and they'd not been large. The gatherers had each drunk four or five. Yet he'd made it seem as if he was taking as much as them.

She turned away, crouched down to remove her boots, then, barefoot, stood again, keeping the knife behind her as she faced him. He was stripping off his shirt; it covered his face as she watched, exposing his ribs and stomach. But the strike would need to go to the neck. If he had a chance to cry out, the gatherers would come running. Then his arms were in the way of a clean strike. The moment had gone. His dark eyes were watching her again and the shirt was thrown to the floor.

"I'm not going to hurt you," he said. "Unless you give me cause."

She was holding the knife hilt so tightly that her muscles ached. "I won't sleep with you."

"Good," he said. "There's no room for two."

She looked to the furs on the floor, then back to his eyes.

"Bed down where you will. But don't shame me. Don't go sneaking out in the night. I'd have to kill you then. That'd cost me. Your mistress would want compensation."

"But I thought…"

He sneered. "You're not my type."

She watched him stripping. His only oath-marks were the words of the law written large across his chest, distorted and stretched so that the writing spread out to left and right but remained dense and small over his sternum. She averted her eyes as he dropped his last garments. He lay back on the furs.

His smile was cold. "When you're done gawping, you can snuff out the light."

With the darkness as her blanket, she retreated to sit on the chest in the corner of the room. Thoughts tumbled. His actions made no sense. All through the meal he'd indicated his designs on her. In word and gesture, he'd let his gatherers know that she was his. In fulfilment of which, he'd dragged her off towards his bed. Either he was keeping her safe for some other purpose, or his real desires were not for women at all, and he wished to hide this from his men.

The floor was too cold to sleep on and the chest impossible. At last she moved the wash basin and curled up on the table, using her arm as a pillow. She was accustomed to sleeping on hard surfaces, but this was too small. However she arranged herself, a limb would be left dangling in the air and the the table edge pressed into her skin. Each time she woke, it was to wonder how she'd managed to drift off at all.

In the early hours she heard a door slamming somewhere in the distance. Jago was snoring gently. A crack of light lay over the barrel of his chest, half-covered in furs. Back in New Whitby, he'd seemed merely a brute. But perhaps that was what he needed people to think. He had sprung from a line of ambitious men, willing to challenge tradition to achieve their aims. She'd had one glimpse behind the facade and seen something quite unexpected.

She thought of the beating he'd ordered on Elias. Jago could certainly use violence when he wanted. But he'd never offered a reason. Elias had crawled away from the church on hands and knees, leaving a trail of blood in the dirt. But the entire show could have been for the benefit of his men. His sexual behaviour towards her proved he was capable of a charade.

Picking up her knife she slipped off the table and stood over him. They were each of them acting a part. For the moment, his disguise was protecting her. She crouched to slip her knife into its sheath within her boot. Then she climbed back onto the table. This time sleep came more easily.

Oh, the irony of feeling homesick for anywhere on Newfoundland, the very place she most needed to leave. But the Salt Ray had been her sanctuary and Maria Rosa the saviour of herself and her companions.

The column of men and horses had been riding towards New Whitby for hours, making far better speed than the ox cart had done going the other way. She'd been catching glimpses of the town in the distance. But on passing the cairn that marked the limit of unaligned land, they branched from the East Road, heading inland, and she knew for the first time that she wasn't going home. The feeling of loss came sudden and unexpected. Her eyes stung as she fought back her tears.

She'd been bumping along on one of the pack animals, thighs and bottom uncomfortable. When she caught up with one of the gatherers and asked for a proper riding saddle to be fitted he just laughed.

"Are you sore from the pony or the Patron?"

There'd been similar talk all morning, which Jago's swagger

and smile had encouraged. All seemed delighted, except for the giant gatherer, who glowered in her direction. Perhaps he'd displeased his master, for he'd been sent to bring up the rear of the column, riding just behind her own place. Three times that morning she'd turned, making it seem as if there was some other cause for a backward glance. Each time she'd found him staring at her, eyes full of hatred.

The track had been narrow as it climbed away from the sea. But levelling off, it widened. Elizabeth had to dig in her heels a couple of times before the pack horse responded by breaking into a trot. She passed Tinker and three pack animals. Then came the line of gatherers riding behind Jago himself. The first few paid her no mind. But as she moved to draw level with the Patron, one of them grabbed the bridle of her horse and pulled her back.

"What's your business?" He hissed his words, as if not wanting Jago to hear.

"That's between him and me."

"You'll answer!"

"I will not!"

"Then you'll go back to your place. Baggage!"

Elizabeth narrowed her eyes. "Tonight, do you want me to tell the Patron that you barred my way?"

She felt the heat rising in her cheeks. But the gatherer's eyes flicked to Jago, riding just ahead. Blanching, he released the halter. So there was power as well as shame in what they thought of her. She dug in her heels and trotted up level with the Patron. He didn't turn, but even from the side she could tell that he was grinning.

"Clever girl," he whispered. "You and I are going to get on fine."

He was the most brutal of men. But somehow she'd become his conspirator. Her skin crawled, as if with lice. "How long till we stop?" she asked.

"As long as it takes."

"Your man at the back – what's his name?"

"He answers to Firehand. Not what his mommy called him. But if you'd seen him in battle, you'd say it suits him well enough."

"He watches me."

"That's his job."

"I don't mean like that. He hates me."

"I know."

"I'm scared with him so close."

"Wisely scared, I'd say. He's a warrior right down to his bones. That's all he's ever been good for. His old Patron wasn't the warring type, so he came to me. Somehow he thinks you bested him. Now he must kill you to save his honour."

"Then let me return to the inn!"

"There's no need. I ordered him not to touch you. That'll hold him, so long as you're with me. My binding oath is on his right arm. He can't lose that as well. I like each of you just where you are. Testing each other. See how well he's tamed you for me. The moment you disobey or run, he'll be free to go after you.

"So here you are, playing your part. I should pay him more, though that would ruin the man. They all need different training. He's the sort needs to be kept hungry and cold. And angry. That way he's grateful for scraps. And when I tell him to fight, he'll cut through half an army."

"What about me?" she asked. "What training do I need?"

He glanced across at her. But whatever he was thinking remained unspoken. A cry came from the outrider who'd been scouting the land ahead. He was standing in his stirrups and waving back towards them. Jago broke away, riding off at a canter, leaving Elizabeth kicking at her horse's flanks in vain until the gatherer she'd mortified herself before came up level and grabbed the reins from her hand. Then all she could do was hold on as they cantered towards the top of the rise. But Jago had turned and was holding up his hand, a sign for the column to come no further. The gatherer with the reins pulled up suddenly. She found herself sliding and had to throw her arms around the pony's neck to keep from falling.

Silhouetted against the sky, Jago and his outrider had their heads close together. The Patron gestured, as if giving orders. Then the outrider came back down from the ridge.

"Turn the column round. You're heading home."

"Back to the fortress?"

"That's the Patron's order."

"Then what's this ride been for?"

"That's the Patron's order! Understand?"

The gatherer who'd been holding the reins of Elizabeth's horse nodded, though he seemed angry.

"Jago's got business to attend to," the outrider said. "He wants me as bodyguard. You'll take charge of the column."

At this the gatherer brightened.

"Logan's to come with us," said the outrider. "And Firehand…"

Elizabeth felt a wash of relief. She'd be free from the giant's hate-filled gaze.

"I don't like it. He shouldn't be unguarded."

"And what do you call Firehand? What's Logan? What am I?"

"Three men? Away from home. On the road. What if you run into an army?"

"The Patron knows what he's doing. Trust him."

There was a nodding of heads at that. A kind of truce, if not an agreement.

"We'll need two pack horses," the outrider said. "Food and bedding."

Firehand rode his carthorse up to the Patron on the brow of the hill. She watched the two men exchanging words.

Then the giant turned and started back down towards her. Her pony must have picked up the tension through her body because its ears went back and it seemed about to bolt. Letting go of his own horse's reins, Firehand reached down and grabbed her pony's halter. She didn't know how he controlled his beast with feet alone, turning it until its flank pushed into her. Then he was off up the slope with her being dragged along.

"Good of you to join us," Jago said, flashing his teeth.

He must have seen the panic in her eyes as she understood what was happening.

She snatched a backward glance to the column of men, already turning away, and Tinker among them.

"Don't try to run," the Patron said.

Then they were descending the other side of the hill. Just the five of them. The North Road lay ahead. A way-sign pointed left towards New Whitby and right towards the North.

Underneath the sign stood a man in a familiar threadbare cloak. He turned and she saw a face so patterned with bruises that she might not have recognised him.

"Well met, Elias," Jago said.

CHAPTER 19

The North Road had been built broad and shaped to slope out to the ditches on either side. Keeping it clear of potholes had become a competition between the Patrons through whose land it cut. None wanted their own stretch to be worse than the others. They all had cause to use it, bringing goods from New Whitby and travelling towards the Reckoning once a year.

But with enough miles, even a good road will wear a man's feet. Or his arse if he's riding. Which Elias was.

Once they passed beyond view of Jago's other men, the Patron ordered things rearranged. Firehand brought up the rear, then Elizabeth, jolting along on her pack pony, then the gatherer called Logan – the squat man with a missing ear. Jago rode in front of them, wearing a battered travelling cloak instead of his finery. Elias had been set to ride the horse in front of the Patron, as if he were a man of importance, despite the bruises. The final gatherer, whose name was Saul, had been sent to scout the road ahead.

A group of traders they might have seemed from a distance. Or navvies seeking work. The arrangement of the travelling party was a kind of disguise. Far from his own lands and in the company of so few, Jago was putting himself at risk.

The first evening, while the others made camp, Jago had

taken his horse to water at a stream. The beast was in a poor state when he returned, tail matted, a cake of black mud over its back and one side, as if it had been rolling in a mire. There was no hiding its fine breeding. But the distinctive pattern of the piebald coat had been covered over.

With the camp pitched, Jago called for Elizabeth to be brought. Elias forced himself not to react as she was pushed into the tent. The flaps dropped and he glanced around, catching sight of Firehand's glaring eyes, staring after his master.

From Elizabeth's reaction, it wasn't the first time she'd been made to go to his bed. Yet there was no sign that her false oath-marks had been found. He needed to talk to her alone. But all they'd been able to pass between them had been glances. Perhaps the light inside the tent had been too thin for Jago to see that the writing on her neck had not been tattooed. Or perhaps she'd used some art to keep him from looking.

His guts churned as he thought on it. He wanted it to be her fault. But whenever his mind went to her ordeal, he found his hands clenching to fists. If he'd not upset her, she wouldn't have rushed into Rooth Bay alone. None of this would have happened.

He couldn't even untangle his own affairs, let alone help her. For the time being Elizabeth must be mistress of her own fate.

When Saul cantered back the next day, shouting news that a party of merchants were on the road and would be with them soon, Jago took himself off to hide. The land was open thereabouts, but a thicket of low spruce gave cover.

Each day brought two or three such meetings. Once they had to pass a work party, filling in the road where a stream had cut through it. This time, the Patron unsaddled his horse and walked next to it like a servant. Logan played the part of their leader, spinning the workers a yarn that the horse had evil in him and was being taken to a witch for the spirit to be cast out.

Having shared gossip and traded a tin of tobacco for two chickens and a bottle of rough whisky, they carried on north.

Elias plucked the birds, but they didn't trust him to roast them. Logan did that, turning them while Firehand kept watch from the top of a pile of rocks some distance from the track.

Drizzle and wind had made for a wretched afternoon. But as the meat was roasting, the clouds cleared from the west, unclothing an orange sunset against pale blue. Through all their days on the road, Elizabeth had been kept from him. Now she sat on the opposite side of the fire. Several times she held his gaze, as if wanting to ask or tell him something, but he couldn't fathom it.

Jago took a couple of swigs then passed the whisky to her. At first she didn't drink. But when most eyes were on Logan turning the chickens, she cleaned the neck of the bottle with the loose cloth of her sleeve. It was a slight movement, but Elias saw it and she saw him see. She made a small nod, which could have meant anything. Then Logan sat back and was licking his fingers.

Elizabeth put the bottle to her mouth and tipped it before passing it on. A man might draw a knife rather than kiss another man. But they'd share a bottle nonetheless. And the two would feel bonded through it. To wipe the neck with her sleeve was an insult.

The bottle passed on to Saul and then it came to Elias. She was watching, but so was Jago. He put it to his lips and tipped it back, allowing a good measure into his mouth. The taste was harsh and it burned his throat as it went down.

"Tell us a tale, Mr No-Thumbs," Jago said. "Tell us of the Hudson Bay."

"It's cold," Elias said.

"Eighteen months you spent there. Have you no stories?"

"Only bad ones."

Jago frowned. "You know your problem? You take each lump in your bed as an insult. And since you now sleep on the dirt, you think the very earth is against you. That's the highborn in you. But look at me. I'm sired from a line of scum and salt. That's what they say. But every bit of my bed that's not a lump is an ally. None of the other Patrons would take this road without a retinue that stretched…" He waved his hand as if measuring out a half-mile of the track.

The bottle had reached him again. This time when he threw it back, Elias saw the bubbles rise. The upstart Patron was drinking a good measure.

"What about you, wench? I bet you've stories to tell."

All eyes turned to Elizabeth. She seemed startled by it.

"Where were you born?" Jago asked. "Come. Don't be shy."

Jago was showing signs of the drink, but he'd stumbled on the right question. Elizabeth would have a cover story. But if she said a place and one of the others happened to know it, she'd be asked about someone who lived there.

Elias stood. Everyone turned to look at him.

"There's a market in Churchill," he said, gesturing towards the west. "Fur traders and leather workers come from all over to buy and sell. But they have to pay a tax to bring their wares into town. Or to leave it."

"Who do they pay?" Jago asked.

"A warlord. His men protect the market."

The Patron nodded, as if to say that was fair.

"Whatever a trader brings or takes, he must pay ten percent."

"Who decides the value?" Jago asked.

The story seemed to have sharpened him. A moment before, he'd looked set to take another drink, but now he passed the bottle to Elizabeth.

"The value is the trader's to say…"

Saul grunted in scorn. "They'd say too low, to make the tax small."

Elias shook his head. "Whatever price he gives, the Warlord's men can buy it for that. So the traders can't risk it."

Jago's eyes had been narrowing but now he smiled. "You should take an oath, No-Thumbs. The things you've seen! A Patron might use such stories."

Elias held out his hands. "I can't afford to lose more limbs."

"Is obedience so disagreeable?"

Elizabeth seemed forgotten by the others. She'd passed the bottle on already. Elias sat.

Logan turned the chickens again, prodding them with a grubby finger, testing the flesh. "They're done," he said, then ripped off a leg and handed it to his Patron, who took a bite before passing it to Elizabeth.

He received another for himself, then gestured for his gatherers to eat. When one of the carcasses had been mostly stripped, Logan took it away to Firehand, who still kept his lonely watch.

Elias's hands were empty. His stomach gurgled in protest. Jago was watching him.

"You wish to eat?"

"Yes, Patron."

"What've you done to earn a portion of my chickens?"

"Didn't you like my story?"

Jago nodded slowly. "It's a good system, that tax. I might use it for myself. But you should have set a price before the telling. You gave it free. These men are oath-bound. I feed them as a farmer feeds his stock. And the wench… I have reason to keep her strong." The men grinned at that. "But you… Elias. I have no debt to you. No reason for care. Have you nothing more to trade?"

"I have another story."

"Then tell it."

"For a leg of chicken?"

"What does your story concern?"

"Tax."

Jago reached forward, tore the wings from the remaining carcass and threw them. Elias managed a double-handed catch, taking them both from the air. The hot fat scalded, but he didn't let his face show pain.

"A trader went to the market in Churchill. 'What's in your wagon?' the guard asked. 'One hundred leather boots,' said the trader. The guard said, 'Tell me their worth so I can tax you.' 'Twenty silver dollars,' said the trader. The guard pulled out some boots from the wagon. They were fine. Worth many times what the trader had said. So the guard gave him twenty silver dollars and bought the whole load."

Elias took a bite of chicken wing. There wasn't much meat on it. But hunger made it delicious.

"That's it?" asked Jago.

"That's it."

"Then you cheated me. This story has no worth!"

"It has the greatest worth. Because when the guard took out the boots and laid them on the ground, he saw that every one of them was for a left foot. He'd bought a load of boots that no one would ever buy. Except the trader. In the end, he bought them back cheap, making a profit."

The gatherers were frowning.

But Jago smiled. "You sell your stories cheap," he said.

"I was hungry."

Jago gestured to the remains of the chicken on its spit. "Help yourself."

All this time, Elizabeth had been staring into the fire. She'd understood, he thought. Of course she had. Such riddles would be bread and butter to a woman like her.

"What did the trader do with the boots?" Logan asked.

Jago reclaimed the whisky and took a long draft. When he'd wiped his mouth on the back of his hand, he said, "Tell him, No-Thumbs."

"The trader had a brother," Elias said. "The brother brought in a load of boots through the gate on the other side of town. He paid his tax to a different guard. One hundred boots of fine leather. Each for a right foot."

The bottle was empty. A lesser man might have swayed. But when Jago got to his feet, it was with a sailor's stance. He filled his lungs with the relish of a man drinking fine wine. Then he stomped off beyond the edge of the firelight, unbuttoned himself and pissed into the dirt.

When he faced them again, Elizabeth stood, meek and dutiful. The Patron took her by the wrist and led her to his tent. That at least the men could understand.

The gatherers may not have had the sharp mind of their oath-holder, but Elias had noticed in them a kind of trusting loyalty. None had asked why they shared the road with a one-time outlaw. Jago had willed it. That was enough.

At first Elias had seen Firehand as a lumbering idiot. But there was more to him than that. From time to time the giant seemed to fall asleep at his watch post. But his position in sleep was wrong. And when he sat back up again, there was no sign of grogginess or guilt. He was a half-tamed wolf, yearning to be let off the leash of Jago's rule. His hunger was for violence itself, Elias thought.

When at last the watch was over and Saul was roused to take his place, Firehand bedded down under the sky next to his master's tent.

All this Elias watched as he lay, without moving. It wasn't

that he couldn't sleep. He'd been fighting to keep his eyes open. But every night of the journey, Elizabeth had taken herself off before going to bed, walking a distance from the fire before doing whatever she needed to do. And this night she had not.

He awoke with a start to no movement or sound, but to a feeling that something had just happened. His heart beat three times before he understood what had changed. The left flap of Jago's tent hung slack where it had been stretched tight before. The dark form of Firehand lay unmoving close by. A man's form lay on the rocks where a wakeful guard should have been sitting.

Elias didn't hear a footfall behind him. But there was the slightest darkening of the already dark ground. He was reaching for his knife when a hand clamped over his mouth. Soft skin, slim fingers and the fine silhouette of Elizabeth's face.

CHAPTER 20

It was a low tent, suited to the storms of Newfoundland. Each night the men gathered rocks to pile around the edges of the canvas. With enough weight placed, the cords could be stretched taut from pole to pole, keeping the structure rigid, even with the wind keening around it. The brown canvas might have been cut from the sail of a cargo barge. It blended into the landscape.

Each night as she followed Jago to his bed she'd caught Elias's eyes on her. She couldn't read that intense gaze. The irony of it was that of the two men whose beds she'd been forced to share, it was Elias who'd taken the liberty of kissing her. Jago, the brutal Patron, hadn't even looked at her body. She wouldn't have needed to keep her false oath-marks hidden.

The furs he kept for himself. And most of the space within the tent. He sprawled, indifferent to her presence, whilst she shivered under the sharp angle of canvas, with only a blanket for covering.

Though she'd been prevented from talking to Elias, his presence told her much. Most of Jago's men had been dismissed. That was the first clue. The journey was being kept secret from whoever might be watching. And from Jago's gatherers also. Even the oath-bound man may change allegiance if the reward is great enough.

They were travelling north, towards Short Harbour. A bruised face surely couldn't fool Jago's trusted men, now that Elias was travelling with them. And it was Short Harbour to which Elias had sent his message. A bargain had been struck in the sacristy of the church, where no one else could witness it. That explained why she was brought along. Jago was using her as security on the deal, whatever it was. He must have mistakenly thought that Elias cared for her.

All this she'd worked out within an hour of Elias joining them. But each time she tried to approach him, to share a few whispered words, Firehand or one of the others had been there to stop her.

Jago lay facing away from her, his breath slack. The air in the tent stank of spirits. She'd taken only a taste. But for the first time, he had drunk deeply. Reaching out a hand towards the warm furs, she touched him. His breathing didn't change. But when she prodded him harder in the ribs he sighed, rolled onto his back and began to snore.

The air was colder outside the tent. The moon had sunk low. By its thin light she made out the sleeping forms of Firehand, Logan and Elias. Saul she couldn't see. That meant he must be on watch duty. She stepped away from the tent, placing her feet so as to make little sound. Saul could have shouted out at any moment. She was braced for it. But thirty yards from the camp, she'd still not been challenged. Stepping off the track she hitched up her skirts and squatted to relieve herself. That had been her plan. Her excuse to cover the midnight excursion. But everything she did after would be a risk.

Elias woke before she touched him. There was a moment when she feared he might call out. But then he recognised her and came willingly, following along the track, away from the others. His footfalls were not so quiet as hers. She winced at the crackle of gravel settling under his boots and looked back to the dark shapes of the sleeping men. None of them stirred.

"I'm sorry," he whispered, when they'd stopped. And again, "I'm sorry." As if she might not have heard the first time, or as if once wasn't enough.

"Where's Jago heading?" she asked.

"A village. It's near Short Harbour. One more day's ride."

"You lost a tooth," she said.

Distractedly, he put a hand to his mouth, touching the healing lip. "When we reach the north coast, there'll be villages. I mean, there should be chances to escape. I can make a distraction for you. So long as I'm there at the end, my bargain with Jago won't have been broken. He has no claim over you."

"You think I'd get away with Firehand after me? And what about *our* bargain? It seems you're still trying to be rid of me. What happens when we get to Short Harbour?"

He sighed. "We go see the man who smuggled me to Labrador. Jago talks to him. I get my reward. That's all."

"And he'll help me?"

"I can't say. That's between you and him."

She'd seen no movement in the camp, but Elias glanced back as if he'd heard something.

"Is Jago... hurting you?" he asked.

It was the question she'd been expecting. The Patron's indifference to her body in the privacy of his bed was still a puzzle. But even though she didn't understand, she felt safer keeping it secret. Instead of a direct lie she put on a pained expression, which she hoped he might catch, even in the darkness. Then she looked away as if trying to hide it.

"What's to be your reward?" she asked.

"That's my business. You'll be gone by then."

"Don't I deserve to know? After what I've gone through?"

She couldn't see his face, but sensed that her words had hurt him. She would have felt guilty for the deception. Perhaps she should have. But not in the midst of danger.

"You do deserve it," he said. "Yes. You do. I'm sorry. I never meant for any of this to happen."

"So tell me. What will Jago give you?"

"A kind of revenge," Elias said. "He'll take me to the Reckoning. The other Patrons hate him. But they can't stop him giving protection where he wants. That means I can be there, with the people who cut off my thumbs."

It was the first thing he'd told her that really made sense. She knew it for the truth. "That's why you practiced your card tricks," she said. "They caught you cheating last time. So you're going to cheat them again. And this time get away with it."

"No," Elias said. "Last time I didn't cheat. They did. They trapped me. This time I will. And I'll make them sorry."

"That's why it had to be Jago," she said, the realisation breaking across her mind. "None of the other Patrons would do. It could only be Jago – the upstart. He's the only one who'd help you get revenge."

"I wasn't sure," Elias said. "At first, I thought another might do it. But then he found me and I had no choice."

She was about to ask what Jago would get out of it, but Elias straightened and angled his head, turning as if seeking out something half-heard. Then she caught it too: a soft sound, not the gravel but something wetter – the mud in the ditch.

Dropping to a crouch, she pulled Elias down. Then she started backing away, over the camber of the road, onto the moss by its side, then further down as the land fell away towards a low outcrop.

They had no cover except stillness and the dark. But she'd been raised in shadows and trusted them. Elias seemed intent on going further but she grabbed his arm and pulled him onto his knees. Water seeped through her skirts where she knelt. Ignoring the pain of the cold, she focused on keeping her back bowed, presenting the same curved profile as the rocks behind them.

A silhouette rose up from the road. Not Saul's angular frame, but an unmistakable outline, seven foot tall and with half a missing arm. Firehand turned slowly. She imagined his gaze passing across the land like the beam of a lamp. She held her breath. But the darkness was doing its work. Once he'd turned a full circle he tilted back his head. It could have been her imagination but she thought she heard him sniffing the air. Just when her chest had started to heave for breath, his silhouette began to recede. She imagined him stepping back into the ditch on the far side, along which he must have left the camp, bent low. Then there was just the road and the outline of the far hills. She opened her mouth wide and filled her lungs. Her hands were shaking.

"Did he see us leave?"

"No," Elias said. "Or he'd have followed sooner."

Elizabeth wasn't so sure. If he'd thought she was trying to escape, he might have chosen to give her a few minutes start, hoping to catch them far from the camp, out of Jago's hearing. Out of his control. Then he'd finish the battle she had started in the storeroom of the inn. He'd tell her to draw her knife, to make it a real fight. Then he'd run her through. The skin on the back of her neck tightened and she shuddered.

"He'll know I've gone wandering," Elias said. "But he'll not know we're together. I'll go back first – let him see me bedding down. You wait half an hour. Go to Jago's tent from his blind side."

She was about to object, but the angle of his head made her change her mind. He was still holding something back. She closed her mouth and waited.

"Tomorrow…" He faltered.

She thought she heard the sound of his teeth grinding against each other.

"Tomorrow what?"

"We'll reach Short Harbour."

"You said that already. I'll meet your smuggler."

He nodded. It was a tiny movement.

She had first thought Elias a man built of revenge, violence and trickery. But something else ran deeper in him. For all his bravado, there was a core of morality buried below the surface. It made him vulnerable to guilt.

"When I meet him," she said, "all I've endured by Jago's hand will have paid off."

Elias's shoulders drooped lower.

"I haven't told you everything," he said. "That man… it's true he can get you to Labrador. If he wishes. But… you shouldn't trust him. Once he knows your need, you'll have put yourself in his power. It may be worse than anything Jago could do."

"But he did help you to escape," she said.

"You think me free? I'm no more than the bait in a trap."

"Bait to catch Jago?"

"Jago's already caught. Now they will catch all the other Patrons. And in their place they'll put an upstart king."

CHAPTER 21

On the last day of the journey north, memories rushed at Elias from every rock and hollow. He tried to push them away, but the land of his childhood would not be forgotten. Living beyond the rule of his great uncle's fortress, he had ridden, fished and hunted as he pleased. Such remembered happiness left a bitter taste.

They stopped a mile before Short Harbour, making camp a good way from the road. A messenger rider passed as they were putting up the tents, pausing to look at them before galloping on. It was Calvary land as far as the eye could see. A Calvary messenger, then.

Elias had little fear of being recognised in his present state, but waited till dusk anyway before walking that last mile. The outcrop that he and Fitz used to sit below. The stream where they tickled fish from under rocks. After that it was too dark to see, but he remembered the places anyway.

He clambered onto the boatshed's slipway, feeling the sharp barnacles on the edge. The building smelled as it had always smelled. His hand found the ladder from memory. Food and drink had been left for him, and a tinderbox next to the storm lantern. He lit it on such a low wick that it would barely show in the window. And only if the watcher was looking for it.

He'd eaten a cold sausage and a hunk of bread when the

door creaked below. Salt in the food had made him thirsty, but he hadn't touched the wine.

The trapdoor swung up and Fitz climbed through, a pistol in one hand. He had aged, Elias thought. Perhaps it was the low light, but his cheeks seemed to have hollowed and there were dark moons under his eyes. He seated himself so that the food and drink lay between them.

"What happened to your face?" Fitz asked.

"You care?"

"Shouldn't I?"

"You didn't carry a gun last time we met here."

"Perhaps you didn't see it," Fitz said, placing the pistol on the boards next to him. It was still in reach, Elias noted. And still cocked.

"You betrayed me," he said.

"You're alive thanks to me."

"You sold me into slavery."

"But here you are. A free man."

"You believe that? They'll only give me more glycer-fortis if I do what they say. I'll never be free."

"Then you'd rather I'd turned you away?"

"Sometimes."

Fitz uncorked the bottle then poured. There was only the one cup. Elias watched him take a drink, their eyes locked all the while.

"Not poisoned, see?"

Elias accepted it but didn't drink. "I've brought the Patron."

"Where?"

"Over the hill."

"How many men?"

"Three."

"I said two."

"He's a long way from home. You can't blame him for wanting protection. You have him hooked or he wouldn't have risked coming this far."

"We've all of us come a long way," said Fitz.

"He wants you to come to his camp."

"I'll see him here. You can bring him. No other."

"Then what?"

Fitz's teeth showed, seeming yellow in the lamplight. It was a smile of sorts. "When it's done, you'll get your reward. Enough of the drug to keep you alive."

"You have the glycer-fortis here?"

"No."

"Do you think me stupid?"

"It's coming. You have my word."

"I'm down to my last few days. You know I'll die without it."

Fitz's smile had disappeared. "Bring the Patron. If he's willing to take the shipment, there'll be enough glycer-fortis for all your life and more to spare."

Elias suppressed a shudder. The control and the chill of Fitz's voice had touched him like an icy finger on the nape of the neck. This was more than the negotiation of the end of a contract.

Fitz held out his hand and took back the wine cup. He stared at Elias as he drank. Elias tried to hold the gaze, but couldn't stop himself from glancing at the gun. It was a mere flick of the eyes but he knew it had been seen. How easily were his thoughts betrayed.

Their childhood friendship had been uneven. Elias was of the Blood. Fitz, a commoner, reaped the benefits. Often he sat at the high table, eating rich food his parents could never have tasted. The two boys were tutored together, learning letters, shooting and swordplay. When Fitz ran with him, they could go where they liked. No one could turn them away. They rode horses from the Patron's own stables.

The drifting apart had seemed natural. There'd been no

argument or sudden break. It was just that they each had other things to do, the duties of adult life.

"There's one more thing I need," Elias said.

Fitz refilled the cup and offered it. "How can I help?"

This time Elias took a sip. It was good wine. Expensive. "There's a woman," he said.

"She's your lover?"

"No."

"Is there no room for love in your life, my friend?"

"I owe her a favour, that's all. She helped me get the message to you. Without her you wouldn't have Jago here. I said I'd introduce you. She needs..." He hesitated, trying to find a less harmful way of saying it. "She wants to help someone get across the water. If I brought her here, would you see her?"

Fitz seemed interested. "Then she does mean something to you. If not love, what would you call it? Pity?"

"Honour," Elias said.

"I'll see her, then. But I'm sorry you've still found no love. You bedded so many girls when we were young. Always the ones that I had an eye for."

"That's not true," Elias said.

"Then your memory is different from mine."

A man who can't live without whisky may blame himself. If he'd die without medicine, he'll blame the gods of chance. But if he comes to need a lie, he may never know, for it's the nature of that disease to hide itself.

Picking his way back along the road from Short Harbour by the light of the stars, Elias replayed the conversation. Other people may have seen them as the child of a Patron and the child of a commoner. But they'd seen no such difference. They'd shared everything: toys, clothes, he even thought he might once have been laid down to sleep next to Fitz in a cot. But that seemed unlikely, since the child of the memory was little more than two years old. Perhaps he'd been told about it. The point was, he couldn't think of a time when they weren't helping each other.

Yet there'd been a bitter tang of poison in Fitz's words.

It was true that they'd fought. But only as young men do. Each time they'd made up, swearing oaths of friendship. Blood and honour. Perhaps they had gone after the same girl from time to time. It was true that Elias often won those battles. Or his Blood won them. He tried to picture the faces of the girls they'd courted, searching for one among them for whom Fitz might have had a special fondness. None came to mind. Or they all did. It was years ago and there was no telling any more. From such shared whispers as he could recall, they'd both lusted after most of the girls and women who walked the Calvary lands.

A childhood grudge couldn't still be a thorn in Fitz's skin. Their friendship hadn't ended in an explosion of rage. It just withered as they grew apart.

The track out of Short Harbour had reached the top of a ridge. Dropping down the other side, he lost sight of the ocean and the few lights of the village. The hill behind him was black edging to the Milky Way. Crouching in the dry ditch to be out of the wind, he struck his flint and steel, catching a spark in the tinderbox. With cupped hands, he lit the stub of a candle in his shuttered lantern. Even such little light as the candle gave made his footfalls sure. But more important was to be seen. More friends had been knifed than enemies on dark nights in Newfoundland.

He couldn't see the camp. But he smelled the remains of a fire doused with coffee dregs. Knowing he was close, he waved the light slowly over his head, three times back and forth.

A call came from the black. "Are you alone?"

"I am."

He waited, hearing nothing but the wind passing through dry grasses. Then a light appeared, revealing an edge of rock some forty paces ahead, and Jago's face next to it. If there'd been a doubt about how well the trap had worked, this alone would have calmed it. The Patron had come himself to guide Elias in.

Close up he saw that Jago had put on a sneer. But eagerness was betrayed in the slight forward tilt of his body, the focus of his eyes. Elias made his own shoulders slump lower and put on an expression of regret, as if he'd failed.

He couldn't see Elizabeth. She would be in the tent, he thought, listening.

"Speak!" Jago said.

Elias glanced at the gatherers. The Patron waved a hand to send them away.

"Well?"

"Bad news," Elias whispered. "He won't come here."

"But he will meet?"

"Not as you asked. It must be only you and I and the girl. The men are to stay here."

"Why the girl?"

"He knows my message was sent through the mistress of the Salt Ray. I suppose he wants to question Elizabeth."

It was too dark to see whether the lie had been believed. But Jago's stillness suggested that he was pondering.

"I told him you wouldn't go without your guard," Elias whispered, even quieter than before.

"Why wouldn't I?"

"This land is Calvary clan. If you were caught on your own…"

There was a long pause before Jago spoke again, a whisper little louder than a breath. "I know what you're doing, No-Thumbs. If another man tried to twist me like this, he'd only do it once."

"All I've said is true."

"Maybe it is. And maybe you're leading me into a trap. But I'm thinking that if you'd wanted just to kill me, you'd have tried some other way. What would happen if old man Calvary found you back here?"

"I don't know," Elias said.

"I've been asking myself all along the North Road, if maybe you're hoping to get back into your great uncle's favour. Perhaps you think that delivering me into his hands will win you a place back in the clan.

"But I was there at the Reckoning when he disowned you. I saw your thumbs cut off. I saw you weeping like a baby. You shamed him with your cheating. And by not dying. He'd never deal with you now. Not even if you gave him my head in a sack. If he found you here – if he found us together – he'd kill you himself.

"I'll always be an upstart to the likes of him. I'm knit from commoners, from fishermen. But I'm Patron now. And if people start killing Patrons, where would it end? That's what they ask themselves. That's why Calvary would ransom me. Just in case one day it falls the other way and he's the prisoner.

"But they're right in one thing. I am different. I'd kill anyone. Blood is blood. Same in a fisherman, same in Patron Calvary, and in all of them. The wind's veering, Elias. Do you feel it? That's why we're going to see your friend in Short Harbour. The air smells of change."

Elias's mind was working hard to keep up with all he was being told. Jago's openness seemed to have come out of nothing. But there were reasons for everything the Patron did. His face was a black void against a bank of clouds edged by starlight.

"What about your gatherers?" Elias asked.

"We leave them here. That's what your smuggler friend asked for. That's what we'll give him."

"And Elizabeth?"

"Elizabeth. Elizabeth. What shall we do with your lovely Elizabeth?"

"She's not mine."

"You keep saying that. But Firehand tells me you went off together. A midnight walk. Whispers in the dark, eh? Or was it more than that? But if you're ever tempted to say what she told you… I'm a creative man, Elias. Some say I'm vicious. But torture is just another tool. An artist has his brush. I have pain. Do you understand?"

Elias did not. "I don't know what you think she's told me."

"Very good," Jago whispered. "You keep it like that." His words were the purr of a tiger. "We'll leave her with the men. If your friend does want to see her, he can deal through me. Though I'm not so sure that part of your story was true."

CHAPTER 22

The only sounds had been the flapping of canvas above her and whispered voices just outside the tent. Elias's words she'd been able to hear clearly enough. And some of Jago's. Towards the end, the Patron had become so quiet that it was impossible to make sense of what he was saying. But the hushed rise and fall of syllables had given her a sense of his mood.

When she'd seen him for the first time, tormenting Elias next to the fire in the saloon of the Salt Ray Inn, it had seemed to her that the man delighted in cruelty. The thrashing of the boy's back over the altar in the corrugated iron church had confirmed it. She'd been appalled but not surprised when Elias was beaten to a bloody mess and thrown onto the dirt. But through the northward journey her opinion had changed.

The sadistic joy was an act, put on for the benefit of his men and anyone else who happened to be watching. He took no particular pleasure in it, she thought. But neither did the suffering of others disquiet him.

He might have a man beaten to death with as little compunction as ordering a goose slaughtered for a feast. But in each case, the act would not be for its own sake. Everything was driven by calculations of advantage and disadvantage. He went through the pretence of bedding her every night so that his men might see him as the same as themselves. But once the tent flaps were dropped, she was of no more interest.

The disturbing thing about Jago's whispered conversation with Elias was not the meaning of the words. It was their steely focus and excitement: the drive towards a great and terrible goal. He'd spoken more than she'd ever heard before. That, too, seemed an omen. Danger was closing in.

When Jago's voice rang clear again, it was to throw insults and threats at Elias. The man was an idiot, he said. No thumbs and no talents. Born with a fortune he was too stupid to keep. A drunk. An impotent. A shit. A boy-lover riddled with lice and pox. In short, this pathetic great nephew of a Patron couldn't even find Short Harbour when the path led directly to it. Therefore Jago, beneficent Jago, would walk the road himself. And when he returned, he would perhaps have Elias's fingernails pulled out, to remind him of the lesson.

The gatherers laughed at first, only becoming agitated when their oath-holder announced that he would walk off into the night without a guard. None of them would dare to question him. That was the genius of his sadistic act. But perhaps its weakness also.

"We go!" Jago said.

It was the word "we" that made her heart constrict. Both of the men who might have tried to protect her were walking away.

"Come, No-Thumbs. Let me help you along the road you couldn't follow on your own."

She heard the impact of a boot hitting a man. She heard a man stumble and fall. Elias groaned. Another kick.

"Get up!"

A scrabbling sound. And then Jago's call, from further away. "Are you too drunk to walk?"

Elizabeth lay, looking up at the canvas, lit faintly from outside by a lamp, which was being carried on a wide circle around the tent. Saul, the outrider, would be too afraid to hurt her, she thought. He'd see it as damaging his oath-holder's property. Sour-faced Logan was harder to read. But Firehand's desire for revenge would surely be too powerful for him to resist, if she gave him any excuse.

She reached into her boot and slipped her knife from its hidden sheath. The blade was a silhouette in front of her face. Gripping the shagreen hilt, she rolled over onto her stomach propping herself up on her elbows, so as to face anyone who opened the flaps.

It wouldn't do. A knife is a fine weapon for surprise. Or to hold while dodging and ducking. If she'd been standing, dancing on the balls of her feet, she'd give him pause, as she'd done before. But not if he was the one choosing the moment, and she lying constricted in a tent.

Outside, the lamp continued to circle.

One man would be set to keep watch, posted at a distance from the camp but close to the road. They wouldn't risk their master returning to find no one alert. Logan had taken his turn earlier in the evening. If it was Firehand next, all would be well for a few hours. The real danger was Saul taking his turn away from the camp and Logan sleeping.

Still, she would be safe so long as the guard could see the tent.

The lamp went out. She widened her eyes but couldn't even see the dark lines of the tent poles. She might still call out, if he came for her. Her voice would carry to the road and beyond.

Tugging the furs of Jago's bed into a ridge, she moulded the rough shape of a sleeping figure, then rolled over, bringing herself close under the angle where the canvas met the ground. However much his eyes grew accustomed to the dark outside, the interior of the tent would still be a shadow to him. That would give her a couple of seconds. She could crawl out under the back edge of the tent, bringing the whole thing down on top of him. Or she could bring the knife around and stab into the dark. An inch this way or that could be the difference between a man bleeding to death and a wound that might heal in a couple of weeks. She didn't know which outcome would be better: a chastened enemy or a dead one and Jago enraged from the loss of his most powerful fighting man.

Whilst the lamp had been lit outside, she'd not heard any movement. But now, with the darkness so complete that her eyes still couldn't make out the slightest detail, she began hearing tiny sounds. They weren't footsteps, nor the whisper that clothing makes when a man tries to move silently. Something was moving around the tent closer in than the lamp had done. She was hearing the touch of grass stems against a boot or shoe. For a giant, Firehand could move with extraordinary stealth. She remembered the way he'd sneaked up on them the night before, following the ditch that ran alongside the track.

The wind began to gust. Flapping and rustling drowned out all other sounds. Then she heard him again: the slightest stumble just a few feet to the side of where she lay. The next gust was strong enough to make the tent poles creak. A lash of rain hit the canvas. Then another. Then the beat of it was continuous, the noise loud. She crawled to the entrance and pulled the flaps an inch to the side. All was black.

She'd lived by her wits before ever coming to Newfoundland. Quick choices had mostly turned out well. And now instinct was saying that she should choose her own ground. The drumming of the rainstorm would cover her movements just as surely as it covered his. The dark would hide her.

She charged out on hands and knees, head first, wrenching the canvas free from the rocks that held it down. Her face was soaked in an instant. She ran blind, stumbling across the tussocks and dips, her hair whipping her face in rats' tails.

All she could hear over the storm was the squelch of her footfalls and the ragged breath in her own throat. She fell, not knowing what had tripped her, jarred her wrist, then sprang up again, running on, the faint outline of the hills her only guide, black against grey. The ground became firm under her feet then disappeared entirely and she dropped, this time hitting water. Her face went under. But only for a heartbeat. She reached out, felt for the edge of the ditch. The road must lie directly ahead. The lookout would be close.

The rain doubled, and the wind, stinging one side of her face. The shivering started then: a tremor of the arms that spread until her entire body was shaking. In the tent she'd risked attack. Running in the dark she might have broken a leg. But only now it came to her that stillness and the cold might kill her. She wasn't numb yet, but her knife hand was starting to go. She'd been gripping too tight. Swapping it to her left, she wedged her right hand under her armpit and held it there. Another bout of shivering took her. But that was good. Her body was making heat. Her fingers started to tingle and burn as the blood returned to them.

She stood, staring into the blackness where the camp must lie.

Then the sky turned blue-white and thunder hit her like a blow to the chest. She saw her shadow flicker over the edge of the ditch. She saw the grasses beyond it and in the far distance a line of low hills. Then the light became a darkness more complete than before, seared with an after-image of Jago's tent in the mid-distance. She had seen no man.

The echo of the thunder was still rolling around the hills. She stood, but kept her back bent so as not to present a clear picture. There would be more lightning. She needed to find Logan when the next flash came. She'd be safe with him. Firehand wouldn't risk attacking her in front of a fellow gatherer. Scrambling out of the ditch, she turned to look in the direction of the road.

This time she saw the fork of the lightning arcing across the sky underneath a lid of cloud. On the road stood a man, barely ten paces distant. The black swallowed him before she could make out who it was. He'd not got Firehand's shoulders. It must be Logan, she thought, or Saul on guard duty. She splashed through the ditch again and clambered up to the road towards him, shouting. Her words were torn away by the wind and lost in the thunder, which rolled on and on.

Sweeping her hands before her, she advanced towards the place he'd been standing, shouting, "Here! Hello! I'm over here!"

The wind lashed her hair across her face. He must have heard her. He would be close now. There was a darker form in the near-black over to her left. She stepped out towards it. Perhaps he hadn't recognised her. No watchman will announce himself until he's sure of what he faces.

The intensity of the rain suddenly dropped. And the wind. Then the lightning flashed again and she saw him. It was Saul, bathed in blue-white, looking straight at her. His eyes wide as hers must have been, trying to pierce the darkness.

Relief washed through her. "I'm here!" she called again, stepping towards him.

Her hand found his. He pulled her closer. In the blackness she felt something flat against her neck.

"Shout and I slit your throat," he said, his face pressed against her ear.

"It's me! It's Elizabeth!"

"I know who you are," he whispered. "You shouldn't have tried to escape."

"I'm not! You heard me call your name!"

"But no one else did. We're going to have some fun, you and me. While the Patron's away." She felt the knife stroking down her neck. The lightning flickered, fainter now, but enough for her to see his face very close. She knew his intent but was not afraid. She angled her own knife, ready to drive it into him, the blade level with his crotch.

But as she drew back her hand, a dark shape detached itself from the skyline behind Saul. It lurched towards them. Saul's grip was off her. She felt him lifted from the ground. Another flash showed him suspended by an arm hooked underneath his neck. The face behind was Firehand's. Saul swung his knife back towards the giant. The arm that held him flexed. She heard the crackle of breaking bones. Saul's hand dropped limp. The knife fell.

Darkness returned. She heard the body drop like a sack of grain. She heard Firehand's breathing, laboured from exertion.

"Go back," he growled, then grabbed her wrist and shook it, forcing her to drop her own knife.

In the dying flickers of the storm he led her across the ditch and over the rough land to the camp. At the mouth of the tent he stopped.

"Get dry," he said. "Be ready. For the Patron."

CHAPTER 23

Jago's kicks had been for show. Elias knew that. His insults had been for the ears of his own men. Under starlight, he followed the Patron, like a whipped dog creeping behind its master. Only when they were beyond view of the camp did Jago suffer him to walk alongside.

Then, from the northern skyline came clouds. The weather changed with frightening speed. As the light fell away, so the wind began to gust, pushing them along the road, as if the coming storm was eager to draw them in.

"Run," Jago said.

Elias didn't question it, though at any moment he could have gone sprawling. It had grown so dark that even staying on the road was guesswork. The first drops of rain hit, lashing his back.

Jago had pulled ahead. "How far?" he shouted.

"Over this hill," Elias shouted back, stumbling but righting himself.

Once they saw the lights of the village, they'd be able to find their way. His feet were on soft ground. He'd strayed from the road.

The weight of rain doubled. He'd lost sight of Jago entirely. Nor could he hear him. The wind was screaming over something close. There were no trees. It had to be the rocks at the crest of the ridge. Turning towards the sound, he found himself pushing into the wind, which had been behind him before. The road was lost entirely.

The sky turned blue-white, revealing everything beneath. He'd veered away to the right. On the road lay the figure of Jago. Darkness rushed in. Elias cupped his hands around his mouth and shouted.

A reply came back, thinned by the gale, but angry. "Here!" Jago cried. "Over here!"

Another flash showed the Patron, lying on his side, holding one of his ankles. Elias knelt next to him.

"Get my fucking boot off!"

Elias found the Patron's arm and followed it to the ankle. If it was a break or a twist, pulling off the boot might do more hurt than good.

"What's wrong?"

"Get it off!"

Gripping the leather, he began to pull. The toes pointed within. Jago roared. Not a cry of pain, but a scream of rage, like a man charging into battle. The boot slid away. Jago rolled onto his back, bringing the knee to his chest. Lightning flickered again and Elias saw blood running from the pale flesh of the foot. The Patron was holding out a hip flask.

"Douse it!" he shouted.

The cap squeaked as Elias unscrewed it. He sniffed, checking it was whisky, then felt for the injured foot, knowing what he'd been ordered to do would hurt. Working blind between the lightning flickers, he lifted the leg and trickled spirits over the wound.

The Patron roared again. "Rub it in deep!"

"With what?"

"With your fingers!"

Elias did, finding a small puncture in the instep. Pouring more of the spirits, he massaged the ragged flesh around the wound. Jago's calf muscle tensed. The man howled, venting rage.

Finding the boot, Elias felt along the underside. Something sharp and metal poked from the leather sole. He eased it out and turned it in his hand, feeling the four outward pointing spikes of a caltrop. Designed to maim horses or men, they were common enough: devilish, simple and cheap to make.

He found the Patron's hand and placed the caltrop in it. Then, bringing his head low to the ground, he waited for the next flash. When it came he saw the road around them scattered with spikes.

"You came this way before?" Jago asked, his voice ominously controlled.

"Yes, Patron."

"There and back?"

"Yes."

It was either luck that he hadn't trodden on one himself or they'd been scattered in the brief span since he'd last used the road. There weren't so many to make wounding certain. And yet enough. He'd had a lucky escape.

The storm had begun to move away. The lightning had faded. The rain slackened as suddenly as it had begun. Jago ripped a strip from his inner shirt, winding it around his foot and ankle. He took back the hip flask. Elias could just make out the Patron dousing the bandage with the last of the whisky. The boot was tighter going on than it had been coming off. There were no more battle cries, though it must have hurt.

"Can you stand?"

Jago rolled over then got to his knees. "Fuck you, Elias," he growled. "I'm not a cripple."

He stood.

It was a slow walk from there. Elias shuffled forwards, Jago leaning heavily on his shoulder with each limping step as they topped the ridge. The downward slope seemed harder on the Patron than the climb. But they could see a few lights in the village and the clouds were clearing. Soon he could make out the ocean and the arms of land that formed the bay.

Neither of them spoke the question, but they must both have been thinking it: who had sown the road with caltrops? Nor did he dare give voice to the turn in their fortunes. Without Elias, Jago might have remained on the road for hours. No one would have come by until dawn at the earliest. With soaked clothes and a cold wind, he'd probably have died. In the ordinary way of things, a man might be grateful for rescue. But Patrons were not ordinary men. It didn't always go well for those who'd seen them helpless.

For the last stretch, they picked their way along the beach. The waters of the bay had stayed calm, despite the storm. Ragged patches of stars marked out the roofs of shacks and boathouses above them. The dark didn't trouble Elias here. He knew the lie of the land from his childhood and easily found the door, though Jago stumbled on the threshold.

"It's up a ladder," he whispered, placing the Patron's hand on a rung, not making the mistake of offering help.

A lamp and tinderbox lay waiting, just as they had on his first visit, earlier in the night. Light revealed the small loft space. A fresh bottle of wine had replaced the empty one. This time there were two cups.

"What is this place?" Jago asked. He was propped against the wall, easing the boot off his bandaged foot.

"Just a boathouse."

"A boathouse on Calvary land. You were raised near here?"

"Here. Yes."

"He didn't keep you in the fortress?"

Elias shook his head. "If I'd been one of the heirs. But I was twelfth in line. He thought it was best I lived outside. To toughen me."

"And did it?"

"No."

Jago unwrapped the bandage. Elias watched as he brought the lamp close to the sole of the foot. The wound seemed small: a clot of blood no bigger than the tip of a woman's finger. But that was the way with caltrops. Many the man left crippled by such a small wound. The Patron was flexing his toes, which meant none of the tendons had been severed. The set of his body spoke of pain, though none showed on his face.

"Did you want to be Patron?" Jago asked.

"I never thought of it."

Jago sneered. "And now?"

"It can't be."

"My great-grandfather was a fisherman. And then a mercenary. And now here we are. Change is coming."

"I don't want to be Patron," Elias said.

"But you do want revenge. I tell you now – that would be the best revenge of all."

"It's impossible."

"You were twelfth in line."

"I was cast out. There must be fifty men of the Blood in the Calvary line by now. Even the bastards would inherit before they'd let me back."

"Only fifty?" Jago's teeth showed in the lamplight. It might have been a smile. "You lack ambition. We're going to kill more than that before this is done."

The word "we" snagged in Elias's mind like a burr in wool. It was a strange turn of events that had left them alone together with the Patron depending on him for knowledge and aid. It felt like a dangerous word.

He bowed his head. "I've no wish to be an oath-holder," he said.

"Then you've no imagination. How about Elizabeth? You'd like to own her."

Elias shook his head. "I've no more taste for slavery."

"You're some kind of monk? Only a Patron isn't owned. Even if you don't have a mark round your neck, you're someone's property. Or do you think you're different?"

"No, Patron. I'm sorry if I offended."

A dangerous light had been growing in Jago's eyes. He was a man who might burn down the world to be king of the ashes. And yet it seemed that something was sacred to him: the idea of power itself.

Jago uncorked the wine. Instead of pouring into a cup, he put the bottle to his lips and tilted it back. Veins were standing in his neck. Elias watched as he swallowed again and again.

The boathouse door latch clicked below. Jago put down the bottle and drew his knife. The ladder creaked and Fitz's face emerged above the floor. Elias held his breath as the two men regarded each other. He thought that perhaps Fitz might be holding his pistol, but when he clambered up, the gun was holstered.

"Is this the one?" Jago asked.

"I am," said Fitz. "And you're the Upstart Patron."

Elias tensed, ready to leap up. Fitz's eyes flicked to Jago's wounded foot and back to his face.

But the Patron was smiling. "They don't call me that to my face," he said. And then, "You can bring guns from Labrador?"

"I can," said Fitz.

"And horses?"

"No," said Fitz. "But something better."

"What's better than horses?"

"What is it you most desire?"

Jago didn't answer.

"I can give it to you," Fitz said.

"Is this a Calvary trap?" Jago asked.

"Patron Calvary would have me skinned if he knew what I was saying."

"And worse," said Jago.

"So what is it you desire?"

"A war. And the weapons to win it."

"I don't believe you."

"You dare say that? Who are you?"

"I'm no one."

Jago frowned. "Then what is it you want for yourself?"

"In this, I represent the King of Crown Point in the Oregon Territories."

"I've never heard of him."

"Nevertheless, he would have you become his brother king. You on the East, he on the West. And between, a trade route all the way from the Pacific to the Atlantic. Wealth beyond measure. And power. That's what you're being offered. Is it not what you want?"

Jago took another drink from the bottle. Then he held it out to Fitz. "I have gold for you, in exchange for guns. That's what I want. But it must be secret. A few men only on either side can know. How quick could it be done?"

Fitz wiped the mouth of the bottle with his sleeve, holding Jago's gaze all the while. Then he took a long draft. Again Elias tensed. But the Patron's smile had remained.

"It's done already," said Fitz. "The weapon is ready to be brought across the water."

"*The* weapon? I'll need many weapons to wage this war."

Fitz shook his head. "This will be a war of one act. You'll take the weapon to the Reckoning. You'll kill all the other Patrons and all the heirs. You'll do it in one instant."

"It can't be. Not at the Reckoning. The powder dogs would find it, whatever it is. They'd sniff it out from a mile away."

"The dogs don't know its smell," said Fitz. "Elias is the proof of that."

They both turned to look at him. From being ignored he was suddenly the focus of their attention.

"Is it true?" Jago demanded. "Will the dogs not know it? And what manner of gun has he devised?"

At last Elias found his voice. "It is not a gun. They have made a substance that detonates like black powder. But with many times the strength. It can do all you've been told. If you take enough of it to the Reckoning... it *will* kill them all."

Jago closed his eyes, as if in thought. His chest rose and fell as he breathed, long and slow. Elias looked to Fitz, who seemed content to wait. The only sounds were the wash of the sea outside and, once, the rattle of window glass against a gust of wind.

Then Jago opened his eyes again and offered a hand.

Fitz leaned forward to take it. "Do we have an agreement?" he asked.

And the Patron said, "We do."

Elizabeth had tried to get warm in the tent. It hadn't worked. Her clothes were soaked through, her fingers numb. She forced her hands to grip and release, to grip and release, until the muscles started to move more easily. By then she was losing feeling in her toes.

The rain had stopped and the wind no longer whipped the slack canvas. She crawled out, thinking to run on the spot or do some other exercise. The fire had gone out hours before, and the storm lantern. Fingers shaking she unscrewed the cap from the lamp and poured its oil over the blackened sticks and sodden ash. A flame caught with her first strike of the steel, but the wind snuffed it out before she could shield it with her hands. On the second try it caught and held. The flames spread, catching quickly in the oil-soaked charcoal.

Logan sat up from where he'd been lying under a sheet of waxed canvas. He'd slept through the storm. And the fight. Blinking in the firelight, he came over to sit next to her. He didn't ask about her wet clothes. Nor did he ask where the others had gone.

Firehand still wished to kill her. She had no doubt of that. And yet, obedience to his oath-holder had been the stronger force. As for Saul: he'd kept his true thoughts hidden. She shuddered, from the cold, she thought. The clothes on her body had started to steam. She'd met bad men before, men who'd done unspeakable things. Yet few of them had managed to so completely hide their evil. Somehow that made it worse.

She stole a glance at Logan, who squatted, hands held to the fire.

"Saul is gone," she said.

"Gone?"

"Dead."

He looked at her, disbelieving for a couple of seconds. Then he nodded, as if it somehow made sense.

"He attacked me," she said.

He nodded again. "It was coming."

"I didn't kill him." Logan seemed confused by her suggestion. "Firehand did it."

"Of course," he said, then looked away.

Neither of them spoke again. It was the strangest silence. He got up and brought the coffee pot. As the water boiled she caught a sound from away in the darkness: the methodical crunch and scrape of a shovel digging a grave in stony soil.

PART FOUR

CHAPTER 24

No one asked to see the grave. Indeed, Saul's attack on her wasn't spoken of. They had been a party of six. Now they were a party of five. That's all there was to it. But after Jago limped back from Short Harbour, the morning light revealing the landscape of the night's hidden battles, he went off at a distance from the camp and stood very close to Firehand. From the angle of his head, Elizabeth could tell that he was listening. And then, when it was done, he received something from the giant's hand, which he tucked inside his coat.

Logan did the work of striking camp, rolling the furs and strapping the baggage to the poor horses, who had been obliged to weather the storm unprotected. Jago seemed preoccupied. He rode his horse off the track and up the slope of the nearest hill.

"What happened here?" Elias whispered.

For once, no one seemed to mind that they were talking.

"When am I going to see your friend?" she asked.

"I tried to make it happen. He agreed to a meeting, but…"

"You're breaking our deal?"

"It's Jago who's stopping you. You want to go ask him to change his mind?"

"You're breaking our deal!"

"It's not my fault!"

She knew he was right. Somehow that made her angrier. The Patron still had her in his grip. There was no explanation she could give for wanting to speak to the smuggler. None that wouldn't give her away.

"But I've come so far!"

"I'm sorry."

Shielding her eyes against the morning sun, she watched Jago in the distance, dismounting to clamber the last few yards of the hill on foot.

"Why's he limping?"

Elias held out a metal spike. She took it.

"Someone scattered them over the road," he said.

"Who knew we were coming this way?"

"Few enough. Most likely it was bad luck. But I'd like to know for sure." He turned full circle, scanning the landscape. "Where's Saul?"

Elizabeth's scalp itched at the mention of his name. She didn't scratch. "He tried to take something of Jago's."

"What?"

"It doesn't matter. He's gone."

She turned away lest her face betray her.

"Gone?"

Jago had reached the top of the hill. He stood there, feet spread in a fighting stance, hands resting on hips. For a moment he seemed more statue than man. A rehearsal perhaps for the greatness he hoped to achieve. How tall might that statue be, she wondered, if he were the one to order it made.

"You mean... gone home?" Elias seemed incapable of dropping the subject.

"He's dead. Firehand did it. He's buried somewhere over there. I haven't looked."

"How?"

"Snapped his neck."

"I mean why?"

"I told you already! Now can we talk about getting me off Newfoundland!"

Elias stepped in front of her. She tried turning again but he put his hand on her shoulder and brought his face close. It was impossible to avoid his gaze or to hide her own. His expression was combative, but only for a second. Then understanding took hold. His eyes widened. He released her shoulder as if it were hot metal. He turned away.

"How do I get to Labrador?" she asked.

"We're going to the Reckoning." Elias's voice sounded flat, as if the emotions had been stripped from him, or hidden.

"We?"

"Jago and me. I'm sorry it didn't work out for you. Really. But I've given all the help I can. We're turning south. Back to New Whitby. When we get close… I mean to say, you should escape. Get away from the Patron. He says things are going to change. I do believe him. Everything's going to be turned upside down. So steal some food. Find somewhere to hide till we're gone. Then get yourself to the Salt Ray. That's your best chance."

Jago was limping back from the top of the hill. She watched as he mounted his horse from the left, using his good foot in the stirrup.

"If I run, he'll come after me," she said.

"He won't have time to search. And now he's only got the two men…"

"Why won't he have time?"

"We have to go somewhere. Before the Reckoning."

"Where?"

"It's safer you don't know."

"Safer for who? Elias, you promised to get me to your friend. You don't know what I've gone through to be here!" He winced. She only felt slightly guilty for the false impression. "You can't just wish me away. Where does he have to go before the Reckoning?"

"Something's going to be smuggled in. We have to collect it. That's all."

"From the smugglers?"

He nodded.

"Then I'll come with you. They're the ones I need to see."

Elias's face seemed paler than when she'd first met him. His cheeks more hollowed. She watched as he reached within his cloak and pulled out a small pot of green glass. She thought she saw his hands shaking as he twisted out the stopper. He dipped his little finger into the pot and then put it to his mouth.

"A tonic," he said, as if she'd asked.

It was what he'd told her before. This time she knew it for a lie.

"The smugglers are dangerous," he said. "You need to find a different way."

"Why didn't you tell me that before?"

"Sometimes the truth costs too much. I needed your help. I'm sorry. But that's it. We're finished."

"When you wanted the use of me you said one thing. Now you're done, you say another! Tell me how you're different from Jago?"

His knuckle whitened as he clutched the green glass pot. The Patron was approaching, his horse picking its way across the rough ground. Too close for them to speak further without the risk of being overheard. She stepped away from Elias in time for Jago to ride between them.

"The day waits for us!" the Patron proclaimed, as if all the rocks and moss in sight should also be witness to his truth. "A finer day, I've never seen. Are we packed?"

"Yes, Patron."

Perhaps it was the new energy that sparked in Jago's eyes.

But Logan bowed as he spoke. She'd never seen him bow before.

Firehand went down on one knee, as if about to pledge his oaths afresh. She looked up and saw that Jago was gesturing for them to rise. This was no longer the Patron. He seemed more a king, gracing the earth with his presence. His men could sense it. How soon, she wondered, till others saw it too.

He took more risks that day, on the southward ride. The storm had washed the mud from his horse's flanks. He did nothing to disguise its markings. Nor did he dismount on meeting a party of wool traders heading the other way. They called greetings, which he ignored. News of their passing would spread.

But if enemies did set out in pursuit, they would need to be quick. Jago had struck up a pace so brisk that it seemed to Elizabeth the beasts might not sustain it. There were no more detours to hide. No dissimulation.

When it was too dark to continue along the road, they pitched camp. The night was dry. Jago ordered a large fire built next to an outcrop, though it would surely be seen for many miles. His men obeyed without question. He had them spread his furs on the rock in such a manner that he could recline in comfort with them sitting on the ground below. When the eating was done, he had them carry the furs into his tent. Instead of leading her by the wrist as he'd done every night of the journey, he strode on ahead. Knowing her part in the display, she followed behind, meekly, her gaze lowered: this for the benefit of the gatherers. And perhaps for Elias too, in exchange for the lies and half-truths he'd been throwing her way.

On the previous nights of the journey Jago had fallen asleep directly, his breathing becoming more regular and shallow, whilst she'd lain awake, her mind turning over the details of the day and the permutations of her future. But on this night she could sense no sleep in him. He turned over to face the canvas wall and then again to face her.

"I'll reward you," he breathed.

"For what?"

"For your loyalty to me."

"When have I been loyal?"

"You walked behind me just now."

"I had a choice?"

He held something above her. She couldn't make it out. A thin line of deeper darkness. Then he changed his grip, holding it as it should be held, and she knew it was a knife.

"You had a choice to use this on me while I slept."

"I... I'm not a killer."

"I'm told you were going to use it on my gatherer."

She wondered how much Firehand had seen of her struggle in the storm before he'd stepped in. "It wasn't his heart I was going to stab," she said.

Jago chuckled then laughed out loud. They'd hear it outside the tent.

He rolled onto his back and sighed. "You're more than you seem, girl. You're an entertainment. Your mistress will hate me for taking you."

"Why do you keep me here every night?" It was a dangerous question. But it seemed the least dangerous moment to ask.

"You'd like to sleep outside?"

"No."

She heard him turning towards her again. Then his hand was on her, feeling for her neck until his fingers closed around it. He began to squeeze. She panicked, trying to grab air through her open mouth. Her mind was clouding as pressure grew on the artery.

"I could have you make noise," he whispered. "I could put bruises on your face so they think I treat you harder."

He tightened his grip further and her senses faded. The

breath hissed in her constricted throat. But she could still hear his voice.

"Would that be better, do you think? You're a beauty. I can see it. They can see it. Saul died for it. You cost me a man. A talented one at that." He released his grip and his hand moved to her jaw, one thumb caressing her cheek. "I'd rather know his weakness than find out later, in a fight. So you saved me that."

Her senses came rushing back. She became aware of the sound of air in her throat. She must have been gasping all along.

"They want gold," he whispered. "They want women. Or men. Or to be loved. Or admired. Or feared. It's weakness – all of it. There was a Patron once, in Norway – my grandfather told me about him. A handsome man, they say. He loved to be admired. But that made him weak. So he stopped washing and combing his hair. After a month it started to stink. Women wouldn't go near him. But he vowed never to wash it till he was king of all Norway. That's what you have to do – to get what you want.

"You think I'm different from Saul? You think my cock doesn't get hard? But I made a vow to take no pleasure. When I'm king, I'll sire ten thousand sons by ten thousand different mothers. But for now, I like having you by my side, Elizabeth. You prove my resolve."

His fingers followed her arm to her hand. And then something was pressed into her grip. The rough shagreen hilt of her dagger. He rolled away.

This time he did fall asleep. It was as if he'd been a boiler, pressurised with steam, which his confession had released. The tautness left his muscles. She couldn't see it, but she could feel it somehow as he subsided into the furs. She listened to the steadying of his breath.

Once she'd thought him a simple brute. And then later,

when she understood his control, she'd known the brutality to be an element of some greater plan. But there had been a strand of delusion in the certainty of his words. So great was his belief in a glorious destiny that he'd put the knife in her hand and drifted to a peaceful sleep. Were he to become the king of Newfoundland, how would the people suffer.

She changed her grip on the knife. In her mind she rehearsed the motion of slamming it down into his chest. But if she were to do it, there'd be nothing to hold back Firehand. And anyway, what she'd said to him had been true. Killing wasn't in her nature. Not an act carried out in cold blood. She felt for her boot and slipped the blade away inside its hidden sheath. Perhaps he was destined for kingship after all.

CHAPTER 25

It took a day less to reach the turning than it had to travel the other way. Each morning Jago roused them earlier. Each night he drove them on until the light was too far gone to ride in safety. Making camp was a fumbled affair in darkness. Men might keep up such a pace, saddle-sore but resigned to the will of their Patron. But the horses were doing the real work. And horses can't understand kingship and the promise of glory. Their dream is a dry stable and a trough of feed.

On the day they reached the New Whitby road, Jago allowed them the luxury of pitching the tent while it was still light. With the fire built and himself seated above it on a throne of rocks and furs, they set about their evening meal: a stew made from strips of dried meat boiled with barley, onions and hot peppers.

As they sat eating, a caravan of mules passed, trying to make the town before dark, Elias thought. He looked to see what Jago would do, but the Patron made no move to hide. The lead mule driver wisely kept his eyes on the path. But a lad at the back did a double take, his mouth gaping as he stared. Such a guileless boy might not have long to live.

Elias tensed, expecting a reaction. But Jago didn't seem to mind and the lad was left to catch up with the train. News of them would reach the town that night. Maria Rosa would hear of it. So would the spies of the other clans. All the land from the turning southwards was unaligned. That meant they should have been safe. But nothing was certain. He remembered the caltrops on the road. It wasn't only Jago who could feel a change in the air. As darkness folded in around them, he crept off to a hollow away from the fire, somewhere he might be missed if trouble came.

But in the morning they were all still alive and Elizabeth had not taken her chance to escape. He watched her emerge from the tent, her hair tangled and eyes bleary. She didn't notice him. He'd tried not to think about her suffering, but it nagged whenever he looked at her. It was, after all, his own stupid mistake that made them argue. And that had driven her off into Rooth Bay. From there she'd fallen into Jago's hands. There'd been no word of her false oath-marks. But from the way she now acted, obedient to the Patron, he could only think the secret must be known.

"There you are, No-Thumbs!" Jago had spotted him.

"Yes, Patron."

"Hiding in a hole?"

"It was comfortable."

"A coward as well as a cripple. What would your great uncle say if he saw you now? You're a smear of shit on the Calvary name. That's what you are." Jago's voice echoed around the rocks.

The insults meant nothing any more, except they might be followed by a beating. Through the turning of less than two years, he'd lost his clan, his wealth, his thumbs. For a time, he'd fooled himself to thinking there might be some virtue left in him. But when it came to it, he'd washed his hands of Elizabeth. All dignity was gone. What did he have left but one slim chance of revenge? He bowed his head low.

"Are you a coward?" Jago demanded.

"I am a coward."

"Are you a smear of shit?"

"Yes, Patron."

"That should be your name, I think, from now on. Mr No-Thumbs Shit Smear."

Firehand grinned. Logan laughed. Elizabeth's face was turned away.

Patron Williams was known to travel with a drummer by his side, beating time, and a line of warriors marching behind. Patron Locke surrounded himself with the young men of his Blood, so the greatness of his line would be seen by all. And Patron Wattlington kept a girl with him on his horse, clinging to his waist. A different one each time.

Entering New Whitby that morning, Jago's train had only two gatherers, a few pack animals, someone else's woman slave and Elias, the thumbless fool, tagging along at the back. Yet by some strange alchemy, Jago seemed more powerful for his pathetic retinue. An upstart he might be. But what other clan leader would dare venture from his fortress home without a small army for protection. Many was the ambush on the roads of Newfoundland. Other clans told of brave deeds, the battles of their ancestors. Jago seemed to have ridden from the pages of just such a saga. If his sword had been dripping with fresh blood, no one could have been surprised.

Standing high in his stirrups, he led the meagre column down the last slope into the town. The clattering of hooves and harnesses echoed from the walls. There was no other sound except the low boom of waves on rocks in the distance. He could see no people, though the whole town would be watching. The very emptiness of the streets seemed to cry out Jago's glory.

Only one door opened. Maria Rosa stepped from the Salt Ray Inn and stood facing the Patron, arms folded in front of her chest. He dismounted and stepped towards her, his limp hardly showing. Elizabeth seemed about to climb down from the pack horse, but Jago shook his finger at her in warning.

"A room and a bath," he said.

Maria Rosa didn't respond.

"And rooms for my men. Stabling for the horses. We'll need fresh pack animals."

Elias watched as the mistress calculated the risks. Her eyes kept returning to Elizabeth. "Will you be paying?" she asked.

Jago patted the purse hanging from his belt. "With gold," he said. "And there'll be compensation for the use of your oath-bound maid."

Maria Rosa curtsied and then stepped into the yard. She called a name. The old man and Tinker came running around the corner of the inn to take the reins of the horses. They must have been waiting just out of sight. The boy could have been released by Jago's gatherers. Or he'd escaped.

Jago stepped inside, followed by Logan and Elizabeth. Firehand ducked under the lintel and then turned, blocking the way. Elias made to push past, but the giant shoved him back, hard enough to send him sprawling. The door closed and Elias was alone.

He knew there would always be someone watching in New Whitby. But his feet took him along the road anyway. It was as if all his willpower had been used up on the journey. The track traced a broad curve over a low ridge and down until the shingles of Charity's roof came into view, then its limewashed walls, its windows. A cart filled the roadway just outside. One man stood on the back of it, rolling heavy kegs to be taken by a second man in the street. Beer or wine, Elias thought. There was no telling, really. Not that it mattered. A voice in his head was shouting at him to turn back. But that would have looked worse. And he was close enough now to see that the man on the cart shared Charity's blunt features. It was an easy puzzle to solve. He was her brother. That meant the one in the road must be her husband.

Elias had been thinking to turn off before reaching the house. A side alley ran through towards the beach. But now he wanted to see the husband properly, not half-hidden behind a wagon. So he carried on walking. At the last moment, as he drew level, he turned his head and looked.

He was a powerful man, the husband, shoulders rounded. He lifted a keg so easily that it might have been empty, but for the bunching of the muscles in his arms. His face showed no emotion. No humanity, Elias thought. But it was his hands that drew the eye. Each fist was like a hammer, the knuckles scarred from use. A fighter, then. The image of Charity's crooked nose flashed into his mind. He felt sick.

"Looking for something?" the man growled.

Elias hadn't been aware of stopping. But there he was, facing the men straight on, close enough to reach out and touch.

"Well?"

"Oats," Elias said. His voice sounded dry. "Where can I buy oats in this town?"

The man on the back of the cart scratched his head. "How much do you need?"

"Never mind... I just thought..."

"Try Spooner's place. The blue house over by West Jetty." He pointed.

"Thanks."

"You're the one just in with the Patron."

"I... yes."

"You were here before. At the Salt Ray. The cards and dice man."

It wasn't a question but he found himself nodding anyway. The man on the cart jumped down and stepped towards him.

His sleeves were rolled up despite the chill. Straw dust had caught in the hairs of his arms. There was no weapon at his belt. But he'd be carrying a knife somewhere.

"You talked to my sister," he said.

"I... I don't know."

The two men glanced at each other.

"I have to go," Elias said. "The Patron..."

He walked away, not knowing where he was going, not looking back, following around another curve until the track petered out at the edge of town. Then he carried on for a quarter of a mile, until there was a ridge of rocks between him and the men and Charity. If she was even there. He sat down, staring at nothing.

How easy it had been for her to say that ink was just ink. Unaligned, she had no loyalty, bore no mark, had no way to understand what he'd lost. He put his face in his hands and wished for the world to disappear and blackness to swallow him.

A trickle of customers arrived at the inn, through the early evening. Not so many as on a normal night. Everyone knew that Jago had chosen to board there. Those crossing the threshold would be spies working for one clan or another. Or they'd be freelancers, gathering news to sell to the highest bidder.

When Elias opened the saloon door, he found himself facing the wall of Firehand's chest. Again. The usual fug of tobacco, wood smoke, warmth and ale wafted out to the step where he stood. An inviting splash of yellow lamplight. The giant reached, as if to shove him back. But this time, Elias dodged it, surprised to find a shred of dignity worth protecting.

Tinker was waiting for him when he slunk into the stable-yard.

"I'm to give you this," the boy said, holding out a candle

lantern. Whether it came from Elizabeth or the mistress, he couldn't tell. "She said careful not to burn the place down."

By such thin light, he found his way inside. Each pony or horse had been given its own stall, its own feed. Animals had ranks, he'd been told. The top beast will bite the ones below if it thinks they stand too tall. He wondered if they felt the humiliation: the pack horses that had to follow behind Jago's stallion. Their breathing sounded gentle. Relaxed.

He climbed the ladder to the hayloft and found a jug of ale set on the boards and two potatoes with charred skins, still hot from the embers of a fire. He broke one open and inhaled the steam. He ate slowly at first, speeding as it cooled and as his body remembered its own hunger. Afterwards, he climbed back down with the bar of soap from his bag and stripped naked to wash in the yard, dousing himself in water from the trough, cold enough to set his teeth chattering.

But Charity might come to him again. He didn't want the stink of ditches, sweat and campfire smoke to put her off. They'd have one more turn in the hay together. Then she'd be gone and that would be an end to it.

Back in the loft he sat waiting, filling his belly with ale. His eyes drifted closed. Three times he woke himself with a start. Until it was clear that he wouldn't see her. Then he bedded down and fell into a dead sleep.

At some time in the night he dreamed that she'd come to him.

When the cold woke him, it was still dark. From the memory of the dream he reached out a hand expecting to touch her. But he was alone. There was little hay above. Not remembering if that was the way he'd left it, he dug himself in deeper. This time his dreams were uneasy.

In the first grey light he gave up trying to sleep. The remains of the ale put some strength back into his belly, though it was bitterly cold. No one else was about but the horses had woken, their ears twitching as he walked along the line. Pausing in front of the smallest of the pack animals, he stroked its flank. Jago's stallion stamped in the next stall. The animal didn't choose its master. It wasn't its fault. Yet Elias made a point of giving feed and water to all the others first.

The old stable master arrived just after dawn. He scowled at Elias, who was working with a brush on the flank of one of the pack horses.

"What y' doin'?"

"Earning my keep."

"It's the boy's work."

"If they'd let me inside, I'd scrub the hearth. But..."

The old man spat before hobbling away.

Next in was Tinker, sucking on a straw. He seemed content to watch. But on hearing a shout from outside, he dropped himself from the barrel he'd been sitting on, grabbed the brush from Elias's hand and set to work.

By sunrise, a fine rain was falling. The cobblestones of the yard shone in the thin light. There being nowhere else to go, Elias sat on the barrel, and tried to get the boy to talk. But Tinker had few words for him.

"How did you come to work for Maria Rosa?"

"Just did."

"Then tell me how you got away from Jago's men."

"Ran."

It couldn't have been so simple.

"Where are your parents?"

A shrug.

"How long have you known Elizabeth?"

At this question the boy turned away and busied himself with some small detail on the side of the stall. His devotion to her was plain. His loyalty.

"Elizabeth's a good woman," Elias said. "And clever, I think. I've never met another like her." The boy's shoulders dropped a little, suggesting this new approach had put him more at ease. "I guess she'd stand out in any land. Though she hides it well. You're right to look after her."

The boy glanced back at him, a smile creasing that dirt-smeared face.

"Hold onto her," Elias said. "That's my advice."

"Yeah," said the boy, and seemed about to say more, but footsteps echoed from the walls of the yard outside and the moment had gone. The boy patted the horse's neck and moved on to the next stall.

"Good morning." It was Maria Rosa, her expression businesslike.

"Morning," Elias said.

"Tinker," she called. The boy poked his head up from behind the stall. "There's hot oatmeal waiting for you in the kitchen. Go."

The brush clattered to the ground and the boy ran out into the rain.

"Oatmeal for everyone?" Elias asked.

She shook her head.

"How are things in there?" He nodded towards the main building.

"How do you think, with that bastard making use of Elizabeth." Her eyes narrowed.

"It's not my fault," he said.

"It is every bit your fault. You said there was a way for her to get to Labrador. You served her a false hope and she swallowed it."

"She forced it out of me. With threats! Don't you remember?" He moved his hands together in front of him, a gesture of helpless submission.

"Jago thinks he's taking her to the Reckoning," Maria Rosa said. "She could run, but she tells me she wants it. You have to talk to her."

"I've tried. She won't listen."

"She says you're going – to the Reckoning."

He nodded.

"And she says you're set on revenge. Is it true?"

"What does it matter?"

"Such plans mean ruin in the end. If she's with you, you'll drag her down."

"What is she to you?" he asked.

Maria Rosa stepped along the line of stalls, stroking the nose of one of the horses. Others stretched out to sniff the air as she passed. Then she turned to face him again. "I'm in her debt," she said. "But it's more than that. She's become dear to me. I never had a daughter. And she…"

"She wants to leave," Elias said. "But you want to keep her. That's the truth of it. You're no better than me."

"The path you've set her on will lead to ruin. That's the truth!"

"Perhaps," he said. "But you're afraid she'll get what she wants and you'll lose her forever. Have you told her how you feel?"

The mistress nodded, but he could see doubt in her eyes. "Not in such plain words," she said.

"Then tell her straight. It'll have more chance of changing her mind than anything I could say."

"It's not for herself she takes such risks. There are two others. She'll do anything to help them. Even if it meant her own death."

"The stable boy," Elias said. "Tinker. Is he one of the two?"

She didn't deny it.

"Where's the other one?"

"Not here."

"Elizabeth's going to leave you," Elias said. "One way or another."

"Then I want you to protect her," Maria Rosa said. "As far

as you can. I'll reward you for it."

"You won't even have me at the inn!"

"That's Jago's doing. Not mine."

"Will you tell me something?" he asked.

Maria Rosa nodded.

"The woman who was talking to me in the saloon that night…"

"Charity?"

"Her. You said something about a husband. Then she ran off."

"I do remember."

"What did you mean by it?"

"She's married. That's all. Some people need reminding."

"Do you know how she got her broken nose?"

Maria Rosa tilted her head, as if assessing him afresh. "Like I said. She's married. Don't you have enough trouble in your life?"

"I was just curious."

Maria Rosa frowned, sceptical. "Jago told me they're moving out tomorrow. And taking my Elizabeth. Be sure to keep a watch for her. I'll not forgive you if she suffers."

A kitchen girl brought him a plate of mutton and potatoes, a jug of ale and a fresh candle for the lantern. He asked for blankets, which Tinker brought afterwards. From sleeping in a cold hollow under a rainy sky, to the luxury of a hayloft. With blankets, no less. All in the space of two days. But none of it pleased him. The only comfort came from knowing that he was truly alone. The world could turn to ashes and he wouldn't care.

In a few days the glycer-fortis would be used up. After that he would die. Or perhaps be given more. Either way, he would set the wheels moving. Jago would take his bomb to the Reckoning. He'd kill all the other Patrons and their sons and advisors. The men who'd destroyed his life would themselves be dead.

He dipped his cloak pin into the greasy medicine and smeared it on the underside of his tongue. A good measure. The heat of it filled his mouth. His chest relaxed. His heart rate slowed.

He was nothing. Jago was right. But he would have his revenge. The world would burn.

The sound of footsteps below made him open his eyes. He knew them even before hearing the familiar creak of the ladder flexing under her weight. He felt the blankets lift as she slipped in next to him. His reaction to the sound of her breathing and the scent of her skin caught him by surprise. In that moment, he needed her and the knowing of it terrified him.

Then her full lips were on his and she was climbing onto him. His face wasn't bruised any more. Or at least, it wasn't tender. Her kisses were firm but didn't hurt. He felt himself sinking deeper into the hay.

"Charity," he whispered.

She put her mouth to his ear. "Say my name again." Her next kiss was more passionate but he needed to understand.

"What happened to you?"

"Happened?"

"Your nose was broken."

He felt her pull back, as if to look at him, though it was perfectly dark. "A fight," she said. "Long ago."

He remembered the scarring on her husband's fists. "Will you be in trouble? For this, I mean."

"What more trouble can there be?"

"I don't know."

"Then put it away."

"But I want to understand."

He felt her hand on his chest, searching lower over his

stomach. "Your body understands," she said.

"I saw your brother. And your husband. I shouldn't have gone to your house. I'm sorry. But he asked who I was. I had to tell him."

She placed a kiss on his brow, on each of his eyes.

"And now you're here," he said, his voice shaking. "He'll know. Everyone knows everything in this place. And…"

"No, they don't!" Her words were emphatic. "It wasn't him that broke my nose. Now say my name again."

So he did, whispering it close to her ear: "Charity."

CHAPTER 26

Fog: the world reduced to white and grey. Slick cobbles. Condensation running on the small panes of glass in the houses of New Whitby. Had it been London, everyone would have huddled indoors around smoky fireplaces. But this was Newfoundland. Where there was fog there could also be smugglers.

It wasn't the prospect of a public execution that brought peasants out onto the beach. There were rewards for anyone who sighted a smuggling boat. The property of the smugglers would be divided. By custom and precedent, first sight was generally held to be worth one-twentieth of the total. Though naturally, there was no binding law. A sum great enough to lift a peasant out of poverty. The fog was a kind of lottery, free to play, but for the bone chill and the slow, inevitable dampness. But Elizabeth had other reasons to venture out.

Though sounds were muffled, she could hear the clanking of boats at anchor in the bay. That gave her a direction, guiding her through the stumbling white, over the rocks at the headland point. The sucking and scouring of the shingle told her the beach was close.

A fog had cloaked her unwonted arrival on Newfoundland. Even then, she would have been discovered but for the remoteness of the cove. Only afterwards had Maria Rosa explained how lucky she'd been. Since then, and once she had grown to understand the parameters of her problem, each new fog had called her out to watch and listen.

She'd found a kind of safety at the Salt Ray Inn. But if she remained, the day would eventually come when she was discovered. Of the two who'd come with her, she was least concerned about Tinker. The boy fitted in. He could adapt. It was Julia she worried about. Her looks would attract attention. Her accent might give her away. Or someone could simply ask the place of her birth. Elizabeth had long ago given up trying to teach her friend to lie. Julia's straightforward and direct nature made it impossible. Even to think of speaking an untruth lit her face up red. Hiding in the hills had kept her safe so far. But that could not last.

Maria Rosa couldn't take them across the waters to Labrador or Nova Scotia. Nor would Elizabeth have asked her to chance it. But smugglers did sometimes make the crossing. If only she could find one, she might demand passage in return for silence.

From out in the bay came the regular beat of a steam engine. That would be a gunboat, she thought. Each time she'd seen the fog lift, the water had been dotted with fast launches, positioned ready to race after any boat making a break for it. On other stretches of coast, the spoils went mainly to the local Patron. Thus the unaligned coast around New Whitby yielded the richest bounty.

Like all lotteries, it was played more for hope than reward. The odds were too low to be meaningful. Better to come home frozen and yet to have dreams than to stay by a sluggish fire as a dead soul.

Elizabeth felt the wind against the side of her face. She shivered. She could see the shingle fading away into the white on either side, and small waves tumbling the stones against each other. It was a wider view than she'd had at the start. There were strands in the fog now, tentacles of denser or thinner white. And more light was making it through from above.

The sound of another steam engine reached her, more distant than the first. And then yet another. They were all starting up, preparing for the race to intercept.

Something dark floated in the water directly out from where she sat. She'd taken it to be a rock. But now she saw that it rose and fell with each wave. Size and distance were hard to estimate, but it seemed not unlike a floating body. The fog thickened and she lost it for a moment. The next clear patch revealed it closer to the shore.

It resolved into the dark face of a seal, only its head above water, looking directly at her. She found herself laughing. Footsteps ground the shingle away to her right. A shadow became the familiar figure of Elias.

"I recognise that voice," he said. "Though I can't remember hearing you laugh."

He approached and the seal pulled away from the shore.

"What are you doing out?" she asked.

"They won't let me in the saloon," he said. "What about you?"

"Looking for a way to cross the water."

"You'll not find one. Not here." He sat himself on the rock next to her. The seal dipped under, reappearing closer to the shore. "If I had a gun, I could shoot him," Elias said.

"No!"

"You eat sheep, don't you? There must be twenty or thirty peasants round this bay. Any one of them would kill him if he came in close enough. The oil from that one beast could be the difference between starving and a good winter. But look at him, he stays just far enough out. Too deep for us to wade in and get the body. We'd freeze if we tried to swim it. And it's foggy so he knows he could escape if we moved to launch a boat. He's learned it. So he takes the risk. Comes in to steal from crab pots in the bay."

"He isn't stealing."

"Then his belly must be full."

"He's watching us."

"He knows what he's doing. Not like you. If you went to the Reckoning, it'd be like him coming up on the beach right here. He'd be dead in a second."

"You want revenge," she said.

He picked up a stone and cast it into the water. The seal dipped under. She peered into the grey.

"Yes, I want revenge," Elias said. "And don't you judge me for it. You don't know what they did."

"They cut off your thumbs."

"That was the start of it. They think I escaped from this place. But the smugglers took me prisoner." He pointed west and seemed to be staring into the far distance, though there was nothing to see beyond a few yards of rock and beach shingle. "They carried me as a slave. All the way to the Yukon. I wasn't the first from here to take that road. There's been others before. But I was the first to survive it."

He dipped into the pocket of his cloak then held out his thumbless hand. The green jar rested on his upturned palm. She reached out to take it, but he closed his fingers round the glass.

"Your tonic," she said.

He nodded. "More than a tonic. This is what we made in the Yukon. So much of it, you can't imagine. A touch of it can save a man's life if his heart's wrong. But making it gets to be a one way road. First it gives you headaches. You throw up. You're dizzy. Then you're used to it. And then... well, it worms its way into your body so you can't live without it."

"Can you make it yourself?"

"With all the stuff we had out there – I could do it in my

sleep. But…" He shrugged.

"You don't have them."

"Nor any chance."

He held the jar up so the light came through the glass, revealing a pea-sized lump.

"How long will it last?"

"A week," he said. "Maybe. I skipped my dose this morning. I can feel it now. Across here." He rubbed a hand over his chest. "It's tight. And it hurts."

She watched him remove the stopper. With the tip of his cloak pin he excavated a smear of the tonic and wiped it inside his mouth. She could see the relaxation spreading over his face and shoulders. And then, as he pushed back the stopper, a new expression formed. It was, she thought, a kind of fey despair.

"They'll give me more when I've done my task."

"You've snared Jago already. That was what they wanted."

"I have. He's mad with dreams of power."

"Then you'll have your tonic."

"Maybe. But they'd never give me enough. Why would they? So long as they have what I need, I must do all they say. They'll want to keep me like this. On a short leash."

"I'm sorry," she said.

"I'm not. They want to bring down the Patrons. I want revenge. We'll change the map together."

He picked up a handful of small stones and flung them towards the water. Some landed short. The seal had long gone.

"Why do they want to kill the Patrons?" she asked.

"They've a kingdom in the west. From the Oregon territories up into the Yukon. If they place a king here – a puppet in their power – they'll have both coasts. That means both oceans. Why does anyone want to conquer?"

"I don't know."

"My great uncle told me once that Alexander wept when it was done. When there was nothing more to take. He grabbed the world because it was there – all laid out for him. There was no reason beyond that. There never is. But if they have the two oceans, they'll get the land between."

"What then?"

"Then the rest. The Gas-Lit Empire. They'll take it all. This..." He held up the pot again for her to see. "This is a poison. Also a medicine. And yet also an explosive. There's more death packed into it than anything else. Why wouldn't they draw a new map, with their own names written large across it?

"You should stay here. When the Reckoning comes, I'll go with Jago. There'll be... I don't know what. A bomb. The death of many. The Patrons, their bloodlines, they'll all be together. One moment – one great explosion. There's going to be chaos after. Every clan at war. For a time nowhere's going to be safe.

"But just after it happens, there's going to be thousands trying to cross the water. That's the time you should go. In the chaos. Your odds will be better. You'll find a place on one of the boats."

A shout came from the direction of the inn, made soft as a whisper by the fog. A man's voice, calling Elizabeth's name. One of the gatherers, she thought, though she couldn't tell which. New men had ridden in during the night. Jago was still lightly guarded by the standards of the Patrons. But no longer quite so vulnerable.

She got to her feet. Her skirts were soaked through where she'd been sitting. The shout came again. Two voices this time.

"Walk away," Elias said.

She looked down at him, weighing his words. The thing was, she'd lived for years on the edge of a knife. There'd been a few months of peace here and there. A few months of love. But she'd had to walk towards death as many times as she'd run away from it. If it was just for herself, she might have taken the odds he suggested. But she couldn't calculate the lives of her friends in the same way. If she went to meet the smugglers again and failed, Julia and Tinker could still risk a crossing in the chaos, as Elias had suggested.

"Walk away," Elias said. "Escape. They'll never find you in this fog."

"You can't escape from yourself," she said. Then, picking her way towards the voices, she called out. "I'm here. I'm coming."

Everyone was up and moving inside the Salt Ray. Except for Jago, who sat in the chair next to the fire with his feet up on the stool. It was the same position he'd occupied the first time she saw him. But something was different: the set of his face, the position of his hands on the arm rests. He looked like a king.

Maria Rosa caught her arm and pulled her into the counting house, closing the door behind them, sealing them in. It was a room with no windows. No other way out. The bolts were iron bars, thick as Elizabeth's finger. It would be the door frame that gave way if they kicked it down. Firehand might do it without breaking sweat.

"He's leaving," Maria Rosa said. "A man rode in half an hour ago. Went straight to Jago. And now this."

"Which road did he come by?" Elizabeth asked.

The mistress shook her head. "The fog's too thick to say."

She went to the corner safe, unlocked it and lifted out a purse. It clinked as she placed it in Elizabeth's hand. It was heavy. Inside was mostly gold: whole coins, parts of coins and a quantity of jewellery scrap.

"He gave me this. Jago. For you – or, for the use of you. He wants to take you with him. He just put it in my hand and walked away. I tried to give it back, but he won't listen."

"How much does this buy?"

"He said he's taking you to the Reckoning."

"Is the price... reasonable?"

"You can't go!"

"But if I was a slave..." She hefted the purse in her hand, making the metal sound within.

"He's paying a fortune. If I asked for that amount from any other Patron for a month of your time, he'd take it as an insult. But Jago... I don't understand what's happening."

Elizabeth gave the purse back and closed Maria Rosa's fingers around it. "Be grateful," she said, wondering how much Jago would have in his treasury, how quickly he'd go through it at this rate. In his mind, he'd already become the king. It had given him a kind of dark charisma. Over the last couple of days she'd seen the force of his personality pushing others aside like the bow wave of a great ship. They might not have understood what was happening, but she remembered how shallowly they'd bowed when entering his presence before. Those bows had now turned deep.

"Keep the money," Elizabeth said. "I would have gone with him for free. He won't touch me until he gets what he wants – which is to wear a crown. He's taken a vow. I'm safer sleeping next to him than I would be anywhere else in Newfoundland. Right up to the last moment. And then... Well, we'll see. Please look after my friends. If all goes well, I'll be back to take them. We'll leave safely."

"And if it doesn't go well?"

"Then you'll be looking after them for longer. Use that gold."

"Either way, I'll lose you."

Maria Rosa took her shoulders. Elizabeth felt the full

intensity of her gaze. Then she was being enfolded in a hug so tight it made her ribs flex. She was held, her face pressed into the mistress's hair, breathing her scent. And then just as suddenly as the embrace had begun she was released and Maria Rosa had turned away to kneel in the hearth. Out came the bricks from the rear wall of the fireplace. She laid them in order on either side of her knees, then reached in and unlocked the hidden safe. When she stood again she was cradling a hessian bag.

"You'll want these," she said, extracting Elias's last few trick cards.

Elizabeth tucked them into her left sleeve. Next out was a flask of indigo and a fine brush.

"The tattoo marks will fade. I don't know who you'll find to freshen them. But keep it hidden."

She wasn't meeting Elizabeth's eyes.

"And my gun?"

"You can't take that to the Reckoning. The powder dogs would sniff it out."

"It hasn't been fired for months."

"They'd smell it if it hadn't been fired for years."

"Then I'll hide it before I get there."

"You want to be stripped and searched? They'll smell it on your hands. You think your oath-marks are good enough to pass?"

"It was my father's gun," Elizabeth said. "I'll find a way."

Maria Rosa shook her head. But when Elizabeth took the hessian bag, there was no resistance. She reached inside it and withdrew the gun. It was a thing of fine craftsmanship. The symbol of a leaping hare had been inlaid in turquoise in the stock. She turned it, letting the reflections of the lamplight move over its surfaces. It was beautiful, yet its one purpose was to kill.

• • •

The horses were saddled and ready in the stable-yard. Ears turned and muscles twitched. All the servants had come out to hold bridles and were having a hard job of it, for the beasts could sense that it was time to be off. A line of gatherers marched out from the rear door, their boots making a din, which agitated the horses still further. Then the men were mounting and out came Jago's most trusted guards, Logan and Firehand.

Finally the Patron Protector emerged. The limp had gone from him entirely. He took his time, surveying the assembled crowd of servants and fighting men. Other villagers were looking in from a distance, using the fog to half hide themselves.

If it had been her, Elizabeth thought, she'd have feared stumbling, or the horse might try to step away as she mounted and she'd be left standing like a fool. But Jago made it look like a dance move: stepping into the stirrup and up onto the back of his fine stallion.

Everyone waited. Everyone watched.

He shifted his heels and the horse stepped forwards. Suddenly they were looking at Elizabeth instead, for the Patron had stopped next to her and was reaching down. She could feel Maria Rosa just behind, fussing with the ties on her back pack.

Elizabeth offered her hand to Jago. He gripped her wrist and hoisted her into the air so that she landed in front of him, in the manner of a side saddle rider, but without the pommels to stop her from slipping. He kicked his heels and they were away, all the other horses following behind, the din of hooves on cobbles half-deafening, even in the fog. Villagers scattered before them. She thought she would fall, but Jago brought in his arms to keep her precarious balance.

She felt his face close to hers. "Play your part," he growled.

• • •

Elizabeth's stomach told her it must be midday. There'd been moments through the morning when the fog thinned enough to let her see the path ahead for a hundred yards or more. Once, at the peak of a headland, she'd glimpsed the disk of the sun, pale as the moon behind cloud. It had seemed as if it might burn through. But as they descended the other side of the hill, it thickened again.

Clear of New Whitby, Jago had let her down and she was back to a pack horse, though not the one that had carried her before. She was glad to be away from the smell of him. Away, too, from the eyes of the peasants they passed along the track. All focused on the Patron and his kingly progress.

It must have been mid-afternoon before the stop was called. They'd come across a gang of beachcombers hauling a quantity of driftwood. Logan paid them to build a great fire with the entire load. And presently the gatherers were standing near it, warming themselves. Stoneware cooking pots had been placed around the edge, with dried meat, carrots, swede, onions and river water. One of the gatherers tipped powder from a tin into each of the pots. Some kind of herb, Elizabeth thought. But when she came to taste the broth, she felt the burn of hot Guinea spice.

"Make camp," someone called, and the work of pitching began, though it was still early and she knew that a village lay not many miles ahead.

It seemed there would be tents for everyone.

"Will one be mine, do you suppose?" Elias asked.

She hadn't noticed his approach.

"You can swap places with me. If you want." Casting him a side glance she caught the pain of his reaction and regretted it. But the secret of Jago's self-imposed celibacy was too dangerous to share.

"I'm sorry," he said.

"I'm not treated so badly as you think." This she gave him in a whisper.

It only seemed to intensify his misery.

"Do you know why we're stopping here?" she asked.

They were standing quite alone but he looked over his shoulder before answering. "The smugglers should be bringing in a delivery."

"Here?"

"Not far. We're to meet at the peak of high tide. It could have been tomorrow. But it'll be tonight, I think. Since the weather's like this."

"It is a boat then?"

"What else could it be?"

"I thought perhaps an airship?"

At least that made him smile. "An airship could never be hidden. No, this is a ship of the waters."

"I want to see it."

He shook his head. "Jago will take as few men as he dares. I know what's happening. So I'll be one of them. There'll be Logan and Firehand as well. He trusts them more than the other men. He'll only send for the rest once the smugglers are gone."

"But I must see them!" she hissed.

He seemed about to answer, but closed his mouth and stood away from her.

Logan was marching towards them. "There's work to do," he called.

CHAPTER 27

Tents there were enough, and bedding, blankets, furs, even pillows, though not for Elias. He'd been a fool to hope. But there was a fire at the top of the beach and wood to feed it, though that lay half a mile up the hill, and him with the job of fetching.

The peasants owned a sledge, for hauling their scant treasures from the beach. At first they wouldn't let him use it. Its runners were sheathed in iron to make for a smooth run over the turf. It must have been the most expensive thing they owned. But when he told them it was Jago's fire that must be fed and that they'd best not anger a Patron, they changed their minds.

Such power in a name. And such danger in using it.

They kept close on either side of him, as if he might try to steal the sledge. They wouldn't help him pull. But gravity was with him going down from the woodpile to the beach. It was done quicker than he'd feared. If Logan hadn't been there, he would have left it at that. But a second load was ordered, so up the hill he went again. Climbing was harder work, even with an empty sledge. The rope cut into his shoulder. By the time he had the second load delivered the skin had been rubbed raw.

He tipped the logs and sticks next to the fire. The peasants scowled at him.

"You gotta take it back," said one, meaning the sledge.

Elias turned away.

Night closed in and the camp grew quiet. One gatherer had been left to watch. From some of the tents he could hear the slack breath of sleep. The fire, which had been huge before, had fallen in on itself to become a wide circle of glowing coals. He threw some sticks on the top, which crackled into flame. By that light, he hefted in a log. Sparks flew up from its fall.

The beach stones had dried near the fire, despite the fog. He lay on them, trying to make himself comfortable. The watch guard stopped to warm himself, then moved on out of the circle of light. Elias listened to the scrunch of his boots. Then there was just the crackle of burning wood and the sound of the shingle being sifted by the waves. They'd built the fire at the very top of the beach, where the stones gave way to grass. The tide was low, but coming in, he thought. It would peak before dawn. Out there, somewhere, the submarine boat would be waiting.

His thoughts were broken by a shout from the dark: a wordless noise. It seemed almost joyful. But as it trailed away, he knew it for a cry of pain. The watch guard. Without thinking, Elias rolled over and over, out of the firelight. An arrow hissed through the air, near where he'd been lying, clattering on the stones beyond.

The guard's cry cut to a sharp silence.

More shafts landed, one arrowhead sending up a spark. Elias scrambled over the lip of the beach, getting his head down behind a ridge of stones. Only now, he found his voice: "Attack! Attack! Archers on the hill!"

Shadows were moving through the camp, spreading out. Light footfalls. Darting forms. Jago's men. Metal clashed on metal somewhere to his right. The sound of combat. Men began roaring battle cries.

He'd been born for the fight, trained for it. It had been his life once. But all he had with him was a short knife. Little use in open combat. He drew it anyway.

A crunch of stones made him look back. Three figures were advancing towards him. Two held swords, one a chain mace. Elias swore and jumped to his feet. They charged. Pebbles rolled and slid under his boots as he scrambled away up the beach. They'd halved the distance when a thought of Elizabeth hit him. He'd been leading them towards her tent, so turned in his path, jagging off to the side, drawing them away. He'd put the fire between him and them. The two swordsmen started around it to the left. He'd have no chance against them. So he dived right, towards the swinging mace.

The spiked iron ball droned as it cut through the air. He'd seen a man's arm smashed to pulp by such a weapon. A touch would rip through flesh and bone. He stepped towards it, counting, then dived in between swings, driving his knife under the man's guard arm. Something thwacked against his shoulder. The handle, not the ball. The man had lost his grip and the whole thing was flying, thudding into the turf. Elias tried to pull out his knife, but the tip had wedged in bone. The man dropped. Elias fell with him, still gripping the hilt.

A blade hissed above his head.

The swordsmen were on him.

Letting go of the knife, Elias threw himself into a shoulder roll, winning a couple of extra yards, twisting in the air so he landed in a crouch, facing them. The sword he'd dodged was two-handed. A bad choice for a night fight. That gave him a chance. But the second man had a quicker weapon. Some kind of scimitar.

The two-hander swung again. Damn, but the thing had a long reach. Elias jumped away, feeling too late the hard line of a tent rope against the back of his calf. It flipped him clean. His shoulders hit the ground hard. The breath knocked out of him. The two-hander lifted, ready for a downward cut. Then it was falling, and one of the arms was falling with it. A spray of blood caught Elias in the face.

The man screamed. Behind him, Firehand swung against the scimitar man. A huge blade. Once. Twice. The third blow cut half through his neck. The man crumpled. Joy was written over Firehand's face.

All had seemed slow, like a clock about to stop, the sounds of battle far away. Now it came rushing back: gunshots, shouts of anger, grunts of effort. And everything was moving fast. Metal and death.

The man whose arm had been severed was slumped over the tent rope, bleeding out in spurts. He groaned as Firehand hauled him across the ground. Then the giant took the severed stump and thrust it onto the red hot stones at the fire's edge.

Flames licked from the ragged end of the man's sleeve. But the fountain of blood had stopped. Too late, perhaps, for there'd been no scream or recoil. Firehand threw him down on the pebbles.

The battle was over. From here and there, men called out that they were safe or that they needed help. But not the attackers. Logan was shouting orders. Survivors began to gather on the beach, but away from the fire. There might still be archers on the hill behind. Elizabeth was there. He saw her shivering. Not from the cold, he thought.

Jago strode among his men. His own sleeve was dark with blood. Elias couldn't see a wound.

"We've lost three killed," said Logan. "And three wounded. The worst is Caricks. He'll lose an eye."

"And them?"

"Six dead. Two got away at least. Maybe more. And there's him." Logan pointed to the swordsman with the severed arm, who lay near Elias.

"What are their marks?"

"Unaligned."

"Paid men?"

"Yes, Patron."

The man with the severed arm was still breathing but his eyes hadn't been open since he fell. The Patron knelt and slapped his face.

"Who sent you?"

Saliva dribbled from the corner of the mouth.

Jago selected a large pebble, lifted it, then brought it down hard on the severed end of the arm. A spasm gripped the man's chest. His eyes snapped open.

"Who sent you?" The pebble lifted again.

The man shook his head and breathed something, which Elias couldn't hear. But the lips had said "Patron Williams".

"How many came with you?"

"Ten."

"Where are you camped?"

At this the man looked away. There was terror in his eyes. Elias knew well enough what it meant. He didn't want to betray his brothers in arms.

"I respect your trade," Jago said. "My grandfather was a mercenary, before he was Patron. I've no grudge. But you know the price. So I'll offer you this deal. You tell me freely where you camped. I'll go there and kill your friends. I'll do it clean. Or you can try to hold out. You will tell me, though. They always do. But if we go that way, I'll kill them slow. A special death."

Jago held out a hand towards Logan and received a thin blade. This he showed, holding the point so close to the man's eyeball that a tremor would have been enough to blind him.

"Where did you make camp? I'll not ask again."

The answer came all in a rush. Jago smiled. Along the woodmen's trail and over the brow of the hill. Away to the left between a low outcrop and a stream.

"Well chosen," Jago said, then felt along the underside of the man's ribs, as might a butcher inspect the carcass of a pig. The narrow blade slipped in with little effort. The man began to breathe hard. He opened his mouth like a beached fish, hungry for air, then began thrashing his one arm. But his heart had been skewered. The eyes lost focus. All the while, Jago stroked the man's forehead like a lover.

Patron Williams could have been sold a lie. Or a story out of date. Either way, he'd sent eleven mercenaries, which might have been enough if Jago's force hadn't grown. But since riding into New Whitby, he'd gone from two guards to twenty-five.

A pack of warriors and hunting dogs left camp, following the woodmen's track. Elias lay watching the tide creep up the beach. Somewhere around its mid flow, he fell asleep.

CHAPTER 28

Caltrops and ambush. The other Patrons could scent change in the air. But they didn't know what form it would take. They were throwing punches in the dark, hoping to connect. Their spies would have told them of Jago's journey along the North Road and back. They would feel a plot hatching.

Elizabeth lay on her side, facing away from the Patron, pretending to sleep. The smugglers were close. She couldn't let him know that she needed to talk to them. But neither could she give up the chance.

Jago wasn't sleeping either, though he didn't pretend. From time to time, his fingers drummed on his chest. She could hear him swallowing. Then footsteps approached.

Logan's voice, a whisper: "It's time."

With the Patron gone, she sat up and listened to them assembling on the path. No words were spoken as they set off. She waited until the sound of their footsteps had thinned to nothing before looking out of the tent.

One gatherer had been left to guard the camp. As she watched, he squatted to warm himself by the fire, throwing on more driftwood. He wouldn't have done that in Jago's presence. He wouldn't be able to see anything beyond the bright new flames.

Placing her feet, she set off along the grassy ridge in

the middle of the track, avoiding the stones to either side, quickening her pace as the camp fell further behind. The fog had thinned. There still wasn't enough moonlight to safely run on the potholed road. But she had to risk it or she'd never catch up. Cresting the rise, she slowed to a walk, back bent, keeping her head lower than the tuckamore, presenting no profile against the top of the hill.

But halfway down the other side, she was stopped by a noise in the blackness ahead. Someone was swearing in a low growl, coming her way. They surely couldn't be returning already, yet it was Jago she'd heard. Banks stood tall to left and right. In a panic she tried to clamber up the downwind side. But the top was fringed with a tangle of low spruce, too dense to push through. She made out Elias's voice.

"It'll be here, Patron."

"It had better be!"

She scrambled up the bank again, not trying to push through this time, but lying herself flat along the top.

"Fitz said it's like a goat track."

"Mess this up and I'll skin the soles of your feet."

"Yes, Patron."

She could see them: darker shadows moving in the shadow of the sunken track, much closer than she'd thought. She spread hair over her face and lay still. Elias was leading the way, followed by Jago, Logan and Firehand.

"How long till high tide?" Jago asked.

No one answered.

"If we miss it…"

"We won't, Patron."

Elias was passing her, then Jago. Her eyes were level with his shoulder. If one of them reached out, he could have touched her. She could smell them. Unwashed bodies and the smoke of campfires. Then they had passed. Her skin itched with sweat, despite the cold.

"It's here!"

She caught the relief in Elias's voice, then a scrambling of feet, then quiet.

No wonder he'd missed it the first time. It was little more than a notch in the bank. Elias hauled himself up over the lip, pushing through a tangle of scratching branches onto a slope so steep that he could touch the ground on the uphill side without leaning over. If he fell, there'd be nothing to stop him, tumbling till he reached the sea.

The path, such as it was, cut down and across the hillside, which steepened even further until the upward slope had become a cliff and they were edging around a narrow shelf of rock. The waves were small, but breaking they sent up fine spray, wetting the ground, which was in any case slick with slime. The ledge curved as it skirted the base of the headland. Elias could just make out a cleft in the rock ahead. The waves boomed from within.

It was the place, sure enough, just as Fitz had described it. The way had been so narrow that they had to flatten themselves against the cliff to pass. But now it widened. Within ten paces he no longer felt the need to cling to handholds. A mooring ring hung from the rock, wide as a dinner plate. His fingers traced the corroded metal. The bolts that held it in place were each an inch across.

Logan crouched down and struck steel to flint, using his body to shield the flash from anyone who might be in a boat out to sea. A yellow flame grew in the tinder. It took a moment for the candle wick to catch inside the dark lantern. He closed the shutter, hiding all but a thin strip of light.

They were standing in a cleft in the headland, a deep inlet just wide enough for the submarine boat to enter. Waves washed in only a few feet below the ledge. The boom of them reverberated, as if they were inside a cavern, though a narrowing strip of stars showed between black cliffs above.

"What now?" Logan whispered, though they were the only ones to hear.

Jago didn't answer. He stood, arms folded, feet slightly spread, staring out to the ocean.

"We wait," Elias said.

When he was young and in the bosom of wealth, Elias never had to wait for anything. If he was hungry, food would be brought. If bored, distraction. Pleasure was a whim. It felt like the story of someone else's childhood. Poverty was all about waiting. It was other people's clocks, other people's choices. He had learned to accept it. But this was different.

His back pressed into the rock wall behind him. The narrow anchorage lay directly in front. A fine spray touched his face from time to time when one of the waves broke against the rocks. Logan stood on his left, Firehand on his right. Jago had begun to pace the widest section of the ledge. Patrons were not used to waiting. What would he do, Elias wondered, if the smugglers failed to arrive with the peak of high tide? If the dream of kingship were snatched from him, even for a short time, Jago's terrible resolve would surely turn to white-hot rage.

At first he wasn't sure he'd seen it. The light blinked in and out, catching on the waves. He knew its soft reddish colour. It sent a shiver of revulsion down his neck. The others had seen it too.

"Is that it?" Jago asked.

"Yes, Patron." Elias's words came as a croak.

"Then where's it gone? The lantern! Open the lantern!"

Logan did, pulling the shutter wide, letting the yellow candlelight show. With nothing to see but a dot of red, it was impossible to know if the submarine boat was getting closer.

"Wave it, man! Wave it around!"

The shadows swung madly as Logan shifted the lantern above his head.

Out in the ocean, the red dot had started to take on a definite form. It was still beyond the arms of the rocky cleft. But reflections picked out the edges of the craft. It formed an oval in the waters like the back of a whale. The light was shining from the barrel structure in the middle, the hatchway to the deck below.

The captain would be standing there, keeping watch, guiding them in. The shifting of his body would sometimes block the light, sometimes reveal it.

The nose of the submarine edged between the cliffs. He could see the captain now and hear the strange whine of the motors. A second figure appeared, clambering out onto the back of the machine with rope fenders, which he threw over the side.

Logan waved the lantern.

"Who's there?" shouted the captain.

"Elias."

"And who else?"

"It's all as Fitz said."

"The Patron?"

"I'm here!" Jago called.

The man peered at them, shifting his head as if for a better view. A wave sluiced over the back of the submarine.

At last he called, "Make us fast!" Then dipped into the hatch, emerging a moment later with ropes, which the other sailor tied to mooring cleats fore and aft before flinging the coils towards them. Firehand caught one and Logan the other. They heaved the submarine in with both lines until the fenders were tight to the rocks.

The captain gripped the aft rope and pulled himself up onto the ledge. Oh, the wonder of thumbs.

"Well met," he said.

It was only now, face to face, that Elias knew him for sure. He'd been there on that first voyage under the water. He'd been the one watching as the others chained Elias to the wall. The skin on his back itched from the memory of the metal girder pressing into his spine.

"I've done my job," Elias said.

"We'll see," said the man.

"I was promised a supply of the glycer-fortis."

"I'm the one you've come to see!" said Jago. His voice sounded bright, though Elias caught the note of irritation.

"You're the Patron then?"

"I am. And you?"

"Captain Fanshaw," said the man.

Jago gestured to the submarine. "Well, Captain Fanshaw. This… This marvel… This boat. How can I own it?"

"It's not for sale."

"I'll pay any price."

"There's no need," Fanshaw said. "We're giving you what you want."

"Giving what?"

"A kingdom."

Below them, a wave washed the back of the submarine and slapped against the rock. A low boom reverberated in the depths of the cleft.

"I've twenty-three barrels to bring up," said Fanshaw. "But. With. Care."

"They're delicate then?"

He nodded.

"I can help," Elias said.

Logan swung the lamp towards him. Shadows lurched. Jago's expression was like vitriol.

"I've worked with glycer-fortis. In the factory where it's made. I know how to handle it. I know how it's used."

"Is this true?" Jago demanded.

"It's true," said Fanshaw. "But I think Elias is more easily controlled if we don't let him have the free use of it. Here…" He dipped into his pocket and held a small object out towards Elias. It was Jago who snatched it.

"Gently!" said Fanshaw. "Gently."

Jago held it to the lantern, another green glass pot with a stopper in the top. The lump within was the size of a musket ball.

"Elias's reward," Fanshaw said. "For services rendered. There'll be many more, I've no doubt. Now, if you're ready. The tide isn't going to wait on us."

It took seven men to do it. Logan, Firehand and Elias heaved on a rope, which had been set to run through the iron mooring ring. Two submariners below kept each barrel clear of the cliff as it was lifted, hand over hand. That left Jago and Fanshaw to manoeuvre it over the lip of rock and place it on the ledge. But carefully. Carefully.

At first it seemed Jago might refuse to do such menial work. But the prize was almost close enough to touch. The Patron knelt on the rock and sweated with the rest of them. It seemed to Elias a dangerous thing to witness. A king might not be so happy with the thought that some of his subjects had seen the potholes and filth along the road to power. A king shouldn't sweat. But a king can write his own history, so long as no one else is left to tell how it really happened.

Five barrels filled the ledge. The tide had just passed its peak. But they could bring up no more until those five had been shifted away. The men worked in threes to carry them deeper into the cleft, one at the front, one at the back and one walking beside, ready to help if the others should falter. An overhanging rock became the roof of a shallow cave. At the very back they stacked them.

By the time they returned to the cave with the next five

barrels, the tide had dropped a foot. Elias's muscles were aching. His back, his arms, his thighs. His hands felt clumsy. Raising the next barrel, the rope slipped through his grip. Firehand stumbled forwards with the sudden shift of weight. But he had it. The men shouted up from below, cursing them to hell.

"Time to go," Fanshaw said.

He turned to the mooring ring, as if to untie the ropes. But Jago stepped in his way.

"There's cargo still to unload."

"The tide," said Fanshaw.

"You said twenty-three barrels."

"We've only the clearance for an hour and a half around high tide. That's used up."

"You've left a few minutes for safety?"

"We'll not be using it."

The two men stared at each other. It was a battle of no consequence. They'd unloaded enough explosive already to do the job many times over. Three barrels would make little difference. Yet the contest was everything.

No good would come if one of them were forced to back down. Elias turned and stared out at the ocean between the arms of the rock cleft. He shifted his head, as if trying to make out some detail in the distance.

"Look!" He pointed, pretending to have seen something.

"What?" Jago growled.

"It's a boat! Someone's coming."

Elizabeth had understood as soon as she saw the profile of the approaching craft. Though submarine boats were unknown within the Gas-Lit Empire, she'd encountered them on her travels in the Sargasso Sea. The technology of the wilds was leaping forwards. And that technology was being harnessed to the service of war.

She recognised the whine of the electric engine as it crept forwards into the cleft. Once it had been moored, she could only see the place where the waves broke over the stern. Any further along the ledge and she'd risk being seen.

She could hear them though, their voices echoing within the hollow as they worked to unload the cargo. If she waited till Jago and the others had gone, she might be able to speak to the boat's captain. But for that, she'd need to find another way into the cleft, perhaps from the other side.

It would have been a hazardous climb on a calm day in full light. Under a thin moon with the wind blowing her hair across her eyes it was foolhardy. Her boots slipped on loose stones. Three times she almost fell. At the top of the headland, a dark V marked the inlet within which they worked. Lying on the ground she wormed out until her head was over the drop and she could see the full length of the submarine below, a red glow coming from within. A strip of lantern light picked out a pile of barrels on the ledge.

The climb down the other side of the headland proved easier. There was even a ledge leading out above the waves. But it narrowed as it came around towards the cleft. By the time she could see the stern of the submarine, there wasn't enough room for her feet. Facing the cliff, with only her toes on the rock, she inched a few yards further.

Jago's voice came suddenly clear. An argument. Three more barrels needed unloading. The boat captain refused. The tide was going out.

"Look!" shouted Elias.

She could just see him, pointing out into the water, as if something was there. The lantern snapped dark. Suddenly everyone was on the move. The red glow blinked out. The electric engine whined into life and the submarine was reversing, passing so close to her it seemed she might be able to jump into the water and swim to it.

She wanted to shout, to call it back. They could carry her and her friends under the waters of the straits in perfect safety. But any noise would have echoed around the rocks and come to Jago on the other side.

The grey of pre-dawn had separated the ocean from the sky. She edged back, the rock widening under her feet with each step. The men were leaving. She had to get back to the camp before them. Firehand and Logan had gone already. Elias was following, but Jago grabbed his arm.

"I know what you did," the Patron said, his words reverberating. "There was no boat. I will remember this. Don't ever step in my way again!"

CHAPTER 29

On leaving the coast, they followed a valley inland. Starting next to a tumbling river, the way climbed gradually until it reached the tops, whereupon it cut a straight path over a treeless landscape. The road was more regular than anything Elizabeth had seen before on Newfoundland. It had been built with a gentle camber on each side and was easily wide enough for the carts that carried their delicate cargo. Most amazing of all, she had not seen a single pothole.

Elizabeth had lost count of the cuttings and embankments they'd ridden past. Stone-lined culverts channelled streams harmlessly underneath. There had even been a short stretch of tunnel. One of the gatherers told her that Jago's grandfather had started the building of it but hadn't lived to see it finished. It had been just as much a part of their rise to power as the acquisition of an oath-wright. The sheer willpower of building it had transformed a worthless hill and the barren slopes around into a fortress that could be supplied from the coast.

She'd imagined some kind of stockade built at the edge of a slope with huts inside, functional, makeshift and grim. But when they crested the last ridge and she saw it laid out before her, it was like a vision from a dream. She let the reins go slack. Her horse slowed then stopped to eat from the thin grass by the roadside.

The path ahead dropped into a narrow valley, then climbed a rocky escarpment on the far side, at the top of which stood a stone wall. Towers flanked a gateway, banners flying from their tops. The fortress must have been the work of many men over many years. The whole thing – towers, walls, even the rocks below down to the valley floor – had been painted bone white.

A man shouted, "Move on!" In stopping she'd caused the column to back up.

As always, Elias had been set to ride close to the rear. She'd seen little of him through the journey. But under the shadow of the towers as they approached, she found herself wanting his company. The stones that made up the base of the walls had looked large from a distance. Closer, she realised they were huge. Big enough to withstand the cannon fire which had been directed at them over the years.

The sounds of horses and wagons were suddenly loud as they came between the walls. Looking up she could see loopholes on either side, through which guns or bows might be fired. Even if the other clans united, they wouldn't be able to storm it. But it was more than a defence. The structure had been built to inspire awe. After some twenty yards, the passage turned a sharp left, emerging through a second set of gates into a wide space, which was the flat summit of the hill. A few hundred souls had gathered around to wave and cheer, though not so ardently as to suggest it was by choice.

Riders dismounted. Some led their horses away towards the watering troughs. Others greeted women and children in the crowd. Looking beyond them, Elizabeth was surprised by the dilapidated state of the buildings. With all the whitewash they'd painted on the cliffs outside, it seemed strange that they'd not spared a few gallons for their own homes. If anything, the place was in a worse state than New Whitby.

The chief difference being the arrangement of the houses. Here the buildings had been crammed tight together. She caught a whiff of sewage on the air.

Jago had ridden into the crowd. His people reached up to touch his outstretched hand. Then he seemed to grow bored and spurred his stallion forwards, knocking one woman onto her back in the process. Once clear, he circled to the wagons. Elizabeth couldn't hear the instructions he gave, but a moment later Logan was relaying them to the crowd.

"You're all to go back to work! Everyone."

The crowd dispersed. Mothers scooped up their children and hurried off. Some ran.

"You…" Logan pointed to one of the gatherers who'd been riding with them. "See the storehouse is clear. I want everyone out."

The man set off towards a large, low building, which abutted the outer wall. The carts rolled after him, following in a line. The cargo of barrels had been treated with extreme caution on the journey. Each cart carried but four, though they might have room for twice that number. The rest of the space had been packed tight with straw. And over the top of each, a tarpaulin had been tied, so that an observer looking on would see nothing beyond the ordinary.

Even in Jago's fortress there would be spies and secrets. Dismounting, Elizabeth patted her pony's flank, whilst watching the doors of the storehouse being pulled open and the line of carts heading inside.

"Welcome to the viper's nest."

She jumped at Elias's whisper, close behind. "Don't creep up on me like that!"

"That's all I can do – creep. When I'm not playing the fool."

"What happens next?"

"We set off for the Reckoning."

"And then?"

"We can't talk here. Odds are, Jago will have me sleep in the stables. Unless... well... If you can't find me there, try the dog kennels."

When she'd first met him, Elias might have said such things as dark humour. But this was different. It seemed almost as if he'd accepted his role as Jago's idiot. It was a ragged garment that fit him too well.

The grand hall lay within a tower built directly above the cliffs. Hangings draped the walls. Not tapestry. Elizabeth took a hem between finger and thumb. It was sail canvas onto which scenes had been painted. Knights in armour. Battles and blood. Women posed to provoke. Muscles, swords and naked breasts: everything was larger and more defined than in real life. If only she could have simply dismissed it as bad taste and bad art, which it was.

"You like it?" Jago asked, calling from his throne, over the heads of his councillors.

Instead of attempting a lie, she turned towards him and curtsied.

"Come," he beckoned.

The men parted for her. Jago wasn't the first self-proclaimed ruler she'd encountered on her travels. And this wasn't the first throne set on a dais that she'd approached. Before, in another hall, she'd been afraid and awed. But here there was also a queasy revulsion, which she was finding hard to conceal.

She reached the lowest step and he held out his hand to take hers. The eyes of the men were on her. He drew her closer until her knees were touching the white fur on which he sat. It was polar bear, she thought. He seemed about to pull her onto his lap, but at the last moment pushed her down to a kneeling position, and then to sit on the floor next to his feet, looking out over the room.

Jago clapped his hands and silence fell.

"To oath matters," he said.

A man in a moss-green robe detached himself from the crowd and stepped to the foot of the dais. The front of his scalp had been shaved and on the dome of bare skin a design like a barbed arrowhead had been tattooed in blue-black ink, the tip pointing down towards the bridge of his nose.

She'd never before seen an oath-wright. Streaks of white in the long hair that fell over his shoulders suggested he might be twenty years older than the Patron. The son, perhaps, of the original oath-wright acquired by Jago's grandfather.

He did not bow, she noted.

"What news?" Jago asked.

"One of your farmers wishes to be severed. And the daughter of the stable master also."

"The ones who wanted to marry last year?"

"The same."

Another man, older still, stepped forwards. His face creased in pain as he got down onto one knee. He bowed low. "If I may, Patron."

"Speak."

"I know the girl. She's young and wilful. But not bad. If you were to talk to her. Tell her that in a few years you might consent. I believe she'd see reason."

"Where's her mark?"

"Right hand and forearm," said the oath-wright, his voice emotionless.

"And his?"

"Left ear and part of the cheek."

Two gatherers carried in a lit brazier, suspended between wooden poles. Sparks jumped as they placed it on the floor before the dais. Then a knife and a sword were thrust into the midst of the coals and a boy set to work with bellows. Air roared. The coals brightened from red to yellow and then towards white. Elizabeth could feel the heat of it on her face even from a distance.

The old councillor had said the girl was young. But how young still came as a shock. She might have been sixteen, Elizabeth thought. The farmer seemed older, but not by many years. His shoulders had yet to fill out. He was handsome though. A face to turn heads.

When they'd been positioned, one on each side of the fire, Jago said, "Is it true you want to sever your oaths?"

"We do," said the farmer boy, his voice small but resolute.

"He speaks for you?"

The girl nodded. The farmer boy looked at her and Elizabeth saw for the first time the oath-mark across his ear and the side of his face. Sparks leapt into the air between the lovers with each exhalation of the bellows.

"I'm advised to tell you that I might change my mind," Jago said, addressing them directly. "I might allow you to marry. In a couple of years. Would you stay oath-bound to me if I did?"

Her eyes widened with hope. "Yes," she said. It was barely a whisper.

"But if I changed my mind once, people might think I'd change it again. And again. I can't have that. Other people change their minds. You could. But not your oath-holder."

He snapped his fingers. One of the gatherers grabbed the farmer boy, hauling him to his knees, then holding his head at an angle to expose the oath-marked ear. The oath-wright drew the long knife from the fire. The blade shone white. Elizabeth turned away. But she couldn't stop herself from hearing the boy's cry and smelling the acrid smoke.

"You are severed," the oath-wright pronounced in that same dead tone.

The girl retched. There was no colour left in her.

"He'll live," said Jago. "And he's still got his looks. On one side. Show her."

The girl was turned, her head held so she could not look away from the ruined side of her lover's face. His ear had gone. But the sickening part was the blackened cheek where the flat of the blade had seared him. There was no blood. Threads of smoke still rose from his hair.

The girl's knees folded. The gatherer behind took her sudden weight.

"Your turn," Jago said. "Extend your arm."

She struggled, but there was another man holding her hand now, pulling it away from her body, and she was a slight thing. The sword blade rang as the oath-wright drew it from the coals. He stepped across and positioned his feet to take the blow. The girl's face had seemed to turn red, but it was only the light from the glowing metal. The sword raised high.

"Are you ready?" Jago asked. When she didn't reply, he said, "You could do it another day, if you wanted. Would you like that?"

This time she nodded. The oath-wright stepped back and handed the sword to a gatherer, who took it, and the long knife, and hurried from the hall. A moment later, the brazier was being carried away. They had to drag the farmer boy, who kept shouting the girl's name.

She didn't once meet his eyes.

"Put him out of the fortress," Jago called. "We'll deal with the girl another time. Next year, perhaps."

It would never happen. Elizabeth had seen defeat in the girl's eyes. Perhaps she'd desired the handsome farmer's son. Not so much the disfigured outcast. Jago had won completely. And the girl had learned the limits of her love. It might have been easier learning to live without a hand.

Jago's personal apartment lay immediately behind the hall. One room with a map-strewn table. Behind that a room for washing. And behind that, the bedchamber itself. The scale was smaller, except for the doors. He closed and bolted each behind them. The first two were thick wood, strengthened with studs and bands of metal. The final door sealing them in was solid iron. He leaned his weight into it before it started to swing on its hinges. No one would be able to get through. But somehow the smell of burned flesh had followed them.

The bed was huge and there were furs enough for her to stay warm without coming close to where he lay. Jago was even quicker to sleep than usual, his breath slackening within seconds of the candles going dark. The security of the stronghold had taken away his cares.

For Elizabeth it was the other way around. Her mind replayed the horror that she'd just witnessed. She tried to picture other things to block it out, concentrating on memories from her childhood. The bow top wagon that had been home to her family. The skewbald horse that she'd fed with pieces of stolen apple. But every time she began to relax, her concentration wavered and she saw again the image of the boy's ruined face.

Rolling out from under the furs, she sat on the edge of the bed and rubbed her own face, as if needing to feel the undamaged skin. Had the doors not been barred, she would have tried to steal away to the stables. Elias was the closest thing she had to a confidant. She wanted to tell him what she'd seen. As if speaking it out loud might make the memory more bearable.

The windows of the bedchamber were narrow and deep as arrow slits. But they were glazed. The glass might be broken, she supposed, if the need came to shoot out of them. There was little enough moonlight, but when she got her head close and looked down, she could just see the escarpment below the cliff, ghostly white. Painting the side of the mountain had been an elegant trick. It united the fortress and the hill on which it stood. The eye saw the two as one, as if the whole thing was a single immense structure.

There would be a way out of the bedchamber, she thought. A secret way. Men like Jago never go into a room without thinking of how they might escape. A trapdoor, perhaps. She walked across the chamber, hitting her heels onto the flagstones with each step, then back to the opposite wall, taking a different line. But every stone she trod was solid.

Somewhere out there, Elias would be waiting. But she wouldn't reach him that night.

CHAPTER 30

Starvation has a more perfect aim than any marksman. Since two rats can breed a nation, wars have come to turn on the workings of a spring-loaded trap, and a fortress is only as good as its storehouse.

Elias watched as three dogs fought over a bucket of offal. It had been emptied out of a window, slopping down to steam on the cobbles, the bloody juices trickling away towards an open drain. Two small mongrels got there first, but a large white hound had come to drive them away, growling through its teeth, saliva dripping.

It was the morning after their arrival in Jago's fortress. There'd been no food for him in that time. And no drink, but for the water in the stable-yard trough. He'd selected a good-sized stick from the woodpile behind the kitchen and was considering the best way of using it. The white hound looked mean. A dog's bite will fester, even a scratch. But one good strike might send it away.

A boy came running around the corner of the building. "No-Thumbs! You're to go to the storehouse."

Elias sighed. But there would be other tables. Other feasts.

One of the storehouse doors swung inwards to his knock. Just enough for him to side-step through. The mixture of scents inside set his heart accelerating like an engine. At first he couldn't pin down what he was smelling. There was dust and dryness, for sure, and the sourness of curing salts. Hams must be hanging somewhere within. It could have been hunger driving his body's reaction. There was hemp and pine resin and gunpowder and tanned hides. And some other odour he couldn't name but which his body craved.

The barrels stood between the doors and the first line of shelving. One of them had been opened, its contents spread out on a canvas sheet. He might have thought them to be unfired bricks, had he not seen such things before. Row after row of them. Enough glycer-fortis to keep him alive into old age.

Without thinking, he lurched towards the precious cargo. But a hand grabbed his arm, hauling him back. Logan stepped in front of him. The man's face was even grimmer than usual.

"Stand!"

Elias did, looking around properly for the first time. Firehand was there, of course. And Jago, though the Patron stood back. Not far enough to live if it exploded. Not nearly far enough for that.

"You said you've worked with it before?" Jago asked.

"Yes, Patron."

"My men are sick. Yet they've not swallowed even a crumb. You knew this would happen?"

Elias nodded. "It works through the skin."

"You sicken without it?"

"Yes, Patron."

"If I put you to work unpacking it, you'd suffer no harm?"

Elias dared not answer. It was the thing he wished for above all. Every day he handled it would be another day of life without dipping into his own meagre supply. And who would notice if he were to gouge a few extra pieces under his fingernails?

"Will this kill them?"

Elias shook his head.

"How long before they need it as you need it?"

The old thermometer man in the far Yukon had said it took months. Burying the memory deep, Elias said, "I don't know."

Jago advanced to the edge of the sheet and knelt. He angled his head, peering at the blocks from different angles. He wrinkled his nose.

"If I put a flame to it?"

"It will burn."

"And if I drop it?"

"Maybe nothing."

"But a blow from a hammer..."

"It would explode. I know how to handle it. I've done it before. I can unpack the barrels. I can do whatever's needed and your men won't sicken."

Jago pulled off his gloves, finger by finger. They were fine leather. Calfskin, perhaps. Logan's hands were a similar size. "Put these on," he said. "And bring one of the bricks."

Logan's face had been sickly before. But now his skin was the colour of tallow. Sweat glistened on his forehead. It wasn't the nausea, Elias thought. It was the knowledge that if he tripped on a cobblestone, it might be his death. He'd in any case be feeling dizzy. That came after the headaches had set in, and the weak stomach.

Carrying his burden in front of his chest, two-handed, he stepped out from the shadow of the walls, wobbling slightly as they began the descent towards the valley floor.

Elias slowed, allowing a gap to open up between himself and the explosive brick. At twenty feet, he might still be killed, should it detonate. Thirty foot would be enough, he thought. But Firehand, walking just behind, gave him a shove between the shoulders, forcing him to speed up. The Patron was away at the front, striding out into his lands with the gait of an immortal.

Once over the river, they followed a track away from the road across marshy ground scattered with bog cotton, then up over a rise and down again. It took two more ridges before they lost sight of the white painted fortress walls.

Logan knelt in a cleft between two rocks and placed the brick. At a distance of forty paces it seemed a tiny thing. Elias kept himself just behind Jago and Firehand.

The other gatherer staggered back to join them. The Patron handed him a pistol. All he had to do was pull the hammer and fire. There would be no shame in missing such a small target. But Logan was shaking so wildly it seemed he might be in danger of shooting himself.

When his hand dropped at last, Jago took back the gun. That had been the point, Elias supposed. Let someone else fail first. Then if Jago's own aim turned out to be faulty there'd be no loss of face.

The Patron levelled the gun, breathed out slow, fired. The bang of the pistol caught Elias first. Then, with no time that he could have measured in between, a white flash lit the rocks. He felt the thump of it in his chest. A rain of dirt and pebbles landed in front of them.

Jago was first to advance to the place where the brick had lain. The turf had been stripped away. The crater was smaller than he'd expected, but the large rocks to either side had gone. Tongues of white smoke clung to the ground, clearing as he watched. Jago raised a fist and shook it at the sky, grinning and laughing like a madman.

There were two forms of the explosive. The first and most dangerous was the greasy liquid they'd mixed in the factory. Too hot and it would detonate, or too roughly stirred or frozen and thawed. A store of it had gone up once during a storm. It wasn't struck by lightning. The sound of the thunder had done it, or so they thought. He didn't know how they'd discovered the trick of mixing it with powdered rock to make this other form.

The rock they'd used came from the Oregon Territory, arriving at the camp in wagons. It was pale and light in weight, powdering easily when they pounded it, raising clouds of choking dust. To this they added other chemicals and finally the greasy explosive liquid, drop by drop, until they could mould it into bricks which they called "inert glycer-fortis". Inert indeed. It must have been a joke.

What might twenty full barrels do, Elias wondered. Easy enough to destroy a fortress or make a hole in the earth. But gather the right people around it, or the wrong people, and it would tip the whole world out of balance.

The Patron asked if the bricks could be squeezed and shaped like clay. Elias told him no. Not safely. So the thing itself had to be built to leave room for the bricks as they were. The joiner and his lads were never told the purpose of their work. And every bit of it was done in the storehouse, away from the gaze of spies.

At last the bricks could be packed within the frame they'd made. But by then the joiner had been sent away. The only ones to see it done were Firehand, Logan, Jago and Elias. Packed around the bricks – the most devilish part – were thousands upon thousands of musket balls.

When it was finished, when all the explosives had been placed and sealed in and the last covering board screwed down, Logan and Firehand went on their knees before their Patron. He placed a hand on each forehead.

Their bodies must have grown used to the glycer-fortis by then. They'd been handling it for twelve days. Jago hadn't spoken of his plans in all that time, so far as Elias knew. But the thing they'd made was its own explanation. Their master would be the king of Newfoundland. And they were the first to know his true station.

"You've been faithful to your oaths," he said. "I'm well pleased with you."

Elias watched from the shadows, as he'd watched the entire time, speaking only when asked for guidance.

Jago lifted his hands but the men remained on their knees. Firehand lowered his forehead to the dirt. Logan was staring at his oath-holder, his mouth slack in awe, as if he could see the crown already.

"What about my faithless dog?"

Elias stepped out of the shadows and knelt. There was no hand on his forehead, of course. He hadn't expected it. Instead, Jago stepped around him, stopping just behind.

"Some dogs can be trained," the Patron said. "Let them off the leash and they'll come back. But a chained dog can still be useful. That's what you are, No-Thumbs. A chained dog that once belonged to another man. If your great uncle watches me stamping on your fingers, will he feel the pain?"

"No, Patron," Elias said. The back of his neck was itching. He thought he could feel Jago's breath on it, though that must have been imagination.

"Show me that precious jar of yours."

Elias pulled it from his pocket and held it out. The ball of glycer-fortis rolled within. Stepping around to the front of him again, Jago took it and held it up to the lamplight.

"I've watched men die from belly wounds," he said. "From hanging, from burning, severed arteries, gangrene. Each way is different. But I never watched a man die for want of poison. I'd like to see it."

"But I can help you."

"And so you shall," Jago said, tossing back the jar. "And so you shall."

CHAPTER 31

There'd been little chance for Elizabeth to wash on the journey to Jago's fortress. On the first morning after their arrival, three maids came to take her dirty clothes. She didn't object. In exchange they gave her a short dressing robe made of yellow linen. Thus attired, with legs bare below the knee, she confined herself to the private apartment.

Food was brought for her: roast chicken and bread cut from the upper crust of a loaf. There was wine also, though she'd have preferred water. Or better still, tea. She hadn't seen tea in all her months on Newfoundland. Banishing an unexpected pang of homesickness, she got on with the job of eating.

When the maids returned that afternoon to clean the rooms, she asked when her clothes would be ready. This made them giggle, as if she'd have no need of such things. As if she hadn't realised the nature of her job.

"Bring my things!" she said, positioning herself in the doorway, hands on hips. When they tried to push past, she caught one of them by the arm, turning the wrist back on itself until she yelped.

"My clothes!" she said again.

There was no more laughter after that. No more knowing glances at her expense. But she felt angry that they'd made her temper break. Violence was the grease that turned the wheels of the fortress. It was a language they all understood, but not one she wanted to learn.

The maids returned before the evening meal carrying heaps of dresses of different sizes, which they laid out on the bed, and stockings, bloomers, chemise and corsets, which were too stiffly ribbed to be practical. She turned to ask for her own things, but the maids had already gone.

All the dresses were heavy with embroidery and of a style that might have been fashionable in London some thirty years before. She chose the least objectionable from among them: a cerise cotton, embroidered with floral designs in greens and darker reds. It was an immodest thing, cut low at the front to draw the eye to the wearer's breasts. She hated it. But the other dresses were heavier and had wider skirts, which would give her no chance if the need came to run.

Jago seemed to approve. On returning that evening, he showed his teeth in a smile, then grabbed her wrist and dragged her out to the hall. There followed an hour of the men staring at her as she sat meekly by his feet. He held court, dispensing judgement on all manner of small matters: the repair of rotten woodwork, a dispute between fishermen over the ownership of a net, the number of rats caught over previous weeks.

That night Jago bolted the doors of his private chamber, as he'd done the day before. She stripped to chemise and bloomers, then slipped under the furs.

"How long till we leave for the Reckoning?" she asked.

"As long as it takes."

The manic focus she'd glimpsed in him before had taken on a steely edge. She lay silent for a moment, weighing the risks of pressing him with another question.

"I'd like to explore the fortress tomorrow."

"Why?"

"I'm... curious."

"That's a dangerous thing to be."

The days that followed saw no more oath business. She was glad of that. The oath-wright had departed on his way to the Reckoning, so such matters would have to wait. It was the only improvement. Whenever she ventured into the hall, men still stared at her body. And when she tried to go out into the ward beyond, the guards barred her way. Time dragged slow.

Jago left early every morning. There was a window in the map room through which she could watch him striding across to the storehouse. On the third day she glimpsed Elias following him in. And again on the fifth.

At such times as the outer rooms were empty, she took the chance to search on hands and knees, testing again each of the exposed flagstones. When she was certain that none of them concealed a trapdoor, she turned her attention to the walls of the bedchamber. Some of the furniture she couldn't move without making noise. If there *was* a hidden door, it had to be below or behind one of those.

Each evening, Jago returned, tired as if he'd been labouring. His hands and fingernails were always clean, but she caught the smell of sawdust from his clothes. She did try to question him once more, pushing though she knew the danger. But his focus had turned inwards. Some all-consuming puzzle had possession of his mind.

She desperately wanted to talk to Elias. Whatever was happening in the storehouse, he must know. But all she saw of him were glimpses, and he never looked up towards her window.

The morning of the twelfth day dawned as each of the days before. But watching Jago stride away across the cobbles, she saw a change. His gait was easier yet more purposeful, as if a way forward had been revealed to him in the night. For almost two weeks, helplessness had gnawed at her. And now she could feel time running out. Something was about to happen.

The great doors of the storehouse closed. Jago and his oath-bound men were within. And Elias, most likely. Behind her the maids were carrying away the dishes from breakfast. Her breath fogged the glass.

She might not get another chance.

Stepping down from the window alcove, she slipped back into the bedchamber. Leaning her weight against the door, she eased it closed. At the end it made a low boom, surely loud enough to turn heads outside. But she had the iron bolts slid closed before anyone could react. For the first time since leaving the Salt Ray Inn, she was truly alone.

The bed frame grated over the floor as she heaved it away from the wall. One of the maids was calling from the other side of the door, her voice muffled by the thickness of metal. Ignoring it, Elizabeth got down on her knees and thumped the flagstones that had been hidden by the bed. The flanks of the frame went down to the floor all around. But behind the head there was a narrow gap.

She stood and began to undo her buttons. They were knocking on the door now. Quiet but urgent. Extracting herself from the dress, Elizabeth cast it aside and dropped down low. She had to lie full length to worm into the dark void beneath the bed. One by one she knocked on the flagstones underneath. All were solid.

By the time she emerged, spitting dust, the knocking on the door had become heavier. Men's fists, she thought, as she heaved the bed back against the wall. The guards must have been called. But not yet the Patron. They would hesitate before disturbing his work.

There were two more things to move, a cabinet of drawers containing some of Jago's clothing and a locked wooden chest. She might only have the time for one of them. Testing its weight, she pulled on the side of the cabinet, shifting it an inch. But when she tried the chest, it wouldn't budge. Built of oak and banded metal, she'd expected it to be heavy. But surely not too heavy to move. She braced herself against the wall and pushed again. The joints in the chest groaned but it moved not a fraction over the floor.

That was wrong. She found herself smiling. It had to be the answer.

The guards were shouting outside. Angry voices. She grabbed one of the other dresses and held it to her chest, covering the dust smears over the front of the chemise and corset.

When she pulled back the door-bolts, it began to swing inwards immediately. As soon as the gap was big enough, the first guard was shouldering through. His eyes widened when he saw her.

"I'm not dressed!" she shouted.

"But…"

"I'm changing my clothes!"

"I… you…"

The second guard was in the room now. The three maids crowded just behind, squabbling to peer through the gap.

Elizabeth pointed at them. "They're always watching me."

"I'm sorry," said the guard. "But you mustn't lock the door again."

Waiting had been difficult before, but the discovery of the immobile chest made it almost unbearable. The guards must have spoken harshly to the three maids, because they scowled whenever they looked at her. When she asked for a comb and hairpins, one was left to loiter in the outer apartment, watching through the door. If Elizabeth tried to close it again, she'd surely be stopped.

They brought leek and potato soup for her evening meal. This she pushed aside, certain they'd all have spat into her bowl. But the bread and butter was easier to trust.

She wore her hair up for the daily audience in the hall, sitting straight and still at Jago's feet while he worked through the business of the day. An unaligned boy wanted to take the oath. It couldn't be done until the oath-wright returned. But the positioning of the mark could be discussed. One of the councillors suggested that it should be marked on the boy's foot. The boy's father begged for a finger or an ear instead. Jago pronounced that it should be tattooed onto his tongue.

Afterwards Jago went through the nightly ritual: sliding the bolts, retreating to the bedchamber, pushing the metal door, the dull reverberations as it closed.

"He's a spy," Jago said.

It was so unlike the Patron to volunteer information that Elizabeth at first thought she'd misheard.

"He?"

"The boy. They bring him to me now, when the wheels are turning. Oh, but they're longing to know my secrets."

"His tongue…" Elizabeth said, as the thought hit her.

"Yes," said Jago. He seemed dangerously pleased with himself. "A mark there doesn't last long. A couple of years, perhaps. But he'll be planning to betray me before that. When he does, we'll cut the tongue from his mouth. Then everyone will know that I saw the truth of it from the start. Let him try to tell my secrets after that. His father sees my reason already. Did you mark how he sweated?"

He stretched, seeming to enjoy the pull of tendons and muscles across his arms and back. Then he began to strip, casting off his clothes. Elizabeth hurriedly turned away. He laughed.

"Soon I'll be king," he said. "My vow will be complete."

He dropped himself onto the furs, limbs loose and spread

wide so that once she'd done her duty and snuffed out the lights, she was obliged to lie at the very edge of the bed for fear of touching him. His change of mood was startling. She'd seen enough to know that relaxed he might be more dangerous than when wrestling with his thoughts.

His breathing slowed as if in sleep. But tonight she felt more uncertain of it. So she waited, counting to five hundred in her head before feeling on the floor for the hairpins and sliding out from under the covers.

Her bare feet made no sound on the flagstones. But when she turned a pin within the lock of the chest, it made a metallic click. Jago's breathing caught for a second. She probed inside the lock again, finding the levers, putting a twist on them and feeling a slight movement. Only when she'd put her free hand over the metal to muffle the sound did she give it a final push. The click sounded loud even then.

Jago turned onto his side. When his breath had gone back to its slow rhythm, she lifted the lid of the chest and felt within. Her hand went down into nothingness, continuing below the level of the floor. She had found his secret escape route.

There were rungs inside the chest: a ladder leading down a narrow shaft. Descending, she reckoned herself to be within the outer wall. After ten steps down she found a floor. All light had gone. From the echoes, she knew she'd entered a small chamber. Following the wall, she came to the mouth of a low passage and began feeling her way along it, expecting it to end at any moment. After one hundred paces she stopped counting. She'd surely passed beyond the apartments and the hall. Beyond the space outside over which she'd watched Jago stride every morning.

The door at the end was studded metal. She slid the bolts and swung it inwards, leaning all her weight into the task until there was a gap big enough to slip through.

She'd arrived inside the storehouse. There was no other building large enough within the fortress to encompass such a room. The smells of produce hung in the air. A single lamp illuminated the space in front of her, and a structure which seemed to be an elevated platform or a stage.

Only when she reached it and placed a hand on the edge did understanding spark. It was a wooden table of great length, rounded at each end. She could smell the fresh sawdust. It had to be the thing that Jago was working on.

"Elizabeth?"

She spun on her heel, ready to sprint back towards the door. But it was a voice she knew. Elias was sitting on the floor at the edge of the room. A collar circled his neck, fixed by a chain to the storehouse wall.

"What is the meaning of this thing?" she asked. "What have you helped him build?"

PART FIVE

CHAPTER 32

Dice rattled in the cup of the gatherer's hand. He closed his eyes, blew on them three times then let them fly. They tumbled over the flat rock and came to rest. Everyone leaned forwards.

"Seven!" he shouted, raising his arms to heaven as if born anew.

"That one's not level! Throw again." This from the supplies man, who'd wagered a clipping from a silver coin.

"It's no less level than yours was."

"The two don't compare!"

It was true that one of the bones had fallen at a tilt. But only because the rock there tilted also. That meant, Elias supposed, that the throw should stand. But when the two men looked to him, he shrugged.

"I can't call it," he said, not falling into the trap of taking sides. For once, being the fool was a help. It put him so far beneath them that neither would have taken his say in any case.

They called over one of the other camp followers, and when he pronounced that it should be thrown again, a second opinion was demanded, which then became a new quarrel. Others from the caravan began to gather around them, everyone with an opinion, but no two the same. Elias sat back and watched the magic flow. Gambling was its own advertisement.

By the time the two men agreed to each take back their own stake and play no more, there were half a dozen others, all eager to have a go. Such was life in the train of a Patron's progress towards the Reckoning.

They'd made camp for the night at the side of the road. Fires burned here and there, marking out the length of the train of wagons and tents. Jago had been riding near the front all day, as befits a leader, but would sleep somewhere in the middle of it all, surrounded by his most trusted men. It was the custom and practice of Newfoundland that clans not wage war on the journey to the Reckoning. But it was also the time when every Patron knew the whereabouts of every other. Before crossing to the Island, the oath-wrights would take their weapons and all chance of war would be gone. Until then, the odds of each choice had to be weighed. They were living in strange times.

The bones rattled and spun. Foreign coins went down on the rock, and silver scrap and a spoon and a decorated pewter mug. One of the camp followers tried to gamble with a poem written on a length of parchment. The others wouldn't have it so she put down a boiled egg instead. But when the numbers turned up, they were a pair of ones and thus Elias got to claim his reward, being the man who set up the game. He scooped the bric-á-brac of his winnings into a pocket and wrapped the egg in a cloth, which he slipped into his tote. His belly grumbled. But to eat it there and then would have been an insult to the losers.

That was the end of the game, as it turned out. Seeing the house take its cut, and in any case being spent out, the gamblers got up and wandered off. Elias walked away from them and found a dark hollow in which to lie. There was no telling whether one of the losers might feel bitter enough to seek him out.

None of them had seen the trick, though. He was pleased with that. He'd swapped out one of the true-cut die for the weighted one he'd been carrying in his sleeve. It was good work for a thumbless man. He'd palmed it, trapping it in the crease of his hand. The life line, a fortune teller might have said. The move was smooth enough in any case. But as the firelight danced, so had the shadows, giving better cover still. That had tipped the odds towards him. The egg had been too much to resist.

Lying on his side in the hollow, he bashed it on a stone until the shell came away clean. There was a tang of sulphur about it. Not enough to stop a hungry man. A chicken's egg in the wilderness was a feast. A pinch of salt would have made it heaven. Later he'd trade the pewter mug for some bread. It was a baker who'd gambled it. The man would get his treasure back. That was the way of things at the shoddy end of the line. A currency of trinkets.

They'd be gambling towards the front as well, those grand men. The stakes would be higher. Gold instead of pewter. They might use cards. Dice were a poor man's game. But the need was no different. A stallion in the vanguard shits no different to a mule in the train.

All day, he'd been able to see Elizabeth riding up there behind the Patron. The huge pink dress drew stares from peasants by the roadside. It matched her character not a bit.

The ill-smelling and ill-dressed were not welcomed towards the front of the line. He'd had no chance to speak with her since leaving Jago's fortress. He still didn't know how she'd managed to find her way into the storehouse that night. She'd stepped into the lamplight and seen his low state. They'd left him facing the great table they'd been building. All the glycer-fortis he'd have needed to last for a hundred years lay just beyond his reach, hidden behind panels in the sections of the table.

She'd rushed to him. "I don't have long," she'd said, then lifted the padlock, as if about to pick it. But there could have been no way out of the fortress. Least of all carrying a hundredweight of explosive bricks. So he put his hand over hers and told her what she needed to know. The table was a bomb. It would kill all who stood within thirty yards. Beyond that, the flying metal and splinters would maim to fifty yards or so.

Two questions remained: how Jago planned to get all the Patrons within the circle of death, and how he would ignite the thing without himself also being killed.

"How would you do it?" she asked.

"I don't know. But I'm thinking that he hasn't built it big enough for all the Patrons to sit. It might be they'll squabble to be close enough to grab a seat."

"Like a game of musical chairs?" she asked.

He'd never heard of the game. But when she explained it he nodded. "Yes. Just like that."

It had seemed so clear before, thinking it through. But reasoning the idea out loud made it seem fantastical. Elizabeth smiled anyway.

She'd been searching the table when a noise brought their time to an end: footsteps at the storehouse door, the clanking of the lock. She'd met his eyes one more time before running back into the shadows and away.

The next day, the six sections of the great table were brought out of the storehouse and loaded onto wagons, wedged in with straw and covered over with canvases.

"Gentle" was the watchword. And the lash for any who scratched or bumped its precious surface. Only four people knew the true reason for the care and they stood far back. Five, counting Elizabeth, though the others didn't know she knew.

When all was done, Jago had walked along the line, testing

each rope and knot. In each wagon he placed a framed mirror. The carters were brought together. He drew his sword and showed them its edge.

"Break one mirror on the journey," he said, "and I will sever all your oaths myself."

Lying in a hollow away from the camp, Elias tried to make his meal last. But there are only so many bites one can take from a chicken's egg. When it was eaten, he worked his tongue around his teeth to get every last smear of it, then sat up from the hollow. Men and women clustered around the campfires, warming themselves, passing the time, smoking and drinking. A man was picking his way from one group to the next, searching it seemed. Logan. He stood aloof, one hand hovering near the hilt of his sword.

Slinging the tote over one shoulder Elias climbed out of his hollow and started towards the gatherer, stepping on the larger rocks to approach in silence.

"Boo," he whispered.

Logan spun, the sword already half-drawn.

"What brings you to the back of the train?" Elias asked.

"You... You!" Logan couldn't seem to find a word strong enough for his loathing.

"Looking for dirty pleasures?"

The sword slid back. "You're to come with me. The Patron will see you."

Three tents had been set in the middle of the camp, each tall enough for a standing man, each facing a central fire. There was nothing to choose between them. That was the point. An attacker wouldn't know in which the Patron slept. Logan knew though. He gave another sharp shove, so that Elias stumbled in through the mouth of the tent.

Jago lay on his side on a pile of furs, eating what looked to be a turkey leg. A map of Newfoundland had been unrolled on the ground in front of him, the corners held down with stones. Lanterns hung from the four corner posts. The air smelled of tobacco.

Elias lowered his head, keeping it down until at last Jago spoke.

"Tomorrow we'll see the Island." He waved the turkey leg towards the map. "You've given me what I want, Elias. My side of the bargain was to bring you to the Reckoning. And to set you up in a game of chance against those who ruined you. I'm going to do that. Because I want to see it. You'll be there under my protection. That means you'll obey me to the letter. At all times. I'll be the one to set the time and place of the game. Those are my terms. Do you accept?"

"Yes, Patron."

Jago took another bite. As he chewed he said, "You know why you're such fine entertainment, Mr No-Thumbs? I could have you beaten for the pleasure of my men. I could have you pulled apart by horses. No one would complain. But I've no need. You torture yourself in ways more inventive than anything I could devise. Your wounds are always raw. You cut them fresh each day. Even in your dreams."

Elias tried to swallow the spit pooling in his mouth, but it stuck halfway.

The camp was long but narrow. Elias picked his way a distance off to the side and, finding a rock to serve as a backrest, sat himself facing the three large tents around the central fire. After a time in which the moon shifted across the sky, Jago emerged and strode around, seeming to say a few words to some of the gatherers on guard duty before stepping away from the road. For a moment, it seemed that he'd somehow pierced the darkness, for he was heading directly towards Elias. But then he stopped, unbuttoned his trousers and pissed onto the ground. When he turned back to the tents, one of his men was there to pour water over his hands. Another passed him a cloth to dry them. The tent he stepped into would be his sleeping quarters.

Elias thought that the job of assassin might not be so hard after all. Except for the killing part. Killing in battle was different. Facing armed men on the beach, fear had driven his arm. But to cut a throat in cold blood would take a store of malice. He considered Aaron Weaverbright, the man who'd demanded his thumbs be cut away. He imagined himself slipping a knife under the ribs, in the same way that Jago had slaughtered the mercenary. But even if he could do it, the act would not be enough. His enemies must know that they had lost because he was the better man.

When Elizabeth emerged from Jago's sleeping tent, Elias found himself leaning forwards from the rock. If she set off in the other direction, he'd have to run in the dark, circling the entire camp to reach her. He tensed in readiness, only relaxing when she left the road on his side. One of the guards followed her, but only for a few paces. She picked her way over the uneven ground, coming further than the Patron had done. Twice as far and then some more. She stopped and was looking around for a place to squat when he whistled: a small sound that wouldn't carry, yet loud enough to make her freeze.

"Elias?" She whispered his name.

"Over here."

He whistled again, guiding her approach. He couldn't see her expression as she crouched next to him. But then she threw her arms around his shoulders and held him tight. He found himself hugging her back, though he didn't understand what she meant by it. The image of Charity's blunt features flashed in his mind. Then he felt Elizabeth shaking. She was sobbing. Knowing it came as a relief.

Pulling away, he tried to see her face. "What's wrong?"

"Nothing. Everything. I don't know."

"Has he hurt you?"

"No."

"Are you ill?"

"No."

"Then, are you… pregnant?"

He felt a fool for saying it and doubly so when her sob turned into something that was akin to a laugh, though more desperate.

"No," she said. "It's just, I've had too much to carry: secrets, other things. And for too long. I've had no one to confide in. And now… finding you here. I just didn't expect it. I thought I'd never get it back. But you… You can help."

Wrapped in darkness, Elias found himself frowning. "Get what back?"

The fabric of her skirts rustled. Dimly he made out her exposed leg. Something had been strapped to her thigh. Then she was covered again and a heavy object rested in his hands, still warm from her skin. A pistol. He touched the single barrel, the hammer and pan, the wooden stock. He could feel an inlaid design where the hand would grip. He didn't need his eyes to know it for a work of quality.

"I was going to bury it," she said. "And hope to find it again when we came back this way."

"You can yield it to the oath-wrights when we get to the Island," he said.

"How could a slave girl own such a thing? And it's not from here. They'd know. They'd ask questions. They'd demand to see my marks. Any oath-wright would know in a second that I'm not what I seem. But you – you could hand it in. Everyone knows you've been over the water. You might have found a gun like this on your travels and brought it back."

"Smuggled it back," he said. "Why did you risk bringing it?"

"It's all I have left of my father. I know it's stupid, but I couldn't let go. Each step on this journey, I've thought I might find a way to escape. So I've carried it with me."

"You managed to hide it from Jago all this time?"

"Yes."

"But how? If he's…"

Elizabeth shook her head. "He hasn't. I'm sorry, Elias. Sorry I didn't tell you. But he hasn't touched me all this time. Not in *that* way. He's taken a vow to have no pleasure from women until he's the king of Newfoundland."

"But you made me think…"

"I'm sorry."

"All this time!"

"It would cost my life if he knew I'd told it. But if I don't trust someone… I just don't know how long I could carry on."

He weighed the pistol in his hand. "I deserved it," he said. "I sent you into his hands."

There was silence for a moment. Then she said, "My father told me that you can't throw a feather to land in a hat, but you can move a hat to catch a falling feather."

"What does that mean?"

"Some things can be controlled. Some things can't. I guess it means you have to know the limit of your power and work with what you've got."

"It's good," he said. "Your father was a wise man."

"Will you give my gun to the oath-wrights?"

"I will," he said.

"And bring it back when we leave?"

"I will," he said again. And then, because she'd been honest with him and it seemed he owed her at least the same in return, he added, "You know we won't make it away from the Island. Most likely."

For a moment he thought he'd shocked her into silence.

But then she said, "Neither of us knew Jago would be waiting in that church."

Most of the camp followers had bedded down by the time he arrived back at the flat rock on which he'd set the dice game. The fire had burned itself down to a mound of glowing coals. He sat nearby, easing himself in the last of its warmth. The baker would be asleep. No chance to trade the pewter mug till morning. At least that gave a promise of breakfast, when the bread would be fresh.

Checking that no one was watching, he dipped into his cloak and slipped Elizabeth's pistol onto his lap. He could make out the design in the stock, now: a leaping hare. The inlay was cold to the touch. It would be some semi-precious stone, he thought. It seemed dark in the orange light of the fire embers, almost black. But from somewhere deep in his mind came the thought of turquoise, pale and beautiful under the sun.

It took him a moment to realise that it was a remembered thing. He'd seen just such a gun before. All in a rush, the design came back to him, sharp and clear. He'd been in the far Yukon. The gun had been in the hand of a traveller, a man who'd come through to observe the glycer-fortis factory. The man with the same strange accent that he'd caught in Elizabeth's voice.

Closing his eyes, he tried to picture the man's face. But the only image he could conjure was Elizabeth herself. Confused, he slipped the gun into his tote and then laid that on the floor as a pillow. He would study it in the morning light and think on the puzzle again.

CHAPTER 33

All the way from Jago's fortress, they'd spoken about the Island of the Reckoning. The sun was warmer there, they said. It couldn't be true, but they seemed to believe it. The soft green turf lay under a sapphire sky. She would see all manner of wildflowers there. And wrestling contests and more food and drink than moderation would allow, yet all would be consumed by the end.

But when the road rounded the final bluff and the trees thinned so that Elizabeth could see it with her own eyes, she understood for the first time that they'd missed one crucial detail from their descriptions. The Island was not an island. The promontory before her pinched to a ridge of rock, not much wider than the road itself. But then it opened out again to a treeless landscape, low and rolling, surrounded by the ocean. One winter of hard storms might break that rock ridge, she thought. Then it would be an island. Or it might stand for another hundred years.

Three round stone buildings with conical roofs stood just before the narrowest point. Without chimneys or windows, they seemed like the towers of a castle. Jago led the column of horses and wagons down the slope towards them. Oathwrights emerged from between the stone walls and gathered in the road in front of the ridge, barring their way. They wore the same long robes as Jago's own oath-wright and the front of their scalps had been shaved. Each forehead bore a different design.

Jago reined in his stallion to stop before them. "I wish to cross to the Island," he announced.

"Will you first yield up your arms?" the oath-wrights intoned.

"I will."

"And all those who follow you?"

"It will be done."

Jago turned his horse to face the column. Elizabeth found herself the closest to him.

"All weapons will be yielded here. Any found carrying an instrument of death beyond this point will be done to death by my hand."

As they began to dismount, he advanced his horse towards her. "That means the stinger you carry in your boot."

When it was all laid out on the ground, Elizabeth marvelled at the quantity of weaponry they'd been carrying: swords and pistols for the most part, but long guns also and maces, throwing knives, crossbows and spiked and bladed things the names of which she didn't know. The oath-wrights entered each into a ledger. Then all the weapons were carried into the nearest of the stone towers. One by one, Jago's followers were cleared, to pass onto the Island. On the other side of the rock ridge they were searched by a second contingent of oath-wrights. Powder dogs sniffed around, yowling in excitement, tails wagging. One man was forced to strip naked when the dogs paid him too much interest. He had nothing.

"Stop!" one of the oath-wrights commanded, pointing to the first of Jago's wagons as it rolled towards the rock ridge. It had moments before been uncovered and its curious cargo revealed. "What's that?" There was no deference, though he was addressing a Patron.

"Part of a table," Jago said.

"Why?"

"Is it allowed?"

"Why bring a table?"

"Is it allowed?" Jago asked again in the same flat tone.

"It is."

Jago gestured to the carter, who flicked his whip. Onwards it rolled. Elizabeth arranged herself so as to watch its progress without seeming interested. On the far side it stopped and the dogs sniffed around it. Two of them jumped into the back and put their noses to the woodwork and the straw it rested in. To her untrained eye, they seemed agitated. But none of them sat and barked or lifted a paw or any of the other indications that dogs were trained to make on smelling contraband. Out they jumped and it was done.

Focused on the scene beyond the rock ridge, she only became aware that Elias was himself crossing when he stepped past her. And then it was too late to catch his eye. The oath-wrights on the other side paid him no attention. The dogs must have become inured to the scent of glycer-fortis because they gave him only a passing sniff. He followed on behind the carts, hardly noticed, it seemed. Though news of his arrival would surely fly like beach sand in a gale.

"You next," said Logan.

He gave her pony a smack on the rump and it started forwards. Walking beside it, she found herself led by the beast instead of the other way around. Halfway across she looked down and saw the waves surging some forty feet below. An experienced climber might scale such a cliff, but not easily. By controlling that pinch point, the oath-wrights could give or deny access to all the land beyond. A perfect setting, then, for the Reckoning. With all their weapons outside, the Patrons could play their games of politics with no thought that it might turn to deadly violence.

The land widened out again. The dogs were all around her. After giving her pistol to Elias, she'd scrubbed her hands until the skin was red. She held them out now to the dogs. Their noses touched her and then just as swiftly they moved on to Logan and Jago himself, the last of the column to cross.

Other than Elias, the train of camp followers had been left on the other side. Looking back she saw them traversing the slope of the final headland, moving towards a shantytown of tents that had already sprung up there.

Another clan had begun to descend the hill towards the oath-wrights. What would have happened, she wondered, had two different Patrons arrived at the same time? On the journey, she'd seen outriders from other clans. Each Patron would know the position and speed of other trains nearby. They would keep their distance.

Elizabeth watched as the men of Jago's upstart clan erected the tents and made stacks of firewood. Some practised their wrestling moves. Jago and his closest advisors huddled in consultation, too quiet and distant for her to hear. Passivity was eating her up from the inside. With the voluminous skirts he'd made her wear, the only thing she could do was stroll slowly from tent to tent. He'd made her into an ornament and she hated it.

Elias had for the first time been granted shelter: a mean-looking sailcloth tent. He'd been made to pitch it away from the main body of the camp, between the latrine pit and the cliff edge. Whenever she tried to wander over and speak to him, one of Jago's men would shepherd her back.

More clans arrived through the afternoon and the Island became like a map of Newfoundland itself. Jago's lands were on the south coast, so his clan made camp near the south coast of the Island. The Williams clan were immediately to the west, the Fotheringills to the east. There were perhaps fifty yards of open ground between each cluster of tents. Such proximity might have caused trouble. But without their weapons the men seemed more relaxed.

On the first morning after their arrival, Jago sent a wagon back over the rock ridge to the shantytown of traders on the headland. It returned stacked with more firewood as well as food and wine. A crowd of camp followers had gathered beyond the rock ridge, waiting to be offered work. There were menial tasks to be done: washing and cooking, digging latrines and any other service that the sons of the Patrons might require. Elizabeth watched through the morning as small groups of them were called across.

Spatchcocked chickens had been set on spikes to roast around the fire. The smell of them grew maddening as her hunger built. If it hadn't been for the great volume of skirts they'd made her wear, she'd have twisted a leg from one of them. But she couldn't approach the fire without risk of sending her entire dress up in flames. When at last the cook announced that it was ready, she had to wait for a portion to be brought: a strip of white meat, entirely too small.

As she took her first bite, the clan milling around the fire began to part and Jago strode through. His eyes were on her. She looked away and stuffed the remains of the chicken into her mouth.

"Hungry?" he said, when close enough.

She struggled to swallow. But with it down, he wouldn't be able to take it from her.

He pulled a cloth from his sleeve and wiped the grease from her chin, as if she were a child.

"Time for a stroll," he said, taking her arm.

A stroll should meander. Instead they cut a straight line across the turf towards the tents of the Williams clan. Logan had tried to follow but the Patron dismissed him with a shake of the head. A wall of young men faced them as they arrived: arms folded, not a smile between them. Jago didn't break step. At the last moment the man in the centre of the line shifted to the side, making space for them to pass.

"Patron Williams," Jago said, addressing a corpulent man with a pockmarked face.

The man scowled. "What do you want, Upstart?"

Elizabeth glanced at Jago. But his smile had, if anything, widened. "A fine day, don't you think?"

"Good enough. Who's the whore?"

"You want the use of her? My gift."

"You've no taste. No class."

"Yet here I am." Jago flourished his arms.

"Why? Why are you here at all?"

"For your company. Your wit. It always makes me laugh."

And then, as if to prove it, Jago did begin a kind of laugh: a cold sound, forced from his throat. Talk fell silent around the camp. All that remained was Jago's mirthless aping of merriment. It went on and on. Elizabeth felt sick.

"Filthy upstart," Patron Williams hissed.

On that moment, Jago's laughter stopped dead. He bowed low, squeezing Elizabeth's arm until she curtsied. Then they were walking away, the wall of young men parting for them.

When they were far enough, he leaned closer to her and said, "Next time bow. Like you're play-acting a man."

"But why?"

"So they'll despise me more."

Next they came to the camp of Patron Tarrik. At first the reception wasn't so cold. But Jago goaded them and by the time Elizabeth made her deep bow, the young men were spitting on the turf.

"Better," Jago said to her. "Much better."

She glanced back and saw a figure following. But not from within the Tarrik camp. He had skirted it and was trying to

seem casual. She looked quickly away, not wanting to direct
Jago's attention. But he'd seen already and was beckoning.

"Enjoying your walk, No-Thumbs?"

"Yes, Patron."

"I'm paying my respects to your Great Uncle Calvary.
Perhaps you'd like to come along?"

"No, Patron."

"No matter," said Jago. "His spies are watching. They'll be
following you for sure. Go set the first section of the table.
Firehand will help. Take it over there."

He pointed to a patch of flat land near the rock ridge. If the
Island was indeed a map, it would represent the unaligned
tract around New Whitby.

"No one can set camp there," Elias said, alarmed it seemed.

Jago smiled. "It's not a camp. It's a table. For all of them
to use. And for you." Then, turning towards her, he added,
"You can go with the fool. That'll draw a crowd. The whole
Reckoning is itching to know who you are."

Elizabeth had been yearning to talk with Elias again. But now
they were together, she could find no words. Each time she
made to speak, there was someone in earshot. And when it
was safe, a new idea would spark and she'd feel suddenly
uncertain.

She'd been brought up among showmen, and knew their
ways. But it hadn't come to her before that Jago possessed
some of those same instincts. The table itself, with not enough
places for all the Patrons. The insulting visits, each calculated
for its effect, stirring up the kind of loathing that would
stop them thinking straight. And now this – the placing of a
segment of the table where all must pass to enter or leave the
Island. He could have had it all assembled at once. But no.
He would tease his audience one segment at a time, hooking
their curiosity. Every Patron would be asking about it. And

every councillor would be failing to answer. Oh, Jago was a ringmaster to his core.

"Run away," Elias whispered, at last.

"How?"

"There's a cove – I can take you. It's out of view. If you wait till low tide, you can scramble to the mainland and no one will see. I did it after they outlawed me."

She should have run the first time he'd told her to, way back on the New Whitby turning. "Can I really get away?"

"There are three headlands. You'll need to do some climbing to get around them. But you're strong enough. If you've got the nerve."

"And then?"

"Head away under the mainland cliff till you're almost out of view. There's an easy place to climb up. It's like a ladder. Then hide with the camp followers. Leave with them when it's all over."

"Come with me," she said.

"I need glycer-fortis. I can't live without it."

"We can wean you off it."

He shook his head. "I've tried."

"But never with my help."

"Even if it worked, I'd not be alive. Not like you." He opened his thumbless hands for her to see.

"You still want revenge?"

"They did this to me, Elizabeth. And now they laugh. Jago was right. Every day I open the wounds so they're fresh. I cut myself raw. I need to see them hurting. I need to see them wish they'd not plotted against me. If I can't do that, I don't want to be alive. I know you think I'm a fool. And you're right. I hate myself for it. But I can't escape from who I am."

"I don't think you see yourself so clearly," she said. "There's more in you than revenge."

"You don't know me."

"I hated a man once," she said.

"What did he do?"

"He ruined my family. My father died in debtors' prison because of him."

"So you killed him?"

"I tried. I even had my knife to his throat. But... I don't know... Somehow I didn't do it. I think it's because I'd learned to love myself. A little bit. And to love my friends."

"I don't know how to do that," Elias said. Then the pain left his face like a candle flame being snuffed. The confession was over.

"We know that Jago wants to kill them all," Elias said, his tone suddenly practical. "The other Patrons, I mean. But we don't know how he's going to trigger the bomb. I've been thinking that with the table set near the rock ridge, he could shoot at it from the mainland. If a bullet went through the timber, it would blow for sure. But then, if a man raised a gun there, the camp followers would set on him."

"Jago will do whatever he'll do," she said. "The men who hurt you will be dead."

"But I need to see them when they know they're beaten."

"Let it go."

But he would not be reasoned with. She sighed. "I'll need a set of men's clothes. I wouldn't get ten paces in this dress. And a man's hat. Wide brim is best. Could you get that for me?"

"I'll try," he said.

"Then you can show me the way to escape and I'll be gone."

CHAPTER 34

Elizabeth didn't come with them. Elias watched her walking away, as if she didn't care about the Patron's order, though he knew she did. When she was gone, he followed behind Firehand, who in turn followed behind the wagon. The framed mirror rattled in the straw as the wheels bumped over stones. With each new judder, he found himself tensing. The urge to reach for his own small jar of glycer-fortis seemed ironic. But his heartbeat skittered with the thought of the bomb and the thousands upon thousands of musket balls that surrounded it. He touched the glass in his pocket but pulled his hand away again. He'd had his morning dose.

People stared at the section of the table as they passed. Some laughed. But if any of the watchers thought the placing of it was a breach of custom and practice, they kept it to themselves.

When it was done and he stood back to look at the piece of table standing on the turf, he found himself marvelling at Jago's genius. Fully assembled, it would have suited a grand hall. But there was something mesmerizingly wrong about a single section, placed alone on the green swathe next to the cliffs. A crowd had already gathered by the time the empty cart began rolling its way back. At first they kept a distance, but then one was touching. Others followed. Please be gentle,

Elias thought.

The slice of table wasn't itself in the way of anything, but onlookers were blocking the track. A wagon of kegs and crates had been forced to stop and the oath-wrights were shouting for a way to be cleared. The crowd parted and the cart rolled forwards again. Wine bottles clinked against each other as it moved.

Elias caught sight of the carter and felt a stab of pain in his chest. His heart stopped for a space of three beats and was then racing to catch up. The carter was the man with scarred knuckles that he'd seen outside Charity's house. It was the brute, her husband. Her brother was there as well, stepping around the cart.

It seemed that neither had seen him. But then he glimpsed a woman in the crowd. He only caught view of her shoulder and part of her head before she was hidden again, but he knew her. It was Charity herself.

She began to shoulder her way in his direction. He angled his face, hoping she wouldn't see him. For a moment he couldn't move his feet. Only when she started up the slope did he find the power to turn away. He was weaving back through the crowds towards the camp when she caught up.

"Elias." She grabbed his arm.

"You shouldn't be here!" he hissed.

"Don't you want to see me?"

There was no time to explain the danger. Even such contact as they'd had might have been seen. He broke her grip but she followed. He cut right, away from the crowd, towards the edge of the cliff.

"Elias!"

"We can't be seen together."

"Are you ashamed of me?"

"No! Look, there's a way down to the rocks. Just follow behind."

"Is it where you men go to bed the camp followers?" It hadn't sounded like a joke.

"It's where we can be alone."

"They told me you're sweet on Jago's woman. They said you slept with her."

"Who said?"

"Someone. Is it not true?"

"It wasn't true like that."

"So you did sleep with her?"

"We were taking shelter. There was only the one bed. It's not as if you haven't had other men."

"Not since I met you!" Again, that catch in her voice.

They'd been tracing the edge of the cliff. Now they came to the place where a steep scree slope gave access to the beach. But looking down he saw that the cove was already in use. A man and a woman lay on the pebbles, her underneath, his bare arse showing above as he pounded away.

"Is that where you're taking me?" she asked.

They stepped back, out of view of the rutting couple.

"I'm sorry," he said.

"Take me to your tent."

"We'd be seen. They'd think…"

"What?"

"This place is all gossip. Your husband will get to hear."

"Take me there!"

So he did, not running, but walking swiftly. Clouds had gathered, making it feel like dusk, though it was mid-afternoon. Hoping the low light would hide them, he strode towards his decrepit tent, as if to pass it. Then, at the last moment he crouched down and crawled in through the flaps.

"Why did you come here?" he whispered, when they were lying facing each other.

"You asked me that already."

"I thought you stayed at home when they took their trips."

"Would you rather I had?"

"It's not safe here."

"Then why did you come? Was it to follow that woman?"

He couldn't explain. But neither could he bear the hurt in her. So he placed a kiss on her lips, just as he'd done once with Elizabeth. But it wasn't the same. Instead of staring at him in shock, Charity closed her eyes. Instead of going rigid and turning away, she shifted closer. And he, instead of trying to stifle her question, was answering it.

Somewhere between the first touch of her lips and the moment when the heat of her body made him forget, he wondered if he had changed. But he didn't even know what that meant.

Elias woke to see the shifting light of a campfire cast on one side of the tent and blackness on the other. He pushed himself up onto his elbows. The movement roused her.

"You can't be here," he whispered. Then he kissed her again, unsure how he'd been tempted to bring her so close to Jago and his men.

"I can't not be here," she said, when the kiss broke for a moment and they were holding each other.

"If they found you…"

There'd been so many girls and women. Each he'd let go without regret. A few had tried to trick him into staying. He'd thought that perhaps, if he found the most perfect one, the most beautiful, then he might feel something in return.

He looked into Charity's face. There was a sturdiness about her, a homeliness, a weight like the ballast that stops the boat from rolling. If she'd been beautiful, perhaps he'd never have seen what lay beneath. Or perhaps it was his desperation that had done it: the impossibility of any relationship between this married woman and himself, a man whose only purpose and destiny were revenge. Yet somehow he'd glimpsed her.

In the few nights they'd spent together, he'd crossed the border into an unknown land. Ink is ink, she'd said, as if such things mattered not at all, as if her innocence stopped her from knowing the truth. But now it seemed she knew things which he would never be able to grasp.

"Charity," he said.

She kissed him again, more passionately than before. It was an answer to the question he hadn't thought to ask. He yielded to it, feeling as though he was vanishing into her.

"I didn't mean it to happen," she said, when the kiss was over. "It was a game. We were having fun, weren't we? And then... I shouldn't have come back to you. But I'd never felt it like that. Not before."

"Not with your husband? Not ever?"

"I loved him. I still do."

"But he broke your nose."

She pulled back as if stung. "No. That was when we were children. Some boys were hitting my brother. I knocked one of them down. I got this in return. I always had to look after him."

"Why?"

"Because he's my brother."

"But why did they pick on him?"

"He was different. He's different still. You asked if I'd get in trouble – if my husband would find out I've been with you. He knows. He always knows. I told him I was coming. That's the way we do it. I love him. But our marriage has never been..." She seemed unable to find the word she was looking for.

"I don't understand," said Elias.

She took his hand and placed it above her breast. He could feel her heartbeat, fast and heavy. "There are three of us in the house," she said. "My husband, my brother and me. But I'm the only one who sleeps alone."

Mind reeling, Elias dropped onto his back. He stared at the canvas and the tent poles above. Those few words had changed his world into another. Everything he understood about her had been turned around.

"Your brother… he likes men?"

"No. Just one man."

"Your husband."

"Yes."

"You married so they could be together."

"It wasn't anyone's business," she said. "But they'd have made it their business. There was talk already. And threats. They'd have killed them. There was no one to stand for them, except me. He's my brother. He found love. I never did. It seemed easy. And I wasn't losing by it. I could have my fun when they were away. We agreed it all from the start. Let people think what they wanted. I didn't mind. If they were happier to think me a trull than to know my dear, sweet brother loved another man – that was their shame, not ours. But then you came to the inn that night. And now I don't know what I'm doing any more."

The picture of them outside her house flashed in his mind. They'd stared at him as if making some great discovery. He'd thought they might attack.

"When I saw them that day…"

"They knew who you were," she said. "They knew what we'd done. And what I felt for you."

"What do you feel?"

"Love," she said.

The word stung. "But you don't know me!"

"You're right. I don't know you."

"I'm a bad man."

"I know you are. You bedded a married woman, remember?" There was laughter in her voice this time. But compassion also. For them both, perhaps.

"I was acting. Playing the rogue for your fantasies."

"We were both acting."

"But when I told you I'd come back to take revenge – that part was true. That's who I am. It's why I'm here, at the Reckoning. There's something rotten in me. You can't love me!"

She put her fingertips on his mouth, stopping his words. It took him a fraction of a second to understand that something had changed. She'd tensed. Her head was angled to listen.

He held his breath. At first it seemed to be the wind in the canvas of a tent. But there were no tents near enough for that. The same sound came again: a footstep close outside. From instinct his hand shifted to where his knife would have been. But there were no knives on the Island.

Their voices had grown louder in the heat of confession. What they'd said would put her in danger. Her brother and husband, too. But only if they'd been heard.

"What is it?" Her whisper was little more than a breath.

Elias felt for his trousers, slipping his legs into them before crawling to the mouth of the tent. He crouched outside, then stood to look around. If someone had been listening, they were now hiding themselves.

"Get dressed," he whispered.

There was no need to say more. She'd picked up the urgency of his tone. In the space of five heavy heartbeats, he'd pulled on his shirt and she was crawling out to join him. He grabbed for his cloak and began to lead her away, taking a line closer to the cliff than the camp.

"What's happening?" she whispered when they were beyond the camp.

"We need to get you off the Island. Fast."

"Why?"

"Go to your husband. Leave here tonight."

"But when will I see you?"

He didn't answer because every truth he might have said would have hurt. And there was no more way for him to lie to her. His world had changed with a sickening lurch. He'd been ready to greet death. His own and his enemies'. That had made him powerful. But suddenly, he wanted to live. The fact of it was terrifying.

They skirted the Williams camp and started off across the rolling land towards the rock ridge. He pulled her along. She stumbled but he kept going, faster if anything. The watch fires of the oath-wrights lay ahead, one on either side of the ridge. At last he could see the turf in front of them and there was no more stumbling.

But as they ran the last few yards, an oath-wright stepped into their path. Elias's first thought was to dodge around him, but that would have meant a swift death. He slowed and stopped, almost losing balance on the slippery mud. He was still holding Charity's hand.

"Who are you?" the oath-wright demanded, not quietly.

"Elias," he said. "Here under Jago's protection."

"And the woman?"

"Charity of New Whitby," she said. "Unaligned. I was delivering wine."

"And stayed after sunset?"

She nodded.

"Why?"

"Business."

"A whore as well as a wine trader?"

"Yes," she said.

She'd said she didn't mind how other people thought of her. It had made a kind of sense. But as the oath-wright stared at her body Elias felt sick.

"It's irregular," the man said. "She should have left while it was light."

"Is it against the rules?"

"I have to search her."

"No," said Elias.

But Charity stepped forwards and raised her arms. The oath-wright kept his eyes on Elias's as he began feeling down her sides. Elias clenched his fists. Then it was finished and Charity stepped back.

"Can I go?"

"You may," said the oath-wright.

Elias caught her eyes one more time before she started away across the rock ridge.

"Wait!"

Jago strode down the slope towards them, flanked by Firehand and Logan.

The oath-wright stepped in front of Charity, barring her way.

"Stop that woman!" Jago called. "We have business to discuss."

CHAPTER 35

It was Logan's voice that woke Elizabeth. Or perhaps it was the movement of the furs as Jago stood. There'd been urgency in both. At the fortress the Patron had slept naked. Here he slept fully clothed and ready for action. She opened her eyes to see him leaving the tent and listened to his footsteps running away in the direction of the rock ridge. Then there was only the rippling of canvas and the wind hissing over the guy ropes outside.

It felt strange to be alone and unwatched. Her heart quickened as she slipped through the tent flaps. The campfires had burned themselves out. She shivered as the chill air cut through the thin fabric of her night shirt and the chemise beneath. There were no voices, no distant songs. Closer to dawn then, than to midnight. The moon seemed to drift in the sky. The shadow of a cloud swept over the rolling turf of the Island. Grabbing a blanket from the tent to wrap around her shoulders, she stepped out in the direction of the wagons, unable to see the ground or even her own feet. The moonlight returned as abruptly as it had left. She crouched and waited. If she'd been the only person on the Island, the scene would have been no different. But knowing there were sleepers all around, her senses tingled. The tiniest noise sounded like a shout.

Under the cover of another cloud she set off again. This time she reached her destination before the moon returned. The wagon cast its own shadow. Crouched next to a wheel she was well-hidden. The tarpaulin covering the load hung loose around the rear, trailing almost to the ground. Even if someone had been watching, they wouldn't have been able to see her clambering up underneath it. She hardly noticed the prick of a loose nail on her ankle as she wormed herself in. But lying on her back in the wagon, she felt the sting of it. The scratch was nothing. But blood on the white linen of her nightshirt would be awkward to explain. So she licked her finger and rubbed the drop away, waiting for it to dry.

The tarpaulin blocked out the moonlight, but for a thin strip at the back. Feeling blind, she touched her fingertips to the table.

The previous night she'd sneaked out and gone through other wagons, exploring three different sections. They had yielded no clue. Another two parts had already been set up near the rock ridge, where they stood like a strange statue. Everyone who passed took time to stare at them. So close to the oath-wrights, those sections were out of her reach.

With the flat of her hand she followed each of the table legs, and then began to sweep the underside, searching for any irregularity. Elias had seen the construction of the table, but they'd not shown him the trigger. That was what she needed to find. If they were to live through the next few days, they had to figure out how Jago planned to detonate the bomb.

She didn't know what the trigger would feel like. But she'd surely recognise it when she found it. It would need to be hidden from view. And now she knew that Jago was having the pieces placed one by one, it seemed clear that what she hunted for would be in the final part. Once that part had been placed, even the Patron couldn't go back.

She almost missed it in the sweep of her hand: a slight ridge where there should have been sanded timber. She traced it around four sides: a square, roughly the size of her hand, standing a fraction proud of the surface. Working her fingernails into the edge, she began to ease it free. It shifted then stuck then shifted again and finally fell, revealing a void.

Her eyes had adjusted to the dark as well as they might, but she couldn't see what lay within. She held her breath and inched her fingers into it. Touching metal, she stopped. Something smooth and rounded had been fixed to the side of the hole. Out of context, it took her a moment to realise that she was feeling the casing of a large watch. The glass had been left open. She felt the dial and the hands. A taut thread ran from the winding key. Steadying her finger, she followed it with the gentlest touch, reaching the opposite wall of the void, where another object had been fixed, a contraption of wood and wire. Her mind flashed back to the storehouse in Jago's fortress. Rat traps had been strewn about the floor. And here was another. But this one had not been rigged to break a rodent's back.

Understanding came to her. The watch would not be a simple thing. It would have one vital complication: an alarm that could be set to a certain time. When the alarm chimed, the unwinding spring would turn the key, reeling in the thread, which would pull on the trigger of the rat trap. She felt under the arm of the trap, expecting to find a small lump of the glycer-fortis. Fearing it. For if the arm of the trap snapped closed, the explosive would detonate, setting off the entire thing.

But the trap had not been primed. There was no glycer-fortis. She breathed again, feeling light-headed with the knowledge. No one would need to shoot at the table to set it off and Jago wouldn't need to be anywhere near. All could be regulated with clockwork. The agent of destruction would be time itself.

Unless she had misunderstood.

With one hand she triggered the trap, the other holding back the killing arm and bringing it down gently. This left the thread slack. Turning the winder, she tightened it again. The watch began to tick. The minute hand moved easily under her finger. She rotated it around the dial, once, twice. Halfway around the third time she heard a click, barely audible and the whirring breath of an escapement. The winder began to turn, reeling in the thread. Then it chimed: a small metallic noise, a nursery tune entirely unlike the night wind and distant boom of waves. Panicking, she wound the hand back. The chiming stopped. The quiet returned.

But there was another noise. A voice. Not close. But she'd recognised Jago's commanding tone.

Hand shaking, she reset the trap, tightening the thread as much as she dared, then pushed the square block of wood back in place to cover the hole.

Worming out from under the edge of the tarpaulin, she dropped to a crouch in the shadow of the wagon.

Figures were approaching from the direction of the rock ridge. There might be four people, or five. She couldn't tell without standing up, and that would give her away. Elias was among them, she'd caught his voice.

She set off in a stooped run towards the latrine pit, then stood to her full height and began walking directly back to the tents. There were four figures, she saw them clearly now, approaching from the far side: Jago, Elias, Logan and one more, shorter and plumper than the rest. Only when they stopped did she recognise Charity.

"Out for a stroll?" asked Jago.

Instead of answering she glanced back to the latrine and then met his gaze for a moment before lowering her head.

• • •

The grey line of the horizon began to separate the sky from the sea. The men pushed Charity into one of the three identical tents facing the remains of the feast fire. By the light of a candle lantern, Elizabeth saw that they had driven an iron stake into the ground next to the tent pole. From the ring at its top ran a short chain, ending in a hinged collar. Logan closed it around Charity's neck, fixing the two ends with a padlock. Misery wreathed her face.

By the time the last of the men were leaving Charity had begun to cry. Elizabeth knelt close.

"There'll be a way out," she whispered.

Tears became heaving sobs.

Elizabeth hugged her. "I'll find a way."

"I've ruined it all!"

"Not you. You must never say that. It's them. They did this to us."

"I had to see him."

"Elias?"

"I've never wanted things… Not for me… And now I do… And I've ruined it all."

Elizabeth pulled back, keeping a gentle hold on Charity's shoulders. She wanted to ask why it was important to see Elias. But the answer was written over that sorrow-riven face. Only love could bring such suffering. It seemed impossible that he felt the same way in return. But remembering the anguish of looks between the two of them as he was ordered back to his tent, she felt a fool. Amid all the extraordinary events of the last few weeks, a bigger drama had been going on that she'd entirely missed.

Jago must have seen it, though. Oh, but the man was so much more dangerous than the brute he seemed. More subtle and more controlled. He used casual violence to hide the sharpness of his mind. In the last weeks he'd used glycer-fortis to keep Elias obedient: the chance of another lease of life, a few more weeks to walk the Earth. But such a threat or promise can only go so far. To have a man go willingly to death would need a more terrible threat. In this new hostage, the Patron had found exactly that. To the extent that Elias loved her, he would do as he was told.

Perhaps Charity had ruined everything after all.

"It's not your fault," Elizabeth said. "None of it." And then, making her voice practical, "The Patron has ordered that I sleep here with you. I can fetch a chamber pot if you need it. And they'll let me bring food. But not much, I think. Wine is easy, though. He always wants me to drink."

"What will become of me?" Charity asked.

"You'll stay here. Until something happens."

"What?"

"I don't know."

The sun was just up by the time Charity had cried herself to sleep. Elizabeth emerged from the tent to the sounds of low voices from around the Island. Fires were being lit and breakfasts prepared. The chores of morning carried out by servants, while those of the Blood slept on.

Creeping around in daylight would only attract attention, so she set off across the turf as if on some errand of her own. Reaching the wagon, she dipped under the tarpaulin and found the nail that had caught her ankle. Half an inch of it projected from the wood. Wiggled from side to side, it began to loosen. It squeaked as she pulled it free.

Then she was walking on again, not looking down as she worked the nail into the hem of her cuff. No one watching would have known what she had done.

CHAPTER 36

Jago's humours had seemed to change as fast as Newfoundland's fickle weather. One hour would see him focused on practical matters, the buying of firewood, the hiring of servants. The next he'd turn bilious, serving insults and punishments to any who came near. By turns he would be arrogant, lazy, sullen. Perhaps some of it was an act.

But with the taking of Charity, a new mood had grown in him. As Elias crumbled from within, so the upstart was seen to relax. His smile became almost warm.

"Come, Elias, we have work."

"Yes, Patron."

"I made you a promise. And my word is good."

"Yes, Patron."

"You will have what you asked. And in every detail. I have a gift for you. It will be ready soon."

"Thank you, Patron."

"Tell me how it felt when they cut off your thumbs."

Elias stopped dead. They'd been walking across the turf towards the northwest of the Island. Jago continued for a couple of paces before turning. "Which was worse: the pain or the humiliation?"

"I don't know."

"That I don't believe. You're a man who would have

thought about it. That's what I like about you, Elias. You've wits enough to suffer. A stupid man can feel pain. But does he understand it? You'll have thought about what they did to you every day. You'll have picked the bones white. Except that kind of carcass can't ever be cleaned. Not unless you get your revenge. Does your woman know what you're wanting to do?"

Elias had given up denying his connection to her. He shook his head. There was no saliva in his mouth.

"I'm not often wrong. But I didn't think you the type to fall for a woman." He prodded Elias in the chest. "Is there room in that cage for anything more than hate? And what a woman to choose! They say she bedded every man in New Whitby before she came to you."

With that, the Patron walked on.

"Don't hurt her," Elias said, following. "Please."

"Once you had nothing. There's strength in that. But now… I don't know, Elias. Do you still want your game of chance?"

"Yes, Patron." It was true and Elias despised himself for it.

"Then you will have it. And if you do all as I tell, your ugly woman will go free. That's my promise. See my generosity! But cut against me and she'll suffer for it. I'll have you watch the whole thing. Understand?" Then he put his arm over Elias's shoulder as if embracing a brother. "Be happy," he said. "Tonight your wishes will come true. Tonight I'll set the game."

Angry faces greeted them in the Weaverbright camp. But there was something more, Elias thought. They despised him. And they hated the upstart Patron. He had no doubt of that. But Jago had an arm over his shoulder and that would be a puzzle they couldn't solve. There was uncertainty behind their anger. And fear, perhaps.

"My dear friend wishes your company in a game of chance," Jago said. "One of you against him."

"It's not happening," said Patron Weaverbright. His arms were folded. His son and daughter flanked him like faithful dogs.

"Are you afraid he'll win?"

"He's a cheat! Everyone knows it."

"A good one, do you think?"

"A cheat is a cheat."

"You're not afraid he'll cheat. You're afraid he'll win."

Patron Weaverbright bared his yellowed teeth. "What's the stake?"

"Gold."

"He's got none."

"Ah, but I have. Whatever your boy brings to the table, I'll set No-Thumbs up with ten times that. Unless you're too much of a coward."

Hands twitched. One young man reached for where his sword would have hung.

"Sit!" Weaverbright spat the word. "We'll do it here and now!"

"We'll do it tonight," Jago said. "Your son against this thumbless beggar. I've brought a table specially for the game."

Then he turned and Elias turned with him. A wall of faces barred the way, reddened with anger. Elias tried to shoulder through but a punch landed at the side of his stomach. He stumbled, tensing every muscle for the blows that would follow. But a shout from Patron Weaverbright had all the men pulling back.

"That would be a coward's way out," Jago said. "Killing a man with no thumbs because you've not the guts to face him over a table."

"No one's been killed!"

"Then we'll see you tonight."

Elias felt the sweat break in the middle of his back. The pain of the punch hadn't masked the pain in his chest.

"Why must I play at the table?" he asked.

"You have somewhere better?"

He wanted to say that anywhere would be better than over a giant bomb. Instead he asked, "How does it serve you?"

"Did you never talk to trappers when you were in Churchill?"

"They were all drunk."

"They put a trap out where the wolves can see it and smell it. They leave it out for days and weeks until one wolf starts to think that it's just another tree or a rock. It goes closer and closer and then..." Jago clapped his hands together like the arms of a trap.

"You're just getting them used to the table. That's all."

The story seemed too reasonable.

"I only passed through Churchill," Elias said.

"Oh? I thought you lived there."

"It was a story to cover the truth. They took me out to the Yukon as a slave. Had me making the glycer-fortis for over a year. When they had me so I couldn't live without it, they sent me back."

"To find me," Jago said.

"I could have chosen someone else."

"Am I supposed to be impressed?"

"No. But I'm doing everything you ask. I just need you to let her go."

"I will," said Jago. "And I'll give you enough of the drug to keep you alive. But first... Boom." He spread his hands, as if following the shape of an explosion.

"When will that be?"

"When I'm ready. Your job is to get them used to sitting around that table."

"Will you be there?" Elias asked. "Tonight, I mean."

The Patron nodded. "I will."

• • •

Elizabeth sat in the triangle of sunshine where the tent flaps had been pulled back. She waited and she watched. It was noon by the time Elias came into view, picking his way across the turf towards his tent. She made her excuses. For once Jago seemed too absorbed in his thoughts to question her. She lifted up his chamber pot, which had been left under the guy ropes. Carrying it in front of her, held away from her body, she set out towards the latrine.

Elias must have seen her, for he slowed. Though he didn't look at her directly, nor did he deviate from his course. For an observer, their paths might have seemed to cross by chance.

"They put in the last piece of the table," she said, not whispering but neither moving her lips. "Half an hour ago. I know how it's to be triggered. There's a clock. It will all be done by time. Logan crawled underneath as they were setting the table in place. Like he was fixing the sections together. But he was rigging the clock. They couldn't have carried it across the ground with the trigger set."

Elias had stopped walking. They were facing each other and someone was sure to be watching.

"Jago will be there for the dice game," Elias said.

"Then he'll go before the bomb detonates. You can't do this."

"If I don't..." He glanced back to the tent where Charity was held. "I couldn't live with her death on my soul. I have no choice."

"But if it goes off, hundreds will die."

"And if I tell the other Patrons there's a bomb, Charity dies."

"Some of them are innocent," she said.

"I've made my choice."

"You could go to your great uncle, tell him everything. He can tell the other Patrons. If they act together, they can rescue Charity and keep everyone away from the bomb. No one dies."

"Look, Elizabeth. I know you mean it for the best. But you don't know this place. You don't understand. This... Newfoundland... the Patrons... everything... it's over. Now they can bring weapons across the water, there's going to be a war. Not like it ever was. This time someone's going to win. There's going to be a king of Newfoundland. If it's not today, it'll be next year. If it's not Jago, it'll be one of the others."

"Then let it be one of the others! That man... I've seen him close. I've slept in his bed! He'll murder and rape his way through the people till the only ones alive have his blood in them."

"You think the others are better? I know them. That was my life once."

"They can't all be as bad as him."

"He's going to kill Charity if I go against him! Don't you understand?"

"I'll rescue her."

"How?"

"I'll find a way."

"Jago will be there for the dice game," he said, as if trying to find a different way of seeing things, a way in which he might not be responsible for the massacre of hundreds. But from his eyes, she knew he was doubting it.

"When I've got her free, I'll get a message to you. All you have to do is get them clear of the table before it goes off. The three of us can escape together. We'll take the path you told me about – around the cliffs."

His head dropped. "I'll die without the glycer-fortis and Jago will hunt you down."

"Your great uncle will help us. All of us."

"I can't tell him anything while Charity's still a prisoner."

"I'm going to work on that. Go to him. You're his blood. He'll hear you, whatever the law says."

"I'm afraid," Elias said.

"You'd be a fool if you weren't. But we can still escape."

"I'll never escape from myself," he said. "There's no hope for a man like me. I'm better dead."

Elias sat on the edge of the cliff and stared at his feet, dangling above the breaking waves. He'd walked away from Elizabeth, not wanting to think that she might be right about the bomb. His neck felt tired, as if all the different odds he'd been carrying in his head were pulling him down. If he jumped over the edge, Charity would die. If he warned the other Patrons, she would die. Or if he refused to play the game.

But what if she could be freed?

He stood, the toes of his battered boots poking over the edge. The cliff wasn't high enough to be sure of a quick death. The explosion would be an instant.

Not quite knowing why, he turned and began to walk, skirting wide of each camp until he reached the northwest tip of the Island.

Patron Calvary looked up from the feast fire as he approached. Around him sat men and women of the clan, advisors and family. Seeing the familiar faces, Elias felt a pang in his chest. For once it wasn't his misbehaving heart. It caught him so sharply that he broke step. A kind of homesickness, he supposed.

All around him were cousins, nephews and aunts, removed to one degree or another. But they weren't his family any more. They hadn't been from the moment he was severed. They stood as he came closer, staring. A woman spat onto the floor. It was his niece, he realised: a girl who'd once clung to him, demanding his attention to play make-believe games. Some of the young men turned their backs. But his great uncle's old advisor shuffled closer, eyes lowered, perhaps in deference.

"You can't be here, boy," he said.

"I need to see him."

"There's no way back."

Elias dropped his voice to a whisper. "I have information."

"Then tell it to me."

"I can't."

The old man sighed. "I had hopes for you once, Elias. There was something about you as a child. But when you came to your maturity…" He shook his head. "Every path has been wrong since then. Now here you are, come to the Reckoning, trailing behind the Upstart. You embarrass me. You embarrass Patron Calvary. Coming here, reminding us of your failure. You may not approach him. Not now. Not ever."

Elias moved close and put his arms around the old man. An embrace, it might seem to the others. Only he could feel how the advisor struggled to escape. He kissed the man on the desiccated cheek and whispered.

"The Patron, your oath-holder, my great uncle: he will be dead within the week unless I can speak to him. Alone. If he wants to find me, I'll be at the cove below the south cliff."

He kissed the man's other cheek before letting go. His bow in the direction of the Patron brought sneers of disgust from the others. But they thought no worse of him than he thought of himself. He turned and walked out of the firelight.

Waves were always close on the Island. Cliffs muffled the sound for the most part, but stepping to the very edge Elias heard the scouring and crashing with sudden clarity. Stones slid under his heels as he clambered down to the little cove.

It was a scramble. He hadn't thought about that when he suggested the place. Patron Calvary hid his years well. But there was always a man to either side of him. They might have looked like guards. But the real job was to catch their oath-holder if he stumbled.

A sharp wind blew off the sea, making it too cold for him to sit still. The sand was wet from the last high tide. He walked to the bluff of rock that walled in the cove on one side, then back across to the other.

It was said that the Island had been chosen because of its shape. It wasn't exactly a map of Newfoundland, but close enough for every clan to know where to pitch camp. The northwest had been the only problem, being too small to fit all the clans who wanted to make camp there. There'd been arguments at first. But over the years, the placing of their fires had shifted apart and no one seemed to mind any more.

It was the cliffs though that made the Island perfect. There were few ways down to the water. That made it hard to cross to the mainland by any means other than the rock ridge. With the ridge held by the oath-wrights, the Patrons could yield their weapons, knowing others couldn't be smuggled across.

Elias lowered his gaze to the pebbles and marched hard from rock to rock, trying to warm himself. The wind found its way too easily through his thinning cloak. When he stopped to empty a pebble from his boot, his uncovered fingers started to go numb.

When Patron Calvary didn't follow him, Elias had thought it might be a waiting game. He'd be left to freeze in the cove for an hour to remind him of his place outside the family. But when an hour or more had passed, it seemed the Patron would likely not come at all.

He decided to wait until the bright stars that made up the constellation of Cassiopeia had wheeled behind the silhouette of the cliff. But clouds came in and he lost that measure of time.

The waves were growing smaller and the tide was going out. By stages he could get further around the rock buttresses.

Another thought had come to him. If anyone did want him dead – and the heavens knew he'd annoyed enough of them by playing Jago's fool – then this would be a place they could get it done. The beach was scattered with weapons, from spars of driftwood to the rocks themselves. If his body washed up with a staved-in skull, who could say he hadn't been staggering near the edge of the cliff and stepped drunkenly into blackness.

The waves had gone out far enough for him to venture onto the barnacle-crusted rocks. The rough surface gave him a good enough grip to start rounding the headland. If he could get around a little further, he'd be beyond view of anyone coming down to do him harm. He could watch from safety. But the tide wasn't out far enough yet for that.

A scatter of falling stones made him stop mid-movement. Three figures were sliding down the scree towards the beach. Two he might have been able to get past, to scramble back into public view.

If he risked the water, he might be able to wade around into the next cove. But his legs would freeze if he didn't get to a fire quickly after that. He'd rather face three men armed with rocks.

Then the middle figure stumbled and the men on either side grabbed his arms to stop the fall. Elias breathed again. It was Patron Calvary.

First they searched him. Then they tied his wrists behind his back. His cloak went over the top, so his fingers wouldn't freeze. That was a kindness of a sort. Then the two guards climbed back up the scree, out of hearing.

The Patron stepped around him, one slow circle before coming back to stare into his face. He was taller than Elias by a few inches, his back unbowed by age.

"It's piteous to see you like this," Patron Calvary said. "You should have the dignity to know when to give up."

"I don't want to come back."

"Then why the threats?"

"I made none."

"Death within the week, you said."

"A prediction. Not a threat."

"That's a fine distinction, Elias. Foretelling the death of a Patron Protector – that's a dangerous prediction to make. The words of one man become the actions of another. There's so much I could have taught you. But here you are. If you've something to say to me, do it now."

"And then your men will come back to stave in my skull?"

"Is that what you think of me?"

Elias shook his head. "I don't know. But you've trussed me like a fowl for the oven."

Cold saliva was pooling in his mouth. He knew what he had to say, though he couldn't put a finger on the moment when he'd decided. It would change everything, for better or worse. He swallowed.

"Would you like to be the king of Newfoundland?" he asked.

A slap came in response, too weak to sting but it stung nonetheless. Calvary's eyes were daggers. It was as if he resented being forced to strike a bound man.

"Don't even whisper such things!"

"Because you don't want to answer?"

"Newfoundland will never have a king."

"It will have one," Elias said. "I could tell you something now that would stop it happening. But only for a month or a year."

"Lies!"

"The only reason we don't have a king is because we fight our wars with weapons that can never finish the job. But if we couldn't keep out the smugglers – what then? Do you know how I got away when I was outlawed?"

Patron Calvary tilted his head. There was interest there, mixed with disgust. A hatred for the idea. But a desire to know, nonetheless. Perhaps that was why he'd come at all.

"I got away on a vessel that can never be seen or caught. It can come and go as it pleases. The blockade of arms is over. You just don't know it yet."

"Is it a ship made of glass? A ship of the air? Is it a tunnel?" Calvary was leaning forwards. Both their voices had dropped, though the guards would have been too far distant to hear in any case.

"You didn't answer my question," Elias said. "Do you want to be king?"

"No," said the Patron.

"No because you don't want? Or no because you think it's impossible?"

"Is there a difference?"

"Yes. A thousand times yes! There *is* going to be a king. Won't you listen to me? The Patrons will die or they'll submit. And then they might die anyway."

"You've a sickness of the mind," Calvary said.

"If I could make you king, would you want it?"

"No. A thousand times no!"

"Why not?" Elias asked.

"Do you think I was cruel to cut you off, Elias, when they found you cheating? How do you think I felt watching – when they put the pincers to your thumbs? I had no choice. I could lose you or I could take the responsibility, and then others would have died. There would have been war after that."

"I didn't cheat."

"What difference does it make?"

"It makes a difference to me!"

Calvary nodded. For a moment he seemed more a tired old man on a cold seashore than the proud Patron Protector, more the great uncle that Elias had lost.

"A Patron must do terrible things," he said. "A king must do all that a hundredfold. I wouldn't submit to it. Even if it could be done."

"I'm sorry I caused you pain," Elias said.

Calvary bowed his head. "I can't take you back. Though I'd do so in a moment – if it was in my gift."

Elias leaned closer still. "New weapons have come to Newfoundland. More will follow. If you won't be king, then another will."

"Jago?"

"Yes. In his mind he's king already. You must have seen it in the way he carries himself. But if he's crowned, he'll be let loose. You'll never have seen such cruelty. He'll use terror to rule. Everyone who's looked down on him, everyone who's called him upstart – he'll have them in agony. He'll keep them alive to make the humiliation last. I've ridden with him. I know what he'll become."

"He has the means of it?"

Elias nodded. "But I'm offering you the crown."

"And I refuse it."

His great uncle dropped a shoulder, as if about to turn away and walk back towards his men. Elias knelt, his knees digging into the stones of the beach.

"Please. I'm begging you. If I call, or send a message, you must know to answer. You must know what's about to happen."

Patron Calvary shook his head. "You're impudent to say this even though I've told you I don't want to be king."

"I'm saying it *because* you don't want to be king! That's why it has to be you."

The Patron gave a final questioning look. His cloak swirled

out as he wheeled. His men came running down the slope to help him away. They didn't beat Elias to death. Nor did they unbind his hands. It took him another hour to free himself, and cost the skin of his wrists.

CHAPTER 37

From the placing of the first section, the table had gathered onlookers, much to the annoyance of the oath-wrights, who were obliged to keep the track to the rock ridge clear. From time to time, Elizabeth had returned to see more pieces joined. The initial crowd had thinned. But with the placing of the final piece, the rounded end section, they returned in numbers. Some of the watchers sprinted off, carrying the news to their clans. Presently, men and women of the Blood arrived, as if they just happened to be passing.

The crowd became a press. But there was always a small space left around the table. It attracted them. But it repelled them also. As well it might, Elizabeth thought.

Everyone must have been talking about it from the start. The placing of the pieces had been a kind of clock, counting down the hours. Now the thing was complete, they knew something would happen. She could see it in their faces.

She began picking her way back to the tents, to Charity. The turf had been churned up around the path, so she took a wide line, following the cliff edge. Approaching Jago's camp from the seaward side. The hem of her dress was now muddied all the way around, making it heavy. Before, it had seemed a thing of childish colours. But without the means of cleaning, it had become a mockery of grace. Everywhere she went, people turned to look, their lips curling into expressions of disgust. That was the way Jago seemed to like it. The more they looked down on him and the company he kept, the less of a threat he would seem.

All she needed was a pair of trousers and a shirt small enough to fit, and a coat to go with it. She could disguise herself well enough. Then she could escape. If she could take Charity with her, all the better. As for Elias, he was lost somewhere inside himself. The only thing she'd asked him for was a set of clothes. He'd failed to deliver. And the closer he came to his game of chance, the more distant he seemed. It was a sickness of the mind.

Approaching his tent, she coughed loud enough to alert him if he were inside. Drawing level, she whispered his name. But there was no response so she let her feet carry her on beyond and back towards the three big tents next to the feast fire.

Charity sat up as she entered, eyes red from crying. "Where's Elias?"

"Doing something good, I'm sure," Elizabeth said.

"Tell him to go. To save himself."

"You think that'll work with you chained here?"

Charity blinked as if about to cry again. "Bring me a knife," she said.

"You know there are none on the Island."

"Then bring a rope. If I kill myself, he'll be able to go."

"We can do better than that," Elizabeth said.

She felt for the nail hidden in the hem of her cuff and worked it towards the loose stitch and out. Kneeling, she lifted the lock that held Charity's neck iron in place.

It seemed a crude thing, with rough edges at the meeting of its metal plates. "Stay still, now," she whispered, then began probing inside the keyhole with the tip of the nail. The crudeness of finish suggested something easy to pick. A simple ward lock, perhaps. But locks could be as deceptive as people.

Charity turned her head, as if trying to see what was happening. But this only pulled the lock from Elizabeth's hand.

"Stay still!"

Using the edge of the keyhole, Elizabeth bent the nail to make an angle at the end. That gave her a deeper reach into the lock. With this she found the levers that stopped it from opening. They were too stiff to move.

Charity was trembling. "Will it work?"

Elizabeth bent an angle on the other end of the nail. With this as a handle she tried again. The first lever shifted but sprang immediately back.

"Pull the lock away from the collar," she whispered. "Keep up a gentle pressure."

Charity obeyed. Having something to do seemed to calm her, which was a bonus. It also kept her still. Elizabeth found the lever again. This time it worked. As did the second lever. But the final one had jammed.

She sat back and shook her head.

Charity tugged at the lock, rattling the chain. Her tears had started again. Elizabeth could see the iron collar digging into her skin with every pull.

"I'll do it," she said, not knowing how. A real locksmith would manage. And so might she, if she had better tools.

The sound of a footstep outside the tent made her jump back. As the flaps opened she palmed the bent nail. Firehand ducked his head inside. He looked from one of them to the other. There was no emotion in his face. Then Jago's voice called from the distance and he was gone.

Elias watched as the Patron assembled his most trusted men. All were dressed in their finery, as if for a grand feast. But the armour they wore was real enough, for all the jewels and ribbons. It made his own frayed and travel-stained clothes more ridiculous.

"Your day of glory," Jago said.

"Thank you, Patron." He felt no thanks.

"Take off your cloak."

Elias frowned.

"Take it off! Do you not think me a man of my word?"

One of the gatherers stepped up, a bundle of grey and green cloth over his arms.

Then Elias understood. It was another cloak. He took it by the collar, unfurled it to hang full length. In colour it was like his old cloak had been when new. But silver thread ran through the hems. The clasps glinted red. They were as big as blackberries. But not garnets, he thought. Coloured glass. How like Jago. Somehow he didn't want to lose his old cloak, but they took it from him. The new one felt heavy over his shoulders, but warm.

Jago pushed him forwards. "Lead us, Elias No-Thumbs."

So he did, stumbling at first, heading the procession down the hill like a jester on the day of fools.

Men, women and children from other clans ran to watch. By the time he reached the final slope, bodies lined the sides of the track. When his feet slipped on the mud, he heard their intake of breath. The laughter when he didn't fall was a nervous sound. They'd come to see a show, but didn't know if it was to be a comedy or a tragedy of horrors.

Elias glanced back. Whilst Jago was with him, it would be a comedy. The Upstart Patron caught his eye then made a mock bow. Laughter rippled through the press. They'd reached the table, and the main mass of the crowd. Faces looked in from all around. Jago pushed him towards the rounded end, the place of honour, where the largest chair had been set. The whole crowd seemed to be holding its breath. Jago pulled out the chair himself, as if he were merely a servant.

Elias's guts churned as he sat. He could see the faces of Patrons in the crowd but it was their sons who pushed forwards to the front. The spectacle and the insults had worked. Everyone had been magnetised to that spot.

Suddenly fearful, Elias stood and turned. But Jago was still standing directly behind his chair.

"It's time," the Patron said, showing his teeth in a false smile. Then calling out to the crowd he said, "This man of no affinity, this No-Thumbs Shit Smear, will now issue a challenge."

There was hatred in every face. "I will... I... will..." Elias's stuttering words came out hoarse, but a deep quiet had fallen. "...I will play a game of Hazard with Aaron of the Weaverbright clan."

The wall of bodies shifted and through it shouldered Patron Weaverbright himself, followed by Aaron, the man who had called for his thumbs to be cut away with hot pincers.

"My son doesn't need to play against this joke."

"True," said Jago. "You can go back on your word if you want. Is it him who's the coward or you?"

"It's you breaking your word! You said he'd have gold. I see none."

Firehand passed a bundle to Jago, who dropped it on the table. It fell with a heavy chinking crash, the noise of soft metal, the sound that every ear was tuned to, the song of wealth.

"Open it," he said.

Elias did, pulling back the corners of the cloth. Foreign coins and hacked plate rolled out. Silver there was. But most was gold. The front row of the crowd leaned towards it. Further back there were whispers as news spread. Another crowd had gathered on the rise overlooking the table, hundreds straining for a glimpse of the drama. The whole Island must be there.

He saw the oath-wrights among them, men usually aloof.

"He's crooked," Aaron said, loud enough to quiet the whispers.

"Is that what you're afraid of?" Jago asked.

"I'm afraid of nothing! But he's a known cheat."

Elias held up his hands. "Remember these?" He'd found his voice. "You did this to me!" He spat out the words, hatred giving them power. He showed his mutilated hands to the crowd, turning until he faced Aaron again. "Do you think I could fool you with these?"

"You'd try!"

"Well, I'd rather have no thumbs than have no wits!"

The crowd erupted: shouts of outrage, barks of laughter.

Jago purred in his ear, "Very good." Then pushed him down into the seat of honour.

Gems glinted among the gold and silver in the cloth. If he won, Jago would surely take the treasure for himself. If he lost, it'd take more than a lifetime to pay it back.

Patron Weaverbright was shouting. A hush fell, moving from the table outwards. The crowd gathered on the rise were the last to know that something was happening.

"This is foolery! You can't put an idiot to play with such a treasure."

"Don't you have the wealth to match it?" Elias asked, saying what Jago would surely have said. Oh, but the task was gripping him now. He would do it. He would bring them low. And if the bomb had been rigged to go while he was sitting there, at least they would die, Charity would be free and his own torment would be over.

Jago's hand still gripped his shoulder.

Weaverbright and his chief councillor had their heads together in a whispered consultation, hands cupped around mouths so no one would be able to read the words on their lips.

"We will play," Weaverbright said at last, pushing his son Aaron towards the seat next to Elias.

"Show the colour of your metal," Elias said, loud enough for all to hear.

Weaverbright's councillor upended a purse on the table in front of Aaron, spilling a pile of Spanish gold coins and silver American dollars. More than the life's earnings of a peasant. But nothing compared to the cloth bundle in front of Elias.

"He'll start with that," Patron Weaverbright said. "More will come."

"We don't gamble on promises," Jago jeered.

"More will come!"

The chair on the other side from Elias pulled back and another purse dropped onto the table. Another Patron's son. "I'm in," he said. The men and women behind him clapped.

Then more were sitting, young men of the Blood from different clans. One against one, his chances had been even. If the dice were fair. But each new player shaved another slice from his odds. Many had been part of his outlawing. But he'd fixed his thoughts of revenge on Aaron Weaverbright. Now they all faced him, ganged together. The table filled.

Men were pushing through to the front of the crowd, tallest among them, his great uncle, Patron Calvary. On reaching the front, he asked, "Who is to assay the bets?"

It was a good question. With no king or government, Newfoundland could have no currency of its own. Thus each bet would need to be appraised, whether it were a love poem or an egg or a gem the size of an egg. In the usual way of things, the balance of wagers could be agreed by the players themselves. But with the highest stakes, an assayer was needed. Chunks of hack silver could be weighed against each other in a hand balance. But it took skill to judge a gem against a pile of gold and silver coins.

"You do it," Jago said to Calvary.

"He's the man's uncle!" Weaverbright growled.

"Then you and he do it together."

There were nods from the councillors.

Elias reached inside his new cloak to his belt pocket. His hand closed around the dice he'd carved at the Salt Ray Inn. That seemed like years ago. He'd taught himself to tell them apart by touch. The weighted one bore a scratch, invisible, though he could feel it. He let that one lie, for the time being.

"I am no cheat," he said, his voice level. "I played fair in that card game."

"Liar," Aaron rumbled.

"It's passed," said Patron Calvary. "Let it go."

Elias selected a handful of silver dollars from the bundle in front of him and pushed them forwards. Then he slapped down his two fair dice.

The other players had coins to match. There would be no need for the assayers on the first bet. Metal sang the song of wealth as coins fell and rolled. Elias took up the dice again and stood.

He would beat them. He would bleed the money from them. And then he'd do as his great uncle had said. He would finally let it go. It would never be revenge enough. But later they would die from Jago's bomb. Then he would rest.

He kissed his clenched knuckles and drew back his hand to cast. But Aaron shouted, "No! I won't play with his dice."

Patron Calvary and Patron Weaverbright nodded to each other. It was Calvary who delivered the verdict: "Elias chose the game. Aaron may demand his own dice be used."

Aaron smiled then, slow and gloating. Elias's heart began to jump. He felt the pain across his chest. His hand dropped, seeking out the glass pot from his pocket. The urge to feel that chemical buzz was almost unbearable.

His enemy stood and held up a small bag of dark velvet. Turning for all to see, he eased back the drawstring and emptied the contents onto his upturned palm. Two dice. But not cubes. These were long dice, cut in the shape of six-sided prisms. He cast them onto the table so they rolled and tumbled towards Elias. Elias found himself reading the numbers carved into the upturned faces. A six and a three. It seemed important for some reason.

Hand shaking, he gathered them up. They were bone dice, like his own. But carved from thin, delicate pieces rather than the leg joint of an ox.

He couldn't speak. Somehow he knew what was coming.

"Do you know them?" Aaron asked. "You should do. They're your own two thumbs."

The lock holding the iron collar in place would not yield. Each time Elizabeth tried to pick it, she got two of the three levers inside to move. The third always jammed. An angry red line on Charity's neck marked the place where rough metal had dragged against her skin.

"One more time," Elizabeth breathed.

But Charity held up a hand to stop her. "Where have the people gone?"

Elizabeth listened. She could hear the whispered boom of waves and the distant cry of a gull. But no voices. She peered outside. There were no people in sight.

"Wait," she said, then set off towards the top of the next rise, which gave a view of four clan encampments. Nothing was moving but a few tethered horses, the turn of an ear, the swish of a tail.

Elias's game of chance was the only answer. But needing to be sure she ran as fast as the stupid dress would allow, down the slope then up another, slowing as she approached the top. Peering towards the rock ridge she saw the massed crowd around the table, like a swarm of ants around a bowl of sugar.

Catching her breath, she took one last turn, scanning the

Island. Everyone was there. If the bomb went off, hundreds would be slaughtered. The most powerful men and women, the oath-holders: all stood near the centre. And the oath-wrights, who'd left their usual places and come to watch. Their robes gave them away.

It was surely the moment that Jago had planned.

She ran. Not back to the tent, but towards the cove that Elias had pointed out to her. At the lip of the cliff she looked down on a scree slope of little stones. But there were bigger rocks on the beach below. She launched herself over the edge, digging in her heels as she slid with the scree tumbling around her. The first rock she tried on the beach was too heavy to lift. The second seemed too small to do the job. It needed to be hard as well. She found what she was looking for in a rounded lump of white quartz. Lifting it two-handed, she struggled back up the scree. For every step she put in she slid back half a step. With a mighty effort she scrambled up the final few feet and cast her burden onto the turf, crawling up after it, exhausted.

There was no time to catch her breath. The watch she'd found hidden in the underside of the table would be ticking, the hands moving towards the alarm. She lifted the stone again and set off towards the tent. If she was right, Jago would soon leave the table with his men. He might come back to the camp. In which case, they'd be found. More likely he'd cross the rock ridge to be near the stored weapons when the explosion hit. Then he'd head back onto the Island, armed, to slaughter the survivors or demand their surrender and their allegiance.

He may have promised to free Charity, but he never would. The fact that Elias had loved her would make her an amusing plaything. And she, Elizabeth, would be condemned to a life of servitude.

She half-collapsed in through the tent flaps, the lump of

quartz rolling to a stop next to the iron spike in the ground. For a moment she couldn't speak to answer the flood of questions. But when her breath calmed, she said, "Stretch the chain..."

Charity understood. She positioned one link over the head of the spike and pulled back her hands, far enough for safety. All they needed was to break that one link. Elizabeth lifted the lump of quartz, took aim and brought it down hard. The sharp noise of it left her ears ringing. The chain had jumped free with the impact. The spike had sunk further into the ground.

Charity held up the link for her to see. It had been dented. She placed it back on top of the spike. Elizabeth lifted the rock again and sent it down on target, letting go at the last moment. A harder impact than the first. A louder noise. Any man standing within a hundred yards would have heard it. But the chain remained whole.

Charity was crying. The link seemed no closer to breaking than before. Less of the iron spike remained above the ground.

"It's sinking in each time," Elizabeth said. "That's cushioning the blow."

"Then what can we do?"

"Pray the end hits something solid down there before we drive it all the way in."

She stood to her full height and raised the rock above her head so that it pressed into the canvas of the tent ridge. Summoning all her strength she brought it down. The rock shattered. Charity fell back. The top of the spike had buckled over. And there, among the white fragments of rock, lay a single iron link, broken and twisted.

Charity stood, a length of chain hanging loose from her neck. A trickle of blood ran down one of her cheeks. A flying shard perhaps. But not a deep cut.

They looked at each other, blinking. Elizabeth was the first to speak.

"Elias – I've got to let him know."

But Charity shook her head. "I should just slip away. He'll find out soon enough. When he's done with his dice game."

Elizabeth took her hand. "You're wrong. We have to tell him somehow. I've no time to explain. But there's going to be an explosion. If he doesn't leave that table, he's going to die. I'm sure of it."

Charity's face fell to horror.

"I'll warn him," Elizabeth said. "You search the other tents. Find clothes. Men's clothes. Anything small enough to fit us. Hats – to hide our hair. As drab as you can find. And a cloth to wind around your neck to hide the irons."

Not waiting for an answer, she ducked out of the tent, gathered up her skirts as best she could and ran back in the direction of the rock ridge.

CHAPTER 38

Elias picked up the long dice. A sweat had broken out all over his body when he saw them. Now, holding them, they seemed to itch, as if they were still attached to him by sinew and flesh. He had to breathe hard to stop himself from throwing up.

Aaron Weaverbright would die. At that moment, Elias had no other wish. Not for gold, not for Elizabeth, not for his own life. Not even for Charity. All his hatred of the man and the misery that he'd suffered came crashing back. Aaron Weaverbright would die. And it wasn't enough for the bomb to take him unawares. He had to know of his own defeat. He had to see death coming. He had to feel regret.

He shook the dice in his cupped hand, meeting Aaron's eyes directly. A hush had fallen.

"Choose your main," said Aaron.

"Eight!" said Elias, then cast the bones down the table. They bounced and clattered and spun and came to rest beyond the range of his reading. Hands reached out to take them.

"Cease!" bellowed Patron Calvary.

The hands withdrew.

Patron Weaverbright pushed through the crowd until he could lean over the dice. "A two and a one," he said. "Three. That's an out."

It took only a moment for Elias's wagered silver to be

scooped away. He watched as they divided it. Aaron leered.

Someone took his hand and placed the dice on his palm. He pushed forward a pile of gold coins. The other players matched the bet.

"Eight," he said, choosing the same main for luck.

This time he threw seven, which became his chance on another throw, but that he lost. By the end of his turn he was down a small fortune.

The dice moved on, scooped from the table by the next caster. Elias flinched at the imagined touch on his thumbs. The noise and stink of people pressed closer around him. If he'd had a sword in his hand, he would have known what to do. His training could have taken over. He could have laid into Aaron's sneering face and suffered the punishment for murder. That would have been a good death. If he'd had his own dice to play with, the sleight of hand he'd practised would have tipped the odds and let him beat them, just as they'd cheated him before.

The dice spun and danced. Some of the other casters won and some lost. Treasure shifted from man to man. But not much. They were saving their big bets for him. Around the table the dice moved. For each throw, he put down a few coins, taking a share of the other men's losses. But it was only a trickle.

Then Aaron's turn came to cast. "Seven!" he shouted.

Elias picked a large sapphire from his pile and pushed it forwards. A whisper passed through the crowd. Patron Weaverbright took the gem and held it close to his eye. "It's flawed," he said. "The value is three ounces of gold."

Everyone must have known that was too low. But Patron Calvary nodded it through. Aaron counted out twelve gold coins. He took the dice, spat on them, shook them in his fist then set them to fly. They spun and stopped in front of Elias. A six and a one.

Aaron took the gemstone between his finger and thumb and licked it. No man should have such a run of luck. He lost on the next throw but the bet was small.

His eyes were still laughing when his turn was over. He scooped up the dice, shaking them in his closed fist as if about to cast again. Then he held them out on his upturned palm. Elias hated him for the touch of skin as he took them for his own throw.

"Seven," he said, trying to breathe confidence into his voice, feeling weak for choosing the same main as his enemy.

Gold and silver went down around the table. Patron Calvary pronounced twenty-three ounces of gold would be required to match the bet.

"Unless you're a coward," Aaron hissed, too quiet for the Patrons to hear.

Elias felt a shift in the press of bodies. Looking around, he saw a flash of bright pink in the crowd. Elizabeth was pushing through in that bloody dress that Jago made her wear. His goading and insults had stirred the Island up into a fever of plot and rumour. Elizabeth had been part of that show. They stepped back from her now, letting her through.

Her arrival had to be Jago's doing. He must be moving his puppets to make the greatest drama. Elias glanced around further, looking for the Patron. A wall of faces stared back at him. The pain in his chest turned to a spike of ice. He fumbled for the green glass pot.

Jago had slipped away.

An extraordinary clarity comes with the proximity of death. Elizabeth took in the scene: men leaning over the table, the baying, the stink of hatred and excitement. Jago had gone. She'd expected it. But it was still somehow a revelation. In that moment she felt as if she could almost see through the timbers of the table to the hidden cavities filled with glycer-fortis, and hear the clockwork ticking away the seconds of life.

On her approach, she'd been watching the man who sat next to Elias. He'd dipped his hand under the table. There'd been a shift in his tension as he brought it back into view. There was a slight cupping of the down-facing palm.

Elias looked back and saw her. He seemed to be struggling to breathe. She pushed closer, put her lips to his ear and shielded her mouth with her hands.

"Charity is free."

Elias didn't move or speak.

"She's free. You can go. Tell them you're giving up."

He seemed frozen. There was something in his eyes that was not Elias. Something fey and bitter, as if the man she'd come to know had been hollowed out.

He grimaced as he took the dice, as if they were made of hot metal. Still he held them. His knuckles had grown white.

She pressed her mouth to his ear again. "They'll all be dead in a few moments. You either come with me or you die here too!"

"I can't."

In her mind, the clockwork ticked. It could go any second. "Know this," she whispered. "The man sitting next to you is cheating. He's got another die in the crease of his palm."

Turning, she stepped away from the table. The crowd jostled each other to back off, as if the touch of her skirts might contaminate them. She didn't look back, but all her focus was behind her, yearning to hear a movement that would mean Elias had chosen to follow.

There was none.

Everyone on the rise was standing. They'd been seated when she arrived. Their whispers stopped as she approached, surrounding her in a circle of silence. Her footsteps in the mud sounded unnaturally loud.

Elias might have helped her to escape. Or he might not. But he had chosen to die. She felt sick. Even with all his lies and plots, he was a good man. If only he could have seen it for himself, he might have let go of the bitterness. He might have lived.

Jago's camp came into view ahead. She would have to tell Charity, somehow. But not until they were off the Island. To save one of them would be a kind of victory. Stepping to the tent, she tried a smile, but knew it wasn't working. So she turned her mind to all things practical. Charity's eyes were bright with excitement or fear.

"I thought you were one of them," she said.

She was dressed in a man's hose and doublet, both a drab russet. The boots were her own, however. The rosy leather and the cut of them, distinctly feminine. The heels were too high. That might be a problem if they had to scramble over the rocks by the sea.

"I couldn't find anything else to fit," she said, following Elizabeth's eyes.

"No matter. It'll be dusk soon. And no one's going to be looking down. Just step in the mud when you have a chance. We've plenty of that."

A heap of clothes had been dumped in the middle of the tent. "I didn't know what to get. I stole a bit of everything."

Elizabeth knelt and began searching for garments small enough to fit.

"Where's Elias?" Charity asked, a tremor in her voice.

"He should meet us when we get to the mainland."

"I thought he'd show us the way."

"He's told me how to get there."

Elizabeth kept her gaze fixed on the clothes. Nothing was right, as if the woman had judged what to bring by her own stout build.

A pair of moss-green canvas breeches were the best of a

bad job. They would reach halfway down her calves, but at least she wouldn't be tripping. A top was easier. There were several shirts that would do. They'd be long and baggy. All the better to hide her figure. She found a plaited rope belt that might be looped round her waist a couple of times.

She laid them out and began to undo the hooks and eyes of the cerise dress.

Charity turned her head, as if hearing a noise. Elizabeth froze. Then the tent flaps ripped open behind her. She twisted to look and jumped away in the same moment. Firehand lunged inside. She dived into a roll, trying to pass under his arm, but the wide skirts collapsed down over her face like a fishing net. One of the tent poles snapped with a sharp crack. She struggled free to see him stooped under the sagging apex. Charity was backed up as far as she could get from him. He rushed her. But his foot caught against the bent top of the iron spike and he stumbled. One missed step. It was enough for Elizabeth to get back to her feet. Grabbing Charity's hand she ran headlong into the wall of canvas, pushing through, bringing the tent down behind them.

They were sprinting. In a snatched back glance she saw him stoop to pull a club-like spar from the pile of firewood, then he was thundering after them. Charity couldn't keep up. Her heels were sinking into the soft turf.

They'd had forty yards on him at the start. Now it was fifteen. He'd have them in seconds. But she would choose the place of it. Dragging Charity by the hand, she veered off towards the cliff edge, out towards the point of a headland. At the brink, she turned to face him. Now that he had them cornered, Firehand slowed to a walk. He smiled as he swished the air with the club.

She'd hoped for a sheer edge behind, something to stop him charging directly at them. But the land sloped away instead, steepening towards a drop. Inching back, she pulled

Charity with her, feeling the angle of the ground under her feet. If they started to slide, there'd be no way to stop.

"Fight," he growled.

"We shan't."

"I caught you running. Now I can kill you." He swung the club, forcing them back again.

"Why?"

"For honour."

"But we give up!"

"You think you can poke your knife at my back and then take the coward's road when things go bad?"

The storeroom of the inn flashed in Elizabeth's mind. "I didn't mean anything by it. I just wanted to escape."

He held up the stub of his left arm. "You know what this means? I was bound to a Patron who wouldn't go to war. I gave this arm to cut that oath! You think I won't fight you now that I can?"

Another swing, another inch, the slope almost too steep to stand on, earth crumbling under her feet.

"Fight me. Die with honour. For die you must. All I am is to fight!"

The faces around the table were a wall, and every eye focused on Elias. All stared poison. He needed a dose of his own poison to slow his heart. His breath was coming fast and shallow, the air stale from so many mouths. He gripped the table edge, steadying himself against a lurch of vertigo.

Elizabeth's words seemed to have come from a dream. The man next to him was cheating. Aaron Weaverbright loomed close.

"Throw the bones, you fucking coward!"

More than anything else, Elias wanted the man to die. He wanted him beaten. He wanted all the wrongs he'd suffered to be done against the Patrons who had plotted his downfall.

Not just those wrongs, but a thousand more. He wanted to see them in agony and their children and all those they loved and the things they cared for brought to ruin.

He squeezed his palm tighter, making the hard edges of the dice bite into his skin. He needed to think. He needed to breathe. His great uncle was at the far end of the table, staring with everyone else.

"The coward won't play," Aaron jeered, then pushed the whole pile of his treasure into the middle of the table. Coins rolled and settled. "I'm all in."

Others followed his lead, pushing their silver and gold towards him.

"Do you agree?" Patron Weaverbright demanded.

Elias found himself nodding.

Hands other than his own pushed Jago's hoard towards the other bets.

He might win. One more throw of the dice and his agony would be over. But not if they were cheating him again. He opened his hand to see the long dice. He took one of them and held it against the scar where his thumb had been severed. It was the right size. If only he could think straight. Elizabeth had said Aaron cheated, that he'd another die palmed.

He could call the man out.

"They're better use as my dice than ever they were as your thumbs!"

Aaron's words stirred and stopped his thoughts again.

"Water!" he called. "Someone bring me water."

The shout went back through the crowd. "Bring him water. He wants water."

"Coward!" Aaron hissed the word under his breath.

Every time he was close to knowing what to do, the man goaded him again. He could feel it blinding him. But he couldn't break the grip of it. He closed his eyes and saw an image of blood and flesh rent by blows from his own sword.

Breathing fast, he tried to picture something else. New Whitby under the sun. The waves rolling in. Charity's house. Her face.

His breathing slowed.

He could call Aaron a cheat, have him searched, perhaps. Within the table, the clockwork was counting off seconds. If the man were humiliated, and then the bomb went off, it would be a kind of victory.

Behind closed eyelids, he imagined Charity's face again. That crooked nose. Those full lips. She smiled at him. He saw her eyes as they were when she looked into his. And in that moment he saw himself as she must see him.

"The coward's crying!" Aaron shouted.

He knew what he had to do. He would die anyway. So would they all, in their time. It felt as if a great boulder was being lifted from his chest.

"Water," someone said.

He opened his eyes. A beaker was held out towards him.

"There's a bomb," he said, his voice becoming louder as his certainty grew. "Within this table, there is a bomb. You all need to go."

Aaron was laughing. Others followed his lead. A wave of mirth spread back into the crowd. Even people who couldn't have heard what he said were laughing.

"The bet is taken," Patron Weaverbright said. "You can't back out."

"There is a bomb!" Elias shouted this time. "Leave the table, or you'll die!"

His great uncle was looking directly at him, alert.

Aaron shoved him in the shoulder, hard enough to make him stagger. "A liar and a coward!"

But Patron Calvary was gesturing to his men, jabbing a finger away from the table, pushing back through the crowd.

"You disgrace yourself," Patron Weaverbright said. "If you

walk from this table, you forfeit your entire treasure."

"Then that's what I do. I give up. You win. But please leave this place or you'll die!"

They were still laughing further back. But for the first time, there was doubt in Aaron's face. He looked to his father.

And there was music. Somewhere. The small, beautiful chime of a watch. A nursery tune.

He shouted, "Run!" Then he was running, himself. Or trying to, for the crowd jostled him as he barged through. They laughed, they jeered, they thumped him on the shoulder.

"Run!"

He screamed at them. He shoulder barged his way through. He wouldn't make the distance in time. There was a rocky outcrop just ahead. A man and two women had perched themselves on top of it for a better view, holding on to each other to keep from falling off.

He dived down behind it and lay flat. They were staring at him, jeering that he was a coward. Then the air turned white and the people were flung away like rag dolls. He never heard the sound.

On the edge of the cliff, Firehand swung the wooden spar. Elizabeth pulled back her head. This time, she felt the waft of air moving against her face. He took another step towards them and pulled his one arm back for the final blow. His feet were on the slope, but not the steepest part. The thin soil kept slipping under her boots.

She must have edged back again because suddenly her feet went from under her. Only Charity's grip stopped her going over the edge. She dropped to one knee as the wooden spar hummed over her head. Clinging to the scrubby grass she hauled herself up towards his feet. If she could catch his ankle, she might pull him off balance.

She lunged up the slope, but the soil under her knee slid

back and she landed short. He raised his club to bring down on her.

Then all the seagulls took off in the same moment. She felt a touch on her face, light as a feather. Firehand must have felt it too. The club lowered. He glanced over his shoulder. Then came the sound: like a thunderclap but many times more powerful. The first wave of it hit and then the echoes, which came rolling back from the cliffs and hills of the mainland.

Releasing Charity's hand, she dived forwards again, under the club that wavered in the air. The damn skirts tangled her legs. She fell, her chin jarring against the ground. Then she was up. Charity had rounded him on the other side. He swung the club. Elizabeth ducked under it. But it was Charity who charged into him, her shoulder crashing against his ribs. He stumbled back, onto the steeper slope, flailing his one arm. The club fell over the edge. Elizabeth ran at him. His feet were sliding down the steepening slope as she hit his chest. His windmilling arm caught her dress. He was falling, but she was being dragged. Charity grabbed at her. They locked hands. The mud-stained fabric of the dress began to rip. And then Firehand was toppling over the edge, a strip of bright satin trailing behind.

CHAPTER 39

The air had turned white. Then there was blackness and a whistling sound, growing louder. He opened his eyes. No, that was wrong. They had been open all the while. The people who'd been looking down at him were gone. He remembered the blur of them being ripped away by the explosion.

The whistle in his ears had grown to a high-pitched scream. He was looking at the sky, though it seemed he'd been lying on his side before. He must have been flipped over. He didn't know how long he'd been lying there.

He turned his head and saw a severed arm beside him.

He sat, pushed himself into a squat then stood. The ground seemed to tilt like the deck of a ship. He turned, stumbled, saw that he'd been facing away from the blast and not towards it. But the landscape made no sense. Dust was still falling. Through it, he made out a great rocky circle, a crater, he supposed, and then a cliff edge and beyond it, a void until the cliffs of the mainland loomed up further away than they should have been.

The table had been standing there. And hundreds of people, the highborn, the oath-holders, the oath-wrights. All were gone. He understood that. But the rock ridge was gone also and that seemed somehow harder to grasp.

In a flash of panic he reached for his pocket and found the

glass pot still whole. Then he was laughing, unable to stop, and crying at the same time.

He'd not been meant to live. Nor would he. Even if he got off the Island, the small lump of glycer-fortis would keep him only for a few days. He'd betrayed Jago. He'd betrayed the smugglers. He'd betrayed the dark power in the west that had plotted it all. There was no way back. When that small bead of poisonous medicine was gone, his heart would seize up in his chest. And yet he felt cut free.

His feet took him around the rim of the crater, limping, for the calf of his left leg was somehow numb. The path ended. He looked down the newly formed cliff and saw two men scrambling away, as if racing each other. At the bottom the waves churned over piles of freshly broken rock. The ridge had collapsed to the left. The Island had become a real island. More men were clambering up the cliff on the other side.

It came to him that time must be flowing more slowly than it should. Or perhaps he was thinking faster. Either way, the dust hadn't cleared enough for him to see what was happening at the round towers. From the distance, he heard the clash of metal on metal.

The two men had reached the bottom of the cliff and were scrambling across the shallows. One picked up a rock and hurled it at the other, catching him on the back of the head, flooring him. There was blood. A wave washed over the body.

Suddenly the world was moving again at normal speed. He heard a scream from the direction of the round towers. The weapons. They were trying to get to the store of weapons.

A movement in the corner of his eye made him duck. A man swinging a knotted rope, catching him on the shoulder with the weight of a punch. He fell. The rope whipped back and swung again. Elias jabbed his elbow at the attacker's knee. The man folded.

Grabbing the rope, Elias scrambled over the edge and

started down the cliff. He had to get hold of a real weapon. Something to defend himself. And Charity. If she'd survived.

The numbness in his leg had turned to a throbbing pain. He didn't want to look. The long bones couldn't have been broken or he wouldn't have been able to climb down at all. That was enough for now.

Halfway across the rubble at the bottom, a wave surged up, tugging at him as it pulled back. He looked down and saw the white foam stained pink. Then he was at the other cliff and climbing.

The jabs of pain were sharper with each step. The rush of men scrambling to cross seemed to be over. There would be others on the Island still alive who'd run in the opposite direction. And what of the Calvary clan? His great uncle had ordered them away. But unless they'd gone far enough, they'd be lying among the corpses. Or they could have crossed the rock ridge and be waiting above to cut down anyone who tried to climb. If so, he was about to find out.

The rock was smoother near the top. He'd run out of handholds. Crouching lower for a moment, he jumped, launching himself upwards to catch a jutting rock that had been just out of reach. He dangled, feet scrabbling, until one found a crevice big enough to wedge in. Then he was clambering the last few feet and over the lip, clawing the turf, hauling himself onto the grass.

No sword ran him through. No words were called. Lying flat out, but with his arms braced, ready to leap, he surveyed the ground ahead. Bodies lay around the two storehouses. Up on the ridge, the shantytown of camp followers seemed like a nest of ants, stirred up with a stick. Riders were leaving at speed, ox carts followed. Tents were coming down. Some seemed to have abandoned their possessions and were running over the rise of the hill and out of sight.

Elias stood. Only now, he realised that the bodies of oath-wrights lay among the dead. He could see no blood on them, but a bruise circled the neck of the nearest corpse. He reached down and turned the head, feeling the vibration of broken bones grinding against each other.

Uncoiling the rope from his shoulder, he began to circle the nearest of the stone towers. The doorway came into view. A hole had been punched through the middle of the iron door, the jagged ends bent inwards. Whoever had killed the oathwrights would surely be inside.

Elizabeth stood frozen, watching the huge dust cloud rolling across the turf. Then figures emerged, running towards the camps, as if they'd find sanctuary anywhere in a world that had just been turned upside down. Most were women or children. The few men among them were low status servants who'd not been able to get close to the dice game.

Firehand had ripped half the dress away from her. But for the first time since she'd set out from New Whitby, no one was looking.

Charity ran, reaching the collapsed tent ahead of her, burrowing under the canvas, hauling out the clothes.

The wounded men and women were passing now, limping, bleeding. One crawled, dragging a leg behind. Elizabeth tore off the remains of the dress and pulled on the breeches.

"Hats!" she ordered. By the time Charity was back from under the canvas, she'd pulled on a couple of loose shirts and had the belt tied. The hats were billycocks, one brown, one black. The brims were too narrow to hide their faces but it would do.

Charity drew in a gulp of air and pointed. A man stumbled over the rise cradling the mangled remains of a girl in his arms, his face blank. He seemed to be sleepwalking.

Charity cast her eyes around. "Where is Elias?"

"We'll find him later."

"You said he was safe."

"He is," said Elizabeth, knowing he would be dead.

She took Charity's hand and set off against the tide of wounded. Walking then running, not breaking step when they crested the rise and saw the crater and the bodies. The worst of the wounded were here. Crawling or dragging themselves or simply lying and waiting to die.

"Don't look!" she shouted as Charity began to lag behind.

Then they were at the crater, with the new cliff ahead of them. In one place the remnants of the ridge made a shallower downward slope. More a scramble than a climb.

"Here," she called.

Charity shook her head. "I can't do it. The drop's too big."

"Then close your eyes. I'll place your feet and hands. But do it now! For Elias."

Her stomach churned. She told herself it was true, in a way. Elias might be dead, but he would want her to escape.

Charity sat, her feet over the edge.

"Now turn around. We're going to make it. Just think of him."

One of Elias's ears seemed blocked. A punctured eardrum, he thought. He could hear some real sounds, but mostly it was just a whining in his head. Standing to one side of the storehouse door, he felt the edge of the ripped metal. It had been punched through, jagged as a blade. It was only glycerfortis that could have done it. That meant it had to be Jago.

If Elias stepped through, he'd block out the daylight. He'd be seen, but he'd not see them. Nor would he be able to see any of the weapons.

"I am a dead man," he said, mouthing the words, touching the truth of them.

Then he stepped through the jagged mouth and immediately to the side, out of the light, expecting the cut of a sword in any case, but not wanting to make it easy. No hearing. No sight. Helpless as a newborn. Waiting for the killing blow.

His eyes began to adjust. Surfaces and edges loomed from blackness. Only oath-wrights had ever been permitted inside the stone towers. He'd somehow imagined there'd be a single space of great height with shelves and ladders reaching up. But from the black, he began to make out a low ceiling supported by beams and an empty circular space. The only feature was a recess opposite, the entrance to a staircase built into the thickness of the wall. He began to climb, placing his feet on the worn steps, deaf to any sound he might be making. Halfway around the first turn, he caught the glow of a light shining down from above. Yellow light. A candle or an oil lamp.

In this light he saw the body of another oath-wright sprawled over the stairs, head low, feet high, shoulder hard against the outer wall. No blood. Head twisted around at an unnatural angle.

Elias patted down the robes, searching for a weapon, finding nothing. He stepped over the body, holding the knotted rope, ready to swing it. An entrance came into view and a room beyond. A round table stood in the centre and shelves lined the walls. There was a ladder on wheels, like in a library. By the glow of the lamplight he saw sword hilts where books might have been. A ledger lay open on the table. He stepped towards it, out of the shadow of the stairs.

The light flickered at the edge of his vision. A blow caught him on the back of his shoulder, a sudden weight crushing him down. He fell. Someone was on his back. A pain like hot metal bit into his body. It seemed a knife stab. He rolled, throwing his attacker's balance. Not a knife. A fist.

Jago reached down and grabbed his hair. Elias felt his head being pulled up from the flagstones. Then slammed back down.

• • •

He became aware of nausea and voices swimming above him, a clatter of metal. Each sound was like a blow to his head. He opened his eyes to see roof beams and the underside of a table.

Logan stepped over him, arms laden with muskets. They crashed onto the table top. Elias winced.

"He's awake," Logan shouted.

Everything hurt. His head. His back where it touched the floor. Logan's boot, jabbing him in the thigh.

Jago's face came close. It seemed upside down. "What did you do? What. Did. You. Do?"

Elias tried to ask what he meant but at first only breath came from his mouth.

"At the dice game. Why did Calvary leave?"

"You… You left."

"That's not an answer."

"Shorry, Patron."

Jago moved too swiftly for Elias to react. An open-handed blow to the cheek. Lights flashed inside his head.

"I'm the King of Newfoundland. Say it."

"You…"

"Say it!"

"You're King. Of Newfoundland."

"Why did Calvary run?"

"I told him."

"Did his men go with him?"

Elias found himself nodding. Jago stood to his full height then brought down a fist. The blow landed in Elias's gut. He curled on his side, trying to breathe.

"They'll be coming," Jago said. "Pick them off the cliffs as they climb down. Shoot anyone who tries to get off the Island."

Logan bowed. "Yes, sire." He gathered up an armful of guns and powder, then left, staggering under its weight.

Elias lay still, eyes open, listening to the whisper and click of the tamping rod as Jago slid bullets into musket after musket. The Calvary clan would be unarmed.

"Where are your men?" Elias asked, not expecting an answer.

The rhythm of Jago's work didn't change. "Some dead. Some I don't know. It doesn't matter. I've an army on the way."

"You killed your own people?" Even as Elias said it, he understood the cold logic. Jago had slipped away. If his men had gone too, the other Patrons would have smelled danger.

"That woman of yours," Jago said. "I'll think of something interesting for her. And everyone you've ever loved. But you – for your betrayal, I'm going to cut off your arms and your legs and I'm going to keep you alive. I'll cut off your tongue. Your ears. Your nose." The words came flat, as if describing some mundane plan.

The rope lay on the flagstones near the stairway. They must have kicked it away from him. Jago tapped gunpowder from a horn into another pan then brought down the cover and picked up the next musket. As a king he would bring such terror as had never been seen, even in the lawless land.

Elias rolled onto his back, bringing his arm closer to the heavy rope. Jago had summoned all his ambition and cruelty into this one act of slaughter. But he had a weakness. He wanted to live. Elias had no such vice. He hoped for death. He longed for it. He rolled again, onto his other side.

"Trying to crawl away on your belly?"

"No," Elias said. "No, Patron."

Businesslike, Jago stepped from the table. "Who am I?"

"An upstart Patron."

"King. Of. Newfoundland." With each word a kick landed on Elias's back.

He rolled again, as if trying to get away from the blows.

The end of the rope lay inches from his face. As Jago's boots scuffed away, Elias took the rope in his thumbless grip. If he stood, the man would knock him down. So he rolled back to face the table. Summoning all his strength, he swung his arm forwards. The rope whipped over the floor, snapping around Jago's ankle. Then he spun his body away, the rope pulled tight. Jago crashed to the ground.

Elias heaved his body over again, tangling himself in the rope, but dragging the Patron, keeping him from the balance he'd need to stand. Jago was trying to kick free. One more pull. Elias braced his free arm over the topmost step of the spiral stairs.

Jago roared in anger. Elias launched himself down the stairs head first. The rope brought him to a wrenching stop. Jago had grabbed hold of the edge of the doorway. But Elias was standing now, the rope wrapped around his shoulders.

He dived again into the void. The rope gave. He fell head-first, knowing he'd break his neck. Welcoming it. But the first impact was soft. His feet arced over his head and crashed down. He'd landed on the dead oath-wright.

Jago shouted again. But this time a bark of pain. Worming free of the rope, Elias clambered back up the stairs. The upstart king lay cradling his right arm. Even in the shadowed stairway, Elias could see the spar of broken bone jutting from the sleeve. He put his foot down on Jago's chest, pinning both arms. Then he looped the rope around the neck and twisted it tight.

Jago stared up at him. They were still the eyes of a king, outraged at such rebellion. Then they were frightened. Elias twisted the rope again. The eyes became unfocused. They flickered. Elias pressed down with all his weight, emptying the lungs. He pulled the twist tighter and tighter until there was no possibility of life remaining.

Through the receding whistle in his damaged ears, he

heard the sound of a gunshot. Then another. And another. He let go of the rope and ran.

Elizabeth and Charity had been halfway across the wave-washed remains of the rock ridge when Logan appeared above them and took aim. They rushed forwards, coming in tight under the cliff, kneeling low, keeping a buttress of rock between themselves and the mouth of his gun.

A wave rolled in, sluicing the tumble of rocks. Elizabeth gasped at the shock of the icy water rushing up to her chest. Bobbing her head out from the cliff, she caught a glimpse of him looking down. She was back against the rocks before he could aim. Another wave washed over them.

"We'll freeze to death," she said.

Charity pointed down the cliff line. "You can climb up there."

"He'll see me."

"I'll keep him looking this way."

"But *you'll* freeze," Elizabeth said.

Charity looked her in the eyes. "That bomb… I know you told me he's safe. I don't blame you for lying. But he was at that table."

Elizabeth took her hand. "Come with me. If we get beyond the next headland, he won't be able to see us at all."

"We'd freeze," Charity said. "But without me you might do it. The thing is, if it happens that I die, I shouldn't much mind."

Elizabeth's fingers were growing numb. Much longer and she wouldn't be able to climb at all. "I'll come back," she said, then waded off through the surge of another wave, feeling it push her and then pull as it drew away. A shot echoed off the cliffs. She looked back and saw Charity ducking her head back in close to the rocks. The water deepened with each step. The foam of the next wave reached her shoulders.

Her feet slid on the submerged rocks as it crashed into her. She might still be in Logan's view, but any further and the sea would have her.

Weed covered the rocks. But the barnacles were sharp enough to give grip. She could no longer feel how hard she was holding onto them. Three footholds up and she was clear of the water. The weight of sodden clothing pulled down but she was climbing. A trickle of blood ran down her arm. Logan came into view, musket aimed down to where Charity crouched. He fired again.

Hand over hand, Elizabeth climbed. A crevice ran up the last few feet of the cliff, making a line of holds like a ladder. Heaving herself over the top and onto the grass, she saw him grab another musket from a pile by his feet. He must have heard her because his aim swung.

Behind him, a figure darted from the storehouse doorway. Elias must surely be dead. But there he was. Or his ghost. Shouting a battle cry.

Logan spun to face this new enemy. He fired and missed. Elias was still advancing. Logan grabbed another musket.

Men were running across the Island towards the cliffs. Calvary's men.

Logan's aim swung from Elias to the Island and then to Elizabeth. Her eyes met his along the length of the barrel. She was about to throw herself to the side.

But Elias shouted, "Jago's dead."

Logan lowered the musket and let it fall. He seemed bewildered, as if unable to believe. Then he pulled a pistol from his belt, put it to the side of his own head and fired.

CHAPTER 40

Calvary's men lifted Charity up the cliff. She emerged blinking, as if startled to be alive. And shivering, which meant the cold had yet to take her. Had she been smaller it would surely have gone worse.

Elizabeth watched as the woman set eyes on Elias, then walked towards him, amazed it seemed. They held each other while Calvary's gatherers clambered up the cliff and swarmed around the stone towers, taking guard.

Charity's husband and brother came charging down the slope, and would have been run through, but Elias managed to call out in time and the guards stepped aside. Charity stripped off the wet things there in the open and warm cloaks were wrapped around her.

After that, Elias fell. When his trouser leg was ripped away they found a long splinter of wood embedded in his calf. How he'd walked at all was a mystery. Elizabeth eased it out while Charity's husband poured spirits into the wound with a delicate hand.

The road was long and slow. When Elizabeth's turn came to ride with Elias in the back of the cart, she found him drifting in and out of sleep. His forehead felt hot. But there was nothing she could do to help. When her watch was nearly over, he opened his eyes and she was able to give him a drink of water.

"The gun," he whispered.

She stroked his forehead. It was cooler than before. "You must rest."

"But I'm dying."

She proffered the cup. "Drink."

He pushed it away, spilling it. "Listen! Your gun! Your father's gun. I saw it in the Yukon."

He'd been delirious in his fever. Mumbling from time to time. Making no sense. But this felt different. Her stomach clenched. "You must rest," she said again.

"There was a man," he said, quieter now. "With your gun." Then he closed his eyes. This time his sleep seemed more peaceful. But his words churned in Elizabeth's mind.

The fever was gone by the following morning. But he seemed too weak and in too much pain to bother with questions. Through the days of the journey, his wound began to heal. But still Elizabeth found herself holding back.

Tinker came running out to meet them as they approached New Whitby, wearing that same carefree smile, as if he'd never had a doubt that she'd be safe. But he submitted to her hug and kisses, so he must have had some idea of what they'd risked.

"Come," he said, taking her hand.

They ran ahead into town, then off on the track to the Salt Ray Inn, where Maria Rosa opened the door and took her inside.

There stood Julia, her fair hair bright in the darkness of the saloon.

Some great deeds must be done in ignorance, for understanding their greatness at the time would make any move impossible. But standing there with Julia and Tinker together again and new roads opening up, Elizabeth did understand. The terror of all the things that might have gone wrong came rushing at her. And the uncontainable joy of reunion. As she embraced her friend, she wept.

"I've missed you," Julia said. "There are no words to say how much."

The house in New Whitby had grown cold and Elias found himself shivering. The first thing the men did was set a fire in the kitchen stove, heaping logs as if they cost nothing. Even when it was blazing, the floor seemed to suck the heat away.

"Show me the glycer-fortis," Elizabeth said.

He gave her the green glass jar and watched as she held it up to the light.

"How many days?" she asked.

"Ten if I'm careful. Twelve, maybe. But I'm not going to have my last days full of pain. I'm not going to cut back. I want to chop wood and carry barrels and eat food and sleep in a bed with Charity, as if that's the way it's going to be forever. Even if it's just a week. And I don't want you to treat me any different or talk about it or anything."

"I understand," Elizabeth said, then handed the jar to Charity, who turned and marched from the room.

Elias set off in pursuit but her husband caught his arm. "You're staying in the warm," he said.

That evening there was a knock and Charity's husband opened the door to the mistress of the Salt Ray Inn, a crock in her arms. A fair-haired woman was with her, and Tinker. Each carried a serving platter.

Elizabeth beamed. "Dear Julia, meet Elias, my friend."

They shook hands, he and the woman Elizabeth had risked so much to protect. It seemed a formal greeting.

Elias, Maria Rosa and Elizabeth were given the three chairs. The rest of them sat on blankets in front of the fire. The crock contained a creamy fish stew, the platters were piled with roasted vegetables. Elias couldn't remember a finer feast, though he'd eaten at the tables of the Patrons in his youth.

"Salt Ray Chowder," Maria Rosa said, with evident pride.

They'd eaten only half the feast, but when he asked for more, Charity merely kissed his brow and took away the bowl.

"No more for the dying man?" he asked.

His words hurt her, he could see that. "You're going to live," she said.

"Then give me my medicine."

But she would not.

He woke in the night and found himself lying on his side. There was pain. Somewhere. Charity began rubbing his back before he'd properly thought that he might be dying. The fire was still blazing in the stove, his bed had been made up in front of it. Elizabeth was there as well, bending over him and holding out the cloak pin. A fist seemed to be squeezing around the raw flesh of his heart. He couldn't lift his hand, so opened his mouth and let her wipe a smear of the poison under his tongue. The chemical buzz filled him. The fist loosened its grip but didn't release. He rolled onto his back.

"Not enough," he whispered.

Charity's thumbs were massaging the sides of his head. He closed his eyes. The women were whispering together: anxious voices. He couldn't tell what they said.

He woke again around dawn with the same fist of pain. But worse. They had to prise open his mouth. His sweat felt cold even though the fire blazed just a few feet away.

Half-asleep, he heard the clank of copper and water being poured nearby. Daylight from the small kitchen windows lit rising steam. Charity was undressing him. Then strong hands lifted him by shoulders and ankles. He was in the air and then they were lowering him into the copper bath. In the first seconds, he thought the shock of the hot water would kill him. Then he began to relax into it and the fist slackened its grip.

Through that day and the next he got used to them carrying him from the fire to the bath and back, eating the small meals that Julia brought over from the Salt Ray Inn: morsels and soups. It all seemed tasteless. Then he thought they might be increasing the dose of glycer-fortis because his head started to clear and for a time he found himself not focused on his own heartbeat.

Someone was always watching. On the morning of the third day it was Elizabeth. Julia would turn her back on his nakedness but Elizabeth never flinched. She'd positioned her chair to the side of the bath.

"How long do I have?" he asked.

"Eighty years or so." Her smile was tight.

He sighed. "At least tell me what's going on out there," he gestured towards the front door.

"The town's in uproar," she said, brightening.

"More than usual?"

"They say there's been a battle."

"They?"

"Well, yes. That's the thing. No one knows for sure. But if it's true, your clan met what's left of Jago's men. On the North Road somewhere."

"I have no clan," he said.

"I'm sorry. How's the water?"

"Cooling."

"Ready to get out?"

He shook his head. He felt better in the water than ever he did dry. "Can you pour in another kettle?"

She held it over the foot of the bath, letting the water trickle in slowly. He pulled back his legs so not to be scalded. The routine had grown familiar. The heat seeped into him and he felt his heart relaxing.

"When you were delirious, you said some things. About my gun. And the Yukon. And a man. I don't know what you meant by it."

He'd been expecting the question. It had hung between them, unspoken through the long journey back to New Whitby. He'd been unwilling to raise it for fear of the trouble it might make.

"I wasn't delirious when I said it."

"Then tell me what you meant."

"It was just that. A man with your gun. He'd travelled up from Oregon. The overseer did everything he asked. So he must have been important."

"What was his name?"

"They never told me. I'm sorry."

"And the gun was like my father's?"

"More than like. I would have sworn it to be the same one. He wore it in a holster strapped across his chest, so you didn't see it except when he took off his jacket. But you've had yours a long time. So it can't be the same. Its twin, perhaps?"

Elizabeth was leaning forwards, her eyes open wide enough for the whites to show all the way around.

"Am I going to die?" he asked again.

"Yes. Wrinkled and grey in old age. Like any other man."

"You won't let me see the glycer-fortis. You've upped my dose, I know. Is it so you can ask me this before I die? I wouldn't mind."

Elizabeth seemed taken aback by his question. "You're carrying two sicknesses, Elias. Only one's the poison in your blood. The other's up here." She tapped the side of her head. "You still believe you'll die without that green jar. I've seen the way you panic when it's out of reach. That's why you can't have it any more. That's why we're not showing you."

"So you haven't increased my dose?"

"You've got to stop thinking on it! Please. Just tell me what that man looked like."

He shook his head. "If I'm going to die, I want to spend my

last days with Charity. She saved me. She brought me back from hell. I need to know!"

"You're getting better," Elizabeth said. "I promise."

"But my dose?"

"We've given you nothing but a sniff of that poison in two days. Your body's strong, Elias. It's over the worst. It can live to be a hundred. But you've got to let it go from your mind."

He'd been sitting forwards, matching Elizabeth's tension. But now he leaned back against the sloping rest. His heart slowed. The beat felt regular for once.

Elizabeth got up and poured cold water from the pail into the kettle. He watched her set it on the stove.

"Your man with the pistol," he said.

"He's not my man."

"Well, that's the thing. I've been trying to picture his face all this time. And I can't. At least, I thought I couldn't. I just kept seeing your face and it seemed like I was getting confused. But that's not the way of it. You asked me what he looked like. The only thing I can say is that he looked just like you. He could have been your brother."

Elizabeth turned away.

On the fourth day he found himself asking for more food. On the fifth he got dressed and walked around the cottage. He wanted to find where they'd hidden his medicine, just to see how much there was left. But he quickly tired and gave up, reminding himself that he didn't need it any more.

The news of battles and politics came quickly after that. He doubted that half of it was true. But the tide seemed to be flowing for Patron Calvary. Scattered clans and leaderless fighters were offering their oaths to him.

"There'll be a king," he said to Charity.

"Your great uncle," she said.

"He cut me off."

"If he's king, he can take you back again." A shadow seemed to have fallen over her.

"It would be difficult," he said. "There's politics, even for a king."

"Oh," she said, still sad.

He touched his fingers to her lips. "I wouldn't want it anyway."

"And why's that?"

"Because I want to stay with you. If I live. And if you'll have me."

All the beautiful women and all the feasts and all the treasures of his old life were cast into shadow by that smile. It lit her face. And the room. And his heart.

"You'll live," she said.

And for the first time, he believed it.

CHAPTER 41

Any king would have been an upstart. But they still came out to see him, the people of New Whitby. He'd approached the unaligned lands at the head of an army greater than any before seen on Newfoundland. Jago would have marched the whole lot of them right in. But Calvary left his host camped beyond the North Road turning. He brought with him only enough warriors to act as guards and five old councillors, who'd once served contending clans.

His first act was a proclamation of peace. There would be no killing or looting, he said. The people of the unaligned lands would be protected. They could go about their trades as before.

It would never be that simple, Elizabeth thought. There would be taxes in exchange for protection and for the mending of roads. Then there would be the other things that governments find the need to spend on. The tyranny of lawlessness would be replaced. It remained to be seen whether the people would warm to their new situation. But Calvary had made a good start.

She'd been thinking about the smugglers in their submarine boat, bringing weapons from the mainland, and before that from the factory in the far Yukon. Beyond that it was hard to see. But Elias had told her the factory was controlled from a kingdom in the Oregon Territory. He didn't know the name of the king.

Whoever it was had wished to establish Newfoundland as a puppet kingdom, a power to trade with, a means of controlling both oceans. He'd backed the wrong man: Jago instead of Calvary. That would sour the diplomacy. But where there was trade and guns, a way would be found, she thought.

Then there was the thing she'd tried not to think about: the man Elias had described with the pistol that looked like hers. The man so like her that he could have been her brother.

There'd been a time when her father pretended she had a brother. It had been part of a trick of stage magic. Sometimes she'd dressed as a boy and played the part. But it was more than pretending. The brother and the sister had each been facets of who she was.

Then there was a time further back. She found it difficult to think about. But on the very edge of her memory there was the warmth and scent of a woman, her mother. She didn't know what her mother's name had been. But there had been another child on the knee. A boy.

Guards came to the cottage to search for dangers. Once they were satisfied, they stepped outside and the King of Newfoundland entered, ducking under the lintel of the door. Elizabeth attempted a curtsy, though it didn't feel right. Charity followed her lead. Then they left Elias and the king together.

"I'm to be a merchant," Elias told her afterwards. "The king approved it. I'll be learning the wine trade."

"You'll be living here then?"

"I will," he said. "I'm to be a lodger with Charity and her family."

"I'm happy for you," Elizabeth said. "Happy for you all."

He blushed, then, that highborn warrior brought low, as if embarrassed to have such blessings heaped upon him.

"The king didn't want you back then?"

"He wanted me. His advisors told him no. It would be an insult to the old clans if I were to be taken so easily into his court. So here I stay. Pretending to be sad about it." Elias stared at his feet, sheepish as a schoolboy, his smile growing slowly until it lit the room.

Charity's husband loaded their things between a cargo of empty barrels. Maria Rosa wept as she said goodbye to Elizabeth. She ruffled Tinker's hair, then hurried back to the inn, not waiting to see the boat go.

With Tinker and Julia boarded, Elizabeth turned to him. "You're sure this is safe?" she asked.

"You're under the king's warrant," Elias said.

"Do all accept it?"

"Those that don't are hiding in the hills."

They'd neither thanked the other. But words would have been trite after what they'd gone through. It was enough that they both knew it.

"It's time," Charity's husband called, from the launch.

"I had a brother," Elizabeth whispered, getting the words out in a rush. "I think that's who you saw in the Yukon. I only half-remember him. I was very small. And my pistol – it was kept in a wooden box. But there were places for two of them. I thought the other one was lost."

"Go back to your people," said Elias. "Back to the Gas-Lit Empire. I shouldn't have told you. No good comes from hunting ghosts. Especially not out there."

She stepped down into the boat. And then they were moving. She looked back only once, and saw Charity leading him away.

A GLOSSARY OF THE OATH-LAW
AND ITS ORIGINS

AFFINITY
A clan allegiance as defined by oaths and/or blood.

THE BLOOD
To be of the Blood was to be a direct patrilineal descendent of the original Patron Protectors, present at the first Reckoning in 1842.

CUSTOM AND PRACTICE
The system of oaths was established to hold the tyranny of law and government within the narrowest possible limits. Anything that might have appeared to be a rule lying beyond those limits was said to be the custom and practice of Newfoundland. Death might result from contravening such custom and practice, but it was not a law.

THE ISLAND OF THE RECKONING
Situated off the northern coast, the Island was not in truth an island, but a peninsular connected by a narrow rock ridge. It was chosen as the venue for the annual Reckoning due to its shape (being a rough approximation of the shape of Newfoundland itself), and due to the ease with which entry and exit could be controlled.

The Migration

The rapid influx of settlers arriving in the first half of the nineteenth century. Mostly from America and Europe, they travelled in search of lands where they could be free from the strict law of the rapidly expanding Gas-Lit Empire.

Oath-bound

One whose skin had been tattooed with an oath of obedience to another.

Oath-breaking

Any attempt to fraudulently evade oaths. An oath-breaker was by definition an outlaw.

Oath-holder

One who held the oaths of another. Note: a person could be both oath-bound and an oath-holder.

Oath-wright

To be an oath-wright was to be a guardian of the law. It was to make power, inking it under the skin of Patron and slave. But they were not to touch it for themselves. Each bore the oaths of office across his chest:

> *I hold no oaths but these:*
> *to ink with no mercy or favour,*
> *for no payment or honour,*
> *to hold the oath of no other*
> *to mark my work with no seal,*
> *but the one placed in clear seeing,*
> *on my brow for all to witness.*

To separate them from political machinations, the oath-wrights were sworn to poverty and celibacy. Thus they performed roles akin to lawyers but with the ethic and social standing of priests. The extent to which they fulfilled these vows was a matter of controversy.

The number of oath-wrights remained mostly constant. A nephew would normally be apprenticed to learn the craft and the wisdom. On the uncle's death, he would be presented to the conclave of oath-wrights, who would confirm him as successor.

Only a majority vote of all the oath-wrights at the Reckoning could make a new one. Once he had served his apprenticeship, the words of the law would be written across his chest and his seal on his forehead. The fact that new, non-hereditary oath-wrights were occasionally made is an indication that politics was at work even among those sanctified ranks.

OFF-LANDER

One born beyond Newfoundland. Typically these were shipwrecked sailors come unwontedly to those shores. Any Patron could place slave marks around the neck of an off-lander and take them to his service.

When discovered, off-landers usually claimed to be the unaligned descendants of Newfoundland's early settlers. But an investigation of their family trees would easily prove otherwise.

OUTLAWING

To be outlawed meant being put beyond the custom and practice which protected Newfoundlanders from arbitrary killing. Whilst not strictly a code of law, it was understood that to slay an outlaw would result in no direct retribution, and one who harboured an outlaw would have all the clans set against them.

By tradition, the outlawed were permitted a warrant of

as many hours as there would be months in the period of outlawing. The optimum time for fatality was held to be eighteen. Too few hours of warrant to get away. Too many months beyond protection or assistance to survive.

Patron Protector
Traditionally, a Patron had to be a man of the Blood, beholden of no oaths.

The Reckoning
First held in 1842 to decide whether Newfoundland should agree to join the Gas-Lit Empire, the Reckoning became an annual festival. It was at the fifth Reckoning in 1846 that the system of oaths and oath-wrights was first instituted.

Severance
The ending of an oath through the removal of the limb or extremity onto which it had been inked and an amendment to the relevant truth mark.

Slave
Strictly speaking there could be no slaves on Newfoundland, since any oath could be severed. But when the oath-marks were written around the neck, there could be no severance without death. However, it was said that a real slave could not with honour kill themselves without their owner's permission. Whereas those oath-bound in this way would still have that one freedom remaining. Thus the two states were different.

Truth Marks
Whenever an oath was tattooed, an additional "truth mark" was made on the part of the body considered its opposite. (These "opposites", some of which might have appeared

arbitrary, were part of the tradition of the oath-wrights.) Thus it was impossible for the oath-bound to simply cut off the skin where their allegiance had been marked and claim it as a battle wound. An oath-wright seeing such a scar could check for a corresponding truth mark. A precise pairing of opposite scars was held as irrefutable evidence of oath-breaking.

UNALIGNED
The unaligned were those people of no clan affinity. They were typically descended from the inhabitants of Newfoundland present before the Migration. Most lived in and around New Whitby.

ACKNOWLEDGMENTS

I'm struck by the sheer number of people who've helped me to write this novel. My special thanks go to the team of midwives who brought it into the world, including Marc, Phil, Penny, Nick, Lottie and Ed. I'm indebted to all the members of Leicester Writers Club for their suggestions, guidance and time, particularly Terri, Siobhan, Dave and Jacob who, at various stages, gave formative input. And I'd like to acknowledge the parts played by Stephanie, Joseph and Anya, whose understanding and support made the whole process possible.

Thanks also to readers of the previous books who took time to send supportive messages through the year or wrote reviews or clicked to 'like' or to 'follow'. Those things always give me a lift. They kept me going on days when the story wouldn't cooperate. Finally, books only become complete when they've been read. So if you've just shared the road with Elizabeth and Elias, thank you. We created their world together.

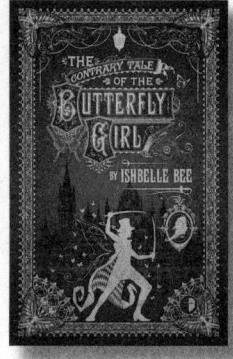